Lewis Campbell

The Seven Plays

Lewis Campbell

The Seven Plays

ISBN/EAN: 9783337418564

Printed in Europe, USA, Canada, Australia, Japan

Cover: Foto ©Andreas Hilbeck / pixelio.de

More available books at **www.hansebooks.com**

PREFATORY NOTE.

I. THE Hellenic spirit has been repeatedly characterized as simple Nature-worship. Even the Higher Paganism has been recently described as "in other words the purified worship of natural forms." * One might suppose, in reading some modern writers, that the Nymphs and Fauns, the River-Gods and Pan, were at least as prominent in all Greek poetry as Zeus, Apollo, and Athena, or that Apollo was only the sweet singer and not also the prophet of retribution.

The fresh and unimpaired enjoyment of the Beautiful is certainly the aspect of ancient life and literature which most attracted the humanists of the sixteenth century, and still most impresses those amongst ourselves who for various reasons desire to point the contrast between Paganism and Juda-ism. The two great groups of forces vaguely

* "Natural Religion," p. 79.

known as the Renaissance and the Revolution have both contributed to this result. Men who were weary of conventionality and of the weight of custom "heavy as frost and deep almost as life," have longed for the vision of "Oread or Dryad glancing through the shade," or to "hear old Triton blow his wreathèd horn." Meanwhile, that in which the Greeks most resembled us, "the human heart by which we live," for the very reason that it lies so near to us, is too apt to be lost from our conception of them. Another cause of this one-sided view is the illusion produced by the contemplation of statuary, together with the unapproachable perfection of form which every relic of Greek antiquity indisputably possesses.

But on turning from the forms of Greek art to the substance of Greek literature, we find that Beauty, although everywhere an important element, is by no means the sole or even the chief attribute of the greatest writings, nor is the Hellenic consciousness confined within the life of Nature, unless this term is allowed to comprehend man with all his thoughts and aspirations. It was in this latter sense that Hegel recognized the union of depth with brightness in Greek culture: "If the first paradise was the paradise of nature, this is the second, the higher paradise of the human spirit, which in its fair naturalness, freedom, depth and brightness here comes forth like a bride out of her chamber. The first wild majesty of the rise of spiritual life in the East is here circumscribed by the dignity of form, and softened into beauty. Its depth shows itself no longer in confusion, obscurity, and inflation, but lies open before us in simple clearness. Its brightness (Heiterkeit) is not a childish play, but covers a sadness which knows the hardness of fate but is not by that knowledge driven out of freedom and measure." Hegels Werke, vol. xvi. p. 139 (translated by Prof. Caird). The simplicity of Herodotus, for example, does not exclude far-reaching thoughts on the political advantages of liberty, nor such reflections on experience as are implied in the saying of Artabanus that the transitoriness of human life is the least of its evils. And in what modern writing is more of the wisdom of life condensed than in the History of Thucydides? It is surely more true to say of Greek literature that it contains types of all things human, stamped with the freshness, simplicity, and directness which belong to first impressions, and to the first impressions of genius.

Now the "thoughts and aspirations," which are nowhere absent from Greek literature, and make a centre of growing warmth and light in its Periclean period,—when the conception of human nature for the first time takes definite shape,—have no less of Religion in them than underlay the "creed out-worn." To think otherwise would be an error of the same kind as that "abuse of the word Atheism" against which the author of the work above alluded to protests so forcibly.

Religion, in the sense here indicated, is the main-spring and vital principle of Tragedy. The efforts of Æschylus and Sophocles were sustained by it, and its inevitable decay through the scepticism which preceded Socrates was the chief hindrance to the tragic genius of Euripides. Yet the hollow-ness of which we have consequently to complain in him is redeemed by occasional hints of something yet "more deeply interfused," which in him, as in his two great predecessors, is sometimes felt as "modern," because it is not of an age but for all time. The most valuable part of every literature is something which transcends the period and nation out of which it springs.

On the other hand, much that at first sight seems primitive in Greek tragedy belongs more to the subject than to the mode of handling. The age of Pericles was in advance of that in which the legends were first Hellenized and humanized, just as this must have been already far removed from the earliest stages of mythopœic imagination. The reader of Æschylus or Sophocles should therefore

be warned against attributing to the poet's inven-
tion that which is given in the fable.

An educated student of Italian painting knows
how to discriminate,—say in an Assumption by
Botticelli,—between the traditional conventions,
the contemporary ideas, and the refinements of the
artist's own fancy. The same indulgence must be
extended to dramatic art. The tragedy of "King
Lear" is not rude or primitive, although the subject
belongs to prehistoric times in Britain. Nor is
Goethe's "Faust" medieval in spirit as in theme.
So neither is the Œdipus Rex the product of
"lawless and uncertain thoughts," notwithstanding
the unspeakable horror of the story; but is pene-
trated by the most profound estimate of all in
human life that is saddest, and all that is most
precious.

Far from being naïve naturalists after the Keats
fashion, the Greek tragic poets had succeeded to a
pessimistic reaction from simple Pagan enjoyment;
they were surrounded with gloomy questionings
about human destiny and Divine Justice, and they
replied by looking steadily at the facts of life and
asserting the supreme worth of innocence, equity,
and mercy.

They were not philosophers, for they spoke
the language of feeling; but the civilization of

which they were the strongest outcome was already tinged with influences derived from early philosophy,—especially from the gnomic wisdom of the sixth century and from the spirit of theosophic speculation, which in Æschylus goes far even to recast mythology. The latter influence was probably reinforced, through channels no longer traceable, by the Eleusinian worship, in which the mystery of life and death and of human sorrow had replaced the primitive wonder at the phenomena of the year.

And whatever elements of philosophic theory or mystic exaltation the drama may have reflected, it was still more emphatically the repository of some of the most precious traditions of civilized humanity—traditions which philosophy has sometimes tended to extenuate, if not to destroy.

Plato's Gorgias contains one of the most eloquent vindications of the transcendent value of righteousness and faithfulness as such. But when we ask, " Righteousness in what relation ? "—" Faithfulness to whom ? "—the Gorgias is silent ; and when the vacant outline is filled up in the Republic, we are presented with an ideal of man's social relations, which, although it may be regarded as the ultimate development of existing tendencies, yet has no immediate bearing on any actual condition of the world.

The ideal of the tragic poet may be less perfect; or rather he does not attempt to set before us abstractedly any single ideal. But the grand types of character which he presents to the world are not merely imaginary. They are creatures of flesh and blood, men and women, to whom the unsullied purity of their homes, the freedom and power of their country, the respect and love of their fellow-citizens, are inestimably dear. From a Platonic and still more from a Christian point of view, the best morality of the age of Pericles is no doubt defective. Such counsels of perfection as "Love your enemies," or "A good man can harm no one, not even an enemy,"—are beyond the horizon of tragedy, unless dimly seen in the person of Antigone. The co-existence of savage vindictiveness with the most affectionate tenderness is characteristic of heroes and heroines alike, and produces some of the most moving contrasts. But the tenderness is no less deep and real for this, and while the chief persons are thus passionate, the Greek lesson of moderation and reasonableness is taught by the event, whether expressed or not by the mouth of sage or prophet or of the "ideal bystander."

Greek tragedy, then, is a religious art, not merely because associated with the festival of Dionys us, nor because the life which it represented was that of men who believed, with all the Hellenes, in Zeus,

Apollo, and Athena, or in the power of Moira and the Erinyes,—not merely because it represented

> "the dread strife
> Of poor humanity's afflicted will
> Struggling in vain with ruthless destiny,"

but much more because it awakened in the Athenian spectator emotions of wonder concerning human life, and of admiration for nobleness in the unfortunate,—a sense of the infinite value of personal uprightness and of domestic purity,—which in the most universal sense of the word were deeply religious ;—because it expressed a consciousness of depths which Plato never fathomed, and an ideal of character which, if less complete than Shakespeare's, is not less noble. It is indeed a "rough" generalization that ranks the Agamemnon with the Adoniazusæ as a religious composition.

II. This spiritual side of tragic poetry deserves to be emphasized both as the most essential aspect of it, and as giving it the most permanent claim to lasting recognition. And yet apart from this, merely as dramas, the works of Æschylus, Sophocles, and Euripides will never cease to be admired. These poets are teachers, but they teach through art. To ask simply, as Carlyle once did, "What did they think?" is not the way to understand or learn from them.

Considered simply as works of art, the plays of Sophocles stand alone amongst dramatic writings in their degree of concentration and complex unity.

1. The interest of a Sophoclean drama is always intensely personal, and is almost always centred in an individual destiny. In other words, it is not historical or mythical, but ethical. Single persons stand out magnificently in Æschylus. But the action is always larger than any single life. Each tragedy or trilogy resembles the fragment of a sublime Epic poem. Mighty issues revolve about the scene, whether this is laid on Earth or amongst the Gods, issues far transcending the fate of Orestes or even of Prometheus. In the perspective painting of Sophocles, these vast surroundings fall into the background, and the feelings of the spectator are absorbed in sympathy with the chief figure on the stage, round whom the other characters—the members of the chorus being included—are grouped with the minutest care.

2. In this grouping of the persons, as well as in the conduct of the action, Sophocles is masterly in his use of pathetic contrast. This motive must of course enter into all tragedy—nothing can be finer than the contrast of Cassandra to Clytemnestra in the Agamemnon,—but in Sophocles it is all-pervading, and some of the minor effects of it are so

subtle that although inevitably felt by the spectator
they are often lost upon the mere reader or student.
And every touch, however transient, is made to
contribute to the main effect.

To recur once more to the much-abused analogy
of statuary :—the work of Æschylus may be com-
pared to a colossal frieze, while that of Sophocles
resembles the pediment of a smaller temple. Or
if, as in considering the Orestean trilogy, the
arrangement of the pediment affords the more
fitting parallel even for Æschylus, yet the forms
are so gigantic that minute touches of characteriza-
tion and of contrast are omitted as superfluous.
Whereas in Sophocles, it is at once the finish of
the chief figure and the studied harmony of the
whole, which have led his work to be compared
with that of his contemporary Pheidias. Such
comparison, however, is useful by way of illustra-
tion merely. It must never be forgotten that, as
Lessing pointed out to some who thought the
Philoctetes too sensational, analogies between the
arts are limited by essential differences of material
and of scope. All poetry represents successive
moments. Its figures are never in repose. And
although the action of Tragedy is concentrated and
revolves around a single point, yet it is a dull
vision that confounds rapidity of motion with rest.

3. Sophocles found the subjects of his dramas

already embodied not only in previous tragedies but in Epic and Lyric poetry. And there were some fables, such as that of the death of Œdipus at Colonos, which seem to have been known to him only through oral tradition. For some reason which is not clearly apparent, both he and Æschylus drew more largely from the Cyclic poets than from "our Homer." The inferior and more recent Epics, which are now lost, were probably more episodical, and thus presented a more inviting repertory of legends than the Iliad and Odyssey.

Arctinus of Lesbos had treated at great length the story of the House of Thebes. The legend of Orestes, to which there are several allusions, not always consistent with each other, in the Homeric poems, had been a favourite and fruitful subject of tradition and of poetical treatment in the intervening period. Passages of the Tale of Troy in which other heroes than Achilles had the pre-eminence had been elaborated by Lesches and other Epic writers of the Post-Homeric time. The voyage of the Argonauts, another favourite heroic theme, supplied the subjects of many dramas which have disappeared. Lastly, the taking of Œchalia by Heracles, and the events which followed it, had been narrated in a long poem, in which one version of that hero's multiform legend was fully set forth.

The subjects of the three plays which come first in this volume, King Œdipus, Œdipus at Colonos, and Antigone, are taken from the Tale of Thebes ; the Aias and the Philoctetes are founded on incidents between the end of the Iliad and the taking of Troy ; the Electra represents the vengeance of Orestes, the crowning event in the tale of " Pelops' line " ; the Trachiniæ recounts the last crisis in the life of Heracles.

4. Of the three Theban plays, the Antigone was first composed, although its subject is the latest. Æschylus in the Seven against Thebes had already represented the young heroine as defying the victorious citizens who forbade the burial of her brother, the rebel Polynices. He allowed her to be supported in her action by a band of sympathizing friends. But in the play of Sophocles she stands alone, and the power which she defies is not that of the citizens generally, but of Creon, whose will is absolute in the State. Thus the struggle is intensified, and both her strength and her desolation become more impressive, while the opposing claims of civic authority and domestic piety are more vividly realized, because either is separately embodied in an individual will. By the same means the situation is humanized to the last degree, and the heart of the spectator, although strained to the uttermost with pity for the heroic

maiden whose life when full of brightest hopes was sacrificed to affection and piety, has still some feeling left for the living desolation of the man, whose patriotic zeal, degenerating into tyranny, brought his city to the brink of ruin, and cost him the lives of his two sons and of his wife, whose dying curse, as well as that of Hæmon, is denounced upon him.

In the Œdipus Tyrannus, Sophocles goes back to the central crisis of the Theban story. And again he fixes our attention, not so much on the fortunes of the city, or of the reigning house, as on the man Œdipus, his glory and his fall.

> "O mirror of our fickle state
>   Since man on earth unparalleled!
>   The rarer thy example stands,
>   By how much from the top of wondrous glory,
>   Strongest of mortal men,
>   To lowest pitch of abject fortune thou art fallen." *

The horror and the pity of it are both enhanced by the character of Œdipus—his essential innocence, his affectionateness, his uncalculating benevolence and public spirit;—while his impetuosity and passionateness make the sequel less incredible.

The essential innocence of Œdipus, which survives the ruin of his hopes in this world, supplies

* Milton, " Samson Agonistes."

the chief motive of the Œdipus at Colonos. This drama, which Sophocles is said to have written late in life, is in many ways contrasted with the former Œdipus. It begins with pity and horror, and ends with peace. It is only in part founded on Epic tradition, the main incident belonging apparently to the local mythology of the poet's birth-place. It also implies a later stage of ethical reflection, and in this respect resembles the Philoctetes ; it depends more on lyrical and melodramatic effects, and allows more room for collateral and subsidiary motives than any other of the seven. Yet in its principal theme, the vindication or redemption of an essentially noble spirit from the consequences of error, it repeats a note which had been struck much earlier in the Aias with great force, although with some crudities of treatment which are absent from the later drama.

5. In one of the Epic poems which narrated the fall of Troy, the figure of Aias was more prominent than in the Iliad. He alone and unassisted was there said to have repulsed Hector from the ships, and he had the chief share, although in this he was aided by Odysseus, in rescuing the dead body of Achilles.* Yet Achilles' arms were awarded by the votes of the chieftains, as the prize of valour, not to

* Is not this, rather than the fight over Patroclus, the subject of the group in the Æginetan marbles?

Aias, but to Odysseus. This, no doubt, meant that wisdom is better than strength. But the wisdom of Odysseus in these later Epics was often less nobly esteemed than in the Iliad and Odyssey, and was represented as alloyed with cunning.

Aias has withdrawn with his Salaminians, in anger, from the fight, and after long brooding by the ships his wrath has broken forth into a blaze which would have endangered the lives of Odysseus and the Atridæ, had not Athena in her care for them changed his wrath into madness. Hence, instead of slaying the generals, he makes havoc amongst the flocks and herds, which as the result of various forays were the common property of the whole army. The truth is discovered by Odysseus with the help of Athena, and from being next to Achilles in renown, Aias becomes the object of universal scorn and hatred. The sequel of this hour of his downfall is the subject of the Aias of Sophocles. After lamenting his fate, the hero eludes the vigilance of his captive bride Tecmessa, and of his Salaminian mariners, and, in complete solitude, falls upon his sword. He is found by Tecmessa and by his halfbrother Teucer, who has returned too late from a raid in the Mysian highlands. The Atridæ would prohibit Aias' funeral; but Odysseus, who has been specially enlightened by Athena, advises generous forbearance, and his counsel prevails. The part representing the disgrace and death of Aias is more affecting to modern readers than the remainder of the drama. But we should bear in mind that the vindication of Aias after death, and his burial with undiminished honours, had an absorbing interest for the Athenian and Salaminian spectator.

Philoctetes also is rejected by man and accepted by Destiny. The Argives in his case, as the Thebans in the case of Œdipus, are blind to the real intentions of the Gods.

The Philoctetes, like the Œdipus at Colonos, was a work of Sophocles' old age; and while it can hardly be said that the fire of tragic feeling is abated in either of these plays, dramatic effect is modified in both of them by the influence of the poet's contemplative mood. The interest of the action in the Philoctetes is more inward and psychological than in any other ancient drama. The change of mind in Neoptolemus, the stubborn fixity of will in Philoctetes, contrasting with the confiding tenderness of his nature, form the elements of a dramatic movement at once extremely simple and wonderfully sustained. No purer ideal of virtuous youth has been imagined than the son of Achilles, who in this play, though sorely tempted, sets faithfulness before ambition.

6. In the Electra, which, though much earlier than the Philoctetes, is still a work of his mature genius, our poet appears at first sight to be in unequal competition with Æschylus. If the Theban trilogy of the elder poet had remained entire, a similar impression might have been produced by the Œdipus Tyrannus. It is best to lay such comparisons aside, and to consider the work of Sophocles simply on its own merits. The subject, as he has chosen to treat it, is the heroic endurance of a woman who devotes her life to the vindication of intolerable wrongs done to her father, and the restoration of her young brother to his hereditary rights. Hers is the human agency which for this purpose works together with Apollo. But the divine intention is concealed from her. She suffers countless indignities from her father's enemies, of whom her own mother is the chief. And, at length, all her hopes are shattered by the false tidings that Orestes is no more. Even then she does not relinquish her resolve. And the revulsion from her deep sorrow to extremity of joy, when she finds Orestes at her side and ready to perform the act of vengeance in his own person, is irresistibly affecting, even when the play is only read.

Sophocles is especially great in the delineation of ideal female characters. The heroic ardour of

Antigone, and the no less heroic persistence and endurance of Electra, are both founded on the strength of their affection. And the affection in both cases is what some moderns too have called the purest of human feelings, the love of a sister for a brother. Another aspect of that world-old marvel, "the love of women," was presented in Aias' captive bride, Tecmessa. This softer type also attains to heroic grandeur in Deianira, the wronged wife of Heracles, whose fatal error is caused by the innocent working of her wounded love.

It is strange that so acute a critic as A. W. Schlegel should have doubted the Sophoclean authorship of the Trachiniæ. If its religious and moral lessons are even less obtrusive than those of either Œdipus and of the Antigone, there is no play which more directly pierces to the very heart of humanity. And it is a superficial judgment which complains that here at all events our sympathies are distracted between the two chief persons, Deianira and Heracles. To one passion of his, to one innocent mistake of hers, the ruin of them both is due. Her love has made their fates inseparable. And the spectator, in sharing Hyllus' grief, is afflicted for them both at once. We may well recognize in this treatment of the death of Heracles the hand of him who wrote—

σὺ καὶ δικαίων ἀδίκους
φρένας παρασπᾷς ἐπὶ λώβᾳ,
*   *   *   *
ἄμαχος γὰρ ἐμπαίζει θεὸς Ἀφροδίτα.*

7. It is unnecessary to expatiate here on the merits of construction in which these seven plays are generally acknowledged to be unrivalled; the natural way in which the main situation is explained, the suddenness and inevitableness of the complications, the steadily sustained climax of emotion until the action culminates, the preservation of the fitting mood until the end, the subtlety and effectiveness of the minor contrasts of situation and character.†

But it may not be irrelevant to observe that the "acting qualities" of Sophocles, as of Shakespeare, are best known to those who have seen him acted, whether in Greek, as by the students at Harvard ‡ and Toronto,§ and more recently at Cambridge,‖ or in English long ago by Miss Helen Faucit (now

---

* "Thou drawest awry
Just minds to wrong and ruin. . . .
. . . . With resistless charm
Great Aphrodite mocks the might of men."
Antigone.

† For detailed observations on these and other points the reader is referred to the little book on Sophocles in Mr. Green's "Classical Writers." Macmillan & Co.

‡ Œd. Tyr., 1881.   § Ant., 1882.
‖ Aj., Nov. 1882.

Lady Martin),* or still earlier and repeatedly in Germany, or in the French version of M. Lacroix at the Théâtre Français, where the part of Œdipe Roi was finely sustained by M. Geoffroy in 1856, and by M. Mounet Sully in 1881.† With reference to the latter performance, which was continued throughout the autumn season, M. Francisque Sarcey wrote an article for the *Temps* newspaper of August 15, 1881, which is full of just and vivid appreciation. At the risk of seeming absurdly "modern," I will quote from this article some of the more striking passages.

"Ce troisième et ce quatrième actes, les plus émouvants qui se soient jamais produits sur aucune scène, se composent d'une suite de narrations, qui viennent l'une après l'autre frapper au cœur d'Œdipe, et qui ont leur contre-coup dans l'âme des spectateurs. Je ne sais qu'une pièce au monde qui soit construite de la sorte, c'est l'*École des Femmes*. Ce rapprochement vous paraîtra singulier, sans doute. . . . Mais . . . c'est dans le vieux drame grec

* Ant., 1845.

† The performance of Greek plays (as of the Agamemnon at Oxford in 1879) is not altogether a new thing in England. The author of Ion, Mr. Serjeant Talfourd, in his Notice prefixed to that drama in 1836, mentions, amongst other reasons for having intended to dedicate it to Dr. Valpy, "the exquisite representations of Greek Tragedy, which he superintended," and which "made its images vital." It would be ungrateful to omit all reference here to some performances of the Trachiniæ in English in Edinburgh and St. Andrew's in 1877, which, though not of a public nature, are still remembered with delight by those who were present at them, and were really the first of a series.

comme dans la comédie du maître français une trouvaille
de génie.

✱ ✱ ✱ ✱ ✱ ✱

"Sophocle a voulu, après des émotions si terribles,
après des angoisses si sèches, ouvrir la source des larmes :
il a écrit un cinquième acte.

✱ ✱ ✱ ✱ ✱ ✱

"Les yeux crevés d'Œdipe ne sont qu'un accident, ou
si vous aimez mieux, un accessoire. Le poète, sans
s'arrêter a ce détail, a mis sur les lèvres de son héros
toute la gamme des sentiments douloureux qu'excite une
si prodigieuse infortune.

✱ ✱ ✱ ✱ ✱ ✱

"À la lecture, elle est un peu longue cette scène de
lamentations. Au théâtre, on n'a pas le temps de la
trouver telle : on pleure de toute son âme et de tous ses
yeux. C'est qu'après avoir eu le cœur si longtemps serré
comme dans un étau, on épreuve comme un soulagement
à sentir en soi jaillir la source des larmes. Sophocle, qui
semble avoir été le plus malin des dramaturges, comme
il est le plus parfait des écrivains dramatiques, a cherché
la un effet de contraste dont l'effet est immanquante sur
la public."

These and other like remarks of one of the best
known critics of the Parisian stage at the present
day show that the dramatic art of Sophocles is
still a living power.

I am well aware how feeble and inadequate the

present attempted reproduction must appear to any
reader who knows the Greek original. There is
much to be said for the view of an eminent scholar
who once declared, that he would never think of
translating a Greek poet. But the end of trans-
lating is not to satisfy fastidious scholars, but to
make the classics partially accessible to those
whose acquaintance with them would otherwise
be still more defective. Part of this version of
Sophocles was printed several years ago in an im-
perfect form. The present volume contains the
seven extant plays entire. As the object has been
to give the effect of each drama as a whole, rather
than to dwell on particular " beauties " (which only
a poet can render), the fragments have not been
included. But the reader should bear in mind that
the seven plays are less than a tithe of the work
produced by the poet in his lifetime.

It may very possibly be asked why verse has
been employed at all. Why not have listened
to Carlyle's rough demand, " Tell us what they
thought ; none of your silly poetry ! " The present
translator can only reply that he began with prose,
but soon found that, for tragic dialogue in English,
blank verse appeared a more natural and effective
vehicle than any prose style which he could hope to
frame. And with the dialogue in verse, it was im-
possible to have the lyric parts in any sort of prose,

simply because the reader would then have felt an intolerable incongruity. These parts have therefore been turned into such familiar lyric measures as seemed at once possible and not unsuitable. And where this method was found impracticable, where the meditative gnomic tone or the tragic earnestness seemed incompatible at least with rhyme in English, blank metres have again been used,—with such liberties as seemed appropriate to the special purpose. The writer's hope throughout has been, not indeed fully to transfuse the poetry of Sophocles into another tongue, but to make the poet's dramatic intention to be understood and felt by English readers. One more such endeavour may possibly find acceptance at a time when many causes have combined to awaken a fresh interest at once in dramatic literature and in Hellenic studies.

The reader who is hitherto unacquainted with the Greek drama, should be warned that the parts assigned to the "Chorus" were often distributed amongst its several members, who spoke or chanted, singly or in groups, alternately or in succession. In some cases, but not in all, *Ch.* 1, *Ch.* 2, etc., have been prefixed, to indicate such an arrangement.

KING ŒDIPUS.

THE PERSONS

ŒDIPUS.

Priest of Zeus.

CREON.

CHORUS *of Theban Elders.*

TEIRESIAS, *the Blind Prophet.*

JOCASTA.

1*st Messenger—a Corinthian Shepherd.*

A Theban Shepherd.

2*nd Messenger.*

The following also appear but do not speak :—

A Train of Suppliants.

The children ANTIGONE *and* ISMENE.

B

Laius, the descendant of Cadmus, and king of Thebes (or Thebè), had been told by an oracle that, if a son were born to him by his wife Jocasta, the boy would be his father's death.

Under such auspices, Œdipus was born, and to elude the prophecy was exposed by his parents on Mount Cithæron. But he was saved by a compassionate shepherd, and became the adopted son of Polybus, king of Corinth. When he grew up he was troubled by a rumour that he was not his father's son. He went to consult the oracle of Apollo at Delphi, and was told—not of his origin but of his destiny—that he should be guilty of parricide and incest.

He was too horror-stricken to return to Corinth, and as he travelled the other way, he met Laius going from Thebes to Delphi. The travellers quarrelled, and the son killed his father, but knew not whom he had slain. He went onward till he came near Thebes, where the Sphinx was making havoc of the noblest citizens. Œdipus solved her riddle and overcame her, and, as Laius did not return, was rewarded with the regal sceptre,—and with the hand of the queen.

He reigned nobly and prosperously, and lived happily with Jocasta, by whom he had four children.

But after some years a plague descended on the people, and Apollo, on being inquired of, answered that it was for Laius' death. The act of regicide must be avenged. Œdipus undertakes the task of discovering the murderer,—and in the same act discovers his own birth, and the fulfilment of both the former oracles.

Jocasta hangs herself, and Œdipus in his despair puts out his eyes.

Scene—Thebes, before the royal palace.

KING ŒDIPUS.

———

ŒDIPUS.   Priest (*with the* Train of Suppliants *grouped before an altar*).

Œdipus. Nurslings of Cadmus, children of my care,
Why press you now to kneel before my gate
With sacred branches in those suppliant hands,
Whilst o'er your city clouds of incense rise
And sounds of praise, mingling with sounds of woe?
I would not learn of your estate, my sons,
Through others; wherefore I myself am come,
Your Œdipus,—a name well known to men.
Speak, aged friend, whose look proclaims thee meet
To be their spokesman :—What desire or fear
Hath brought you?   Doubt not of my earnest will
To lend all succour.   Hard would be the heart
That looked unmoved on such a kneeling throng.
Priest. Great ruler of my fatherland, thou seest
The different ages of our flock who here
Are gathered round thine altar ;—some, whose wing
Hath not yet ventured far from home; and some
Burdened with many years, priests of the Gods,

Myself the arch-priest of Zeus ; and these fresh youths,
A chosen few.   Others there are who crowd
The holy agora and the temples twain
Of Pallas, and Ismenus' hallowed fires,
A suppliant host.   For, as thyself perceivest,
Our city is tempest-tost, and all too weak
To lift above the waves her weary prow
That plunges in a rude and ravenous sea.
Earth's buds are nipped, withering the germs within ;
Our cattle lose their increase, and our wives
Have fruitless travail ; and that scourge from Heaven
The fiery Pestilence abhorred of men
Descending on our people with dire stroke
Lays waste the Home of Cadmus, while dark Death
Hath ample tribute of laments and groans.
    We kneel, then, at thy hearth ; not likening thee
Unto the gods, I nor these children here,
But of men counting thee the first in might
Whether to cope with earthly casualties
Or visitation of unearthly Powers ;
Who, in thy coming to this Theban land,
Didst take away the hateful tax we paid
To that harsh songstress,*—aided not by us
With hint nor counsel, but, as all believe,
Gifted from heaven with life-restoring thought.
Now too, great Œdipus of matchless fame,
We all uplift our suppliant looks to thee,
To find some help for us, whether from man,
Or through the promptings of a voice Divine.

* The Sphinx.

Experienced counsel, we have seen and know,
Hath ever prosperous issue.   Thou then come,
Noblest of mortals, give our city rest
From sorrow ! come, take heed ! seeing this our land
Now calls thee Saviour for thy former zeal ;
And 'twere not well to leave this memory
Of thy great reign among Cadmeian men,
" He raised us, but we afterward fell down."
Let the salvation thou hast wrought for us
Be flawless and assured !   As once erewhile
Thy lucky star gave us prosperity,
Be the same man to-day.   Wouldst thou be king
In power, as in command, 'tis greater far
To rule a people than a wilderness.
Since nought avails or city or buttressed wall
Or gallant vessel, if unmanned and void.

   Œd. Ye touch me to the core.   Full well I know
Your trouble and your desire.   Think not, my sons,
I have no feeling of your misery !
Yet none of you hath heaviness like mine.
Your grief is held within the single breast
Of each man severally.   My burdened heart
Mourns for myself, for Thebe, and for you.
Your coming hath not roused me from repose.
I have watched, and wept right bitter tears.   My soul
Hath travelled many a labyrinth of thought.
And now I have put in proof the one design
Long meditation showed me.   I have sent
My brother-in-law, Creon, Menœceus' son,
To Phœbus' Pythian mansion, there to learn

What word or deed of mine may save this city.
And when I count the time, I am full of pain
To guess his speed ; for he is absent long,
Beyond the limit of expectancy.
But when he shall appear, base then were I
In aught to disobey the voice of Heaven.

Pr. With happy speed to crown thy gracious word,
'Tis told me by these youths, Creon draws near.

Œd. Apollo ! may his coming be as blest
With saving fortune, as his looks are bright.

Pr. Sure he brings joyful news ; else had he ne'er
Worn that full wreath of thickly-berried bay.

Œd. We have not long to doubt.   He can hear now.

Enter CREON.

Son of Menœceus, brother of my queen,
What answer from Apollo dost thou bring ?

Creon. Good ; for my message is that even our woes,
When brought to their right issue, shall be well.

Œd. What saith the oracle ?   Thy words so far
Neither embolden nor dishearten me.

Cr. Say, must I tell it with these standing by,
Or go within ?   I am ready either way.

Œd. Speak forth to all.   The burden of their grief
Weighs more than any danger of my own.

Cr. My lips shall utter what the God hath said.
Sovereign Apollo clearly bids us drive
Forth from this region an accursed thing
(For such is fostered in this land and stains
Our clime), and not to cherish it past cure.

Œd. What is the fault, and how to be redressed ?

Cr. By exile, or by purging blood with blood.
Since murder is the cause that shakes our State.

Œd. Whose life destroyed can Phœbus here intend ?

Cr. My gracious lord, before thy prosperous reign,
King Laius was the leader of our land.

Œd. Though I ne'er saw him, I have heard, and know.

Cr. The God commands us now to punish home
The undetected authors of his death.

Œd. But they, where are they ?   Where shall now be
    traced
The fading record of this ancient guilt ?

Cr. He saith, 'tis in this land.   And what is sought
Is found, while things uncared for glide away.

Œd. But where did Laius meet this violent end ?
At home, afield, or on some foreign soil ?

Cr. He left us, as he said, to visit Delphi ;
But never more returned since he set forth.

Œd. And was there none, no fellow-traveller,
To see, and tell the tale, and help our search ?

Cr. No, they were slain ; save one, who, flying in fear,
Had nought to tell us but one only thing.

Œd. What was that thing ?   A little door of hope,
If opened, may discover much to our view.

Cr. A random troop of robbers, so 'twas told,
Destroyed him, not with one, but many a blow.

Œd. What robber would have ventured such a deed,
Were not the crime procured with Theban gold ?

Cr. We thought of that.   But Laius being dead,
No helper found us in our miseries.

Œd. What misery, when majesty was fallen,
Withheld you from inquiring to the end?

 Cr. A present trouble had engrossed our care.
The riddling Sphinx compelled us to observe
The moment's grief, neglecting things obscure.

 Œd. But I will track this evil to the source
And clear it to the day. Most worthily
Doth great Apollo, worthily dost thou
Prompt this new care for the unthought of dead.
And me too ye shall find a just ally,
Succouring the cause of Phœbus and the land.
Since, in dispelling this dark cloud, I serve
Not some remote collateral claim on me,
But mine own life ; for he that slew the king
May one day turn his guilty hand 'gainst me
With equal wrath. In righting Laius, then,
I forward mine own cause. Now, children, rise
From the altar-steps, and lift your suppliant boughs,
And let some other summon to this place
All Cadmus' people, and assure them, I
Will answer every need. This day shall see us
Blest with glad fortune through God's help, or fallen.

 Pr. Rise then, my children. Even for this we came
Which our good lord hath promised of himself.
Only may Phœbus, who hath sent this word,
With healing power descend, and stay the plague.

[Exeunt severally.

CHORUS (*entering*).

Kind voice of Heaven, soft-breathing from the height
Of Pytho's opulent home to Thebè bright,
  What wilt thou bring to-day?
  Ah, Delian Healer, say!
My heart hangs on thy word with trembling awe:
  What new-giv'n law,
Or what returning in Time's circling round
Wilt thou unfold?   Tell us, immortal sound,
Daughter of golden Hope, we pray, we pray!

First, child of Zeus, Pallas, to thee appealing,
Then to sweet Artemis, thy sister, kneeling,
  Who guards our sacred land
  With blessing from her hand,
Throned o'er the circling mart that hears her praise,
  And thou, whose rays
Pierce evil from afar, ho! come and save,
Ye mighty three! if e'er before ye drave
The threatening fire of woe from Thebè, come to-day!

  For ah! the griefs that on me weigh
  Are numberless; weak are my helpers all,
  And thought finds not a sword to fray
This hated pestilence from hearth or hall.
  Earth's blossoms blasted fall:
  Nor can our women rise
  From childbed after pangs and cries;

But flocking more and more
Towards the western shore,
Soul after soul is found to wing her flight,
Swifter than quenchless flame, to the far realm of Night.

So countless deaths abound.
My city's sons unpitied lie around
Over the plague-encumbered ground.
And wives and matrons old on every hand
Along the altar-strand
Groaning in saddest grief
Pour supplication for relief.
Loud hymns are sounding clear
With wailing voices near.
Then, golden daughter of the heavenly sire,
Send fair-eyed Succour to subdue this fire.

And swiftly speed afar,
Windborne on backward car,
The unshielded War-god with loud onset sweeping,
To oarless Thracian tide,
Or ocean-chambers wide,
Where Amphitritè lone her couch is keeping.
Day ruins what night spares.   O thou whose hand
Wields lightning, blast him with thy thundering brand

Shower from the golden string
Thine arrows, Lycian King !
O Phœbè, let thy fiery lances fly
Resistless, as they rove

Through Xanthus' mountain-grove !
O Theban Bacchus of the lustrous eye,
With torch and trooping Mænads and bright crown
Blaze on the god whom all in Heaven disown.

  [ŒDIPUS *has entered during the Choral song.*

Œd. This help ye pray for, this release from woe,
Is yours, if ye will heed my voice and do
That which the plague demands. Hear it from me,
Who am hitherto a stranger to the tale,
As to the crime. Being nought concerned therewith,
I could not of myself divine the truth.
But now, as one adopted to your state,
To all of you Cadmeians I speak this :
Whoe'er among you knows the murderer
Of Laïus, the son of Labdacus,
I bid him show the deed in full to me.
First, if the man himself be touched with fear,
Let him depart, carrying the guilt away.
No harm shall follow him :—he shall go free.
Or if there be who knows another here,
Come from some other country, to have done
This murder, let him speak. My rich reward
Awaits him and full gratitude besides.
But if ye shall keep silence, and the man
Who might have spoken shall refuse for fear,
Whether on his own behalf or for his friend,
I will execute the word I now proclaim.
Whoever is the author of the deed,
I here prohibit all within this realm
Whereof I wield the sovereignty and sway,

To admit him to their doors or speak with him
Or share with him in vow or sacrifice
Or lustral rite.   All men shall thrust him forth,
Our dark pollution, so to me revealed
By this day's oracle from Pytho's cell.
    Thus firm is mine allegiance to the God
And your dead sovereign in this holy war.
Now on the murderer, whether he lurk
In lonely guilt, or with a numerous band,
I here pronounce this curse : let his crushed life
Perish forlorn in hopeless misery.
Next, I pray Heaven, should he or they be housed
With my own knowledge in my home, that I
May suffer all I imprecate on them.
Last, I enjoin each here to lend his aid
For my sake, and the God's, and for your land
Reft of her increase and renounced by Heaven.
It was not right, when your good king was fallen,
Even had the oracle kept silence still,
To leave this inquisition unperformed.
Long since ye should have purged the crime.   But now
I, to whom fortune has transferred his crown,
And given his wife in marriage, yea, moreover,
His seed and mine had formed one family,
Had not misfortune trampled on his head
Cutting him off from fair posterity,—
All this being so,—I will maintain his cause
As if my father's, racking means and might,
To apprehend the author of the death

Of Laius, son of Labdacus, and heir
Of Polydorus and of Cadmus old,
And wise Agenor of the eldest time.
    Once more, to all who disobey in this
May Heaven deny the produce of the ground
And offspring from their wives, and may they pine
With plagues more horrible than this to-day.
But for the rest of you Cadmeian men,
Who here embrace my word, may Righteousness,
Strong to defend, and all the Gods for aye
Watch over you for blessing in your land.
    Ch. Under the shadow of thy curse, my lord,
I will speak.   I slew him not, nor can I show
The man who slew.   Phœbus, who gave the word,
Should name the criminal.
    Œd.   Thy thought is just,
But man may not compel the Gods.
    Ch.   Again,
That failing, I perceive a second way.
    Œd. Were it a third, spare not to speak it forth.
    Ch. I know of one alone whose royal mind
Sees all King Phœbus sees—Teirésias,—he
Infallibly would guide us in this search.
    Œd. That doth not count among my deeds undone.
By Creon's counsel I have sent twice o'er
To seek him, and I muse at his delay.
    Ch. The rumour that remains is old and dim.
    Œd. What rumour ?   Let no tale be left untried.
    Ch. 'Twas said he perished by some wandering band.
    Œd. But the one witness is removed from ken.

Ch. Well, if the man be capable of fear,
He will not stay when he hath heard thy curse.

Œd. Words have no terror for the soul that dares
Such deeds.

Ch.   Yet is there one who shall convict him.
For see where now they lead the holy seer,
Whom sacred Truth inspires alone of men.

Enter TEIRESIAS.

Œd. O thou whose universal thought surveys
All knowledge and all mysteries, in Heaven
And on the earth beneath, thy mind perceives,
Teirésias, though thine outward eye be dark,
What plague is wasting Thebe, who in thee,
Great Sir, finds her one Saviour, her sole guide.
Phœbus (albeit the messengers perchance
Have told thee this) upon our sending sent
This answer back, that no release might come
From this disaster, till we sought and found
And slew the murderers of king Laïus,
Or drave them exiles from our land.   Thou then
Withhold not any word of augury
Or other divination which thou knowest,
But rescue Thebe, and thyself, and me,
And purge this dire pollution of the dead.
We cast ourselves on thee : and beautiful
It is to use the power one hath for good.

Teiresias. Ah ! terrible is knowledge to the man
Whom knowledge profits not.   This well I knew,
But had forgotten.   Else had I ne'er come hither.

Œd. Why dost thou bring a mind so full of gloom?

Tei. Let me go home. Thy part and mine to-day
ill best be borne, if thou obey me there.

Œd. Rebellious and ungrateful! to deprive
ɪe state that reared thee of thine utterance now.

Tei. Thy speech, I see, is crossing thine intent;
nd I would shield me from the like mishap.

Œd. Nay, if thou knowest, turn thee not away:
ɔ, all these suppliants are entreating thee!

Tei. Yea, for ye all are blind. Never will I
tter the sound that shall reveal thine evil.

Œd. So, then, thou hast the knowledge of the crime
nd wilt not tell, but rather wouldst betray
his people, and destroy thy fatherland!

Tei. You press me to no purpose. I'll not pain
hee, nor myself. Thou wilt hear nought from me.

Œd. How? Miscreant! Thy stubbornness would
    rouse
ʳrath in a breast of stone. Wilt thou still keep
hat silent, hard, impenetrable mien?

Tei. You censure me for my harsh mood. Your own
ᴵwells unsuspected with you. Me you blame!

Œd. Who can be mild and gentle, when thou speakest
uch words to mock this people?

Tei.   It will come:
lthough I bury it in silence here.

Œd. Must not the King be told of what will come?

Tei. No word from me. At this, an if thou wilt,
ᴸage to the height of passionate vehemence.

Œd. Ay, and my passion shall declare my thought.

'Tis clear to me as daylight, thou hast been
The arch-plotter of this deed ; yea, thou hast done
All but the actual blow.   Hadst thou thy sight,
I would pronounce thee the sole murderer.

　　Tei. Ay, say'st thou so ?—I charge thee to abide
By that thou hast proclaimed ; and from this hour
Speak not to any Theban nor to me.
Thou art the vile polluter of the land.

　　Œd. O void of shame !   What wickedness is this ?
What power will give thee refuge for such guilt ?

　　Tei. The might of truth is scatheless.   I am free.

　　Œd. Whence gottest thou this truth ?   Not from thine
　　　　art.

　　Tei. From thee, whose rage impelled my backward
　　　　tongue.

　　Œd. Say it once more, that I may know the drift.

　　Tei. Was it so dark ?   Or wouldst thou tempt my
　　　　voice ?

　　Œd. I cannot say 'twas clear.   Speak it again.

　　Tei. I say thou art the murderer whom thou seekest.

　　Œd. Again that baleful word !   But thou shalt rue.

　　Tei. Shall I speak something more, to feed thy wrath ?

　　Œd. All is but idleness.   Say what thou wilt.

　　Tei. I tell thee thou art living unawares
In shameful commerce with thy near'st of blood,
Ignorant of the abyss wherein thou liest.

　　Œd. Mean'st thou to triumph in offending still ?

　　Tei. Yes, if the might of truth be anything.

　　Œd. It is, for other men, but not for thee,
Blind as thou art in eyes and ears and mind.

Tei. O miserable reproach, which all who now
Behold thee, soon shall thunder forth on thee!

Œd. Nursed in unbroken night, thou canst not harm
Or me, or any man who seëth the day.

Tei. No, not from me proceeds thy fall; the God,
Who cares for this, is able to perform it.

Œd. Came this device from Creon or thyself?

Tei. Not Creon: thou art thy sole enemy.

Œd. O wealth and sovereign power and high success
Attained through wisdom and admired of men,
What boundless jealousies environ you!
When for this rule which to my hand the State
Committed unsolicited and free
Creon, my first of friends, trusted and sure,
Would undermine and cast me from my throne,
Meanly suborning such a mendicant
Botcher of lies, this crafty wizard rogue,
Blind in his art, and seeing but for gain.
Where are the proofs of thy prophetic power?
How came it, when the minstrel-hound * was here,
This folk had no deliverance through thy word?
Her snare could not be loosed by common wit,
But needed divination and deep skill.
No sign whereof proceeded forth from thee
Procured through birds or given by God, till I
The unknowing traveller overmastered her,
The stranger Œdipus, not led by birds,
But ravelling out the secret by my thought:
Whom now you study to supplant, and trust

* The Sphinx.

To stand as a supporter of the throne
Of lordly Creon,—To your bitter pain
Both you and he who plotted this will hunt
Pollution forth.*   But for thy reverend look
Thou hadst atoned thy trespass on the spot.

    Ch. Your friends would humbly deprecate the wrath
That sounds both in your speech, my lord, and his.
That is not what we need, but to discern
How best to solve the heavenly oracle.

    Tei. Though thou art sovereign here, the right of
        speech
Is my prerogative no less.   Not thee
I serve, but Phœbus.   He protects my life.
Small need of Creon's arm to shelter me !
Now, then : my blindness is thy theme :—thou hast
Thine eyes, nor seest where thou art sunk in woe,
What halls thou dost inhabit, or with whom :
Knowest not from whence thou art—nay, to thy kin,
Buried in death and here above the ground,
Unwittingly art a most grievous foe.
And when thy father's and thy mother's curse
With fearful tread shall drive thee from the land,
On both sides lashing thee,—thine eye so clear
Seeing but darkness in that day,—oh, then,
What region will not shudder at thy cry ?
What echo of Cithæron will be mute,
When thou perceiv'st, what bride-song in thy hall

   * The party cry of " driving out the pollution " was raised against
the Alcmæonidæ and other families at Athens, who were supposed
to lie under a traditional curse.

Wafted thy gallant bark with flattering gale
To anchor,—where?   And other store of ill
Thou seest not, that shall show thee as thou art,
Merged with thy children in one horror of birth.
Then slander noble Creon, and revile
My sacred utterance !   No life on earth
More wretchedly shall be crushed out, ~~than thine~~.

    Œd. Must I endure such words from him?   Begone !
Off to thy ruin and with speed !   Away,
And take thy presence from our palace-hall !

    Tei. Had you not sent for me, I ne'er had come.

    Œd. I knew not thou wouldst utter folly here,
Else had I never fetched thee to my door.

    Tei. To thee I am foolish, then ; but to the pair
Who gave thee life, I was wise.

    Œd.   Hold, go not ! who?
Who gave me being ?

    Tei.   This day shall disclose
Thy birth and thy destruction.

    Œd.   Wilt thou still
Speak all in riddles and dark sentences ?

    Tei. Methought thou wast the man to find them out.

    Œd. Ay ! Taunt me with the gift that makes me great.

    Tei. And yet this luck hath been thine overthrow.

    Œd. I care not, if I have preserved this city.

    Tei. Then I will go.   Come, sirrah, guide me forth !

    Œd. Be it so !   For standing here you vex our eye,
But, you being gone, our trouble goes with you.

    Tei. I go, but I will speak.   Why should I fear
Thy frown?   Thou ne'er canst ruin me.   The word

Wherefore I came, is this.   The man you seek
With threatening proclamation of the guilt
Of Laius' blood, that man is here to-day,
An alien sojourner supposed from far,
But by-and-by he shall be certified
A true-born Theban : nor will such event
Bring him great joy ; for, blind from having sight
And beggared from high fortune, with a staff
In stranger lands he shall feel forth his way ;
Shown living with the children of his loins,
Their brother and their sire, and to the womb
That bare him, husband-son, and, to his father,
Parricide and corrival.   Now go in,
Ponder my words ; and if thou find them false,
Then say my power is naught in prophecy.

[Exeunt severally.

Chorus.

Whom hath the voice from Pytho's rocky throne
Loudly declared to have done
Horrors unnameable with blood-stained hand ?
With speed of storm-swift car
'Tis time he fled afar
With mighty footsteps hurrying from the land.
For, armed with lightning brand,
The son of Zeus assails him with fierce bounds,
Hunting with Death's inevitable hounds.

Late from divine Parnassus' snow tipped height
This utterance sprang to light, .

To track by every path the man unknown.
Through woodland caverns deep
And o'er the rocky steep
Like vanquish'd bull he roams the wild alone,
With none to share his moan,
Shunning that prophet-voice's central * sound,
Which ever lives, and haunts him, hovering round.

The reverend Seer hath stirred me with strange awe,
Gainsay I cannot, nor yet think him true.
I know not how to speak.   My fluttering heart
In wild expectancy sees nothing clear.
Things past and future with the present doubt
Are shrouded in one mist.   What quarrel lay
'Twixt Cadmus' issue and Corinthus' heir
Was never shown me, from old times till now,
By one on whose sure word I might rely
In running counter to the King's fair fame,
Wreaking for Laius his mysterious death.

Zeus and Apollo scan the ways of men
With perfect vision.   But of mortals here
Why should the prophet have more gifts than I ?
What certain proof is told ?   A man through wit
May pass another's wisdom in the race.
But never, till I see the word fulfilled,
Will I confirm their clamour against the King.
In open day the female monster came :
Then perfect witness made his wisdom clear.

* *i.e.* Proceeding from Delphi, the centre of the Earth.

Thebe has tried him and delights in him.
Wherefore my heart shall still believe him good.

Enter CREON.

Cr. Citizens, hearing of dire calumnies
Pronounced on me by Œdipus the King,
I am here to make loud protest.   If he think,
In this embroilment of events, one word
Or deed of mine hath wrought him injury,
I am not careful to prolong my life
Beneath such imputation.   For it means
No trifling danger, but disastrous harm,
Making my life dishonoured in the state,
And basely thought of by my friends and you.
Ch. Perchance 'twas but the sudden flash of wrath,
Not the deliberate judgment of the soul.
Cr. Whence came the fancy—that Teirésias spake
False prophecies, set on to this by me?
Ch. Such was the word, I know not how advised.
Cr. And were the eyes and spirit not distraught,
When the tongue uttered this to ruin me?
Ch. I cannot say.   To what my betters do
I am blind.   But see, the King comes forth again.

Enter ŒDIPUS.

Œd. Insolent, art thou here?   Hadst thou the face
To bring thy boldness near my palace-roof,
Convicted of contriving 'gainst my life
And laying robber hands upon my state?

Tell me, by heaven, did you perceive in me
A coward or a fool, when you planned this?
Thought you I would fail to notice your attempt
Craftily creeping on, or, when perceived,
Not ward it off? Is't not a silly scheme,
To think to compass without troops of friends
Power, that is only won by wealth and men?

   Cr. Wilt thou be counselled? Hear as much in turn
As thou hast spoken, and then thyself be judge.

   Œd. I know thy tongue; but I am slow to learn
From thee, whom I have found my grievous foe.

   Cr. First on this very point, hear me declare—
   Œd. I will not hear that thou art not a villain.

   Cr. Thine is a shallow judgment, if thou thinkest
Self-will without true thought can bring thee gain.

   Œd. Thine is a shallow judgment, if thou thinkest
Thou canst abuse thy kinsman and be free.

   Cr. Right. I assent to that. But I would learn
What wrong is that you speak of?

   Œd.   Tell me this,
Didst thou, or not, urge me to send and bring
The reverend-seeming prophet?

   Cr.   Yea, and still
I hold that counsel firm.

   Œd.   How long is't now
Since Laius—

   Cr.   What? I do not catch your drift.

   Œd. Vanished in ruin by a dire défeat?

   Cr. 'Twere long to count the years that come between.

   Œd. And did this prophet then profess his art?

Cr. Wise then as now, nor less in reverence.

Œd. Then at that season did he mention me?

Cr. Not in my hearing.

Œd.   But, I may presume,
Ye held some inquisition for the dead?

Cr. Yes, we inquired, of course: and could not hear.

Œd. How spake this wise man then no word of this?

Cr. I cannot answer, for I do not know.

Œd. This you can answer, for you know it well.

Cr. Say what?   I will not gainsay, if I know.

Œd. That, had you not been by, he ne'er had sought
To attribute Laius'-murder to my hand.

Cr. You know if he said this.   But I in turn
Would be the questioner, and ask thee this.—

Œd. Ask on.   No words will fasten blood on me.

Cr. Tell me.. Hast thou my sister for thy queen?

Œd. The fact is patent, and denial vain.

Cr. And shar'st with her dominion of this realm?

Œd. All she desires is given her by my will.

Cr. Well, am not I third-partner with you twain?

Œd. There is your villany in breaking fealty.

Cr. Not so, if thou wouldst reason with thyself
As I do.   First consider one thing well:
Who would choose rule accompanied with fear
Before safe slumbers with an equal sway?
'Tis not my nature, no, nor any man's,
Whom modest wisdom guides, to love the place
Of domination rather than the power.
Now, without fear, I have my will from thee;
But were I king, I should do much unwillingly.

How then can I desire to be a king,
When masterdom is mine without annoy?
Delusion hath not gone so far with me
As to crave more than honour joined with gain.
Now all men count me happy, all embrace me;
Now he that needs thee calls me to his aid,
For on that chance his fortune wholly turns.
How should I leave this substance for that show?
No man of sense can harbour thoughts of crime.
Such vain ambition hath no charms for me,
Nor could I bear to lend it countenance.
If you would test me, go and ask again
If I brought Phœbus' answer truly back.
Nay more, if I am found to have devised
Aught in collusion with the seer, destroy me,
Not with one vote, but two, mine own with thine.
But do not on a dim suspicion blame me
Of thy mere will. To darken a good name
Without clear cause is heinous wickedness,
And to cast off a worthy friend I call
No less a folly than to fling away
What most we love, the life within our breast.
The certainty of this will come with time;
For time alone can clear the righteous man.
An hour suffices to make known the villain.

 Ch. Prudence bids hearken to such words, my lord,
For fear one fall. Swift is not sure in thought.

 Œd. When he who hath designs on me is swift
In his advance, I must bethink me swiftly.
Should I wait leisurely, his work hath gained

Completion, while my plans have missed success.

   Cr. What would you then? To thrust me from the
     land?

   Œd. Nay, death, not exile, is my wish for thee,
When all have seen what envy brings on men.

   Cr. You'll ne'er relent nor listen to my plea.

   Œd. You'll ne'er be governed or repent your guilt.

   Cr. Because I see thou art blind.

   Œd.   Not to my need.

   Cr. Mine must be thought of too.

   Œd.   You are a villain.

   Cr. Suppose thou art all ignorance?

   Œd.   My power
Must be maintained even then.

   Cr.   Authority
Sorts not with error.

   Œd.   O my citizens!

   Cr. I have a part in them no less than you.

   Ch. Cease, princes. Opportunely I behold
Jocasta coming toward you from the palace.
Her presence may attune your jarring minds.

Enter JOCASTA.

   Jocasta. Unhappy that ye are, why have ye reared
Your wordy rancour 'mid the city's harms?
Have you no shame, to stir up private broils
In such a time as this? Get thee within!
And thou too, Creon! nor enlarge your griefs
To make a mountain out of nothingness.

   Cr. Sister, thy husband Œdipus declares

One of two horrors he will wreak on me,
Banishment from my native land, or death.

 Œd. Yes, for I caught him practising, my queen,
Against our person with malignant guile.

 Cr. May comforts fail me, and a withering curse
Destroy me, if I e'er planned aught of this.

 Jo. I pray thee, husband, listen to his plea ;
Chiefly respecting his appeal to Heaven,
But also me, and these who stand by thee.

 Ch. 1. Incline to our request
Thy mind and heart, O King !

 Œd. What would you I should yield unto your
   prayer ?

 Ch. 2. Respect one ever wise,
Whose oath protects him now.

 Œd. Know ye what thing ye ask ?

 Ch. 3. I know.

 Œd.   Then plainly tell.

 Ch. 4. Thy friend, who is rendered sacred by his oath,
Rob not of honour through obscure surmise.

 Œd. In asking that, you labour for my death
Or banishment. Of this be well assured.

 Ch. 5. No, by the Sun I swear,
Vaunt-courier of the host of heaven.
For may I die the last of deaths,
Unblest of God or friend,
If e'er such thought were mine.
But oh ! this pining land
Afflicts my hapless soul,
To think that to her past and present woe

She must add this, which springs from your debate.

Œd. Then let him range, though I must die outright,
Or be thrust forth with violence from the land !
—Not for his voice, but thine, which wrings my heart :
He, wheresoe'er he live, shall have my hate.

Cr. You show yourself as sullen when you yield,
As unendurable in your fury's height.
Such natures justly give themselves most pain.

Œd. Let me alone, then, and begone !

Cr.   I go,
Untainted in their sight, though thou art blind.

                                 [*Exit.*

Ch. 1. Lady, why tarriest thou
To lead thy husband in ?

Jo. Not till I learn what mischief is befallen.

Ch. 2. Words without knowledge voiced a vague
        surmise ;
And accusations, though unfounded, sting.

Jo. Came this from both of them ?

Ch. 3.   From both alike.

Jo. And what was the dispute ?

Ch. 4.   Enough for me,
Amply enough it seems, when our poor land
Is vexed already, not to wake what sleeps.

Œd. (*To leader of Ch.*). See where thine honest zeal
        hath landed thee,
Bating my wrath, and blunting my desire !

Ch. 5. My prince, not once alone
I have said it, but twice o'er.
I should be clearly mad,

Unfurnished of all sense,
To loose my faith from thee,
Who, when my land was sore distraught,
Didst speed her forth anew with favouring gale.
Now, too, if but thou may'st, be her good guide.

 Jo. Let not thy queen be kept in ignorance
What cause thou hadst to lift thy wrath so high.

 Œd. I'll tell thee, lady, for I honour thee
More than these citizens. 'Twas Creon there,
And his inveterate treason against me.

 Jo. Accuse him, so you make the quarrel plain.

 Œd. He saith I am the murderer of the King.

 Jo. Speaks he from hearsay, or as one who knows?

 Œd. He keeps his own lips free : but hath suborned
A knavish soothsayer to this villany.

 Jo. Hearken to me, and set your heart at rest
On that you speak of, whilst I make you see
No mortal thing is touched by prophecy.
Of that I'll give thee proof concise and clear.
Word came to Laius once, I will not say
From Phœbus' self, but from his ministers,
The King should be destroyed by his own son,
If son were born to him from me. What followed ?
Laius was slain, by robbers from abroad,
Saith Rumour, in a cross-way ; But the child
Grew not three days, ere by my husband's hand
His feet were locked, and he was cast and left
By messengers on the waste mountain wold.
So Phœbus neither brought upon the boy
His father's murder, nor on Laïus

The thing he greatly feared, death by his son.
Such issue came of prophesying words,
Therefore regard them not.   God can himself
With ease bring forth what for his ends he needs.

   Œd. What strange emotions overcloud my soul,
Stirred to her depths on hearing this thy tale !

     Jo. What sudden change is this ?   What is thy
       thought ?

     Œd. Did I not hear thee say, King Laïus
Was at a cross-road overpowered and slain ?

     Jo. So ran the talk that yet is current here.

     Œd. Where was the scene of this unhappy blow ?

     Jo. Phocis the land is named : the parted ways
Lead from one point to Daulia and to Delphi.

     Œd. And since the event how much of time is passed?

     Jo. 'Twas just ere you appeared with prospering
       speed
And took the kingdom, that the tidings came.

     Œd. What are thy purposes against me, Zeus ?

     Jo. Why thus intent on such a thought, O King ?

     Œd. Nay, ask me not.   But tell me first what height
Had Laius, and what share of manly bloom ?

     Jo. Tall, with dark locks just sprinkled o'er with grey :
In shape and bearing much resembling thee.

     Œd. O heavy fate !   How all unknowingly
I laid that dreadful curse on my own head !

     Jo. How?
I tremble as I gaze on thee, O king !

     Œd. The fear appals me that the seer can see.
Tell one thing more, to make me doubly sure.

Jo. I am loth to speak, but, when you ask, I will.

Œd. Had he scant following, or, as princes use,
Full numbers of a well-appointed train?

Jo. There were but five in all : a herald one :
And Laius travelled in the only car.

Œd. Woe ! woe ! 'Tis clear as daylight. Who was he
That brought you this sad message, O my queen?

Jo. A home-slave, who alone returned alive.

Œd. And is he now at hand within the house?

Jo. No, truly. When he came from yonder scene,
And found thee reigning after Laius' death,
He touched my hand, and plied an urgent prayer
That I would send him to o'erlook the flocks
And rural pastures, so to live as far
As might be from the very thought of Thebes.
And he obtained from me his suit. No slave
Had richlier merited such boon than he.

Œd. Can he be brought again immediately?

Jo. Of course he can. But why desire it so?

Œd. Words have by me been spoken, O my queen,
Which furnish too much cause for that desire.

Jo. Then come he shall. But I may surely claim
To hear what in thy state goes heavily.

Œd. Thou shalt not lose thy rights in such an hour,
When I am harrowed thus with doubt and fear.
To whom more worthy should I tell my grief?
My father was Corinthian Polybus,
My mother Dorian Merope.—I lived
A prince among that people, till a chance
Encountered me, worth wonder, but, though strange,

Not worth the anxious thoughts it waked in me.
For at a feasting once over the wine
One deep in liquor called to me aloud,
Hail, thou false foundling of a foster-sire !
That day with pain I held my passion down,
But straightway on the morrow I went near
And questioned both my parents, who were fierce
In wrath at him whose lips had let this fall.
For their part I was satisfied, but still
It galled me, for the rumour would not die.

    Unknown to both my parents then I went
To Pytho, where, as touching my desire,
Phœbus denied me ; but brake forth instead
With other oracles of misery
And horrible misfortune, how that I
Must know my mother's shame, and cause to appear
A birth intolerable to human view,
And do to death the author of my life.
I fled forth at the word, and, measuring now
Corinthia's region by the stars of heaven,
Went roaming, where I never might behold
Those shameful prophecies fulfilled on me.
So travelling on, I came even to the place
Where, as thou tell'st, the King of Thebe fell.
And, O my wife, I will hide nought from thee.
When I drew near the cross-road of your tale,
A herald, and a man upon a car,
Like your description, there encountered me.
And he who went before, and he himself
The grey-beard, sought to thrust me from the path.

Then in mine angry mood I sharply struck
The driver-man that turned me from the way;
Which when the elder saw, he watched for me
As I passed by, and from the chariot-seat
Smote full upon my head with the fork'd goad;
But paid no equal price, for, by a blow
From this right hand, smit with my staff, he fell
Instantly rolled out of the car supine.
 I slew them every one.   Now if that stranger
Had aught in common with king Laïus,
What wretch on earth was e'er so lost as I?
Whom have the Heavens so followed with their hate?
No house of Theban or of foreigner
Must any more receive me, none henceforth
Must speak to me, but push me from the door!
, I have laid this curse on mine own head?
Yea, and this arm that slew him now enfolds
His queen.   O cruel stain! Am I not vile?
Polluted utterly! Yes, I must flee,
And, lost to Thebe, nevermore behold
My friends, nor tread my country, lest I meet
In marriage mine own mother, and bring low
His head that gave me life and reared my youth,
My father, Polybus.   Ah! right were he
Who should declare some god of cruel mood
Had sent this trouble upon my soul! Ye powers,
Worshipped in holiness, ne'er may I see
That day, but perish from the sight of men,
Ere sins like these are branded on my name!

  Ch. Thy fear is ours, O king : yet lose not hope,

D

Till thou hast heard him who beheld the deed.

Œd. Ay, that is all I still have left of hope,
To bide the coming of the shepherd man.

Jo. What eager thought attends his presence here?

Œd. I'll tell thee.   Should his speech accord with thine,
My life stands clear from this calamity.

Jo. What word of mine agreed not with the scene?

Œd. You said he spake of robbers in a band
As having slain him.   Now if he shall still
Persist in the same number, I am free.
One man and many cannot be the same.
But should he tell of one lone traveller,
Then, unavoidably, this falls on me.

Jo. So 'twas given out by him, be sure of that.
He cannot take it back.   Not I alone
But all the people heard him speak it so.
And should he swerve in aught from his first tale,
He ne'er will show the murder of the king
Rightly accordant with the oracle.
For Phœbus said expressly he should fall
Through him whom I brought forth.   But that poor
         babe
Ne'er slew his sire, but perished long-before.
Wherefore henceforth I will pursue my way
Regardless of all words of prophecy.

Œd. Wisely resolved.   But still send one to bring
The labourer-swain, and be not slack in this.

Jo. I will, and promptly.   Pass we now within!
My whole desire is but to work thy will.

[Exeunt.

CHORUS.

O may I live
Sinless and pure in every word and deed
Ordained by those firm laws, that hold their realm on
    high !
Begotten of Heaven, of brightest Ether born,
Created not of man's ephemeral mould,
They ne'er shall sink to slumber in oblivion.
A Power of God is there, untouched by Time.

Pride plants the root from whence the tyrant grows.
Insolent pride, if idly surfeited
With plenty inordinate, injurious wealth,
Mounts to his pinnacle, then leaps amain
Down a precipitous doom, where foothold finds he none.
Beneath the arm of God I would shelter me,
And pray him to maintain the people's cause,
Yea, all who strive for the universal good.

But if there be who walks disdainfully,
Reckless in act or word,
Fearless of Justice, passing without awe
The abodes of Deity,—
Let evil Destiny take him for her own,
And quench his ill-starred wanton spirit, unless
He learn in time to traffic without wrong,
And hold his hands from sacrilegious gain ;
Nor in mad folly grasp at things forbidden.
What man in such a course shall keep his soul

Unblasted by the artillery of Heaven ?
Nay, were such lives continued in renown,
Most idle were our service.

       ,Never again
Will I adore the holy central seat
Of Delphi, nor the famed Abæan shrine,
No, nor the Olympian home of the Most High,
Unless in clear fulfilment Phœbus' word
Be justified for every eye to see.
Zeus, if thy reign be not a fable of men,
If thou art Lord of all things, let thine eye
Behold, let thine eternal Power o'ertake !
They set at nought the fading oracle
Given long ago to Laius; the renown
Of great Apollo in every land grows dim ;
Religion is no more.

Enter JOCASTA.

Jo.   Princes of Thebes,
A sudden thought hath sent me forth again
To worship at the holy altars here
With frankincense and garlands.   For the king,
Transported by the tempest of his thoughts,
Runs wild in grief, nor like a man of sense
Reasons of present fears from what has been.
Each tongue possesses him that tells of woe.
Then since my counsels are of no avail,
To thee, for thou art nearest, Lycian God,
I bring my supplication with full hand,
That thou may'st grant remission and release,

For seeing him our pilot so distraught,
We are all, like mariners, amazed with fear.

Enter Messenger.

Messenger. Are ye the folk to tell me where to find
The mansion of the sovereign Œdipus?
Or better, where he may himself be found?

Ch. Here is the roof you seek, and he, our lord,
Is there within : and stranger, thou behold'st
The mother of his royal progeny.

Mess. May she and hers be always fortunate!
Still may she crown him with the joys of home!

Jo. Be thou, too, blest, kind sir! Thy gracious tongue
Deserves no less.   But tell me what request
Or what intelligence thou bring'st with thee?

Mess. Good tidings for thy house and husband, queen.

Jo. What are they? Who hath sent thee to our hall?

Mess. From Corinth came I, and will quickly tell
What sure will please you; yet perchance 'twill grieve.

Jo. What news can move us thus two ways at once?

Mess. 'Twas rumoured that the people of the land
Of Corinth would make Œdipus their king.

Jo. Is ancient Polybus not still in power?

Mess. No.   Mightier Death controls him in the grave.

Jo. Hold there! How say you? Polybus in his grave?

Mess. May I die for him if I speak not true!

Jo. (To an attendant). Run thou, and tell this quickly
    to my lord.
Voices of prophecy! where are ye now?
Long time hath Œdipus, a homeless man,

Trembled with fear of slaying Polybus,
Who now lies slain by Fortune, not by him.

Enter ŒDIPUS.

Œd. Jocasta, my dear queen, why didst thou send
To fetch me hither from our palace-hall?

Jo. Hear this man's tale, and then consider well
The end of yonder dreadful prophecy.

Œd. Who is the man, and what his errand here?

Jo. He comes from Corinth, to make known to thee
That Polybus, thy father, is no more.

Œd. How, stranger? Let me learn it from thy mouth.

Mess. If my first duty be to make this clear,
Know beyond doubt that he is dead and gone.

Œd. By sickness coming o'er him, or by guile?

Mess. Light force subdues to rest the aged frame.

Œd. He perished, then, by some disease, poor soul!

Mess. And also from the fulness of his years.

Œd. Ah! my Jocasta, who again will heed
The Pythian hearth oracular, and birds
Screaming in air, blind guides! that would have made
My father's death my deed; but he is gone,
Hidden underneath the ground, while I stand here
Harmless and weaponless:—unless, perchance,
My absence killed him,—so he may have died
Through me. But be that as it may, the grave
That covers Polybus from sight, hath closed
One voice of prophecy, worth nothing now.

Jo. Did I not tell thee so, long since?

Œd.　　　　　　　　　　　　　　　Thou didst.

But I was drawn to error by my fear.

   Jo. Now cast it altogether out of mind.

   Œd. Must I not fear my mother's marriage-bed ?

   Jo. Why should man fear, seeing his course is ruled
By fortune, and he nothing can foreknow ?
'Tis best to live at random, as one may.
Then fear not thou thy mother's nuptial hour.
Many a man ere now in dreams hath lain
With her who bare him.   He hath easiest life
Who with such omens troubleth not his mind.

   Œd. All this would be well spoken, were not she
Alive that gave me birth.   But since she lives,
Though you speak well, yet have I cause for fear.

   Jo. Your father's burial might enlighten you.

   Œd. It doth.   But I am darkened by a life.

   Mess. What woman is the occasion of your fears ?

   Œd. Merope, aged sir, who lived with Polybus.

   Mess. What touching her affects you thus with fear ?

   Œd. A heaven-sent oracle of dreadful sound.

   Mess. May it be told, or must no stranger know ?

   Œd. Surely it may.   Word came from Phœbus once
That I must know my mother's shame, and shed
With these my hands my own true father's blood.
Wherefore long since my home hath been removed
Far from Corinthos : not unhappily ;
But still 'tis sweet to see a parent's face.

   Mess. Did fear of this make thee so long an exile ?

   Œd. Of this and parricide, my aged friend.

   Mess. I came with kind intent and, O my king,
I fain would rid thee from this haunting fear.

Œd. Our gratitude should well reward thy love.

Mess. Hope of reward from thee in thy return
Was the chief motive of my journey hither.

Œd. Return ? Not to my parents' dwelling-place !

Mess. Son, 'tis too clear, you know not what you do.

Œd. Why, aged sir ? For Heaven's sake teach me
    this.

Mess. If for these reasons you avoid your home.

Œd. The fear torments me, Phœbus may prove true.

Mess. Lest from your parents you receive a stain ?

Œd. That is the life-long torment of my soul.

Mess. Will you be certified your fears are groundless ?

Œd. How groundless, if I am my parents' child ?

Mess. Because with Polybus thou hast no kin.

Œd. Why? Was not he the author of my life ?

Mess. As much as I am, and no more than I.

Œd. How can my father be no more to me
Than who is nothing ?

Mess.   In begetting thee
Nor I nor he had any part at all.

Œd. Why then did he declare me for his son ?

Mess. Because he took thee once a gift from me.

Œd. Was all that love unto a foundling shown ?

Mess. Heirless affection so inclined his heart.

Œd. A gift from you ! Your purchase or your child ?

Mess. Found in Cithæron's hollowy wilderness.

Œd. What led your travelling footsteps to that ground ?

Mess. The flocks I tended grazed the mountain there.

Œd. A shepherd wast thou, and a wandering hind ?

Mess. Whatever else, my son, thy saviour then.

Œd. From what didst thou release me or relieve?

Mess. Thine instep bears memorial of the pain.

Œd. Ah! what old evil will thy words disclose?

Mess. Thy feet were pierced till I unfastened them.

Œd. So cruel to my tender infancy!

Mess. From this thou hast received thy name.

Œd.   By heaven
I pray thee, did my father do this thing,
Or was't my mother?

Mess.   That I dare not say.
He should know best who gave thee to my hand.

Œd. Another gave me, then? You did not find me?

Mess. Another herdsman passed thee on to me.

Œd. Can you describe him? Tell us what you
      know.

Mess. He was called one of Laius' people, sure.

Œd. Of Laius once the sovereign of this land?

Mess. Yea, surely, he was shepherd of his flock.

Œd. And is he still alive for me to see?

Mess. You Thebans are most likely to know that.

Œd. Speak, any one of you in presence here,
Can you point out the swain he tells us of,
In town or country having known of him?
The time for this discovery is full come.

  Ch. Methinks it is no other than the peasant
Whom thou didst seek before to see : but this
Could best be told by queen Jocasta there.

Œd. We lately sought that one should come, my
      queen.
Know'st thou, is this of whom he speaks the same?

Jo. What matter who?   Regard not, nor desire
Even vainly to remember aught he saith.

Œd. When I have found such tokens of my birth,
I must disclose it.

Jo.   As you love your life,
By heaven I beg you, search no further here !
The sickness in my bosom is enough.

Œd. Nay, never fear.   Were I proved thrice a slave
And waif of bondwomen, you still are noble.

Jo. Yet hearken, I implore you : do not so.

Œd. I cannot hear you.   I must know this through.

Jo. With clear perception I advise the best.

Œd. This " best advice " is ever mine annoy.

Jo. Wretched one, never may you know your birth !

Œd. Will some one go and fetch the herdman hither ?
Leave her to revel in her lordly line !

Jo. O horrible !   O lost one !   This alone
I speak to thee, and no word more for ever.   [*Exit.*

Ch. Œdipus, wherefore is Jocasta gone,
Driven madly by wild grief?   I needs must fear
Lest from this silence she make sorrow spring.

Œd. Leave her to raise what storm she will.   But I
Will persevere to know mine origin,
Though from an humble seed.   Her woman's pride
Is shamed, it may be, by my lowliness.
But I, whilst I account myself the son
Of prospering Fortune, ne'er will be disgraced.
For she is my true mother : and the months
Coheirs with me of the same father, Time,
Have marked my lowness and mine exaltation.

So born, so nurtured, I can fear no change,
That I need shrink to search this to the end.

   [ŒDIPUS *remains, and gazes towards the country,*
      while the Chorus *sing.*

CHORUS.

  If I wield a prophet's might,
  Or have sense to search aright,
Cithæron, when all night the moon rides high,
    Loud thy praise shall be confessed,
    How upon thy rugged breast,
Thou, mighty mother, nursedst tenderly
Great Œdipus, and gav'st his being room
    Within thy spacious home.
    Yea, we will dance and sing
Thy glory for thy friendship to our king.
    Phœbus, unto thee we cry,
    Be this pleasing in thine eye !

    Who, my child, hath given thee birth
Of the long-lived nymphs of earth ?
Say, was she clasped by mountain-roving Faun,
    Or, beguiled she one sweet hour
    With Apollo in her bower,
Who loves to trace the wide uncultured lawn ?
Or was the ruler of Cyllene's height
    The author of thy light ?
    Or did the Bacchic god,
Who makes the top of Helicon to nod,

Take thee for a foundling care
From his playmates that are there?

[*The* Theban Shepherd *is seen approaching, guarded.*

Œd. If haply I, who never saw his face,
Thebans, may guess, methinks I see the hind
Whose coming we have longed for.   Both his age,
Agreeing with this other's wintry locks,
Accords with my conjecture, and the garb
Of his conductors is well-known to me
As that of mine own people.   But methinks
Thy knowledge is more perfect in this case,
Whose eyes have seen the herdman in the past.
Ch. I know him well, believe me.   Laïus
Had no more faithful shepherd than this man.
Œd. Corinthian friend, I first appeal to you:
Was't he you spake of?
Mess.   'Twas the man you see.
Œd. Turn thine eyes hither, aged friend, and tell
What I shall ask thee.   Wast thou Laius' slave?
Theb. Sh. I was, not bought, but bred within the
  house.
Œd. What charge or occupation was thy care?
Theb. Sh. Most of my time was spent in shepherding.
Œd. And where didst thou inhabit with thy flock?
Theb. Sh. 'Twas now Cithæron, now the_neighbouring
  tract.
Œd. And hadst thou there acquaintance of this man?
Theb. Sh. Following what service?   What is he you
  mean?

Œd. The man you see.   Hast thou once met with
   him?

Theb. Sh. I cannot bring him suddenly to mind.

Mess. No marvel, good my lord.   But I will soon
Wake to clear knowledge his oblivious sense.
For sure I am he can recall the time,
When he with his two flocks, and I with one
Beside him, grazed Cithæron's pasture wide
Good six month's space of three successive years,
From spring to rising of Arcturus; then
For the bleak winter-season, I drove mine
To their own folds, he his to Laius' stalls.
Do I talk idly, or is this the truth?

Theb. Sh. The time is far remote.   But all is true.

Mess. Well, dost remember having given me then
A child, that I might nurture him for mine?

Theb. Sh. What means thy question?   Let me know
   thy drift.

Mess. Friend, yonder is the infant whom we knew.

Theb. Sh. Confusion seize thee, and thy evil tongue!

Œd. Check not his speech, I pray thee, for thy words
Call more than his for chastisement, old sir.

Theb. Sh. O my dread lord, wherein do I offend?

Œd. Thou wilt not answer him about the child.

Theb. Sh. He knows not what he speaks.   His end is
   vain.

Œd. So! Thou'lt not tell to please us, but the lash
Will make thee tell.

Theb. Sh.   By all that's merciful,
Scourge not this aged frame!

Œd.   Pinion him straight!

Theb. Sh. Unhappy! wherefore? what is't you would
know?

Œd. Gave you the child he asks of to this man?

Theb. Sh. I gave it him.   Would I had died that
hour!

Œd. Speak rightly, or your wish will soon come true.

Theb. Sh. My ruin comes the sooner, if I speak.

Œd. You mean to keep us in suspense, I see.

Theb. Sh. Not so.   I said long since, "I gave the
child."

Œd. Whence?   Wast your own, or from another's
hand?

Theb. Sh. 'Twas not mine own; another gave it me.

Œd. What Theban gave it, from what home in
Thebes?

Theb. Sh. O, I implore thee, master, ask no more!

Œd. You perish, if I have to ask again.

Theb. Sh. The child was of the stock of Laïus.

Œd. Slave-born, or rightly of the royal line?

Theb. Sh. Ah me!   Now comes the horror to my
tongue!

Œd. And to mine ear.   But thou shalt tell it me!

Theb. Sh. He was described as Laïus' son: but she,
Thy queen, within the palace, best should know.

Œd. How?   Did she give it thee?

Theb. Sh.   My lord, she did.

Œd. With what commission?

Theb. Sh.   I was to destroy him.

Œd. How could a mother's heart be steeled to this?

Theb. Sh. With fear of evil prophecies.

Œd.   What were they?

Theb. Sh. 'Twas said the child should be his father's
  death.

Œd. What then possessed thee to give up the child
To this old man?

Theb. Sh.   Pity, my sovereign lord!
Supposing he would take him far away
Unto the land whence he was come.   But he
Preserved him to great sorrow.   For if thou
Art he this man hath said, be well assured
Thou bear'st a heavy doom.

Œd.   O horrible!
Horrible!   All fulfill'd, as sunlight clear!
Oh may I nevermore behold the day,
Since proved accursèd in my parentage,
In those I live with, and in him I slew!   [*Exeunt.*

CHORUS.

O tribes of living men,
How nothing-worth I count you while ye stand!
For who of all the train
Draws more of happiness into his hand
Than to seem bright, and, seeming, fade in gloom?
O Œdipus, by thine all-hapless doom
Too clearly 'tis expressed
Nought in mortality is blest.
Thou that surpassing all in skill
With perfect aim didst kill

The crook-clawed minstrel, as a tower
Saving my land from death's dark power,
And winning for thyself the name
Of Thebè's king, and noblest fame,
        Thou, thou, art fallen at last
        To misery unsurpassed.
        Who, in life's dark reverse,
        Like thee hath felt the curse
Of destiny, the assault of boundless pain ?

        O Œdipus renowned,
        Who in one haven found
        Harbour for son and sire
When led with nuptial fire !
Ah ! how couldst thou so long remain
The furrower of thy father's field,
Borne patiently and unrevealed ?
        Crimes from thyself concealed
All-searching time hath opened to the day,
        And shown thee with clear ray,
Long while, in hideous bond, spouse, father, child.
        O Laius' fatal son,
        Would I had ne'er thee known !
        My heart cries loud for thee
        In tones of agony,
And frenzied exclamation wild.
For, to speak sooth, thou didst restore my life,
And gav'st my soul sweet respite after strife.

Enter 2nd Messenger.

2nd Mess. O ye whom Thebe still hath chosen in chief
To honour, what a burden of dire woe
Awaits your eyes, your ears ! What piercing grief
Your hearts must suffer, if as kinsmen should
Ye still regard the house of Laïus !
Not Phasis, no, nor Ister's mightiest flood,
Can ever wash away the stains and purge
This mansion of the horror that it hides.
And more it soon shall give to light, not now
Unconsciously determined.   Of all ill,
Self-chosen sorrows are the worst to bear.
    Ch. What hast thou new to add ? the weight of grief
From that we know burdens the heart enough.
    2nd Mess. Soon spoken and soon heard is the chief
        sum.
Jocasta's royal head is sunk in death.
    Ch. The hapless queen ! What was the fatal cause ?
    2nd Mess. Her own determination.   Those who saw
Felt agony that never can be told.
Yet to the utmost of my memory's power
The wretched lady's passion you shall hear.
When she had passed in her rash mood within
The vestibule, straight to the bridal room
She rushes, tearing with both hands her hair.
Then having entered, pulling fast the door,
She called aloud on Laïus, long dead,
With anguished memory of the hour that knew
The embrace wherefrom he died, leaving his queen

                                            E

To breed a dreadful brood for his own son.
And loudly o'er the bed she mourned, where she,
Hapless, in twofold wedlock had brought forth
Husband from husband, children from a child.
We could not know the moment of her death,
Which followed soon, for Œdipus with cries
Swept in, and would not let us see her end,
But held our eyes as he careered the hall,
Demanding arms, and where to find his wife,—
No, not his wife, but fatal mother-croft,
Cropped doubly with himself and his own seed.
And in his rage some god directed him
That way,—for 'twas no man of us at hand.
And with a fearful shout, as following
His leader, he assailed the folding-doors,
Then, battering inwards from the mortised bolts
The bending boards, he breaks into the room;
Where high suspended we beheld the queen,
In twisted cordage resolutely swung.
And he with dreadful outcry when he saw,
Poor king! undid the hanging noose.   But when
She lay upon the ground, 'twas terrible
To see what followed—for he tore away
The brooch-pins that had fastened her attire,
And, lifting, smote his eyeballs to the root,
Saying, Henceforth they should not see the evil
Suffered or done by him in the past time,
But evermore in darkness now should scan
The features he ought never to have seen,
And not discern the souls he longed to know.

Thus crying aloud, not once but oftentimes
He dashed the points into his eyes ; and soon
The bleeding pupils moistened all his beard,
Nor stinted the dark flood, but all at once
The ruddy hail poured down in plenteous shower.
Thus from two springs, from man and wife together,
Burst the joint evil that is now o'erflowing.
And the old happiness in that past day
Was truly happy, but the present hour
Hath groaning, death, disaster, shame, all ill
Without exemption, that hath e'er been named.

   Ch. And finds the sufferer now some pause of woe ?

   2nd Mess. He bids make wide the portal and display
To all the men of Thebes the man who slew
His father, who unto his mother did
What I dare not repeat, and fain would fling
His body from the land, nor calmly bide
The shock of his own curse in his own hall.
Meanwhile he needs some comfort and some guide,
For such a load of misery who can bear ?
Thyself shalt judge : for, lo, the palace-doors
Unfold, and presently thine eyes will see
A hateful sight, yet one thou needs must pity.

Enter ŒDIPUS, *blind.*

   Ch. O horror of the world !
Too great for mortal eye !
More terrible than all I have known of ill !
What madness, O poor head !
Came o'er thee ? Who in heaven

Hath leapt against thy hapless life
With boundings out of measure fierce and huge ?
Ah ! wretched one, I cannot look on thee :
No, though I long to search, to ask, to learn.
Thine aspect is too horrible.—I cannot !

Œd. Me miserable ! Whither am I borne ?
Into what region are these wavering sounds
Wafted on aimless wings ? O ruthless Fate !
To what a height thy fury hath soared !

Ch.   Too far
For human sense to follow, or human thought
To endure the horror.

Œd.   O dark cloud, descending
Unutterably on me ! invincible,
Abhorred, borne onward by too sure a wind.
Woe, woe !
Woe ! Yet again I voice it, with such pangs
Both from these piercing wounds I am assailed
And from within through memory of my grief.

Ch. Nay, tis no marvel if thy matchless woe
Redouble thine affliction and thy moan !

Œd. Ah ! Friend, thou art still constant ! Thou re-
        mainest
To tend me and to care for the blind man.
Alas !
I know thee well, nor fail I to perceive,
Dark though I be, thy kind familiar voice.

Ch. How dreadful is thy deed ! How couldst thou
        bear
Thus to put out thine eyes ? What Power impelled thee ?

Œd. Apollo, O my friends, Apollo brought to pass
In dreadful wise, this my calamitous woe.
But I,—no being else,—I with this hand destroyed them.
[Pointing to his eyes.
For why should I have sight,
To whom nothing now gave pleasure through the eye?
  Ch. There speak'st thou truly.
  Œd.   What could I see, whom hear
With gladness, whom delight in any more?
Lead me away out of the land with speed!
Be rid of the destroyer, the accursed,
Whom most of all the world the Gods abhor.
  Ch. O miserable in thy calamity
And not less miserable in thy despair,
Would thou wert still in ignorance of thy birth!
  Œd. My curse on him who from the cruel bond
That held my feet in that high pasture-land
Freed me, and rescued me from murder there,
And saved my life! Vain kindness! Then to have died
Had spared this agony to me and mine.
  Ch. Ay, would it had been so!
  Œd.   Then had I ne'er
Become a parricide, ne'er borne the shame
Of marriage-bonds incestuous! But now
I am God-abandoned, Son of the unholy,
Rival of him who gave me being. Ah woe!
What sorrow hath precedence over sorrows?
That sorrow Œdipus must bear!

  Ch. I know not how to call thee wise in this,

Better be out of life than live in blindness !
   Œd. That this last act hath not been for the best
Instruct me not, nor counsel me again.
For if I still had eyes, how could I look
In Hades on my father's countenance,
Or my all-hapless mother, when, toward both,
I have done deeds not strangling could atone.
Ah ! but my children were a sight of joy ;—
Offspring of such a marriage ! were they so ?
Never, to eyes of mine ! nor town, nor tower,
Nor holy fanes o' the gods, which I myself,
Dowered with the fairest life of Theban men,
Have forfeited, alas, by mine own law,
Declaring men should drive from every door
One marked by Heaven as impious and impure,
Nay worse, of Laius born ! And was I then,
By mine own edict branded thus, to look
On Theban faces with unaltered eye ?
Nay verily ; but had there been a way
To stop the hearing-fountain through the ear,
I had not faltered, but had closed and barred
Each gate of this poor body ; deaf and blind !
So thought might sweetly dwell at rest from harm.
Cithæron ! Why didst thou receive me ? Why
Not slay me then and there ? So had I not
Told to the world the horror of my birth.
O foster-home of Corinth and her king,
How bright the life ye cherished, filming o'er
What foulness underneath ! For I am vile,
And vile were both my parents. So 'tis proved.

O cross-road in the covert of the glen,
O thicket in the gorge where three ways met,
Bedewed by these my hands with mine own blood
From whence I sprang—have you forgotten me?
Or doth some memory haunt you of the deeds
I did before you, and went on to do
Worse horrors here?   O doubly cursèd womb!
That gave me being, and then again sent forth
Fresh saplings springing from the selfsame seed,
To amaze men's eyes and hearts with dire confusion
Of father, brother, son, bride, mother, wife,
Murder of parents, and all shames that are!
Silence alone befits such deeds.   Then, pray you,
Hide me immediately away from men!
Kill me outright, or fling me far to sea,
Where never ye may look upon me more.
Come, lend your hand unto my misery!
Comply, and fear not, for my strain of woe
Is incommunicable to all but me.

 Ch. With timely presence to fulfil thy need
With act and counsel, Creon comes, who now
Is regent of this country in thy room.

 Œd. Alas, what shall I say to him?   What plea
Will hold for my defence?   My evil part
Toward him in all the past is all too plain.

Enter CREON.

 Cr. I come not, Œdipus, to mock thy woes,
Or to reproach thee for thine evils past.
But ye, (*to* Chorus) if all respect of mortal eye

Be dead, let awe of the universal flame
Of life's great nourisher, our lord the Sun,
Forbid your holding thus unveiled to view
This huge abomination, which nor Earth
Nor sacred Element, nor light of Heaven
Can once endure.   Convey him in with speed.
Religion bids that kindred eyes and ears
Alone should witness kindred crime and woe.

Œd. By Heaven, since thou hast reft away my fear,
So nobly meeting my unworthiness,
I pray thee, hear me for thine own behoof.

Cr. What boon art thou so earnest to secure?

Œd. Fling me with speediest swiftness from the land,
Where never I may speak with mortal more.

Cr. Doubt not I would have done so, but the God
Must be inquired of, ere we act in this.

Œd. Sure unequivocal was his command,
The parricide, the unholy, should be slain.

Cr. Ay, so 'twas spoken : but, in such a time,
We needs must be advised more perfectly.

Œd. Will ye then ask him for a wretch like me?

Cr. Yes.   For even thou methinks wilt now believe.

Œd. Not only so.   But I will charge thee too,
With urgent exhortation, to perform
The funeral-rite for her who lies within—
She is thy kinswoman—howe'er thou wilt.
But never let this city of my sires
Claim me for living habitant !   There, there
Leave me to range the mountain, where my nurse,
Cithæron, echoeth with my name, Cithæron,

Which both my parents destined for my grave
So my true murderers will be my death.
Yet one thing I can tell.   Mine end will come
Not by disease nor ordinary chance.
I had not lived when at the point to die,
But for some terrible doom.   Then let my fate
Run out its full career.   But for my children
Thou, Creon, shalt provide.   As for my sons,
I pray thee burden not thyself with them.
They ne'er will lack subsistence—they are men.
But my poor maidens, hapless and forlorn,
Who never had a meal apart from mine,
But ever shared my table, yea, for them
Take heedful care; and grant me, though but once,
Yea, I beseech thee, with these hands to feel,
Thou noble heart! the forms I love so well,
And weep with them our common misery.
Oh, if my arms were round them, I might seem
To have them as of old when I could see.—
What?   Am I fooled once more, or do I hear
My dear ones weeping?   And hath Creon sent,
Pitying my sorrows, mine own children to me
Whom most I love?   Can this be truth I utter?

   Cr. Yea, I have done it.   For I knew the joy
Thou ever hadst in this, thy comfort now.

   Œd. Fair be thy fortune, and, for this last deed,
May Heaven protect thee better far than me!
Where are ye, O my children?   Come, draw near
To these my hands of brother blood with you,
Hands that have made so piteous to your sight

The spectacle of his once brilliant eyes,
Who all in blindness, with no thought of ill,
Became your father at that fount of life,
Where he himself had being !   Oh ! for you
I weep, not seeing you, when I take thought
Of all the bitter passages of fate
That must attend you amongst men.   For where
Can ye find fellowship, what civic throng
Shall ye resort unto, what festival,
From whence, instead of sights or sounds enjoyed,
Ye will not come in tears unto your home ?
And when ye reach the marriageable bloom,
My daughters, who will be the man to cast
His lot with the unfortunate, and take
All those reproaches on his name, which press
So sorely on my parents and on you ?
What evil is not here ?   Your father slew
His father, and then eared the mother-field
Where he himself was sown, and got you from
The source of his own birth.   Such taunts will fly.
And who will marry you ?   No man, my daughters ;
But ye must wither childless and unwed.
Son of Menœceus, who alone art left
As father to these maidens, for the pair
That gave them birth are both alike undone,
Suffer them not, being your kinswomen,
To wander desolate and poor, nor make
Their lot perforce the counterpart of mine.
But look with pity upon their youth, thus left
Forlorn of all protection save from thee.

Noble one, seal this promise with thy hand !
For you, my children, were ye of an age
To ponder speech, I would have counselled you
Full carefully.   Now I would have you pray
To dwell where 'tis convenient, that your life
May find more blessing than your father knew.

Cr. Thou hast had enough of weeping.   Close thee in
thy chamber walls.

Œd. I must yield, though sore against me.

Cr.   Yea, for strong occasion calls.

Œd. Know'st thou on what terms I yield it ?

Cr.   Tell me, let us hear and know.

Œd. That ye send me from the country.

Cr.   God alone can let thee go.

Œd. But the gods long since abhor me.

Cr.   Thou wilt sooner gain that boon.

Œd. Then consent.

Cr.   'Tis not my wont to venture promises too soon.

Œd. Lead me now within the palace.

Cr.   Come, but leave thy children.

Œd.   Nay !
Tear not these from my embraces !

Cr.   Think not all things to command.
Of the good thou hadst beforetime much hath fleeted
from thy hand.

CHORUS.

Dwellers in our native Thebe, fix on Œdipus your eyes,
Who resolved the dark enigma, noblest champion and
    most wise.
Glorious, like a sun he mounted, envied of the popular
    throng;
Now he sinks in seas of anguish, plunged the lashing
    waves among.
Therefore, with the old-world sages, waiting for the final
    day,
I will call no mortal happy, while he holds his house of
    clay,
Till without one pang of sorrow, all his hours have
    passed away.

ŒDIPUS AT COLONOS.

THE PERSONS.

ŒDIPUS, *old and blind.*

ANTIGONE, *his daughter, a young girl.*

ISMENE, *his daughter, a young girl.*

CHORUS *of Village Guardians.*

An Athenian.

THESEUS, *King of Athens.*

CREON, *Envoy from Thebes.*

POLYNICES, *the elder son of Œdipus.*

Messenger.

ŒDIPUS had remained at Thebes for some time
But he was afterwards banished by the command
consent of his own sons. Their intention at
claim to the throne. But by-and-by ambi
Eteocles, the youngest-born, and he persuaded
to banish his elder brother. Polynices took re
he married the daughter of Adrastus, and lev
iliaries to support his pretentions to the thron
going into exile Œdipus had cursed his sons.

Antigone after a while fled forth to join her fa
in his wanderings. Ismene also once brought hin

Years have now elapsed, and the Delphian o   proclaims
Œdipus dies in a foreign land the enemies
come her.

In ignorance of this fact, Œdipus, now aged as well as blind
led by his daughter Antigone, appears before the grove of
Eumenides, at Colonos, in the neighbourhood of Athens. He
felt an inward intimation, which is strengthened by some w
of the oracle received by him long since at Delphi, that his invo
tary crimes have been atoned for, and that the Avenging Dei
will now receive him kindly and make his cause their own.

After some natural hesitation on the part of the village-co
cillors of Colonos, Œdipus is received with princely magnanir
by Theseus, who takes him under the protection of Athens,
defends him against the machinations of Creon.

Thus the blessing of the Gods, which Œdipus carried with hi
is secured to Athens and denied to Thebes. The craft of Creon a
the prayers of Polynices alike prove unavailing. Then the man
many sorrows, whose essential nobleness has survived them all, pass
away mysteriously from the sight of men.

The scene is laid at Colonos, a suburb of Athens much frequente
by the upper classes, especially the Knights (see Thuc. viii., 67)
and before the sacred grove of the Eumenides, or Gentle Goddesses,
a euphemistic title for the Erinyes, or Goddesses of Vengeance.

ŒDIPUS AT COLONOS.

ŒDIPUS.   ANTIGONE.

Œdipus. Antigone, child of the old blind sire,
What land is here, what people? Who to-day
Shall dole to Œdipus, the wandering exile,
Their meagre gifts? Little I ask, and less
Receive without a murmur, since my woes,
And the long years ripening the noble mind,
Have schooled me to content.—But, O my child,
If thou espiest where we may sit, though near
Some holy precinct, stay me and set me there,
Till we may learn where we are come. 'Tis ours
To hear the will of strangers, and to obey.

Antigone. Poor woe-worn father, yonder city's wall
That shields her, looks far distant ; but this ground
Is surely sacred, thickly planted over
With olive, bay and vine, within whose bowers
Thick-fluttering song-birds make sweet melody.
Here then repose thee on this unhewn stone.
Thou hast travelled far to-day for one so old.

Œd. Seat me, my child, and be the blind man's guard
Ant. Long time hath well instructed me in that.

Œd. Now, canst thou tell me where we have set our
  feet?

Ant. Athens I know, but not the nearer ground.

Œd. Ay, every man that met us in the way
Named Athens.

Ant.   Shall I go, then, and find out
The name of the spot?

Œd.   Yes, if 'tis habitable.

Ant. It is inhabited.   Yet I need not go.
I see a man even now approaching here.

Œd. How? Makes he toward us? Is he drawing
  nigh?

Ant. He is close beside us.   Whatsoe'er thou find'st
Good to be spoken, say it.   The man is here.

Enter an Athenian.

Œd. O stranger, learning from this maid, who sees
Both for herself and me, that thou art come
With timely light to clear our troubled thought—

Athenian. Ere thou ask more, come forth from where
  thou sittest!
Ye encroach on ground forbidden human tread.

Œd. What ground? And to what power thus conse-
  crate?

Ath. None may go near, nor dwell there. 'Tis pos-
  sessed
By the dread sisters, children of Earth and Night.

Œd. What holy name will please them, if I pray?

Ath. "All-seeing Gentle Powers" the dwellers here
Would call them. But each land hath its own rule

Œd. And gently may they look on me, who now
mplore them, and will never leave this grove !

Ath. What saying is this?

Œd.   The watchword of my doom.

Ath. Yet dare I not remove thee, till the town
Iave heard my purpose and confirm the deed.

Œd. By Heaven I pray thee, stranger, scorn me not,
'oor wanderer that I am, but answer me.

Ath. Make clear thy drift. Thou'lt have no scorn
        from me.

Œd. Then, pray thee, tell me how ye name the place
Vhere now I sit.

Ath.   The region all around
s sacred. For 'tis guarded and possessed
ly dread Poseidon, and the Titan mind
'hat brought us fire,—Prometheus. But that floor
Vhereon thy feet are resting, hath been called
'he brazen threshold of our land, the stay
)f glorious Athens, and the neighbouring fields
ire fain to honour for their patron-god
'hee, O Colonos, first of Knights, whose name

                              [*Pointing to a statue.*

'hey bear in brotherhood and own for theirs.
uch, friend, believe me, is this place, not praised
n story, but of many a heart beloved.

Œd. Then is the land inhabited of men?

Ath. By men, who name them from Colonos there.

Œd. Have they a lord, or sways the people's voice ?

Ath. Lord Theseus, child of Ægeus, our late king.

Œd. Will some one of your people bring him hither ?

                                        F

Ath. Wherefore? What urgent cause requires him now ?

Œd. He shall gain mightily by granting little.

Ath. Who can gain profit from the blind ?

Œd.   The words

These lips will utter, shall be full of sight.

Ath. Well, thou look'st nobly, but for thy hard fate.

This course is safe. Thus do. Stay where I found

       thee,

Till I go tell the neighbour townsmen here

Not of the city, but Colonos.   They

Shall judge for thee to abide or to depart.   [*Exit.*

Œd. Tell me, my daughter, is the stranger gone ?

Ant. He is gone, father.   I alone am near.

Speak what thou wilt in peace and quietness.

Œd. Dread Forms of holy Fear, since in this land

Your sanctuary first gives this frame repose,

Be not obdúrate to my prayer, nor spurn

The voice of Phœbus, who that fatal day,

When he proclaimed my host of ills to come,

Told me of rest after a weary time,

Where else but here ? " When I should reach my bourne,

And find repose and refuge with the Powers

Of reverend name, my troubled life should end

With blessing to the men who sheltered me,

And curses on their race who banished me

And sent me wandering forth." Whereof he vouched

       me

Sure tokens, or by earthquake, or by fire

From heaven, or thundrous voices.   And I know

Some aëry message from your shrine hath drawn me

With wingèd whisper to this grove.   Not else
Had ye first met me when I came, nor I
Sate on your dread unchiselled seat of stone,
With dry cold lips greeting your sober shrine.
Then give Apollo's word due course, and give
Pause and completion to my life, if now
Those toils and sorrows past the human bound
Seem not too little in your sight.   Sweet powers,
Offspring of primal darkness, hear my prayer !
Hear it, Athenæ, of all cities queen,
Great Pallas' foster-city ! Look with ruth
On this poor shadow of King Œdipus,
This fading semblance of his ancient form.

Ant. Be silent now.   There comes an aged band
With jealous looks to know thine errand here.

Œd. I will be silent, and thine arm shall guide
My footsteps under covert of the grove
Out of the path, till I make sure what words
These men will utter.   Warily to observe
Is the prime secret of wise heedfulness.   [*Exeunt.*

CHORUS (*entering*).

Look out ! Who can it be ?
Where is he ? Gone !
Vanished ! O where ?
Where stolen away, most impious,
Most uncontrolled of men ?
Look well, inquire him out,
Search keenly in every nook !

—Some wanderer is the aged wight,
A wanderer surely, not a native here.
Else never had he gone within
The untrodden grove
Of these unmarried, unapproachable in might,
Whose names we dare not breathe,
But pass their shrine
Without a look, without the sound of words,
Uttering an unheard voice of reverential thought.
But now, we are told, one is arrived,
Who neither cares nor fears.
Whom, searching all around the sacred place,
I cannot yet discern, where he is hidden from me.

Œd. (*behind*). Behold me! For I " see by sound,"
As some men say.
　Ch. O, O!
With horror I see him, with horror hear him speak.
　Œd. Pray you, regard me not as a transgressor!
　Ch. Defend us, Zeus! Who can the old man be?
　Œd. Not one of happiest fate,
Or enviable, O guardians of this land!
"Tis manifest; else had I not come hither
Led by another's eyes, not sought your port
With princely mien begging a slender boon.
　Ch. Alas! And are thine eyes
Sightless? O full of misery,
As thou look'st full of years!
But know thou, I must hinder thee
From bringing down this curse.

ıou art trespassing.   Yet keep thy foot
om falling in that verdant, voiceless dell,
here running water in the sacred bowl
 mingled with a draught of honied streams.
ɩoid that, hapless stranger, with all care.
ɛmove thee!   Come away!
ɩstance impedes the sound.   Dost hear,
oe-weary wanderer?   If thou bringest aught
ɩfore our council, leave forbidden ground,
ɩd there, where all have liberty,
ɩeak,—but till then, avaunt thee!
Œd. Daughter, what must I think, or do?
Ant.   My sire!
e must conform us to the people's will,
ɩd yield ere they compel.
Œd.   Give me thy hand.
Ant. Thou hast it.
Œd.   —Strangers, let me not
ɩ wronged, when I have trusted you
ɩd come from where I stood!
Ch. Be sure that from this seat
ɔ man shall drag thee off against thy will.
Œd. Farther?
Ch.   Advance thy foot.
Œd.   Yet more?
Ch.   Assist him onward,
aiden; thou hast thy sight.
Ant. Come, follow, this way follow with thy darkened
     steps,
ɩther, the way I am leading thee.

Ch. Content thee, sojourning in a strange land,
O man of woe!
To eschew whate'er the city holds accurs'd,
And honour what she loves!
 Œd.   Then do thou lead me, child,
Where with our feet secure from sin
We may be suffered both to speak and hear.
Let us not war against necessity.
 Ch. There! From that bench of rock
Go not again astray.
 Œd. Even here?
 Ch.   Enough, I tell thee.
 Œd.   May I sit?
 Ch. Ay, crouch thee low adown
Crooking thy limbs upon the stone.
 Ant. Father, this task is mine.—
Frame thou thy motion by my gentle pace—
 Œd. Woe is me!
 Ant. And lean upon this loving hand
Thy reverend aged form.
 Œd. Woe, for my cruel fate! [ŒDIPUS *is seated.*

Ch. Now thou unbendest from thy stubborn ways,
O man of woe!
Declare, what mortal wight thou art,
That, marked by troublous fortune, here art led.
What native country, shall we learn, is thine?
 Œd. O strangers, I have none!
But do not—
 Ch.   What dost thou forbid, old sir?

Œd. Do not, oh, do not ask me who I am,
Nor probe me with more question.
    Ch.   What dost thou mean?
    Œd. My birth is dreadful.
    Ch.   Tell it forth.
    Œd. What should I utter, O my child?   Woe is me!
    Ch. Thy seed, thy father's name, stranger, pronounce!
    Œd. Alas!   What must I do?   My child!
    Ant. Since no resource avails thee, speak!
    Œd. I will.   I cannot hide it further.
    Ch. Ye are long about it.   Haste thee!
    Œd.   Know ye of one
Begotten of Laïus?
    Ch.   Horror!   Horror!   O!
    Œd. Derived from Labdacus?
    Ch.   O Heaven!
    Œd. Fate-wearied Œdipus?
    Ch.   Art thou he?
    Œd. Fear not my words.
    Ch.   Oh!   Oh!
    Œd. Unhappy me!
    Ch.   Oh!
    Œd.   Daughter, what is coming?
    Ch. Away!   Go   forth.   Leave ye   the   land.   Be
        gone!
    Œd. And where, then, is the promise thou hast given?
    Ch. No destined punishment attends the deed
That wreaks precedent wrong.
Deceit, matched with deceit, makes recompense
Of evil, not of kindness.   Get thee forth!

Desert that seat again and from this land
Unmooring speed thee away, lest on our state
Thou bring some further harm!
　　Ant.　　　　　　　　　　　　O strangers,
So full of reverent care!
Since ye cannot endure my father here,
Aged and blind,
Because ye have heard a rumour of the deeds
He did unknowingly,—yet, we entreat you,
Strangers, have pity on me, the hapless girl,
Who pray for mine own sire and for none else,
—Pray, looking in your eyes with eyes not blind,
As if a daughter had appeared to you,
Pleading for mercy to the unfortunate.
We are in your hands as in the hand of God,
Helpless.　O then accord the unhoped-for boon!
By what is dear to thee, thy veriest own,
I pray thee,—chattel or child, or holier name!
Search through the world, thou wilt not find the man
Who could resist the leading of a God.

　　Ch. Daughter of Œdipus, be well assured
We see with pity both thy case and his,
But fear of Heavenly wrath restricts our speech
To that we have already said to thee.
　　Œd. What profit lives in fame and fair renown
By unsubstantial rumour idly spread?
When Athens is extolled with peerless praise
For reverence, and for mercy!—She alone
The sufferer's shield, the exile's comforter!

What have I reaped hereof?   Ye have raised me up
From yonder seat, and now would drive me forth
Fearing a name !   For there is nought in me
Or deeds of mine to make you fear.   My life
Hath more of wrong endured than of wrong done,
Were it but lawful to disclose to you
Wherefore ye dread me,—not my sin but their's,
My mother's and my sire's.   I know your thought.
Yet never can ye fasten guilt on me,
Who, though I had acted with the clear'st intent,
Repaying but ill for ill, were free from sin ?
But as it was, all blindly I went forth
On that dire road, while they who ruined me
Knew well they were accomplishing my fall.
Then, in Heaven's name, as ye have bid me rise,
Be my protectors, gentle sirs, and do not
In jealous reverence for the blessed Gods
Rob them of truest reverence, but know this :—
God looks upon the righteousness of man
And his unrighteousness, nor ever yet
Hath one escaped who wrought iniquity.
Take part, then, with the Gods, nor overcloud
The golden fame of Athens with dark deeds,
But as ye have pledged your faith to shelter me,
Defend me and rescue, not rejecting me
Through mere abhorrence of my ruined face.
For on a holy mission am I come,
Sent with rich blessings for your neighbours here.
And when the head and sovereign of your race
Is present, ye shall be informed of all.

'Till then, be gracious to me, and not perverse.

  Ch. Thy meaning needs must strike our hearts with
     awe,
Old wanderer! so weighty are the words
'That body it forth.   Therefore we are content
The Lord of Athens shall decide this case.

  Œd. And where is he who rules this country, sirs?

  Ch. He keeps his father's citadel.   But one
Is gone to fetch him, he who brought me hither.

  Œd. Think you he will consider the blind man,
And come in person here to visit him?

  Ch. Be sure he will,—when he hath heard thy name.

  Œd. And who will carry that?

  Ch.   'Tis a long road;
But rumour on the tongues of wayfarers
Flies far and wide, so that he needs must hear;
And hearing, never doubt but he will come.
So noised in every land hath been thy name,
Old king, that were he sunk in drowsiness,
'That sound would bring him swiftly to thy side.

  Œd. Well, may he come to bless his city and me!
When hath not goodness blessed the giver of good?

  Ant. O Heavens! What shall I say, what think, my
     sire?

  Œd. Daughter Antigone, what is it?

  Ant.   I see
A woman coming towards us, mounted well
On a fair Sicilian palfrey, and her face
With brow-defending hood of Thessaly

Is shadowed from the sun.   What must I think?
Is it she or no?   Can the eye so far deceive?
It is.   'Tis not.   Unhappy that I am,
I know not.—Yes, 'tis she.   For drawing near
She greets me with bright glances, and declares
Beyond a doubt, Ismene's self is here.

Œd. What say'st thou, daughter?

Ant.   That I see thy child,
My sister.   Soon her voice will make thee sure.

Enter ISMENE.

Ismene. Father and sister!—names how sweet to me!
Hard hath it been to reach you, yea, and hard
I find it now to look on you for grief.

Œd. Child, art thou here?

Ism.   Father! O sight of pain!

Œd. Offspring and sister!

Ism.   Woe for thy dark fate!

Œd. Hast thou come, daughter?

Ism.   On a troublous way.

Œd. Touch me, my child!

Ism.   I give a hand to both.

Œd. To her and me?

Ism.   Three linked in one sad knot.

Œd. Child, wherefore art thou come?

Ism.   In care for thee.

Œd. Because you missed me?

Ism.   Ay, and to bring thee news,
With the only slave whom I could trust.

Œd.   And they,

Thy brethren, what of them?   Were they not there
To take this journey for their father's good?
  Ism. Ask not of them.   Dire deeds are their's to-day.
  Œd. How in all points their life obeys the law
Of Egypt, where the men keep house and weave
Sitting within-doors, while the wives abroad
Provide with ceaseless toil the means of life.
So in your case, my daughters, they who should
Have ta'en this burden on them, stay at home
Like girls, while ye instead of them relieve
My miseries by your toil.   Antigone,
When once her childhood ended, and her frame
Grew firm, began her ceaseless ministry,
In tendance on an old man's wanderings
Oft in the forest ranging up and down
Fasting and barefoot through the burning heat
Or pelting rain, unhappy maid, nor thinks
Of home or comfort, so her father's need
Be satisfied.   And thou, that camest before,
Eluding the Cadmeians, and didst tell me
What words Apollo had pronounced on me,
And when they banished me, wast my firm guard,
What news, Ismene, bring'st thou to thy sire
To-day?   What mission sped thee forth?   I know
Thou com'st not idly, but with fears for me.
  Ism. Father, I will not say what I endured
In searching out the place that sheltered thee.
To tell it o'er would but renew the pain.
But of the danger now encompassing
Thine illstarred sons,—of that I came to speak.

At first they strove with Creon and declared
The throne should be left vacant and the town
Freed from pollution,—paying deep regard
In their debate to the dark heritage
Of ruin that had fastened on thy race.
Far different is the strife which holds them now,
Since Heaven, conspiring with their sinful mind,
Incites them both to seize on sovereign power.
Eteocles, in pride of younger years
Robbed elder Polynices of his right,
Dethroned and banished him.   To Argos then
Goes exiled Polynices, and obtains
Through intermarriage a strong favouring league,
Whose word is, " Either Argos vanquishes
The seed of Cadmus or exalts their fame."
This, father, is no vain array of words,
But dreadful truth, nor can I tell, where Heaven
Is to reveal his mercy to thy woe.

    Œd. And hadst thou ever hoped the Gods would
       care
For mine affliction, and restore my life?

   Ism. My hope rests on the oracle of to-day

   Œd. What oracle hath been declared, my child?

   Ism. That they shall seek thee forth, alive or dead,
To bring salvation to the Theban race.

   Œd. Who can win safety through such help as mine?

   Ism. 'Tis said their victory depends on thee.

   Œd. When shrunk to nothing, am I indeed a man?

   Ism. Yea, for the Gods uphold thee, who then
      destroyed.

Œd. Poor work, to uphold in age who falls whei
    young !

Ism. Know howsoe'er that Creon will be here
For this same end, ere many hours be spent.

Œd. For what end, daughter? Tell me in plaii
    speech.

Ism. To set thee near their land, that thou may'st be
Beyond their borders, but within their power.

Œd. What can my lying at their gates avail?

Ism. 'Twill grieve them should thy burial bring then
    bale

Œd. There needs no oracle to tell one that.

Ism. And therefore they would place thee near thei
    land,
Where thou may'st have no power upon thyself.

Œd. Say then, shall Theban dust o'ershadow me?

Ism. The blood of kindred cleaving to thy hand,
Father, debars thee.

Œd.   Never, then, henceforth,
Shall they lay hold on me !

Ism.   If that be so,
The seed of Cadmus shall be smitten.

Œd.   What cause
Shall spring to light to bring this doom to pass?

Ism. Thine anger, when they halt beside thy tomb.

Œd. From whom hast thou heard this?

Ism.   Sworn messenger:
Brought such report from Delphi's holy shrine.

Œd. Hath Phœbus so pronounced my destiny?

Ism. Such their report, who then returned to Thebes.

Œd. Did my sons hear?

Ism.   They know it both alike.

Œd. Villains, who, being informed of such a word
Turned not their thoughts toward me, but rather chose
Ambition and a throne !

Ism.   It wounds mine ear
To hear it spoken, but the news I bring
Is to that stern effect.

Œd.   Then I pray Heaven
The fury of their fate-appointed strife
May ne'er be quenched, but that the end may come
According to my wish upon them twain
To this contention and arbitrement
Of battle which they now assay and lift
The spear ! So neither he who now usurps
The sceptred power should have possession still,
Nor should his brother out of banishment
Ever return :—who, when their own true sire
Was shamefully thrust from his native land,
Checked not his fall nor saved him, but, for them,
I was driven homeless and proclaimed an exile.
Ye will tell me 'twas in reason that the State
Granted this boon to mine express desire.
Nay; for in those first hours of agony,
When my heart boiled, and it seemed sweetest to me
To die the death, and to be stoned with stones,
There came no minister of such relief.
But after lapse of days, when all my pain
Was softened, and I felt that my hot spirit
Had run to fierce excess of bitterness

In punishing my crime—then, then the State
Drove me for ever from the land, and they,
Their father's sons, who might have saved their father,
Cared not to help him, but betrayed by them,
For lack of one light word, I wandered forth
To homeless banishment and beggary.
But these weak maidens to their nature's power
Have striven to furnish me with means to live
And dwell securely, girt around with love.
My sons have chosen before their father's life
A lordly throne and sceptred sovereignty.
But never shall they win support from me,
Nor shall the Theban throne for which they strive
Bring any comfort to them.   This I know,
Comparing with my daughter's prophecies
Those ancient oracles which Phœbus once
Spake in mine ear.   Then let them send, to seek me,—
Creon, or who is strongest in their State.
For if ye, strangers, will but add your might
To the protection of these awful Powers,
The guardians of your deme, to shelter me,
Ye shall acquire for this your State a saviour
Mighty to save, and ye shall vex my foes.

   Ch. Thou art worthy of all compassion, Œdipus,
And so are these thy daughters.   Now, moreover,
Since thou dost give thyself to save this land,
I would advise thee for the best.

   Œd.   Kind sir,
Be my good guide.   I will obey thy voice.

   Ch. Propitiate then these holy powers, whose grove

Received thee first in entering on our land.

Œd. What are the appointed forms?   Advise me, sirs.

Ch. First see to it that from some perennial fount
Pure hands provide a holy drink-offering.

Œd. And when I have gotten this unpolluted draught?

Ch. You will find bowls, carved by a skilful hand,
Whose brims and jutting handles you must crown.

Œd. With leaves or flocks of wool, or in what way?

Ch. With tender wool ta'en from a young ewe-lamb.

Œd. Well, and what follows to complete the rite?

Ch. Next, make libation toward the earliest dawn.

Œd. Mean'st thou from those same urns whereof thou
          spakest?

Ch. From those three vessels pour three several streams,
Filling the last to the brim.

Œd.   With what contents
Must this be filled?   Instruct me.

Ch.   Not with wine,
But water and the treasure of the bee.

Œd. And when the o'er-shadowed earth has drunk
          of this,
What follows?

Ch.   Thou shalt lay upon her then
From both thy hands a row of olive-twigs—
Counting thrice nine in all—and add this prayer—

Œd. That is the chief thing,—that I long to hear.

Ch. That, as we name them Gentle Powers, so they
From gentle hearts would yield their suppliant aid;—
Be this thy prayer, or theirs who pray for thee,
Spoken not aloud, but so that none may hear;

And in departing, turn not.　This being done,
I can stand by thee without dread.　But else,
I needs must fear concerning thee.

　　Œd.　　　　　　　　　　　My daughters,
Have ye both heard our friends who inhabit here?

　　Ant. Yea, father; and we wait for thy command.

　　Œd. I cannot go.　Two losses hinder me,
Two evils, want of strength and want of sight.
Let one of you go and perform this service.
One soul, methinks, in paying such a debt
May quit a million, so the heart be pure.
Haste, then, to do it.　Only leave me not
Untended.　For I cannot move alone
Nor without some one to support me and guide.

　　Ism. I will be ministrant.　But let me know
Where I must find the place of offering.

　　Ch. Beyond this grove.　And, stranger maid, if aught
Seem wanting, there is one at hand to show it.

　　Ism. Then to my task.　Meantime, Antigone,
Watch by our sire.　We must not make account
Of labour that supplies a parent's need.　　　　[*Exit.*

　　Ch. Thy long since slumbering woe I would not wake
　　　　again
But yet I long to learn.

　　Œd.　　　　　　　　　What hidden lore?

　　Ch.　　　　　　　　　　　　　The pain.
That sprang against thy life with spirit-mastering force.

　　Œd. Ah, sirs, as ye are kind, re-open not that source
Of unavoided shame.

Ch.   Friend, we would hear the tale
Told truly, whose loud breath doth hourly more prevail.
  Œd. Misery!
  Ch.   Be not loth!
  Œd.   O bitterness!
  Ch.   Consent
For all thou didst require we gave to thy content.
  Œd. Oh, strangers, I have borne an all-too-willing
    brand,
Yet not of mine own choice.
  Ch.   Whence? We would understand.
  Œd. Nought knowing of the curse she fastened on my
    head
Thebe in evil bands bound me.
  Ch.   Thy mother's bed,
Say, didst thou fill? mine ear still echoes to the noise.
  Œd. 'Tis death to me to hear, but, these, mine only
    joys,
Friends, are my curse.
  Ch.   O Heaven!
  Œd.   The travail of one womb
Hath gendered all you see, one mother, one dark doom.
  Ch. How? Are they both thy race, and—
  Œd.   Sister branches too,
Nursed at the self-same place with him from whom they
    grew.
  Ch. O horror!
  Œd.   Ay, not one, ten thousand charged me then!
  Ch. O sorrow!
  Œd.   Never done, an ever-sounding strain.

Ch. O crime!

Œd.   By me ne'er wrought.

Ch.   But how?

Œd.   The guerdon fell.
Would I had earned it not from those I served too well.

  Ch. But, hapless, didst thou slay—

Œd.   What seek ye more to know?

Ch. Thy father?

Œd.   O dismay! Ye wound me, blow on blow.

Ch. Thy hand destroyed him.

Œd.   Yes. Yet lacks there not herein
A plea for my redress.

  Ch.   How canst thou clear that sin?

Œd. I'll tell thee. For the deed, 'twas proved mine,—
     O 'tis true.
Yet by Heaven's Law I am freed:—I wot not whom
     I slew.

  Ch. Enough. For lo! where Ægeus' princely son,
Theseus, comes hither, summoned at thy word.

Enter THESEUS.

Theseus. From many voices in the former time
Telling thy cruel tale of sight destroyed
I have known thee, son of Laius, and to-day
I know thee anew, in learning thou art here.
Thy raiment, and the sad change in thy face
Proclaim thee who thou art, and pitying thee,
Dark-fated Œdipus, I fain would hear
What prayer or supplication thou preferrest

To me and to my city, thou and this
Poor maid who moves beside thee.   Full of dread
Must be that fortune thou canst name, which I
Would shrink from, since I know of mine own youth,
How in strange lands a stranger as thou art
I stood the brunt of perilous circumstance
Beyond all others ; nor shall any man,
Like thee an alien from his native home,
Find me turn from him, or not succour him.
 I am a man and know it.   To-morrow's good
Is no more mine than thine or any man's.

Œd. Thy noble spirit, Theseus, in few words
Has made my task of utterance brief indeed.
Thou hast told aright my name and parentage
And native city.   Nought remains for me
But to make known mine errand, and our talk
Is ended.

   The.   Tell me plainly thy desire.

   Œd. I come to offer thee this woe-worn frame,
As a free boon,—not goodly in outward view.
A better gift than beauty is that I bring.

   The. What boon dost thou profess to have brought
     with thee ?

   Œd. Thou shalt know by-and-by,—not yet awhile.

   The. When comes the revelation of thine aid ?

   Œd. When I am dead, and thou hast buried me.

   The. Thou cravest the last kindness.   What's between
Thou dost forget or else neglect.

   Œd.   Herein
One word conveys the assurance of the whole.

The. You sum up your petition in brief form.

Œd. Look to it.   Great issues hang upon this hour.

The. Mean'st thou in this the fortune of thy sons
Or mine?

Œd.   I mean the force of their behest
Compelling my removal hence to Thebes.

The. So thy consent were asked, 'twere fair to yield.

Œd. Once I was ready enow.   They would not then.

The. Wrath is not wisdom in misfortune, man!

Œd. Nay, chide not till thou knowest all.

The.   Say on!
I must not speak without just grounds.

Œd.   O Theseus,
I am cruelly pursued with wrong on wrong.

The. Mean'st thou that prime misfortune of thy birth?

Œd. No.   That hath long been rumoured through the
      world.

The. What, then, can be thy grief?   If more than that,
'Tis more than human.

Œd.   Here is my distress :—
I am made an outcast from my native land
By mine own offspring.   And return is barred
For ever to the man who slew his sire.

The. How should they then require thee to go near,
And yet dwell separate?

Œd.   The voice of Heaven
Will drive them to it.

The.   As fearing what reverse
Prophetically told?

Œd.   Destined defeat
By Athens in the Athenian land.

 The.   What source
Of bitterness 'twixt us and Thebes can rise?
 Œd. Dear son of Ægeus, to the Gods alone
Comes never Age nor Death.   All else i' the world
Time, the all-subduer, merges in oblivion.
Earth and men's bodies weaken, fail, and perish :
Faith withers, breach of faith springs up and grows,
And neither men nor cities that are friends
Breathe the same spirit with continuing breath.
Love shall be turned to hate, and hate to love
With many hereafter, as with some to-day.
And though, this hour, betwixt great Thebes and thee
No cloud be in the heavens, yet moving Time
Enfolds a countless brood of days to come,
Wherein for a light cause they shall destroy
Your now harmonious league with severing war,
Even where my slumbering form, buried in death,
Coldly shall drink the life-blood of my foes,
If Zeus be Zeus, and his son Phœbus true.
I would not speak aloud of mysteries.
Then let me end where I began.   Preserve
Thine own good faith, and thou shalt never say,
Unless the Gods shall fail me, that for nought
Athens took Œdipus to dwell with her.
 Ch. My lord, long since the stranger hath professed
Like promises of blessing to our land.
 The. And who would dare reject his proffered good?
Whose bond with us of warrior amity
Hath ne'er been sundered,—and to-day he comes
A God-sent suppliant, whose sacred hand

Is rich with gifts for Athens and for me.
In reverent heed whereof I ne'er will scorn
His boon, but plant him in Athenian soil.
And if it please our friend to linger here,
Ye shall protect him :—if to go with me
Best likes thee, Œdipus,—reflect, and use
Thy preference.   For my course shall follow thine.

 Œd. Ye Heavens, reward such excellence !

 The.   How, then ?
Is it thy choice now to go home with me?

 Œd. Yea, were it lawful.   But in this same spot—

 The. What wouldst thou do?   I'll not withstand thy
  will.

 Œd. I must have victory o'er my banishers.

 The. Thy dwelling with us, then, is our great gain?

 Œd. Yes, if thou fail me not, but keep thy word.

 The. Nay, fear not me !   I will aye be true to thee.

 Œd. I will not bind thee, like a knave, with oaths.

 The. Oaths were no stronger than my simple word.

 Œd. What will ye do, then ?

 The.   . What is that thou fearest ?

 Œd. They will come hither.

 The.   Thy guards will see to that.

 Œd. Beware, lest, if you leave me—

 The   Tell not me,
I know my part.

 Œd.   Terror will have me speak.

 The. Terror and I are strangers.

 Œd.   But their threats !
Thou canst not know—

The.   I know that none shall force
Thee from this ground against thy will.   Full oft
In wrath have threatening words been voluble,
Yet, when the mind regained her place again,
The threatened evil was no more.   And now
Bold words of boastful meaning have proclaimed
Thy forcible abduction by thy kin.
Yet shall they find (I know it) the voyage from Thebes,
On such a quest, long and scarce navigable.
Whate'er my thought, if Phœbus sent thee forth,
I would bid thee have no fear.   And howsoe'er,
My name will shield thee from all injury.

CHORUS.

Friend, in our land of victor-steeds thou art come
To this Heaven-fostered haunt, Earth's fairest home,
Gleaming Colonos, where the nightingale
In cool green covert warbleth ever clear,
True to the deep-flushed ivy and the dear
Divine, impenetrable shade,
From wildered boughs and myriad fruitage made,
Sunless at noon, stormless in every gale.
Wood-roving Bacchus there, with mazy round,
And his nymph nurses range the unoffended ground.

And nourished day by day with heavenly dew
Bright flowers their never-failing bloom renew,
From eldest time Dêo * and Cora's crown
Clustering narcissus, and the golden beam

* Demeter.

Of crocus, while from many a sleepless spring
Perennial waters duly minist'ring
Cephisus, never withering down,
Daily with quickening power
Revisits Earth in unpolluting shower.
Her wide breast heaves, thrilled by the gentle stream.
The quiring Muses love to seek the spot
And Aphrodite's golden car forsakes it not.

Here too a plant, nobler than e'er was known
On Asian soil, grander than yet hath grown
In Pelops' mighty Dorian isle, unsown,
    Free, self-create, the conquering foeman's fear,
The kind oil-olive, silvery-green,
Chief nourisher of childish life, is seen
To burgeon best in this our mother-land ;
No warrior, young, nor aged in command,
    Shall ravage this, or scathe it with the spear ;
For guardian Zeus' unslumbering eye
Beholds it everlastingly.
    And Athens' grey-eyed Queen, dwelling for ever near.

Yet one more praise mightier than all I tell
O'er this my home, that Ocean loves her well,
    And coursers love her, children of the wave.
To grace these roadways Prince Poseidon first
Framed for the fiery horse, that else had burst
From man's control, the spirit-taming bit.
And the trim bark, rowed by strong arms, doth flit
    O'er briny seas with glancing motion brave.

Thanks ! Lord of waters, for thy glorious gift !
The Sea-nymphs' plashing throng glide not more
   smoothly swift.

Ant. O land exalted thus in blessing and praise,
Now is thy time to prove these brave words true.
   Œd. What hath befallen, my daughter ?
   Ant.   Here at hand,
Not unaccompanied, is Creon, father.
   Œd. Dear aged friends, be it yours now to provide
My safety and the goal of my desire !
   Ch. It shall be so. Fear naught. I am old and weak,
But Athens in her might is ever young.

Enter CREON.

Creon. Noble inhabiters of Attic ground
I see as 'twere conceived within your eyes
A newly-risen alarm at mine approach.
Yet fear me not, nor utter one harsh word.
I come not with intent to act, for I
Am aged, and the state whereto I come
Is mighty,—none in Hellas mightier,—
That know I well. But now I am sent to bring
By fair persuasion to our Theban plain
The reverend form of him now present here.
Nor came this mission from one single will,
But the commands of all my citizens
Are on me, seeing that it becomes my birth
To mourn his sorrows most of all the state.
Thou, then, poor sufferer, lend thine ear to me

And come.   All Cadmus' people rightfully
.Invite thee with one voice unto thy home,
I before all,—since I were worst of men,
Were I not pained at thy misfortunes, sir,
—To see thee wandering in the stranger's land
Aged and miserable, unhoused, unfed,
Singly attended by this girl, whom I,
Alas, could never have believed would fall
Into such depth of undeservèd woe,
Hapless, unshielded maiden ! evermore
Caring for.that poor eyeless head of thine,
Roving in beggary, so young, with no man
To marry her,—exposed to all mischance.
O misery, what deep reproach I have laid
On thee and me and all our ill-starred race !
But who can hide evil that courts the day ?
Thou, therefore, Œdipus, without constraint,
(By all the Gods of Cadmus' race I pray thee)
Withdraw this horror from the sight of men
By coming to the ancestral city and home
Of thy great sires, bidding a kind farewell
To worthiest Athens, as is meet.   But Thebes
Thy native land, yet more deserves thy love.

   Œd. Thou unabashed in knavery, who canst frame
For every cause the semblance of a plea
Pranked up with righteous seeming, why again
Dost thou contrive my ruin, and attempt
To catch me where I most were grieved being caught ?
Beforetime, when the trouble of my soul
Was plaguing me, and I would fain have rushed

To instant banishment, thou wouldst not then
Grant this indulgence to my strong desire.
But when I had fed my passion to the full,
And all my pleasure was to live at home,
Then 'twas thy choice to chase and banish me,
Nor was this name of kindred then so dear.
And now once more, when thou behold'st this city
And people joined in friendly bands with me,
Now thou art bent to drag me off again,
Hiding hard policy with courtly show.
Strange kindness, to love men against their will !
Suppose, when thou wast earnest in some suit
No grace were granted thee, but all denied,
And when thy soul was sated, then the boon
Were offered, when such grace were graceless now ;
—Poor satisfaction then were thine, I trow !
Even such a gift thou profferest me to-day,
Kind in pretence, but really full of evil.
These men shall know thy wickedness.   Thou comest
To take me, not unto my home, but where
I may be lodged beyond your gates, that so
Your Thebe may come off untouched of harm
From her encounter with Athenian men.
Ye shall not have me thus.   But you shall have
My vengeful spirit ever in your land
Abiding for destruction,—and my sons
Shall have this portion in their father's ground,
To die therein.   Know I not things in Thebes
Better than thou ? Yea, for 'tis mine to hear
Safer intelligencers,—Zeus himself,

And Phœbus, high interpreter of Heaven.
Thou bring'st a tongue suborned with false pretence,
Sharpened with insolence;—but in shrewd speech
Thou shalt find less of profit than of bane.
This thou wilt ne'er believe. Therefore begone !
Let me live here. For even such life as mine
Were not amiss, might I but have my will.

   Cr. Which of us twain, believ'st thou, in this talk
Hath more profoundly sinned against thy peace ?

   Œd. If thou prevail'st with these men present here
Even as with me, I shall be well content.

   Cr. Unhappy man, will not even Time bring forth
One spark of wisdom to redeem thine age ?

   Œd. Thou art a clever talker. But I know
No just man who in every cause abounds
With eloquent speech.

   Cr.   'Tis not to abound in speech,
When one speaks fitting words in season.

   Œd.   Oh !
As if thy words were few and seasonable !

   Cr. Not in the dotard's judgment.

   Œd.   Get thee gone !
I speak their mind as well—and dog not me
With watchers to prescribe my dwelling-place !

   Cr. These men shall witness—for thy word is naught ;
And for thy spiteful answer to thy friends,
If once I seize thee—

   Œd.   Who shall seize on me
Without the will of my protectors here ?

   Cr. Well, short of that, thou shalt have pain, I trow.

Œd. What hast thou done, that thou canst threaten
  thus ?

Cr. One of thy daughters I have sent in charge.
This other, I myself will quickly take.

Œd. O, cruel !

Cr. Soon thou'lt have more cause to cry.

Œd. Hast thou my child ?

Cr. I will have both ere long.

Œd. Dear friends, what will ye do ? Will ye forsake
  me ?

Will you not drive the offender from your land ?

Ch. Stranger, depart at once ! Thou hast done wrong,
And wrong art doing.

Cr. (*to attendants*). Now then, lead her away
By force, if she refuse to go with you.

Ant. Ah me ! unhappy ! Whither shall I flee ?
What aid of God or mortal can I find ?

Ch. What dost thou, stranger ?

Cr. I will lay no hand
On him, but on my kinswoman.

Œd. Alas !
Lords of Colonos, will ye suffer it ?

Ch. Thou art transgressing, stranger.

Cr. Nay, I stand
Within my right.

Ch. How so ?

Cr. I take mine own.

Œd. O help me, Athens !

Ch. Stranger, forbear ! What dost thou ?
Let go, or thou shalt try thy strength with us.

Cr. Unhand me!

Ch.   Not while this intent is thine.

Cr. If you harm me, you will have war with Thebes.

Œd. Did I not tell you this would come?

Ch.   Let go
The maid with speed.

Cr.   Command where you have power.

Ch. Leave hold, I say!

Cr.   Away with her, say I!

Ch. Come hither, neighbours, come!
My city suffers violence. Wrongful men
Are hurting her with force. Come hither to me!

Ant. Unhappy, I am dragged away,—O strangers!

Œd. Where art thou, O my child?

Ant.   I go away
Against my will.

Œd.   Reach forth thy hands, my daughter!

Ant. I cannot.

Cr.   Off with her!

Ant.   Alas, undone!

          [Exit, guarded.

Cr. Thou shalt not have these staves henceforth to
  prop
Thy roaming to and fro. Take thine own way!
Since thou hast chosen to thwart thy nearest kin,—
Beneath whose orders, though a royal man,
I am acting now,—and thine own native land.
The time will surely come when thou shalt find
That in this deed and all that thou hast done
In opposition to their friendly will,

Thou hast counselled foolishly against thy peace,
Yielding to anger, thy perpetual bane.   [*Going.*

   Ch. Stranger, stay where thou art!

   Cr.   Hands off, I say!

   Ch. Thou shalt not go, till thou restore the maids.

   Cr. Soon, then, my city shall retain from you
A weightier cause of war.   I will lay hands
Not on the maidens only.

   Ch.   What wilt thou do?

   Cr. Œdipus I will seize and bear away.

   Ch. Great Heaven forefend!

   Cr.   It shall be done forthwith,
Unless the ruler of this land prevent me.

   Œd. O shameless utterance!   Wilt thou lay thy hold
On me?

   Cr.   Be silent! 'Speak no more!

   Œd.   No more?
May these dread Goddesses not close my lips
To this one prayer of evil against thee,
Thou villain, who, when I have lost mine eyes,
Bereavest me of all that I had left
To make my darkness light! Therefore I pray,
For this thy sinful act, may He in heaven
Whose eye sees all things, Helios,* give to thee
Slowly to wither in an age like mine!

   Cr. Men of this land, bear witness to his rage!

   Œd. They see us both, and are aware that I
Pay thee with words for thy remorseless deed.

   Cr. No longer will I curb my wrath.   Though lone

* The Sun-god.

H

And hampered by mine age, I will bear off
This man !

   Œd.   Me miserable !

   Ch.   How bold thou art,
If standing here thou think'st to do this thing !

   Cr. I do.

   Ch.   Then Athens is to me no city.

   Cr. Slight men prevail o'er strength in a just cause.

   Œd. Hear ye his words ?

   Ch.   He shall not make them good.
Be witness, Zeus !

   Cr.   Zeus knows more things than thou.

   Œd. Is not this violence ?

   Cr.   Violence you must bear.

   Ch. Come, chieftain of our land !
Come hither with all speed.   They pass the bound.

Enter THESEUS.

   The. Wherefore that shouting !   Daunted by what fear
Stayed ye me sacrificing to the God
Who guards this deme Colonos ?   Let me know
What cause so hastened my reluctant foot.

   Œd. Dear friend, (I know thy voice addressing us),
One here hath lately done me cruel wrong.

   The. Who is the wrong-doer, say, and what the deed ?

   Œd. This Creon, whom thou seest, hath torn away
The loving pair of girls that were mine all.

   The. Can this be possible ?

   Œd.   Thou hear'st the truth.

   The. Then one of you run to the altar-foot

Hard by, and haste the people from the rite,
Horsemen and footmen at the height of speed
To race unto the parting of the roads
Where travellers from both gorges wont to meet.
Lest there the maidens pass beyond our reach
And I be worsted by this stranger's might
And let him laugh at me. Be swift! Away!
For him, were I as wroth as he deserves,
He should not go unpunished from my hand.
Yet, as he came with colour of a law,
The laws alone shall give him chastisement.
Thou goest not from this land till thou hast brought
And set those maidens full in presence here ;
Since by thine act thou hast disgraced both me
And thine own lineage and thy native land,
Who with unlicenced inroad hast assailed
An ancient city that hath still observed
Justice and equity, and apart from law
Ratifies nothing ; and, being here, hast cast
Authority to the winds, and made thine own
Whate'er thou wouldst, bearing it off perforce,—
Deeming of me forsooth as nothing worth,
And of my city as one enslaved to foes
Or void of manhood.   Not of Thebe's will
Come such wild courses.   It is not her wont
To foster men in sin, nor would she praise
Thy doings, if she knew that thou hast robbed
Me and the gods, and dragged poor suppliant wights
From sanctuary at thy will.   I would not, then,
Had I perchance set foot within thy land,

Even were my cause most righteous, have presumed,
Without consent of him who bore chief sway,
To seize on any man, but would have known
How to behave myself on foreign ground.
Thou bring'st disgrace on thine own mother-state
All undeservedly, and the weight of years
Hath made thee aged, but not wise.—Again
I bid those maids now to be brought with speed,
Unless thou wouldst be made a sojourner
In Athens by compulsion.   This I speak
Not with my lips alone, but from my will.

 Ch. Stranger, dost thou perceive thy plight? Thy
   birth
Is owned as noble, but thine evil deeds
Are blazoned visibly.

 Cr.   Great Ægeus' son !
Not as misprizing this thy city's strength
In arms, or wisdom in debate, I dared
This capture, but in simple confidence
Thy citizens would not so envy me
My blood-relations, as to foster them
Against my will,—nor welcome to their hearths
A man incestuous and a parricide,
The proved defiler of his mother's bed.
Such was the mount of Ares that I knew,
Seat of high wisdom, planted in their soil,
That suffers no such lawless vagabond
To dwell within the borders of your realm.
Relying on that I laid my hands upon
This prey.   Nor had I done so, were it not

For the deep curse he invoked on me and mine.
That moved me to requital, since even Age
Still bears resentment, till the power of death
Frees men from anger, as from all annoy.
Being sovereign here thou wilt do thy will.   For I,
Though I have justice on my side, am weak
Throughbeing alone.   Yet if you meddle with me,
Old as I am, you'll find me dangerous.

  Œd. O boldness void of shame ! Whom dost thou
   think
Thy contumely most harms, this aged head
Or thine, who hast thus let pass thy lips the crimes
I have borne unwittingly.   So Heaven was pleased
To wreak some old offence upon our race.
Since in myself you will find no stain of sin
For which such ruinous error 'gainst myself
And mine own house might be the recompense.
Tell me, I pray thee, if a word from Heaven
Came to my father through the oracle
That he should die by his son's hand,—how then
Can this be justly a reproach to me,
The child not yet begotten of my sire,
An unborn nothing, unconceived?   Or if,
Born as I was to misery, I met
And killed my father in an angry fray,
Nought knowing of what I did or whom I slew,
What reason is 't to blame the unwitting deed?
And, oh, thou wretch ! art not ashamed to force me
To speak that of my mother, thine own sister,
Which I will speak, for I will not withhold it,

Since thou hast been thus impious with thy tongue.
She was my mother, oh, the bitter word !
Though neither knew it, and having borne me, she
Became the mother of children to her son,
An infamous birth !   Yet this I know, thy crime
Of speech against us both is voluntary.
But all involuntary was my deed
In marriage and is this mine utterance now.
No,—mine shall not be called a bosom-sin,
Neither in this, nor in that deed of blood
Against my sire, wherewith thou still revil'st me.
For answer me one question.   If to-day,
Here, now, one struck at thee a murderous stroke,—
At thee, the righteous person,—wouldst thou ask
Who the man was who sought your life, or strike
Forthwith?   Methinks, as you loved life, your hand
Would strike before you questioned of the right,
Or reasoned of his fatherhood you slew.
Yet such the snare I fell into : such woes
Heaven drave me to fulfil.   My father's spirit,
Came he to life, would not gainsay my word.
But thou, no just man, as thou seem'st, but one
To whom nothing is too dreadful or too deep
For words, so rail'st on me, in such a presence.
Well thou dost flatter the great name of Theseus,
And Athens in her glory stablished here,
But midst thy fulsome praises thou forgettest
How of all lands that yield the blessed Gods
Just homage of true piety, this land
Is foremost.   Yet from hence thou wouldst beguile

Me, the aged suppliant.   Nay, from hence thou wouldst
     drag
Myself with violence, and hast reft away
My children.   Wherefore I beseech these powers,
With solemn obsecration and appeal,
To come and take my part, that thou mayst know
What men are they that guard this sacred realm.
  Ch. My lord, the stranger deserves well.   His fate
s grievous, but the more demands our aid.
  The. Enough of words.   The captors and their prey
Are hasting ;—we, they have wronged, are standing still.
  Cr. I am powerless here.   What dost thou bid me
     do ?
  The. I bid thee lead the way they are gone.   But I
Will go along by thee, that if thou keepest
Those maidens from us hereabouts, thou mayest
Thyself disclose them to mine eyes.   But if
They are off and past the boundary, thou and I
May spare our labour.   Others hotly urge
That chase, o'er whom those ravishers shall ne'er
Vaunt their escape in triumph from this land.
Come, lead the way !   Thou hast and hast not.   Fortune
Hath seized thee seizing on thy prey.   So quickly
Passes the gain that's got by wrongful guile.
Nay, thou shalt have no helper.   Well I wot
Thou flew'st not to this pitch of truculent pride
Alone, or unsupported by intrigue.
But thy bold act hath some confederate here.
This I must look into, nor let great Athens
Prove herself weaker than one single man.

Hast caught my drift?   Or is my voice as vain
Now, as you thought it when you planned this thing?
  Cr. I will gainsay naught of what thou utterest here.
But once in Thebes, I too shall know my course.
  The. Threaten, but go !   Thou, Œdipus, wait here
In quietness and perfect trust that I,
If death do not prevent me, will not rest
Till I restore thy children to thy hand.

CHORUS.

Soon shall the wheeling foes
Clash with the din of brazen-throated War.
  Would I were there to see them close,
Be the onset near or far !
  Whether at Daphne's gorge to Phœbus dear,
Or by the torch-lit shore
Where kind maternal powers for evermore
  Guard blessed mysteries of holy fear
To nourish mortal souls ;
Powers, whose dread seal of silent awe controls
  The tongue of each Eumolpid minister.
  There, on that sacred way,
Shall the divinest head
  Of Theseus, rouser of the fray,
And those free maids, in their two squadrons led,
  Meet in the valorous fight
  That conquers for the right.

Else, passing westward of the snow-capped rock,
  Even now they are drawing nigh

The tract beyond the pasture high
　　Where Oea feeds her flock.
The riders ride, the chariots flee
　　At racing speed.—'Tis done !
He shall be vanquished.　Our land's chivalry
　　Are valiant, valiant every warrior son
　　Of Theseus.—On they run !
Their bridles glancing to the light,
Forward each steed is straining to the fight,
　　Forward each eye and hand
　　Of all that mounted band,
Athena's knighthood, champions of her name
And his who doth the mighty waters tame,
　　Rhea's son that from of old
　　Doth the Earth with seas enfold.

Strive they ?　Or is the battle still to be ?
　　　An eager thought in me
Is pleading, " Soon must they restore
The enduring maid, whose kinsmen vex her sore ! "
To-day shall Zeus perform his will.
The righteous cause wakes my prophetic skill.
Oh ! had I wings, and like a storm-swift dove
Poised on some aëry cloud might there descry
　　　The conflict from above,
Scouring the region with mine eye !

Sovran of Heaven, all-seeing Zeus, afford
　　　Unto this nation's lord
Triumphant strength to crown the fair emprize,

Thou, and sage Pallas, thy dread child!
And thou, Apollo, huntsman of the wild,
—With thine own sister, who doth still pursue
Swift many-spotted stags,—arise,
With love we pray you, be our champions true!
  Yea, both together come
To help our people and our home!

Leader of Ch. Ah! wanderer friend, thou wilt not have
  to accuse
 Thy seer of falsehood. I behold the maids
 This way once more in safe protection brought.
Œd. Where? Is it true? How say you?
Ant.   Father, father!
Oh that some God would give thee once to see
This man whose royal virtue brings us hither!
 Œd. My daughters, are ye there?
Ant.   Saved by the arm
Of Theseus and his most dear ministers.
 Œd. Come near me, child, and let your father feel
The treasure he had feared was lost and gone.
 Ant. Not hard the boon which the heart longs to
  give.
 Œd. Where are ye, where?
Ant.   Together we draw near.
 Œd. Loved saplings of a solitary tree!
 Ant. A father's heart hides all.
 Œd.   Staves of mine age!
 Ant. Forlorn supporters of an ill-starred life!
 Œd. I have all I love; nor would the stroke of death

Be wholly bitter, with you standing by.
Press close to either side of me, my children;
Grow to your sire, and ye shall give me rest
From mine else lonely, hapless, wandering life.
And tell your tale as briefly as ye may,
Since at your age short speaking is enough.

Ant. Here is our saviour.   He shall tell thee all,
And save this labour both for us and thee.

Œd. O sir, think it not strange that I prolong
The unhoped-for greeting with my children here.
Full well I know, the joy I find in them
Springs from thee only, and from none beside.
Thou, thou alone hast rescued them.   May Heaven
Fulfil my prayer for thee and for thy land!
Since only in Athens, only here i' the world,
Have I found pious thought and righteous care,
And truth in word and deed.   From a full heart
And thankful mind I thus requite thy love,
Knowing all I have is due to none but thee.
Extend to me, I pray thee, thy right hand,
O King, that I may feel thee, and may kiss,
If that be lawful, thy dear head!   And yet
What am I asking?   How can one like me
Desire of thee to touch an outlawed man,
On whose dark life all stains of sin and woe
Are fixed indelibly?   I will not dare—
No, nor allow thee!—None but only they
Who have experience of such woes as mine
May share their wretchedness.   Thou, where thou art,
Receive my salutation, and henceforth

Continue in thy promised care of me
As true as to this moment thou hast proved.
  The. I marvel not at all if mere delight
In these thy daughters lengthened thy discourse,
Or led thee to address them before me.
That gives me not the shadow of annoy.
Nor am I careful to adorn my life
With words, but with the lustre of good deeds.
And thou hast proof of this.   For I have failed
In nothing of my promise, aged King !
Here stand I with thy children in full life
Unharmed in aught the foe had threatened them.
And now why vaunt the deeds that won the day,
When these dear maids will tell them in thine ear?
But let me crave thy counsel on a thing
That crossed me as I came.   Small though it seem
When told, 'tis worthy of some wonder, too.
Be it small or great, men should not let things pass.
  Œd. What is it, O son of Ægeus ?   Let me hear,
Since I know nought of all whereof thou askest.
  The. 'Tis said that one, though not thy countryman,
Yet kin to thee, appears in suppliant guise,
Fallen prostrate by the altar of the God
To whom I had sacrificed ere we set forth.
  Œd. What countryman, and wherefore suppliant
       there ?
  The. One thing alone I know.   He craves of thee
Some speech, they say, that will not hold thee long.
  Œd. His kneeling there imports no trivial suit.
  The. All he desires, they tell me, is to come,

Have speech with thee, and go unharmed away.

 Œd. Who can he be that kneels for such a boon?

 The. Think, if at Argos thou a kinsman hast
Who might desire to obtain so much of thee.

 Œd. Dear friend! Hold there! No more!

 The.   What ails thee, man?

 Œd. Ask it not of me!

 The.   What? Speak plainly forth.

 Œd. Thy words have shown me who the stranger is.

 The. And who is he that I should say him nay?

 Œd. My son, O King,—hateful to me, whose voice
Least of the world I could endure to hear.

 The. What pain is there in hearing? Canst thou
   not
First hear, and then refuse what thou dislikest?

 Œd. My Lord, I have come to loathe his very voice.
I pray thee force me not to yield in this.

 The. Think that the God must be considered too;
The suppliant's posture may compel thy care.

 Ant. Father, give ear, though I be young that speak.
Yield to the scruple of the King, who claims
This reverence for his people's God;—and yield
To us who beg our brother may come near.
Take heart! He will not force thee from thy will.
What harm can come of listening? Wisdom's ways
Reveal themselves through words. He is thy son:
Whence, were his heartless conduct against thee
Beyond redemption impious, O my sire,
Thy vengeance still would be unnatural.
O let him!—Others have had evil sons

And passionate anger, but the warning voice
Of friends hath charmed them from their mood.   And
     thou
Look not, I pray thee, on thy present griefs,
But on those ancient wrongs thou didst sustain
From father and from mother.   Thence I am sure
Thou wilt learn that evil passion ends in woe.
Thy sightless eyes are no slight argument
To warn thee through the feeling of thy loss.
Relent and hear us !   'Tis a mere disgrace
To beg so long for a just boon.   The King
Is kind to thee.   Be generous in return.

   Œd. Child, your dear pleading to your hard request
Hath won me.   Let this be as ye desire.
Only, my lords, if he is to come near,
Let no man's power molest my liberty.

   The. I need no repetition, aged friend,
Of that request.   Vaunt will I not; but, thou,
Be sure, if Heaven protects me, thou art free.

CHORUS.

Who, loving life, hath sought
   To outrun the appointed span,
Shall be arraigned before my thought
   For an infatuate man.
Since the added years entail
   Much that is bitter ;—joy
Flies out of ken, desire doth fail,
   The wished-for moments cloy.

But when the troublous life
  Be it less or more, is past,
With power to end the strife
  Comes rescuing Death at last.
Lo! the dark bridegroom waits! No festal choir
Shall grace his destined hour, no dance, no lyre!

  Far best were ne'er to be;
    But, once he hath seen the day,
  Next best by far for each to flee
    As swiftly as each may,
  Yonder from whence he came;
    For let but Youth be there
  With her light fooleries, who shall name
    The unnumbered brood of Care?
  No trial spared, no fall!
    Feuds, battles, murders, rage,
  Envy, and last of all, ·
    Despised, dim, friendless age!
Ay, there all evils, crowded in one room,
Each at his worst of ill, augment the gloom.

  Such lot is mine, and round this man of woe,
  —As some grey headland of a northward shore
  Bears buffets of all wintry winds that blow,—
  Fresh storms of Fate are bursting evermore
    In thundrous billows, borne
    Some from the waning light,
Some through mid-noon, some from the rising morn,
    Some from the stars of Night.

Ant. Ah! Who comes here? Sure 'tis the Argive
   man
Approaching hitherward, weeping amain.
And, father, it is he!
   Œd.   Whom dost thou mean?
   Ant. The same our thoughts have dwelt on all this
      while,
Polynices. He is here.
   Polynices.   What shall I do?
I stand in doubt which first I should lament,
My own misfortunes or my father's woes,
Whom now I find an outcast in his age
With you, my sisters, in the stranger land,
Clothed in such raiment, whose inveterate filth
Horridly clings, wasting his reverend form,
While the grey locks over his eye-reft brow
Wave all unkempt upon the ruffling breeze.
And of close kindred to these miseries
Seems yond' provision for his hungry frame.
Wretch that I am! Too late I learn the truth,
And thus give witness to mine own disgrace,
Which is as deep as thy distress. Myself
Declare it. Ask not others of my guilt.
But seeing that Zeus on his almighty throne
Keeps Mercy in all he does to counsel him,
Thou, too, my father, let her plead with thee!
The evil that is done may yet be healed;
It cannot be augmented. Art thou silent?
O turn not from me, father! Speak but once!
Wilt thou not answer me? Must I endure

Shame with thine anger, nor be told the cause?
O ye his daughters, one with me in blood,
Say, will not ye endeavour to unlock
The stern lips of our unrelenting sire?
Let him not thus dismiss in silent scorn
Without reply the suppliant of Heaven!

Ant. Thyself, unhappy one, say why thou camest.
Speech ofttimes, as it flows, touching some root
Of pity or joy, or even of hate, hath stirred
The dumb to utterance.

Pol.   I will tell my need :—
First having claimed protection of the God
From whose dread altar he who rules this land
Hath brought me under safe-guard of his power,
Scatheless to speak and hear and go my way.
Whose word, I am confident, will be made good,
Strangers, by you, and by my sisters twain,
And by our sire.—Now let me tell the cause
Wherefore I come.—Father, thy son is driven
To exile from the country of his birth,
Because, being elder-born, I claimed to sit
Upon thy sovereign throne.   Eteocles,
For this, my younger brother, thrust me forth,
Not having won the advantage in debate
Or trial of manhood, but through guileful art
Gaining the people's will.   Whereof my soul
Acknowledges thine anger as chief cause,
And thereto prophet-voices testify.
For when I had come to Dorian Argolis,
I raised, through marriage with Adrastus' child,

An army bound in friendly league with me,
Headed by those who in the Apian land
Hold first pre-eminence and honour in war,
With whose aid levying all that mighty host
Of seven battalions, I have deeply sworn
Either to die, or cast from Theban soil
The authors of the offence.   So far, so well.
But why come hither?   Father, to entreat thine aid
With earnest supplication for myself
And for my firm allies, who at this hour,
Seven leaders of seven bands embattled there,
Encompass Thebe's plain.   Amphiaráus,
Foremost in augury, foremost in war,
First wields his warlike spear.   Next, Œneus' son,
Ætolian Tydeus ; then Etéoclus
Of Argive lineage : fourth, Hippomedon,
Sent by his father Tálaüs, and the fifth
Is Capaneus, who vaunts he will destroy
Thebe with desolating fire.   The sixth,
Parthenopæus, from the Arcadian glen
Comes down, swift Atalanta's valiant son,
Named from his mother's life of maidenhood
Till she conceived him.   And the seventh am I,
Thy son, or if not thine, but the sad child
Of evil Destiny, yet named thy son,
Who lead this dauntless host from Argolis
Against the Theban land.   Now one and all
We pray thee on our knees, conjuring thee
As thou dost love these maids and thine own life,
My father, to forgive me, ere I go

To be revenged upon my brother there
Who drave me forth and robbed me of my throne.
If aught in prophecy deserves belief,
'Tis certain, whom thou favourest, those shall win.
Now by the wells whereof our fathers drank
And by the Gods they worshipped, hear our prayer,
Grant this petition : since alike in woe,
Alike in poverty and banishment,
Partakers of one destiny, thou and I
Depend on strangers for a dwelling-place.
Whilst he at home, the tyrant, woe is me,
Laughs at us both in soft luxurious pride.
Whose power, so thou wilt favour my design,
With no great effort in one little hour
I will scatter to the winds, and bring thee home
And stablish thee in thine own palace-hall
Near to myself, and cast the usurper forth.
All this with thy consent I shall achieve,
But without thee, not safety even is mine.

 Ch. For his sake who hath brought him, Œdipus,
Say what is meet, and let him go in peace.

 Œd. Ay, were it not the lord of all this land
Theseus, that brought him to me and desired
He might hear words from me,—never again
Had these tones fallen upon his ear.   But now
This boon is granted him : he shall receive,
Ere he depart, such utterance of my tongue,
As ne'er shall give him joy ;—ne'er comfort thee,
Villain, who when possessed of the chief power
Which now thy brother hath in Thebes, didst banish

Me thine own father who stand here, didst make me
To live in exile, wearing this attire
Which moves thy tears now that thine own estate
Is fallen into like depth of struggling woe.
Weeping avails not.   Howsoe'er I live,
I must endure, still counting thee my murderer.
'Tis thou hast thus surrounded me with pain,
'Tis thou didst drive me forth, and driven by thee
I beg my bread, a wandering sojourner.
Yea, had these daughters not been born to me
To tend me, I were dead, for all thou hast done.
They have rescued, they have nursed me.   They are men,
Not women, in the strength of ministry.
Ye are another's, not my sons.—For this
The eye of Destiny pursues thee still
Eager to light on thee with instant doom
If once that army move toward the town
Of ancient Thebes,—the *town;* no dearer name,
'City' or 'Country' shall beseem thy lip
Till ye both fall, stained with fraternal gore.
Long since I launched that curse against you twain
Which here again I summon to mine aid,
That ye may learn what duty children owe
To a parent, nor esteem it a light thing
That ye were cruel sons to your blind sire.
These maidens did not so.   Wherefore my curse
Prevails against thy prayer for Thebe's throne,
If ancient Zeus, the eternal lawgiver,
Keep primal Justice for his counsellor.
Begone, rejected and renounced by me,

And take with thee, thou vilest of the vile,
This imprecation :—Vain be thine attempt
In levying war against thy father's race,
Frustrate be thy return to Argos' vale :
Die foully by a fratricidal hand,
And foully slay him who hath banished thee !
I call moreover from his dread abysm
The Power that waits upon a father's curse
To bear thee off to his confíne : I invoke
The Spirits who haunt this ground, and the fierce God
Who hath filled you both with this unnatural hate.—
Go now with all this in thine ears, and tell
The people of Cadmus and thy firm allies
In whom thou trustest, what inheritance
Œdipus hath divided to his sons.

   Ch. 'Tis pity for thee, prince, to have come at all :
And now we bid thee go the way thou camest.

   Pol. Alas ! Vain enterprise, and hope undone !
Alas, my comrades ! To what fatal end
I led you forth from Argos, woe is me !
I may not tell it you,—no, nor return ;
In silence I must go to meet my doom.
Daughters of this inexorable sire,
Since now ye have heard his cruel curse on me,
Ah ! in Heaven's name, my sisters, do not ye
Treat me despitefully, but, hereafter, if
Our father's execration is fulfilled
And ye shall be restored to Thebes again,
Provide me funeral honours and a grave !
So shall this ample praise which ye receive

For filial ministration, in that day
Be more than doubled through your care for me.
   Ant. Brother, I beg thee, listen to my voice!
   Pol. Dearest Antigone, speak what thou wilt.
   Ant. Turn back thy host to Argos with all speed,
And ruin not thyself and Thebe too.
   Pol. Impossible.   If once I shrink for fear,
I nevermore may lead them to the war.
   Ant. But why renew thy rage?   What benefit
Comes to thee from destroying thine own land?
   Pol. 'Tis shameful to remain in banishment,
And let my brother mock my right of birth.
   Ant. Then seest thou not how straight unto their aim
Our father's prophecies of mutual death
Against you both are sped?
   Pol.   He speaks his wish.
'Tis not for me to yield.
   Ant.   Oh me, unhappy!
But who that hears the deep oracular sound
Of his dark words, will dare to follow thee?
   Pol. They shall not hear of danger from my mouth.
Wise generals tell of vantage, not defeat.
   Ant. Art thou then so resolved, O brother mine?
   Pol. I am.   Retard me not!   I must attend
To my dark enterprise, blasted and foiled
Beforehand by my father's angry curse.
But as for you, Heaven prosper all your way!
If ye will show this kindness to my corse,
For nevermore in life shall ye befriend me.
Nay, cling to me no longer.   Fare ye well.

Ye will behold my living face no more.

Ant. O misery!

Pol.   Bewail me not.

Ant.   And who
That saw thee setting forth to certain death
Would not bewail thee, brother?

Pol.   If Fate wills,
Why, I must die.

Ant.   Nay, but be ruled by me.

Pol. Give me not craven counsel.

Ant.   Woe is me,
To lose thee!

Pol.   Heaven hath power to guide the event
Or thus or otherwise.   Howe'er it prove,
I pray that ye may ne'er encounter pain.
All men may know, ye merit nought but good.

      [The sky is overcast—a storm is threatened.

CHORUS.

New trouble, strange trouble, deep-laden with doom
From the sight-bereft stranger seems dimly to loom!
      Or peers Fate through the gloom?
She will move toward her mark or through shining or
      shade;
Since no purpose of Gods ever idly was made.
Time sees the fulfilment, who lifteth to-day
What was lowly, and trampleth the lofty to clay.
      Thunder! Heavens! what a sound!

Œd. My children! Would but some one in the place

Speed hither Theseus, noblest among men !

   Ant. Wherefore, my father ? What is thy desire ?

   Œd. These winged thunders of the highest will soon
Bear me away to the Unseen.   Send quickly !

CHORUS.

Again, yonder crash through the fire-startled air
Wing'd from Zeus, rushes down, till my thin locks of
     hair,
       Stiff with fear, upward stare.
My soul shrinks and cowers, for yon gleam from on high
Darts again ! Ne'er in vain hath it leapt from the sky,
But rushes amain to the task Zeus hath given.
I fear the unknown fatal edict of Heaven !
       Lightning glares all around !

   Œd. My daughters, the divinely promised end
Here unavoidably descends on me.

   Ant. How dost thou know it ?   By what certain
     sign ?

   Œd. I know it perfectly.   Let some one go
With speed and bring the lord of Athens hither.

CHORUS.

Great Heaven, how above me, beside me, around,
      Peals redoubled the soul-thrilling sound !
O our God, to this land, to our mother, if aught
Thou wouldst send with some darkness of destiny
     fraught,

Smile gently once more ! With the good let me bear
    What of fortune soe'er,—
Taste no cup, touch no food, the doomed sinner may
    share.
    Zeus, to thee, Lord, I cry !

Œd. Is the King coming ? Will he find me alive,
My daughters, and with reason undisturbed ?
  Ant. Say wherefore dost thou crave with such desire
The clearness of an undistracted mind ?
  Œd. I would fully render from a grateful soul
The boon I promised, when I gained my suit.

CHORUS (*looking towards Athens*).

Come, my chief! come with speed ! Or, if haply at
    hand,
    On the height where the curved altars stand,
Thou art hallowing with oxen in sacrifice slain
Yonder shrine of Poseidon, dread lord of the main,
Speed hither ! Be swift ! The blind stranger intends
    To thee, to thy friends,
To thy city, for troubles imposed, just amends.
    Haste thee, King ! Hear our cry !

The. Why sounds again from hence your joint appeal,
Wherein the stranger's voice is loudly heard ?
Is it some lightning-bolt new-fallen from Zeus,
Or cloud-born hail that is come rattling down ?
From Heavens so black with storm nought can surprise.

Œd. Prince, thou art come to my desire.   Some God
Hath happily directed this thy way.

The. What is befallen ?   O son of Laius, tell !

Œd. My path sinks downward, and before my death
I would confirm to Athens and to thee
My promised boon.

The.   Whereon dost thou rely
That proves thine end so near ?

Œd.   The Gods themselves
With herald voices are proclaiming it,
Nought failing of the fore-appointed signs.

The. What are these tokens, aged monarch, say ?

Œd. The many ceaseless thunderings, and the darts
That flash in volleys from the almighty hand.

The. I may not doubt thee ; for thy speech, I feel,
Hath ample witness of prophetic power.
What must I do ?

Œd.   I will instruct thee now
Ægeus' great son ! in rites which shall remain
An ageless treasure to thy countrymen.
I will presently, with no man guiding me,
Myself point out the spot, where I must die.
This is thy secret, not to be revealed
To any one of men, or where 'tis hid
Or whereabout it lies.   So for defence
This shall bestead thee better through all time,
Than many a shield and help of neighbour-spears.
More shalt thou learn, too sacred to divulge,
When yonder thou art come thyself alone.
Since to no other of Athenian men

Nor even unto the children of my love
May I disclose it.   'Tis for thee to keep
Inviolate while thou livest, and when thy days
Have end, then breathe it to the foremost man
Alone, and he in turn unto the next
Successively.   So shalt thou ever hold
Athens unravaged by the dragon brood.
Cities are numberless, and any one
May lightly insult even those who govern well.
For the eye of Heaven though late yet surely sees
When, casting off respect, men turn to crime.
Erectheus' heir ! let that be far from thee !
A warning needless to a man so wise !
Now go we—for this leading of the God
Is urgent—to the place, nor loiter more.
This way, my children ! follow me ! For I
Am now your guide, as ye were mine.   Come on !
Nay, touch me not, but leave me of myself
To find the holy sepulchre, wherein
This form must rest beneath Athenian ground.
This way ! Come, come ! This way are leading me
Guide Hermes and the Queen of realms below.
O Light, all dark to me !   I' the former time
Bright seemed thy shining ! Now thy latest ray
Sheds vital influence o'er this frame.   I go
To hide the close of my disastrous life
With Hades.   Kind Athenian friend, farewell !
May'st thou, thy followers, and this land of thine,
Be happy, and in your endless happiness
Remember him who blessed you in his death.

CHORUS.

Prince of the Powers Unseen,
    Durst we with prayers adore
Thee and thy viewless Queen,
    Your aid, Aïdôneus,* would our lips implore!
By no harsh-sounding doom
    Let him we love descend,
    With calm and cloudless end,
To abide among the people of the tomb!
Long worn with many an undeserved woe,
Just Gods will give thee glory there below.

Dread Forms, who rule this floor,
    And thou, the Unconquered Beast,
    That hugely liest at rest
At the dark-shining adamantine door,
—Still from thy cavernous lair
    Gnarling, so legends tell,
    A tameless guard of Hell,—
Mayest thou this once thy vigilance forbear,
And leave large room for him now entering there.
Hear us, great Son of Darkness and the Deep;
On thee we call, God of the dreamless sleep!

Enter Messenger.

Mess. Athenian citizens, my briefest tale
Were to say simply, Œdipus is gone;
But to describe the scene enacted yonder
Craves no brief speech, nor was the action brief.

* A name of Pluto.

Ch. Then he is gone! Poor man!
Mess.   Know it once for all.
He hath left eternally the light of day.
   Ch. Poor soul!   What?   Ended he with peace
    divine?
Mess. Ay, there is the main marvel.   How he moved
From hence, thou knowest, for thou too wast here,
And saw'st that of his friends none guided him,
But he they loved was leader to them all.
Now, when he came to the steep pavement, rooted
With adamant foundation deep in Earth,
On one of many paths he took his stand
Near the stone basin, where Pirithoüs
And Theseus graved their everlasting league.
There, opposite the mass of Laurian ore,
Turned from the hollow pear-tree and the tomb
Of marble, he sate down, and straight undid
His squalid raiment.   Then he called aloud
Upon his children, and bade some one fetch
Pure water from a running stream.   And they,
Hasting together to the neighbouring hill
Of green Demeter, goddess of the Spring,
Brought back their sire's commission speedily,
And bathed, and clothed him with the sacred robe.
And when his heart was satisfied, and nought
Remained undone of all he bade them do,
The God of darkness thundered, and the maids
Stood horror-stricken at the sound,—then fell
Around their father's knees and wept and wailed
Loudly and long with beatings of the breast.

But he, when all at once he heard that cry,
Caressed them in his arms and said :—" My daughters,
From this day forth you have no more a father.
All that was mine is ended, and no more
Shall ye continue your hard ministry
Of labour for my life. And yet, though hard,
Not unendurable, since all the toil
Was rendered light through love, which ye can find
Nowhere on earth so richly, as from him
Whose loss to-day will leave you to sustain
Your rest of life in virgin orphanhood."
Such was the talk, mingled with sobs and crying,
As each clung fast to each. But when the sounds
Of lamentation had subsided there
And silence reigned, a sudden voice was heard
That urged him onward, making each man's hair
Bristle on end with force of instant fear.
Now here, now there, repeated oftentimes,
A God's voice summoned him. " Ho ! Œdipus,
Why thus delay our going ? This long while
We are stayed for and thou linger'st. Come away ! "
He, when he knew the summons of the God,
Gave word for royal Theseus to go near ;
And when he came, said : " Friend for ever kind,
Reach thy right hand, I pray thee (that first pledge)
To these my children :—daughters, yours to him !—
And pass thy sacred word that thou wilt never
Betray these willingly : but still perform
All that thou mayest with true thoughts for their
   good."

[e, with grand calmness like his noble self,
romised on oath to keep this friendly bond.
nd when he had done so, Œdipus forthwith
roking his daughters with his helpless hands
ᴐake thus :—" My daughters, you must steel your hearts
o noble firmness, and depart from hence,
'or ask to see or hear forbidden things.
o, go at once !   Theseus alone must stay
s rightful witness of these mysteries."
hose accents were the last we all might hear.
hen, following the two maids, with checkless tears
nd groans we took our way.   But by-and-by,
t distance looking round, we saw,—not him,
'ho was not there,—but Theseus all alone
ᴐlding his hand before his eyes, as if
ᴐme apparition unendurable
ᴐad scared his vision.   In a little while,
'e marked him making reverence in one prayer
o the Earth, and to the home of Gods on high.
ut by what fate He perished, mortal man,
ᴠe Theseus, none can say.   No lightning-flash
rom heaven, no tempest rising from the deep,
aused his departure in that hour, but either
ᴐme messenger from heaven, or, from beneath,
he lower part of Earth, that knows no pain,
pening kindly to receive him in.
ot to be mourned, nor with a painful end
f sickness was he taken from the Earth,
ut wondrously, beyond recorded fate.
'any deem my words unwise, I care not

In that man's judgment to be counted wise.

   Ch. Where are those maidens and their escort ?   Say.

   Mess. They are not far off, but here.   The voice of
      weeping

Betokens all too plainly their approach.

   Ant. Alas !

How manifold the inheritance of woe

Drawn from the troubled fountain of our birth !

Indelible, ineradicable grief !

For him erewhile

We had labour infinite and unrelieved,

And now in his last hours we have to tell

Of sights and sorrows beyond thought.

   Ch.   How then ?

   Ant. Friends, ye might understand.

   Ch.   Speak.   Is he gone ?

   Ant. Gone !   Even as heart could wish, had wishes
      power.

How else, when neither war, nor the wide sea

Encountered him, but viewless realms enwrapt him,

Wafted away to some mysterious doom ?

Whence on our hearts a horror of night is fallen.

Woe 's me !   For whither wandering shall we find

Hard livelihood, by land or over seas ?

   Ism. I know not.   Let dark Hades bear me off

To lie in death with mine age-honoured sire !

Death were far better than my life to come.

   Ch. Noblest of maidens, ye must learn to bear

Meekly the sending of the Gods.   Be not

n fire with grief.   Your state is well assured.
Ant. If to be thus is well, then may one long
)r evil to return.   Things nowise dear
ere dear to me, whiles I had him to embrace.
father ! loved one ! thou that wearest now
1e eternal robe of darkness underground,
.d as thou art, think not this maid and I
ill cease from loving thee !
Ch.   He met his doom.
Ant. He met the doom he longed for.
Ch.   How was that ?
Ant. In the strange land where he desired to die
) died.   He rests in shadow undisturbed ;
)r hath he left a tearless funeral.
)r these mine eyes, father, unceasingly
)urn thee with weeping, nor can I subdue
1is ever-mounting sorrow for thy loss.
1 me !   Would thou hadst not desired to die
)re among strangers, but alone with thee
1ere, in the desert, I had seen thee die !
Ism. Unhappy me !   What destiny, dear girl,
7aits us both, bereaved and fatherless ?
Ch. His end was fortunate.   He rests in peace.
)ar maidens, then desist from this complaint.
rrow is swift to overtake us all.

Ant. Thither again, dear girl, let us go speedily !
Ism. Say, for what end.
Ant.   Desire possesses me—
Ism. Whereof?

Ant. To see the darksome dwelling-place—
Ism. Of whom?
Ant.   Woe is me!   Of him, our sire!
Ism.   But how
Can this be lawful?   Seest thou not?
Ant.   How say'st thou?
Why this remonstrance?
Ism.   Seest thou not, again,
He hath no grave and no man buried him.
    Ant. Take me but where he lies.   Then slay me there.
    Ism. Ah! woe is me, doubly unfortunate,
Forlorn and destitute, whither henceforth
For wretched comfort must we go?
    Ch.   Fear naught,
Dear maidens!
    Ism.   Where shall we find refuge?
    Ch.   How so?
Long since, your refuge is secure.
    Ant.   How so?
    Ch. No harm shall touch you.
    Ant.   I know that.
    Ch.   What then
Further engrosses thee?
    Ant.   How to get home
I know not.
    Ch.   Seek not for it.
    Ant.   Weariness
Weighs o'er me.
    Ch.   Hath it not before oppressed thee?
    Ant. Before, it vexed me; now it overwhelms.

Ch. A mighty sea of misery is your lot.

Ant. Woe is me! O Zeus! And whither must we go?
Into what future doth Fate drive me now?

Ch. Children, lament no longer.   'Tis not well
To mourn amongst this people, to whom the dead
Hath left his all-embracing benison.

Enter THESEUS.

Ant. Theseus, behold us falling at thy feet.
The. What boon, my children, are ye bent to obtain?
Ant. Our eyes would see our father's burial-place.
The. 'Tis not permitted to go near that spot.
Ant. Athenæ's sovereign lord, what hast thou said?
The. My children, 'twas your father's spoken will
That no man should approach his resting-place,
Nor human voice should ever violate
The mystery of the tomb wherein he lies.
He promised, if I truly kept this word,
My land should evermore be free from harms.
The power which no man may transgress and live,
The oath of Zeus, bore witness to our troth.
Ant. His wishes are enough.   Then, pray thee, send
An escort to convey us to our home,
Primeval Thebes, if so we may prevent
The death that menaces our brethren there.
The. That will I; and in all that I may do
To prosper you and solace him beneath,—
Who even now passes to eternity,—
I must not falter.   Come, lament no more.
All now is ended, and the end is Peace.

ANTIGONE.

THE PERSONS.

ANTIGONE, } Daughters of Œdipus and Sisters of Polynices.
ISMENE, }

CHORUS *of Theban Elders.*

CREON, *King of Thebes.*

A Watchman.

HÆMON, *Son of Creon, betrothed to Antigone.*

TEIRESIAS, *the blind Prophet.*

A Messenger.

EURYDICE, *the Wife of Creon.*

Another Messenger.

POLYNICES, having been supplanted by his younger brother Eteocles, brought an army of Argives against his native city, Thebes. The army was defeated, and the two brothers slew each other in single combat. On this Creon, the brother-in-law of Œdipus, succeeding to the chief power, forbade the burial of Polynices. But Antigone, placing the dues of affection and piety before her obligation to the magistrate, disobeyed the edict at the sacrifice of her life. Creon carried out his will, but lost his son Hæmon and his wife Eurydice, and received their curses on his head. His other son, Megareus, had previously been devoted as a victim to the good of the state.

SCENE. Before the royal palace at Thebes.

ANTIGONE.

Antigone. Sister, from whom I never hide a thought,
ιene, have the tidings caught thine ear?
ιven surely hath decreed to execute
thee and me, while yet we are alive,
the evil Œdipus bequeathed.   All horror,
pain, all outrage, falls on us!   And now
ι General's proclamation of to-day—
st thou not heard?—Art thou so slow to hear
en harm from foes menaces those we love?
smene. No word of those we love, Antigone,
nful or glad, hath reached me, since we two
re utterly deprived of our two brothers,
: off with mutual stroke, both in one day.
ι since the Argive host this now-past night
;one, I know nought else to make me feel
ιrer to happiness or more in woe.
Ant. I knew it well, and therefore led thee forth
ι palace gate, that none beside might hear.

Ism. Speak ! For thy troubled look bodes some dark
  news.

  Ant. Why, hath not Creon, duly honouring one
Of our two brothers in the burial-rite,
To the other done foul wrong? Eteocles
With lawful consecration he lays out,
And after covers him in earth, adorned
With amplest honours in the world below.
But, for the hapless corse of Polynices,
They say 'tis publicly proclaimed that none
Must bury it out of sight, nor mourn for him ;
But leave him tombless and unwept, a store
Of sweet provision for the carrion fowl
That eye him greedily. Such righteous law
Good Creon hath pronounced for thy behoof—
Ay, and for mine ! I am not left out ! And now
He comes this way to promulgate his will
To such as have not heard, nor lightly holds
The thing he bids, but, whoso disobeys,
The citizens shall stone him to the death.
This is the matter, and thou wilt quickly show
If thou art noble, or fallen below thy birth.

  Ism. Brave heart ! but what, if things be thus, can I
Avail to do or undo?

  Ant.   Wilt thou share
This danger and this labour? Make thy choice.

  Ism. In what wild enterprise? What canst thou
  mean?

  Ant. Wilt thou join hand with mine to lift the dead ?

  Ism. To bury him, when all have been forbidden ?

Is that thy thought?

Ant.   To bury my own brother
And thine, even though thou wilt not do thy part.
I will not be a traitress to my kin.

   Ism. Fool-hardy girl! against the word of Creon?
   Ant. He hath no right to bar me from mine own.
   Ism. Ah, sister, think but how our father fell,
Hated of all and lost to fair renown,
Through self-detected crimes—with his own hand,
Self-wreaking, how he dashed out both his eyes:
Then how the mother-wife, sad two-fold name!
With twisted halter bruised her life away;
And lastly, our two brethren miserable
With internecine conflict at a blow
Wrought out by fratricide their mutual doom.
Now, left alone, O think how beyond all
Most piteously we too shall be destroyed,
If in defiance of authority
We traverse the commandment of the King!
We needs must bear in mind we are but women,
Never created to contend with men;
Nay more, made victims of resistless power,
To obey behests more harsh than this to-day.
I, then, imploring those beneath to grant
Indulgence, seeing I am enforced in this,
Will yield submission to the powers that rule.
Small wisdom were 't to overpass the bound.

   Ant. I will not urge you! no! nor if now you list
To help me, will your help afford me joy.
Be what you choose to be! This single hand

Shall bury our lost brother.   Glorious
For me to take this labour and to die !
Dear to him will my soul be as we rest
In death, when I have dared this holy crime.
My time for pleasing men will soon be over,
Not so my duty toward the Dead !   My home
Yonder will have no end.   You, if you will,
May throw contempt on laws revered on High.

   Ism. Not from irreverence.   But I have no strength
To strive against the citizens' resolve.

   Ant. Thou make excuses !   I will go my way
To raise a burial-mound to my dear brother.

   Ism. Unhappy one, oh, how I fear for thee !

   Ant. Spend not your fears on me !   Guide your own
      fortune.

   Ism. Ah ! yet divulge thine enterprise to none,
But keep the secret close, and so will I.

   Ant. O Heavens ! Nay, tell ! I hate your silence worse,
I had rather you proclaimed it to the world.

   Ism. You are ardent in a chilling enterprise.

   Ant. I know that I please those whom I would please.

   Ism. Yes, if you thrive ; but your desire is bootless.

   Ant. Well, when I fail I shall be stopt I trow !

   Ism. One should not start upon a hopeless quest.

   Ant. Speak in that vein if you would earn my hate
And aye be hated of our lost one.   Peace !
Leave my unwisdom to endure this peril ;
Fate cannot rob me of a noble death.

   Ism. Go, if you must—Not to be checked in folly,
But sure unparalleled in faithful love !   [*Exeunt.*

CHORUS (*entering*).

O fairest beam
That yet hath wakened Thebe's towers with light !
Thou cam'st to our waiting sight,
Eye of the Golden Day,
When the strong Sun-god glanced on Dirce's stream,
And spurred to faster flight
The Argive on his headlong way.

He rose in proud array,
With snow-white panoply on eagle wing,
Ruin on our land to bring,
Roused by the fierce debate
Of Polynices' hate,
With many a shield and many a crest,
Shrilling sharp menace from his breast.

Then stooped above the domes,
With lust of carnage fired,
And, baring teeth of serried spears,
Yawned wide above the gates that guard our homes.
But went, or e'er his hungry jaws had tired
On Theban flesh, or e'er the Fire-god fierce,
Seizing our sacred town,
Had smirched and rent her battlemented crown.
Such noise of battle as he fled
About his back the War-god spread ;
So writhed to hard-fought victory
The serpent, struggling to be free.

For Zeus, who hates the boastful tongue,
Despiser of the clank of gold,
Saw their stream that proudly rolled,
And with hurled fire down flung
One, who in haste had mounted high,
And in that hour from topmost tower
Upraised the exulting cry.
  Then with rude crash to earth was swung,
Who with rash hand on flaming brand
Came breathing madness at the gate
In eager blasts of hate.

  And various were the forms of fight,
As now on these and now on those
The War-god bounded 'midst our foes,
A mighty helper on our right.
  Seven against seven, at each gate one,
Their captains, when the day was done,
Left for our Zeus who turned the scale
The brazen tribute in full tale.
  Only untold remain
The unenviable twain
That from one sire, one mother, drawing breath,
Each with conquering lance in rest
Against a true-born brother's breast,
Found equal lots in death.

  But with blithe greeting to glad Thebe came
Great Victory of glorious fame,

And smiled on all our chariot-throng
With eyes that waken song.
   Then let the battle roar
Sound in our hearts no more,
But with dances of delight
Through the holy night,
Let us visit every Theban shrine.
And let him who shakes the Earth
Be the leader of our mirth,
Thebe's God, the Lord of Wine.

   But lo! where Creon in his new-made power,
Moved by the fortune of the recent hour,
Comes with fresh counsel.   What intelligence
Intends he for our private conference,
That he hath sent his herald to us all,
Gathering the elders with a general call?

Enter CREON.

Creon. My friends, the noble vessel of our State,
After sore shaking her, the Gods have sped
On a smooth course again.   I have brought you hither,
By special messengers selecting you
From all the city, first, because I knew you
Aye loyal to the throne of Laïus ;
Then, both while Œdipus gave prosperous days,
And since his fall, I still beheld you firm
In sound allegiance to the royal issue.
Now since the pair have perished in an hour,
Twinned in their fate, both stricken, striking both,

Staining our clime with guilt of kindred blood,
All rule and potency of sovereign sway,
·In virtue of next kin to the deceased,
Descends on me.   But hard it is to learn
The mind of any mortal or the heart,
Till he be tried in chief authority.
Power shows the man.   For he who, when supreme,
Withholds his hand or voice from the best cause,
Being thwarted by some fear, that man to me
Appears, and ever hath appeared, most vile.
And he too hath no place in mine esteem,
Who sets his friend before his fatherland.
Let Zeus whose eye sees all eternally
Be here my witness.   I will ne'er keep silence
When danger lours upon my citizens
Who looked for safety, nor make him my friend
Who doth not love my country.   For I know
Our country carries us, and whilst her helm
Is held aright we gain good friends and true.
    Following such courses 'tis my steadfast will
To foster Thebe's greatness, and therewith
In brotherly accord is my decree
Touching the sons of Œdipus.   The man—
Eteocles I mean—who died for Thebes
Fighting with eminent prowess on her side,
Shall be entombed with every sacred rite
Which follows to the grave the lordliest dead.
But for his brother, who, a banished man,
Returned to devastate and burn with fire
The land of his nativity, the shrines

Of his ancestral gods, to feed him fat
With Theban carnage, and make captive all
That should escape the sword—for Polynices,
This law hath been proclaimed concerning him :
He shall have no lament, no funeral,
But lie unburied, for the carrion fowl
And dogs to eat his corse, a sight of shame.

Such are the motions of this heart and mind.
Never from me shall villains reap renown
Before the just.   But whoso loves the State,
I will exalt him both in life and death.

Ch. Son of Menœceus, we have heard thy will
Toward him who loves, and him who hates our city.
And sure, 'tis thine to exercise all power
Both on the dead and on all us who live.

Cr. Then be ye watchful to maintain my word.

Ch. Young strength for such a burden were more meet.

Cr. Already there are watchers of the dead.

Ch. What charge then wouldst thou further lay on us ?

Cr. Not to give place to those that disobey.

Ch. Who is so fond, to be in love with death ?

Cr. Such, truly, is the meed.   But hope of gain
Full oft ere now hath been the ruin of men.

Enter Watchman.

Watchman. My lord, I am out of breath, but not with
          speed.
I will not say my foot was fleet.   My thoughts
Cried halt unto me ever as I came
And wheeled me to return.   My mind discoursed

Most volubly within my breast, and said—
Poor wretch ! why go where thou wilt find thy bane ?
Unhappy wight ! say, wilt thou bide aloof?
Then if the king shall hear this from another,
How shalt thou 'scape for't ?   Winding thus about,
I hasted, but I could not speed, and so
Made a long journey of a little way.
At last " yes " carried it, that I should come
To thee ; and tell thee I must needs, and shall,
Though it be nothing that I have to tell.
For I came hither, holding fast by this·—
Nought that is not my fate can happen to me.

 Cr. Speak forth thy cause of fear.   What is the matter?
 Watch. First of my own part in the business.   For
I did it not, nor saw the man that did,
And 'twere not fair that I should come to harm.
 Cr. You fence your ground, and keep well out of
  danger ;
I see you have some strange thing to declare.
 Watch. A man will shrink who carries words of fear.
 Cr. Let us have done with you.   Tell your tale,
  and go.
 Watch. Well, here it is.   The corse hath burial
From some one who is stolen away and gone,
But first hath strown dry dust upon the skin,
And added what religion doth require.
 Cr. Ha !
What man hath been so daring in revolt ?
 Watch. I cannot tell.   There was no mark to show—
No dint of spade, or mattock-loosened sod,—

ıly the hard bare ground, untilled and trackless.
hoe'er he was, the doer left no trace.
ıd, when the scout of our first daylight watch
owed us the thing, we marvelled in dismay.
ıe Prince was out of sight; not in a grave,
.t a thin dust was o'er him, as if thrown
· one who shunned the curse. There was no sign
˙ any hound or any beast o' the field
ıving come near, or pulled at the dead body.
ıen rose high words among us sentinels
ıth bickering noise accusing each his mate,
ıd it seemed like to come to blows, with none
ı hinder. For the hand that thus had wrought
ıs any one of ours, and none; the man
caped all knowledge. And we were prepared
ı lift hot iron with our bare palms; to walk
ırough fire, and swear by all the Gods at once
ıat we were guiltless, ay, and ignorant
 who had plotted or performed this thing.
When further search seemed bootless, at the last
ıe spake, whose words bowed all our heads to the earth
.th fear. We knew not what to answer him,
ır how to act and prosper. He advised
grave a matter must not be concealed,
.t instantly reported to the King.
Well, this prevailed, and the lot seized on me,
lucky man! to be the ministrant
this fair service. So I am present here,
ρinst my will and yours, I know that well.
ne loves the messenger of evil news.

L

Ch. My lord, a thought keeps whispering in my breast,
Some Power divine hath interposed in this.
   Cr. Cease, ere thou quite enrage me, and appear
Foolish and old at once.　Talk not to me
Of Gods who have taken thought for this dead man!
Say, was it for his benefits to them
They hid his corse, preferring him so far,
Who came to set on fire their pillared shrines,
With all the riches of their offerings,
And to make nothing of their land and laws?
Or, hast thou seen them honouring the vile?
That cannot be.　Long time the cause of this
Hath come to me in secret murmurings
From malcontents of Thebes, who under yoke
Turned restive, and would not accept my sway.
Well know I, these have bribed the watchmen here
To do this for some fee.　For nought hath grown
Current among mankind so mischievous
As money.　This brings cities to their fall:
This drives men homeless, and moves honest minds
To base contrivings.　This hath taught mankind
The use of villanies, and how to give
An impious turn to every kind of act.
But whoso hath done this for a reward
Hath found his way at length to punishment.
If Zeus have still my worship, be assured
Of that which here on oath I say to thee—
Unless ye find the man who made this grave
And bring him bodily before mine eye,
Death shall not be enough, till ye have hung

Alive for an example of your guilt,
That henceforth in your rapine ye may know
Whence gain is to be gotten, and may learn
Pelf from all sources is not to be loved.
For in base gettings, 'tis a common proof,
More men have ruin than advantage found.

 Watch. Am I to speak? or must I turn and go?
 Cr. What? know ye not your speech offends even
   now?
 Watch. Doth the mind smart withal, or only the ear?
 Cr. Art thou to probe the place of mine annoy?
 Watch. If I offend, 'tis in your ears alone,
The malefactor wounds ye to the soul.
 Cr. Out on thee! thou art nothing but a tongue.
 Watch. Then was I ne'er the doer of this deed.
 Cr. Yea, verily: self-hired to crime for gold.
 Watch. Pity so clear a mind should clearly err!
 Cr. Gloze now on clearness! But unless ye show
The doer, without glozing ye shall tell,
Craven advantage clearly worketh bane.
 Watch. Well, by all means let him be found; but
   this
I know, that whether he be caught or not,
Howe'er Fate rules it, me you will not see
Standing in presence here. Even now I owe
Deep thanks to Heaven for mine escape, so far
Beyond my hope and highest expectancy.
       [Exeunt severally.

CHORUS.

Many a wonder lives and moves, but the wonder of all
 is man,
That courseth over the grey ocean, borne of stormy
 South-wind,
Faring amidst high-swelling seas that surge around,
And year by year with winding furrow patient wears
 away
  Earth, primal Deity imperishable,
Subduing her unwearied strength with children of the
 steed.*

And wound in woven coils of nets he seizeth for his
 prey
The aëry tribe of birds and wilding armies of the chase,
And sea-born millions of the deep—man is so crafty-wise.
And now with engine of his wit he tameth to his will
The mountain-ranging beast whose lair is in the country
 wild;
  And now his yoke hath passed upon the mane
Of horse with proudly crested neck and tireless mountain
 bull.

Wise utterance and wind-swift thought, and civic, social
 ways,
And where to shelter from the clear-eyed power of biting
 frost,

<hr>

* *Mules* are so-called by Homer.

He hath taught him, and to shun the sharp, roof-
    penetrating rain.—
Full of resource, without device he meets no coming
    time ;
        From death alone he shall not find release :
Even for disease invincible he hath contrived a cure.

Beyond belief endow'd with skill, potent in art, he goes
One while to evil, and one while to good.
Weaving the laws into his life and steadfast oath of
    Heaven,
        High in the State he moves : but outcast he,
Who hugs dishonour to his heart and follows paths of
    crime.
Ne'er may he come beneath my roof, nor think like
    thoughts with me.

        What portent from the Gods is here?
        My mind is mazed with doubt and fear.
        How can I gainsay what I see?
        I know the girl Antigone.
        O hapless child of hapless sire !
        Didst thou, then, recklessly aspire
        To brave kings' laws, and now art brought
        In madness of transgression caught?

    Enter Watchman, *bringing in* ANTIGONE.

Watch. Here is the doer of the deed : this maid.
We caught her burying him.   Where is the King?
    Ch. Look, he comes forth again to meet thy call.

Enter CREON.

Cr. What call so nearly times with mine approach?

Watch. My lord, no mortal should deny on oath;
Judgment is still belied by after-thought.
When quailing 'neath yon tempest of your threats,
Methought no force would drive me to this place.
But joy unlook'd for and surpassing hope
Is out of bound the best of all delight,
And so I am here again,—though I had sworn
I ne'er would come,—bringing in charge this maid,
New-taken in the act of sepulture.
Here was no lot-throwing; this hap was mine
Without dispute.   And now, my sovereign lord,
According to thy pleasure, thine own self
Examine and convict her.   For my part
I have good right to be away and free
From the bad business I am come upon.

 Cr. This maiden!
How came she in thy charge?   Where didst thou find
  her?

 Watch. Burying the prince.   One word hath told thee
  all.

 Cr. But mean'st thou soberly, and hast thy sense?

 Watch. I saw her burying him whom you forbade
To bury.   Is that, now, clearly spoken, or no?

 Cr. And how was she detected, caught, and ta'en?

 Watch. It fell in this wise.   We were come to the spot,
Bearing the dreadful burden of thy threats;
And first with care we swept the dust away

om round the corse, and laid the dank limbs bare :
hen sate below the hill-top, out o' the wind,
here no bad odour from the dead might strike us,
irring each other on with interchange
f loud revilings on the negligent
'tendance on this duty.   So we stayed
ll in mid heaven the sun's resplendent orb
ood high, and the heat strengthened.   Suddenly,
he Storm-god raised a whirlwind from the ground,
exing heaven's concave, and filled all the plain ;
ending the locks of all the orchard groves,
ll the great sky was choked withal.   We closed
ur lips and eyes, and bore the God-sent plague.
hen after a long while this ceased, the maid
as seen, and wailed in high and bitter key,
ke some despairing bird that hath espied
er nest all desolate, the nestlings gone.
, when she saw the body bare, she mourned
udly, and cursed the authors of this deed.
hen nimbly with her hands she brought dry dust,
nd holding high a shapely brazen cruse,
onoured the dead with thrice-poured drink-offering.
e, when we saw, ran in, and straightway seized
ur quarry, nought dismayed, and charged her with
he former crime and this.   And she denied
othing ;—to my delight, and to my grief.
ne's self to escape disaster is great joy ;
t to have drawn a friend into distress
painful.   But my own security
me is of more value than aught else.

Cr. Thou, with thine eyes down-fastened to the earth !
Dost thou confess to have done this, or deny it?
Ant. I deny nothing.   I avow the deed.
    Cr. (*to* Watchman).   Thou may'st betake thyself
        whither thou wilt,
Acquitted of the grievous charge, and free.
(*To* ANTIGONE) And thou,—no prating talk, but briefly
        tell,
Knew'st thou our edict that forbade this thing ?
    Ant. I could not fail to know.   You made it clear.
    Cr. How durst thou then transgress the published
        law?
    Ant. I heard it not from Zeus, nor came it forth
From Justice, where she reigns in the Underworld.
They too have published to mankind a law.
Nor could I think thine edict of such might
That one who is mortal thus could overrule
The infallible, unwritten laws of Heáven.
Their majesty begins not from to-day
But from eternity, and none can tell
The hour that saw their birth.   I would not, I,
For any terrors of a man's resolve,
Incur the God-inflicted penalty
Of doing them violence. Death will come,—I know it,—
Without thine edict ;—if before the time,
I count it gain.   Who does not gain by death,
That lives, as I do, amid boundless woe?
Slight is the sorrow of such doom to me.
But had I suffered my own mother's child,
Fallen in blood, to be without a grave,

That were indeed a sorrow.   This is none.
And if thou deem'st me foolish for my deed,
I am foolish in the judgment of a fool.

    Ch. The maiden shows the fierceness of her sire.
Calamity doth not subdue her will.

    Cr. Ay, but the stubborn spirit first doth fall.
Oft ye shall see the strongest bar of steel,
That fire hath hardened to extremity,
Shattered to pieces.   A small bit doth rule
The fiery steed.   Pride may not be allowed
In one whose life is subject to command.
This maiden hath been conversant with crime
Since first she trampled on the public law;
And now she adds to crime this insolence,
To laugh at her offence, and glory in it.
Truly, if she that hath usurped this power
Shall rest unpunished, she then is a man,
And I am none.   Be she my sister's child,
Or of yet nearer blood to me than all
That take protection from my hearth, the pair
Shall not escape the worst of deaths.   For know,
I count the younger of the twain no less
To have conspired in this rebellious rite.
And now I bid you call her.   Late I saw her
Within the house, beyond herself, and frantic.
—Full oft when one is darkly plotting wrong,
The disturbed spirit hath betrayed itself
Before the act it hides.—But not less hateful
Seems it to me, when one that hath been caught
In wickedness would give it a brave show.

Ant. Wouldst thou aught more of me than merely death?

Cr. No more.   Death closes the account of power.

Ant. Why then delay?   No talk of thine can charm
  me,

Forbid it Heaven !   And my discourse no less

Must evermore sound noisome to thine ear.

Yet whence could I have found a fairer fame

Than giving burial to my own true brother?

All here would tell thee they approve my deed,

Were they not tongue-tied to authority.

But kingship hath much profit, this in chief,

That it may do and say whate'er it will.

  Cr. No Theban sees the matter with thine eye.

  Ant. They see, but curb their voices to thy sway.

  Cr. And art not thou ashamed, acting alone ?

  Ant. A sister's piety hath no touch of shame.

  Cr. Was not Eteocles thy brother too ?

  Ant. My own true brother from both parents' blood.

  Cr. This duty was impiety to him.

  Ant. He that is dead will not confirm that word.

  Cr. If you impart his honours to the vile.

  Ant. It was his brother, not a slave, who fell.

  Cr. But laying waste the land for which he fought.

  Ant. Death knows no difference, but demands his due.

  Cr. Yet not equality 'twixt good and bad.

  Ant. Who knows but this is pious there below ?

  Cr. An enemy is hated even in death.

  Ant. Love, and not hatred, is the path for me.

  Cr. Down then to death ! and, if you must, there love

The dead.   No woman rules me while I live.

Ch. Now comes Ismene forth.   Ah, see,
From clouds above her brow
The sister-loving tear
Is falling wet on her fair cheek,
Distaining her flush'd face, that gloweth red !

Enter ISMENE.

Cr. And thou that like a serpent coiled i' the house
Hast secretly been draining my life-blood,—
Little aware that I was cherishing
Two curses and subverters of my throne,—
Tell us, wilt thou avouch thy part in this
Interment, or forswear all knowledge of it ?
Ism. If her voice go therewith, I did the deed,
And bear my part and burden of the blame.
Ant. Nay, justice will not suffer that.· You would not,
And I refused to let you have a share.
Ism. But now in thy misfortune I would fain
Embark with thee in thy calamity.
Ant. Who did the deed, the powers beneath can tell.
I care not for lip-kindness from my kin.
Ism. Ah ! scorn me not so far as to forbid me
To die with thee, and honour our lost brother.
Ant. Die not with me, nor make your own a deed
You never touched !   My dying is enough.
Ism. How can I joy in life when thou art gone ?
Ant. Ask Creon there.   He hath your care and duty.
Ism. What can it profit thee to vex me so ?
Ant. My heart is pained, though my lip laughs at thee.
Ism. What can I do for thee now, even now ?

Ant. Save your own life. I grudge not your escape.

Ism. Alas ! and must I be debarred thy fate ?

Ant. Life was the choice you made. Mine was to
    die.

Ism. I warned thee——

Ant.   Yes, your prudence is admired
On earth.   My wisdom is approved below.

Ism. Yet surely we are both alike in fault.

Ant. Fear not ; you live.   My life hath long been
    given
To death, to be of service to the dead.

Cr. Of these two girls, the one hath lost her wits :
The other hath had none since she was born.

Ism. My lord, in misery, the mind one hath
Is wont to be dislodged, and will not stay.

Cr. You have ta'en leave of yours at any rate,
When you cast in your portion with the vile.

Ism. What can life profit me without my sister ?

Cr. Say not "my sister ;" she is nothing now.

Ism. What ? wilt thou kill thy son's espousals too ?

Cr. He may find other fields to plough upon.

Ism. Not so as love was plighted 'twixt them twain.

Cr. I hate a wicked consort for my son.

Ant. O dearest Hæmon! how thy father wrongs
    thee !

Cr. Thou and thy marriage are a torment to me.

Ch. And wilt thou sever her from thine own son ?

Cr. 'Tis death must come between him and his joy.

Ch. All doubt is then resolved : the maid must die.

Cr. I am resolved ; and so, 'twould seem, are you.

In with her, slaves !   No more delay !   Henceforth
These maids must have but woman's liberty
And be mewed up ; for even the bold will fly
When they see Death nearing the house of life.

      [Antigone *and* Ismene *are led into the palace.*

Chorus.

Blest is the life that never tasted woe.
    When once the blow
Hath fallen upon a house with Heaven-sent doom,
Trouble descends in ever-widening gloom
Through all the number of the tribe to flow ;
    As when the briny surge
    That Thrace-born tempests urge
(The big wave ever gathering more and more)
Runs o'er the darkness of the deep,
    And with far-searching sweep
Uprolls the storm-heap'd tangle on the shore,
While cliff to beaten cliff resounds with sullen roar.

The stock of Cadmus from old time, I know,
    Hath woe on woe,
Age following age, the living on the dead,
Fresh sorrow falling on each new-ris'n head,
None freed by God from ruthless overthrow.
    E'en now a smiling light
    Was spreading to our sight
O'er one last fibre of a blasted tree,—
When, lo ! the dust of cruel death,
    Tribute of Gods beneath,

you oughts, and furious ecstasy,
And wildering th and mum in dark Nonentity.
Quench the brief glea the choic
                                     s ! can check thy might ?
What froward will of man, O Zeu   months divine,
Not all-enfeebling sleep, nor tireless our pru e
Can touch thee, who through ageless ti below.
Rulest mightily Olympus' dazzling height. fault.
This was in the beginning, and shall be   ath lo.
          Now and eternally,
Not here and there, but everywhere,
A law of misery that shall not spare.   s :

For hope, that wandereth wide, comforting many a head,
Entangleth many more with glamour of desire :
Unknowing they have trode the fire.
Wise was the famous word of one who said,
Evil oft seemeth goodness to the mind
          An angry God doth blind.
Few are the days that such as he
Can live untroubled of calamity.

But see ! the youngest, Hæmon, now is come,
Lamenting haply for the maiden's doom.
Say, is he mourning o'er her young·life lost,
Fiercely indignant for his bridal crossed ?

Enter Hæmon.

Cr. We shall know soon, better than seers could teach
          us.
Can it be so, my son, that thou art brought

By mad distemperature against thy sire,
On hearing the irrevocable decree
Passed on thy promised bride?   Or is thy love
Thy father's, whatsoever he may do?

Hæmon. I am thine, father, and will follow still
Thy good directions; nor would I prefer
The fairest bride to thy wise government.

Cr. That, O my son! should be thy constant mind,
In all to bend thee to thy father's will.
Therefore men pray to have around their hearth
Obedient offspring, to requite their foes
With harm, and honour whom their father loves;
But he whose issue proves unprofitable,
Begets what else but sorrow to himself
And store of laughter to his enemies?
Make not, my son, a shipwreck of thy wit
For a woman.   Thine own heart may teach thee this.
There's but cold comfort in a wicked wife
Yoked in the home inseparably.   What wound
Can be more deadly than a harmful friend?
Then spurn her like an enemy, and cast her
Away to wed with some one down below!
For since of all the city I have found
Her only recusant, caught in the act,
I will not break my word before the state.
I will take her life.   At this let her invoke
The god of kindred blood!   For if at home
I foster rebels, how much more abroad?
Whoso is just in ruling his own house,
Lives rightly in the commonwealth no less:

But he that wantonly defies the law,
Or thinks to dictate to authority,
Shall have no praise from me.   What power soe'er
The city hath ordained, must be obeyed
In little things and great things, right or wrong.
The man who so obeys, I have good hope
Will govern and be governed as he ought,
And in the storm of battle at my side
Will stand a faithful and a trusty comrade.
But what more fatal than the lapse of rule?
This ruins cities, this lays houses waste,
This joins with the assault of war to break
Full-numbered armies into hopeless rout;
And in the unbroken host 'tis nought but rule
That keeps those many bodies from defeat.
I must be zealous for my subjects' good,
And not go down before a woman's will.
Else, if I fall, 'twere best a man should strike me;
Lest one should say, "a woman worsted him."

   Ch. Unless our sense is weakened by long time,
Thou speakest not unwisely.

   Hæm.   O my sire,
Sound wisdom is a God-implanted seed,
Of all possessions highest in regard.
I cannot, and I would not learn to say
That thou art wrong in this; though in another,
It may be such a word were not unmeet.
But as thy son, 'tis surely mine to scan
Men's deeds, and words, and muttered thoughts toward
       thee.

ear of thy frown restrains the citizen
1 talk that would fall harshly on thine ear.
under shadow may o'erhear, how all
'hy people mourn this maiden, and complain
'hat of all women least deservedly
he perishes for a most glorious deed.
Who, when her own true brother on the earth
ay weltering after combat in his gore,
eft him not graveless, for the carrion fowl
nd raw-devouring field-dogs to consume—
[ath she not merited a golden praise ? "
uch the dark rumour spreading silently.
ow, in my valuing, with thy prosperous life,
[y father, no possession can compare.
'here can be found a richer ornament
or children, than their father's high renown ?
r where for fathers, than their children's fame ?
'ear not one changeless humour in thy breast,
hat nothing can be right but as thou sayest.
'hoe'er presumes that he alone hath sense,
r peerless eloquence, or range of soul,
nwrap him, and you'll find but emptiness.
'is no disgrace, even to the wise, to learn
nd lend an ear to reason.   You may see
he plant that yields where torrent waters flow
ives every little twig, when the stout tree
torn away and dies.   The mariner
'ho will not ever slack the sheet that sways
he vessel, but still tightens, oversets,
nd so, keel-upward, ends his voyaging.

M

Relent, I pray thee, and give place to change.
If any judgment hath informed my youth,
I grant it noblest to be always wise,
But,—for omniscience is denied to man—
'Tis good to hearken to admonishment.

Ch. My lord, 'twere wise, if thou wouldst learn of him
In reason ; and thou, Hæmon, from thy sire !
Truth rests between you.

Cr.   Shall our age, forsooth,
Be taught discretion by a peevish boy ?

Hæm. Only in what is right.   Respects of time
Must be outbalanced by the actual need.

Cr. To cringe to rebels cannot be a need.

Hæm. I do not claim observance for the base.

Cr. Why, is not she so tainted ?   Is it not proved ?

Hæm. All Thebes denies it.

Cr.   Am I ruled by Thebes ?

Hæm. If youth be folly, that is youngly said.

Cr. Shall other men prescribe my government ?

Hæm. One only makes not up a city, father.

Cr. Is not the city in the sovereign's hand ?

Hæm. Nobly you'd govern as the desert's king.

Cr. I see, you are the woman's champion.

Hæm. You are the woman, then—for you I care.

Cr. Villain, to bandy justice with your sire !

Hæm. I plead against the injustice of your fault.

Cr. What fault is there in reverencing my power ?

Hæm. There is no reverence when you spurn the Gods.

Cr. Abominable spirit, woman-led !

Hæm. You will not find me following the vile.

Cr. Why, all your speech this day is spent for her.
Hæm. For you and me too, and the Gods below.
Cr. She will not live to be your wife on earth.
Hæm. I know whom she will ruin by her death.
Cr. What, wilt thou threaten, too, thou audacious boy ?
Hæm. It is no threat to answer empty words.
Cr. Witless admonisher, thou shalt pay for this !
Hæm. Thou art my sire, else would I call thee senseless.
Cr. Base woman's minion ! mince not terms with me.
Hæm. Wouldst thou have all the speaking on thy side ?
Cr. Is't possible ? By this heaven ! thou'lt not escape,
For adding contumely to words of blame.
Bring out the hated thing, that she may die
Immediately, before her lover's face !
Hæm. Nay, dream not she shall suffer in my sight.
Nor shalt thou ever see my face again ;
Let those stay with you that can brook your rage ! [*Exit.*
Ch. My lord, he is parted swiftly in deep wrath !
The youthful spirit offended makes wild work.
Cr. Ay, let him do his worst. Let him give scope,
To pride beyond the compass of a man !
He shall not free these maidens from their doom.
Ch. Is death thy destination for them both ?
Cr. Only for her who acted. Thou art right.
Ch. And what hast thou determined for her death ?
Cr. Where human footstep shuns the desert ground,
I'll hide her living in a rocky vault,
With so much provender as may prevent
Pollution from o'ertaking the whole city.
And there, perchance, she may obtain of Death,

Her only deity, to spare her soul;
Or else in that last moment she will learn
— 'Tis labour lost to worship powers unseen. [*Exit* Creon.

CHORUS.

Victorious combatant, spoiler of wealth,
Love, that in ambush of soft youthful cheek
Keep'st night-watch,—over ocean thou dost rove
And where lone cabins harbour thee.   No power
Of God or perishing man avoids thy spell,
And whoso finds thee, raves.

      Thou drawest awry
Just minds to wrong and ruin.   Thou hast roused
This turmoil between men of kindred blood!
Such influence radiates from the sovereign eye
Of fair betrothèd bride, that strong desire
Corrivals the supreme authority
Of high Commandment.   With resistless charm
Great Aphrodite mocks the might of men.

Ah! now myself am carried past the bound
Of law, nor can I stay the rising tear,
When I behold Antigone even here
Touching the quiet bourne where all must rest.

Enter Antigone, *guarded.*

Ant. Ye see me on my way,
   O burghers of my father's land!
   With one last look on Helios' ray,

Led my last path toward the silent strand.
Alive to the wide house of rest I go,
No dawn for me may shine,
No marriage-blessing e'er be mine,
No hymeneal with my praises flow !
The Lord of Night hath won me to his hand.

Ch.　　Yea, but with glory and fame,—
　　Not by award of the sword,
　　Not with blighting disease,
　　But by a law of thine own,—
　　Thou, of mortals alone,
　　Goest alive to the deep
　　Tranquil home of the dead.

Ant. Erewhile I heard men say,
How, in far Phrygia, Thebe's friend,
Tantalus' child, had dreariest end
On heights of Sipylus consumed away :
O'er whom the rock like clinging ivy grows,
And while with moistening dew
Her cheek runs down, the everlasting snows
Weigh o'er her, and the stream renew
That from sad brows her stone-cold breast doth steep.
Like unto her the God lulls me to sleep.

Ch.　　But she was a goddess born,
　　We but of mortal line ;
　　And sure to rival the fate
　　Of one of a race Divine
　　Were no light glory in death.

Ant. O mockery of my woe !
　　I pray you by our fathers' holy Fear,

Why must I hear
Your insults, while in life on earth I stand,
O ye that flow
In wealth, rich burghers of my bounteous land?
O fount of Dirce, and thou spacious grove,
Where Thebe's chariots move!
Ye are my witness, though none else be nigh,
By what enormity of lawless doom,
Without one friendly sigh,
I go to the strong mound of yon strange tomb,—
All hapless, having neither part nor room
With those who live or those who die!
Ch. Thy boldness mounted high,
And thou, my child, 'gainst the great pedestal
Of Justice with unmeasured force didst fall.
Thy father's lot still presseth hard on thee.
Ant. That pains me more than all.
Ah! thou hast touched my father's misery
        Still mourned anew,
With all the world-famed sorrows on us rolled
        Since Cadmus old.
O cursèd marriage that my mother knew!
O wretched fortune of my sire, who lay
Where first he saw the day!
Such were the authors of my burdened life;
To whom, with curses dowered, never a wife,
        I go to dwell beneath.
O brother mine, thy seeming-happy tie
Hath been thy downfall, and in this thy death
Thou hast destroyed me ere I die.

Ch. 'Twas pious, we confess,
Thy fervent deed.   But he, who power would show,
Must let no soul transgress.
A self-willed passion was thine overthrow.
   Ant. Friendless, uncomforted of bridal lay,
Unmourned, they lead me on my destined way.
Woe for my desolate lot !   I may not see
The sacred round of yon great light,
Rising again to greet me from the night;
No friend bemoans my fate, no tear hath fallen for me !

Enter CREON.

   Cr. If criminals were suffered to complain
In dirges before death, they ne'er would end.
Away with her at once, and closing her,
As I commanded, in the vaulty tomb,
Leave her all desolate, whether to die,
Or to live on in that sepulchral cell.
We are guiltless in the matter of this maid ;
Only she shall not share the light of day.
   Ant. O grave ! my bridal chamber, prison-house
Eterne, deep-hollowed, whither I am led
To find mine own,—of whom Persephone
Hath now a mighty number housed in death :—
I last of all, and far most miserably,
Am going, ere my days have reached their term !
Yet lives the hope that, when I go, most surely
Dear will my coming be, father, to thee,
And dear to thee, my mother, and to thee,

O brother mine! since with these hands I decked
And bathed you after death, and ministered
The last libations. And I reap this doom
For 'tending, Polynices, on thy corse.
Indeed I honoured thee, the wise will say.
For neither, had I children, nor if one
I had married were laid bleeding on the earth,
Would I have brav'd the city's will, or ta'en
This burden on me. Wherefore? I will tell.
A husband lost might be replaced; a son,
If son were lost to me, might yet be born;
But, with both parents hidden in the tomb,
No brother can arise to comfort me.
Therefore above all else I honoured thee,
And therefore Creon thought me criminal,
And bold in wickedness, O brother mine!
And now by servile hands, for all to see,
He hastens me away, unhusbanded,
Before my nuptial, having never known
Or married joy or tender infant cares.
But desolate and friendless I go down
Alive, O horror! to the vaults of the dead.
For what transgression of Heaven's ordinance?
Alas! how can I look to Heaven? how pray
For any succour, since I have earned, good sooth!
By piety, .the meed of impious?—
Oh! if these deeds be what the Gods approve,
Death, I presume, will teach me penitence;
But if they sin who judge me, be their doom
No heavier than they wrongly wreak on me!

Ch. With unchanged fury beats the storm of soul
That shakes this maiden.

Cr.   Then for that, be sure
Her warders shall lament their tardiness.

   Ant. Alas! I hear Death's footstep in that sound.

   Cr. I may not reassure thee.—'Tis most true.

   Ant. O' land of Thebes and city of my sires,
Ye too, ancestral Gods! I go—I go!
Even now they lead me to mine end.   Behold!
Princes of Thebes, the only scion left
Of Cadmus' issue, how unworthily,
By what mean instruments my life is crushed,
For reverencing the dues of piety.

                    [*Exit* ANTIGONE, *guarded.*

CHORUS.

Even Danaë's beauty left the lightsome day.
Closed in her strong and brass-bound tower she lay
         In tomb-like deep confine.
Yet she was gendered, O my child!
         From sires of noblest line,
And treasured for the Highest the golden rain.
Fated misfortune hath a power so fell:
         Not wealth, nor warfare wild,
Nor dark spray-dashing coursers of the main
Against great Destiny may e'er rebel.

He too in darksome durance was compressed,
King of Edonians, Dryas' haughty son,*

         * Lycurgus. See Homer, Iliad, vi. 130.

In eyeless vault of stone
Immured by Dionysus' hest,
    All for a wrathful jest.
Fierce madness issueth in such fatal flower.
He found 'twas mad to taunt the Heavenly Power,
    Chilling the Mænad breast
Kindled with Bacchic fire, and with annoy
Angering the Muse that in the flute hath joy.

And near twin rocks that guard the Colchian sea,
Bosporian cliffs 'fore Salmydessus rise,
Where neighbouring Ares from his shrine beheld
Phineus' two sons by female fury quelled,
With cursed wounding of their sight-reft eyes,
That cried to Heaven to 'venge the iniquity.
The shuttle's sharpness in a cruel hand
Dealt the dire blow, not struck with martial brand.*

But chiefly for her piteous lot they pined,
Who was the source of their rejected birth.
She touched the lineage of Erechtheus old ;
Whence in far caves her life did erst unfold,
Cradled 'mid storms, daughter of Northern wind,
Steed-swift o'er all steep places of the earth.
Yet even on her, though reared of heavenly kind,
The long-enduring Fates at last took hold.

* Idothea, the second wife of Phineus, persecuted his two sons by Cleopatra, a daughter of Boreas, whom he had repudiated and immured. The Argonauts saw them in the condition here described.

Enter TEIRESIAS, *led by a boy.*

Teiresias. We are come, my lords of Thebes, joint
    wayfarers,
One having eyes for both.   The blind must still
Thus journey in dependence on a guide.
    Cr. And what hath brought thee, old Teiresias,
      now ?
    Tei. I will instruct thee, if thou wilt hear my voice.
    Cr. I have not heretofore rejected thee.
    Tei. Therefore thy pilotage hath saved this city.
    Cr. Grateful experience owns the benefit.
    Tei. Take heed.   Again thou art on an edge of
      peril.
    Cr. What is it ?   How I shudder at thy word !
    Tei. The tokens of mine art shall make thee know.
As I was sitting on that ancient seat
Of divination, where I might command
Sure cognizance of every bird of the air,
I heard strange clamouring of fowl, that screeched
In furious dissonance ; and, I could tell,
Talons were bloodily engaged—the whirr
Of wings told a clear tale.   At once, in fear,
I tried burnt sacrifice at the high altar :
Where from the offering the fire-god refused
To gleam ; but a dank humour from the bones
Dripped on the embers with a sputtering fume.
The gall was spirtled high in air ; the thighs
Lay wasting, bared of their enclosing fat.
Such failing tokens of blurred augury

This youth reported, who is guide to me,
As I to others.   And this evil state
Is come upon the city from thy will :
Because our altars—yea, our sacred hearths—
Are everywhere infected from the mouths
Of dogs or beak of vulture that hath fed
On Œdipus' unhappy slaughtered son.
And then at sacrifice the Gods refuse
Our prayers and savour of the thigh-bone fat—
And of ill presage is the thickening cry
Of bird that battens upon human gore.
Now, then, my son, take thought.   A man may err;
But he is not insensate or foredoomed
To ruin, who, when he hath lapsed to evil,
Stands not inflexible, but heals the harm.
The obstinate man still earns the name of fool.
Urge not contention with the dead, nor stab
The fallen.   What valour is't to slay the slain ?
I have thought well of this, and say it with care ;
And careful counsel, that brings gain withal,
Is precious to the understanding soul.

 Cr. I am your mark, and ye with one consent
All shoot your shafts at me.   Nought left untried,
Not even the sect of prophets, by whose crew
I am bought and merchandised long since.   Go on !
Traffic, get gain, pale silver from the mine
Of Lydia, and the gold of Ind !   Yet know,
Grey-beard ! ye ne'er shall hide him in a tomb.
No, not if heaven's own eagle chose to snatch
And bear him to the throne supreme for food,

Even that pollution should not daunt my heart
To yield permission for his funeral.
For well know I defilement ne'er can rise
From man to God.   But, old Teiresias, hear!
Even wisest spirits have a shameful fall
That fairly speak base words for love of gain.

 Tei. Ah! where is wisdom? who considereth?
 Cr. Wherefore? what means this universal doubt?
 Tei. How far the best of riches is good counsel?
 Cr. As far as folly is the mightiest bane.
 Tei. Yet thou art sick of that same pestilence.
 Cr. I would not give the prophet blow for blow.
 Tei. What blow is harder than to call me false?
 Cr. Desire of money is the prophet's plague.
 Tei. And ill-sought lucre is the curse of kings.
 Cr. Know'st thou 'tis of thy sovereign thou speak'st
  this?
 Tei. Yea, for my aid gives thee to sway this city.
 Cr. Far-seeing art thou, but dishonest too.
 Tei. Thou wilt provoke the utterance of my tongue
To that even thought refus'd to dwell upon.

 Cr. Say on, so thou speak sooth, and not for gain.
 Tei. You think me likely to seek gain from you?
 Cr. You shall not make your merchandise on me!
 Tei. Not many courses of the racing sun
Shalt thou fulfil, ere of thine own true blood
Thou shalt have given a corse in recompense
For one above whom thou hast cast beneath,
Entombing shamefully a living soul,
And one whom thou hast kept above the ground

And disappointed of all obsequies,
Unsanctified and godlessly forlorn.
Such violence the powers beneath will bear
Not even from the Olympian gods.　For thee
The avengers wait.　Hidden but near at hand,
Lagging but sure, the Furies of the grave
Are watching for thee to thy ruinous harm,
With thine own evil to entangle thee.
Look well to it now whether I speak for gold!
A little while, and thine own palace-halls
Shall flash the truth upon thee with loud noise
Of men and women, shrieking o'er the dead.
And all the cities whose unburied sons,
Mangled and torn, have found a sepulchre
In dogs or jackals or some ravenous bird
That stains their incense with polluted breath,
Are forming leagues in troublous enmity.
Such shafts, since thou hast stung me to the quick,
I like an archer at thee in my wrath
Have loosed unerringly—carrying their pang,
Inevitable, to thy very heart.
Now, sirrah! lead me home, that his hot mood
Be spent on younger objects, till he learn
To keep a safer mind and calmer tongue.　　　[*Exit.*

　　Ch. Sire, there is terror in that prophecy.
He who is gone, since ever these my locks,
Once black, now white with age, waved o'er my brow,
Hath never spoken falsely to the state.

　　Cr. I know it, and it shakes me to the core.
To yield is dreadful: but resistingly

To face the blow of fate, is full of dread.

    Ch. The time calls loud on wisdom, good my lord.

    Cr. What must I do? Advise me. I will obey.

    Ch. Go and release the maiden from the vault,

And make a grave for the unburied dead.

    Cr. Is that your counsel? Think you I will yield?

    Ch. With all the speed thou mayest : swift harms from

        heaven

Are keen to overtake the froward man.

    Cr. O! it is hard. But I am forced to this

Against myself. I cannot fight with Destiny. ——

    Ch. Go now to do it. Trust no second hand.

    Cr. Even as I am, I go. Come, come, my people,

Here or not here, with mattocks in your hands

Set forth immediately to yonder hill !

And, since I have ta'en this sudden turn, myself,

Who bound her, will be present to unloose her—

For now the fear comes over me, 'tis best

To pass one's life in the accustomed round.   [*Exeunt.*

CHORUS.

O God of many a name !

Filling the heart of that Cadmeian bride

With deep delicious pride,

Offspring of him who wields the withering flame !

Thou for Italia's good

Dost care, and 'midst the all-gathering bosom wide *

---

* The plain of Eleusis, where the mysteries were held in honour
of Dêo or Demeter.

Of Dêo dost preside ;
Thou, Bacchus, by Ismenus' winding waters
'Mongst Thebe's frenzied daughters,
Keep'st haunt, commanding the fierce dragon's brood.

Thee o'er the forkèd hill
The pitchy flame beholds, where Bacchai rove,
Nymphs of Corycian grove,
Hard by the flowing of Castalia's rill.
To visit Theban ways,
By bloomy wine-cliffs flushing tender bright
'Neath far Nyseian height
Thou movest o'er the ivy-mantled mound,
While myriad voices sound
Loud strains of ' Evœ'! to thy deathless praise.

For Thebe thou dost still uphold,
First of cities manifold,
Thou and the nymph whom lightning made
Mother of thy radiant head.
Come then with healing for the violent woe
That o'er our peopled land doth largely flow,
Passing the high Parnassian steep
Or moaning narrows of the deep !

Come, leader of the starry quire
Quick-panting with their breath of fire !
Lord of high voices of the night,
Child born to him who dwells in light,
Appear with those who, joying in their madness,

Honour the sole dispenser of their gladness,
Thyiads of the Ægean main
Night-long tripping in thy train.

Enter Messenger.

Mess. Neighbours of Cadmus and Amphion's halls,
No life of mortal, howsoe'er it stand,
Shall once have praise or censure from my mouth.
Since human happiness and human woe
Come even as fickle Fortune smiles or lours ;
And none can augur aught from what we see.
Creon erewhile to me was enviable,
Who saved our Thebe from her enemies ;
Then, vested with supreme authority,
Ruled her aright ; and flourish'd in his home
With noblest progeny.   What hath he now ?
Nothing.   For when a man is lost to joy,
I count him not to live, but reckon him
A living corse.   Riches belike are his,
Great riches and the appearance of a King ;
But if no gladness come to him, all else
Is shadow of a vapour, weighed with joy.
Ch. What new affliction heaped on sovereignty
Com'st thou to tell ?
Mess.   They are dead ; and they that live
Are guilty of the death.
Ch.   The slayer, who ?
And who the slain ? Declare.
Mess.   Hæmon is dead,
And by a desperate hand.

Ch.   His own, or Creon's?

Mess. By his own hand, impelled with violent wrath
At Creon for the murder of the maid.

   Ch. Ah, Seer! how surely didst thou aim thy word!

   Mess. So stands the matter. Make of it what ye
      list.

   Ch. See, from the palace cometh close to us
Creon's unhappy wife, Eurydice.
Is it by chance, or heard she of her son?

Enter EURYDICE.

   Eurydice.   People of Thebes, the tidings met mine
      ear
As I was coming forth to visit Pallas
With prayerful salutation.   I was loosening
The bar of the clos'd gate, when the sharp sound
Of mine own sorrow smote against my heart,
And I fell back astonied on my maids
And fainted.   But the tale? tell me once more;
I am no novice in adversity.

   Mess. Dear lady, I will tell thee what I saw,
And hide no particle of truth; for why
Should I smooth over the harsh fact, which soon
Must prove my tale a lie?   Truth aye is best.
I went among the attendants of thy lord
To the highest point of the plain, where still was
      lying,
Cruelly mangled by the dogs, the corse
Of Polynices.   We besought Persephone
And Pluto gently to restrain their wrath,

And wash'd him pure and clean, and then we burned
The poor remains with brushwood freshly pulled,
And heaped a lofty mound of his own earth
Above him.   Then we turned us to the vault,
The maiden's hollow bride-chamber of death.
And from afar, round the unhallowed cell,
One heard a voice of wailing loud and long,
And went and told his lord : who coming near
Was haunted by the dim and bitter cry,
And suddenly exclaiming on his fate
Said lamentably, " My prophetic heart
Divined aright.   I am going, of all ways
That e'er I went, the unhappiest to-day.
My son's voice strikes me.   Go, my men, approach
With speed, and, where the stones are torn away,
Press through the passage to that door of death,
Look hard, and tell me, if I hear aright
The voice of Hæmon, or the gods deceive me."
Thus urged by our despairing lord, we made
Th' espial.   And i' the farthest nook of the vault
We saw the maiden hanging by the neck
With noose of finest muslin firmly tied,
And clinging to her on his knees the boy,
Lamenting o'er his ruined nuptial-rite,
Consummated in death, his father's crime
And his lost love.   And when the father saw him,
With horrid exclamation bursting in
He went to him and called him piteously :
" What deed is this, unhappy youth ?   What thought
O'ermaster'd thee ?   Where did the force of woe

O'erturn thy reason?   O come forth, my son,
I beg thee!"   But with savage eyes the youth
Glared scowling at him, and without a word
Plucked forth his two-edged blade.   The father then
Fled and escaped: but the unhappy boy,
Wroth with himself, even where he stood, leant heavily
Upon his sword and plunged it in his side.—
And while the sense remained, his slackening arm
Enfolded still the maiden, and his breath,
Gaspingly drawn and panted forth with pain,
Cast ruddy drops upon her pallid face;
Then lay in death upon the dead, at last
Joined to his bride in Hades' dismal hall:—
A monument unto mankind, that rashness
Is the worst evil of this mortal state.   [*Exit* EURYDICE.

    Ch. What augur ye from this?   The queen is gone
Without word spoken either good or bad.

    Mess. I, too, am struck with dread.   But hope con-
        soles me,
That having heard the affliction of her son,
Her pride forbids to publish her lament
Before the town, but to her maids within
She will prescribe to mourn the loss o' the house.
She is too tried in judgment to do ill.

    Ch. I cannot tell.   The extreme of silence, too,
Is dangerous, no less than much vain noise.

    Mess. Well, we may learn, if there be aught unseen
Suppressed within her passion-stricken soul,
By going within the palace.   Ye say well:
There is a danger, even in too much silence.

Ch. Ah ! look where sadly comes our lord the King,
Bearing upon his arm a monument—
If we may speak it—of no foreign woe,
But of his own infirmity the fruit.

Enter CREON *with the body of* HÆMON.

Cr. O error of my senseless soul,
Stubborn, and deadly in the end !
O ye who now behold
Slayer and slain of the same kindred blood !
O bitter consequence of seeming-wise decree !
Alas, my son !
Strange to the world wert thou, and strange the fate
That took thee off, that slew thee ; woe is me !
Not for thy rashness, but my folly.   Ah me !
    Ch. Alas for him who sees the right too late !
    Cr. Alas !
I have learnt it now.   But then upon my head
Some God had smitten with dire weight of doom ;
And plunged me in a furious course, woe is me !
Discomforting and trampling on my joy.
Woe ! for the bitterness of mortal pain !

Enter 2nd Messenger.

2nd Mess. My lord and master ! Thou art master
        here
Of nought but sorrows.   One within thine arms
Thou bring'st with thee, and in thy palace halls
Thou hast possession of another grief,
Which thou wilt soon behold.

Cr. What more of woe,
Or what more woeful, sounds anew from thee ?
　2nd Mess. The honoured mother of that corse, thy queen,
Is dead, and·bleeding with a new-given wound.
　Cr. O ! O ! O !
O charnel gulf of Hades, choked with dead,
Why harrowest thou my soul ?
Ill-boding harbinger of woe, what word
Didst utter ?　Oh, thou hast killed me o'er again,
Before undone !　What say'st ?　What was thy news ?
Ah me !
A slaughter'd wife thrown on the pile of ruin ?
　Ch. No longer hidden in the house.　Behold !
　　　　　　　　[*The Corpse of* EURYDICE *is disclosed.*
　Cr. Alas !
Mine eyes behold a new, a second woe.
What curse awaits me still ?　But now I clasp
My child, and lo ! yon corse before my face !
Ah ! hapless, hapless mother, hapless son !
　2nd Mess. The queen thou seest, with hot impassioned
　　　soul
Had fallen about the altar, when she closed
Her eyes' dark fires ; but first lamented loud
The glorious bed of buried Megareus,*
And then of Hæmon ; lastly clamoured forth
The curse of murdered offspring upon thee.
　Cr. Ai ! Ai !
I am rapt with terror.　Is there none to strike me

---

* Megareus, in sacrificing himself for Thebes, threw himself into
a deep cave, called the Dragon's Lair.

With doubly-sharpened blade a mortal stroke?
Ah! I am plunged in fathomless distress.
   2nd Mess. The guilt of this and of the former grief
By this dead lady was denounced on thee.
   Cr. Tell us, how ended she her life in blood?
   2nd Mess. Herself wounding her side, when she had
      heard
The cry of lamentation for her son.
   Cr. O me! This crime can come
On no man else, exempting me.
I slew thee—I, O misery!
I say the truth, 'twas I! My followers,
Take me with speed—take me away, away!
Me, who am nothing now.
   Ch. Thou sayest the best, if there be best in woe.
Briefest is happiest in calamity.
   Cr. Ah! let it come,
The day of days, that brings my latest doom.
Come! Come! I would not see another day.
   Ch. Time will determine that. We must attend
To present needs. Fate works her own dread work.
   Cr. All my desire was gathered in my prayer.
   Ch. But prayer is bootless. For to mortal men
There is no saviour from appointed woe.
   Cr. Take me away, the vain-proud man that slew
Thee, O my son! unwittingly, and thee!
Me miserable, which way shall I turn,
Which look upon? Since all that I can touch
Is falling,—falling,—round me, and o'erhead
Intolerable destiny descends.

Ch. Wise thought hath the first place in happiness
Before all else, and piety to Heaven
Must be preserved.   High boastings of the proud
Bring sorrows to the height to punish pride :—
A lesson men shall learn when they are old.

AIAS.

THE PERSONS.

Athena.

Odysseus.

Aias, *the son of Telamon.*

Chorus *of Salaminian Mariners.*

Tecmessa.

A Messenger.

Teucer.

Menelaus.

Agamemnon.

The child Eurysakés *appears, but does not speak.*

AFTER the death of Achilles, the armour made for him by
Hephæstus was to be given to the worthiest of the surviving
Greeks. Although Aias was the most valiant, the judges made
the award to Odysseus, because he was the wisest.

Aias in his rage attempts to kill the generals; but Athena sends
madness upon him, and he makes a raid upon the flocks and herds
of the army, imagining the bulls and rams to be the Argive chiefs.
On awakening from his delusion, he finds that he has fallen irre-
coverably from honour and from the favour of the Greeks. He also
imagines that the anger of Athena is unappeasable. Under this
impression he eludes the loving eyes of his captive-bride Tecmessa,
and of his Salaminian comrades, and falls on his sword.

But it is revealed through the prophet Calchas, that the wrath
of Athena will last only for a day; and on the return of Teucer,
his half-brother, Aias receives an honoured funeral; the tyrannical
reclamations of the two sons of Atreus being overcome by the firm
fidelity of Teucer and the magnanimity of Odysseus, who has been
inspired for this purpose by Athena.

SCENE—Before the encampment of Aias on the Trojan shore.
Afterwards, a lonely place towards Rhœteum.

AIAS.

———

ATHENA (*above*).   ODYSSEUS.

Athena. Still have I seen thee, Laërtiades,
Intent on some surprisal of thy foes ;
As now I find thee by the seaward camp,
Where Aias holds the last place in your line,
Lingering in quest, and scanning the fresh print
Of his late footsteps, to be certified
If he keep house or no.   Right well thy sense
Hath led thee like some keen-nosed hound of Sparta !
The man is even but now come home, his head
And slaughterous hands reeking with ardent toil.
Thou then no longer keenly peer within
That doorway, but declare what eager chase
Thou followest, that a god may give thee light.

Odysseus. Athena, 'tis thy voice !   Dearest in heaven,
How well-discerned and welcome to my soul
From yon dim distance doth thine utterance fly
Clearer to me than Tuscan trumpet-clang !
Wisely hast thou perceived my purpose here,
Beating this ground for Aias of the shield,
The lion-quarry whom I track to-day.

For he hath wrought on us to-night a deed
Past thought—if he be doer of this thing ;
We drift in ignorant doubt, unsatisfied :—
And I unbidden have yoked me to this toil.

Brief time hath flown since suddenly we knew
That all our gathered spoils were foully slain,
Flocks, herds, and herdmen, by some human hand.
Of this then all at Aias point the blame.
Yea and a watcher who had marked him, lone,
With new-fleshed weapon raging on the field,
Gave me to know it, when immediately
I darted on the trail, and here in part
I find some trace to guide me, but in part
I halt, amazed, and know not where to look.
Thou com'st full timely. For my venturous course,
Past or to come, is governed by thy will.
  Ath. I knew thy doubts, Odysseus, and came forth
Zealous to guard thy perilous hunting-path.
  Od. Dear Queen ! and am I labouring to an end ?
  Ath. Thou schem'st not idly. This is Aias' deed.
  Od. Say, what could rouse him to a work so wild ?
  Ath. His grievous anger for Pelides' arms.
  Od. But wherefore on the flock this violent raid ?
  Ath. He thought to imbrue his hands with your heart's
    blood.
  Od. What ? Was this planned against the Argives,
    then ?
  Ath. Planned, and performed, had I kept careless
    guard.

Od. What daring spirit, what hardihood, was here!
Ath. Alone by night in craft he sought your tents.
Od. How? Came he near them? Won he to his
    goal?
Ath. He stood in darkness at the generals' gates.
Od. What then restrained his eager hand from murder?
Ath. I turned him backward from his baleful joy,
And overswayed him with blind phantasies,
To swerve against the flocks and well-watched herd
Not yet divided from the public booty.
There plunging in he hewed the horned throng,
And with him Havoc ranged: while now he thought
To kill the Atridæ with hot hand, now this
Now that commander, as the fancy grew.
I, joining with the tumult of his mind,
Flung the wild victim on the fatal net.
Anon, this toil being overpast, he draws
The living oxen and the panting sheep
With cords to his home, not as a goad-driv'n spoil,
But as in triumph marshalling his foes: ·
Whom now he tortures in their bonds within!

    Come, thou shalt see this madness in clear day,
And speak to the Argives all I show thee here.
Only stand firm and shrink not; I will turn
His eyes askance, not to distinguish thee;
Fear nought.—Ho! thou that bindest to thy will
The limbs of those thy captives, come thou forth!
Aias! advance before thy palace-gate!
    Od. My Queen! what dost thou? Never call him
      forth!

Ath. Hush, hush !   Be not so timorous, but endure.
Od. Nay, nay !   Enough.   He is there, and let him
     bide.
Ath. What fear you?   Dates his valour from to-day?
Od. He was and is my valiant enemy.
Ath. Then is not laughter sweetest o'er a foe ?
Od. No more !   I care not hè should pass abroad.
Ath. You flinch from seeing the madman in full view
Od. When sane, I ne'er had flinched before his face.
Ath. Well, but even now he shall not know thee near.
Od. How, if his eyes be not transformed or lost ?
Ath. I will confound his sense although he see.
Od. Well, nothing is too hard for Deity.
Ath. Stand still and keep thy place without a word.
Od. I must.   Would I were far away from here !
Ath. Aias ! again I summon thee.   Why pay
So scanty heed to her who fights for thee ?

Enter AIAS *with a bloody scourge.*

Aias. Hail, offspring of the Highest !   Pallas, hail !
Well hast thou stood by me.   Triumphal gold
Shall crown thy temple for this lordly prey.
Ath. A fair intention !   But resolve me this :
Hast dyed thy falchion deep in Argive blood?
Ai. There is my boast ; that charge I'll ne'er deny.
Ath. Have Atreus' sons felt thy victorious might ?
Ai. They have.   No more they'll make a scorn of
     me !
Ath. I take it then they are dead.
Ai.   Ay, now they are dead,

Let them arise and rob me of mine arms !

   Ath. Good.   Next inform us of Laërtes' son ;
How stands his fortune ?   Hast thou let him go ?

   Ai. The accursed fox !   Dost thou inquire of him ?

   Ath. Ay, of Odysseus, thy late adversary.

   Ai. He sits within, dear lady, to my joy,
Bound ; for I mean him not just yet to die.

   Ath. What fine advantage wouldst thou first achieve ?

   Ai. First, tie him to a pillar of my hall—

   Ath. Poor wretch !   What torment wilt thou wreak
     on him ?

   Ai. Then stain his back with scourging till he die.

   Ath. Nay, 'tis too much.   Poor caitiff !   Not the
     scourge !

   Ai. Pallas, in all things else have thou thy will,
But none shall wrest Odysseus from this doom.

   Ath. Well, since thy pleasure calls thee to the deed,
Spare nought of thine intent : indulge thy hand !

   Ai. (*waving the bloody scourge*).   I go ! But thou, I
     charge thee, let thine aid
Be evermore like valorous, as to-day.   [*Exit.*

   Ath. The gods are strong, Odysseus.   Dost thou see ?
What man than Aias was more provident,
Or who for timeliest action more approved ?

   Od. I know of none.   But, though he hates me sore,
I pity him, poor mortal, thus chained fast
To a wild and cruel fate,—not weighing so much
His fortune as mine own.   For now I feel
All we who live are but an empty show

And idle pageant of a shadowy dream.

   Ath. Then, warned by what.thou seest, be thou not
     rash
To vaunt high words toward Heaven, nor swell thy port
Too proudly, if in puissance of thy hand
Thou passest others, or in mines of wealth.
Since Time abases and uplifts again
All that is human, and the modest heart
Is loved by Heaven, who hates the intemperate will.

                              [*Exeunt.*

           Chorus (*entering*).

     Telamonian chief, whose hand
     Guards our wave-encircled land,
     Salamis that breasts the sea,
     Good of thine is joy to me ;
     But if one who reigns above
     Smite thee, or if murmurs move
     From fierce Danaäns in their hate
     Full of threatening to thy state,
     All my heart for fear doth sigh,
     Shrinking like a dove's soft eye.

     Hardly had the darkness waned,
     When our ears were filled and pained
     With huge scandal on thy fame,
     Telling, thine the arm that came
     To the cattle-browsèd mead,
     Wild with prancing of the steed,
     And that ravaged there and slew
     With a sword of fiery hue

All the spoils that yet remain,
By the sweat of spearmen ta'en.

Such report against thy life,
Whispered words with falsehood rife,
Wise Odysseus bringing near
Shrewdly gaineth many an ear:
Since invention against thee
Findeth hearing speedily,
Tallying with the moment's birth;
And with loudly waxing mirth
Heaping insult on thy grief,
Each who hears it glories more
Than the tongue that told before.
Every slander wins belief
Aimed at souls whose worth is chief:
Shot at me, or one so small,
Such a bolt might harmless fall.
Ever toward the great and high
Creepeth climbing jealousy.
Yet the low without the tall
Make at need a tottering wall.
Let the strong the feeble save
And the mean support the brave.

Ah! 'twere vain to tune such song
'Mid the nought-discerning throng
Who are clamouring now 'gainst thee
Long and loud; and strengthless we,
Mighty chieftain, thou away,

To withstand the gathering fray.
Flocking fowl with carping cry
Seem they, lurking from thine eye;
Till the royal eagle's poise
Overawe the paltry noise :
Till before thy presence hushed
Sudden sink they, mute and crushed.

Oh, can it be 'twas Artemis incited
  (Ah, fearful rumour, fountain of my shame !)
This foolish raid that thy renown hath blighted
  On the full herd stored in our army's name ?
Say, had her blood-stained * temple missed the kindness
  Of some vow-promised fruit of victory,
Foiled of some glorious armour through thy blindness,
 · Or fell some stag ungraced by gift from thee ?
Or did stern Ares venge his thankless spear
Through this night-foray that hath cost thee dear ?

For never, if thy heart were not distracted
  By stings from Heaven, O child of Telamon,
Wouldst thou have bounded leftward, to have acted
  Thus wildly, spoiling all our host hath won !
Madness might fall : some heavenly power forefend it !
  But if Odysseus and the sovereign lords
Suggest a forgèd tale, O rise to end it,
  Nor fan the fierce flame of their withering words !

---

* In some of her temples Artemis was worshipped with sacrifices of bulls, and, according to an old tradition, also with human sacrifices.

Forth from thy tent, and let thine eye confound
The brood of Sisyphus * that would thee wound !

Too long hast thou been fixed in grim repose,
　Heightening the haughty malice of thy foes,
That, while thou porest by the sullen sea,
　Through breezy glades advanceth fearlessly,
A mounting blaze with crackling laughter fed
From myriad throats ; whence pain and sorrow bred
Within my bosom are establishèd.

Enter TECMESSA.

Tecmessa. Helpers of Aias' vessel's speed,
　　Erechtheus' earth-derivèd seed,
　　Sorrows are ours who truly care
　　For the house of Telamon afar.
　　The dread, the grand, the rugged form
　　　　Of him we know,
　　Is stricken with a troublous storm ;
　　　Our Aias' glory stoopeth low.
Chorus. What burden through the darkness fell
　　Where still at eventide 'twas well ?
　　Phrygian Teleutas' daughter, say ;
　　Since Aias, foremost in the fray,
　　Disdaining not the spear-won bride,
　　Still holds thee nearest at his side,
　　And thou mayst solve our doubts aright.
Tec. How shall I speak the dreadful word ?

---

* Amongst his enemies, Odysseus was reputed to be the offspring
of Sisyphus, and not of Laertes.

How shall ye live when ye have heard ?
Madness hath seized our lord by night
And blasted him with hopeless blight.
Such horrid victims mightst thou see
Huddled beneath yon canopy,
Torn by red hands and dyed in blood,
Dread offerings to his direful mood.

Ch. What news of our fierce lord thy story showeth,
    Sharp to endure, impossible to fly !
News that on tongues of Danaäns hourly groweth,
    Which Rumour's myriad voices multiply !
Alas ! the event that cometh wakes my terror.
    The man will die, disgraced in open day,
Whose dark-dyed steel hath dared through mad-brained
    error
    The roving herdsmen with their herds to slay.

Tec. O horror !   Then 'twas there he found
    The flock he brought as captives tied ;
And some he slew upon the ground,
    And some, side-smiting, sundered wide.
Two white-foot rams he backward drew,
And bound.   Of one he share and threw
The tipmost tongue and head away ;
The other to an upright stay
He tied, and with a harness thong
    Doubled in hand, gave whizzing blows,
Echoing his lashes with a song
    More dire than mortal fury knows.

Ch. Ah ! then 'tis time, our heads in mantles hiding,
  Our feet on some stol'n pathway now to ply,
Or with swift oarage o'er the billows gliding,
  With ordered stroke to make the good ship fly.
Such threats the Atridæ, armed with two-fold power,
  Launch to assail us.   Oh, I sadly fear
Stones from fierce hands on us and him will shower,
  Whose heavy plight no comfort may come near.

Tec. 'Tis changed ; his rage, like summer blast,
    Without the lightning-gleam is past.
    And now that Reason's light returns,
    New sorrow in his spirit burns.
    For when we look on self-made woe,
      In which no hand but ours had part,
    Thought of such griefs and whence they flow
      Brings aching misery to the heart.

Ch. If he hath ceased to rave, he should do well.
The account of evil lessens when 'tis past.
    Tec. If choice were given you, would you rather choose
Hurting your friends, yourself to feel delight,
Or share with them in one commingled pain ?
    Ch. The twofold trouble is more terrible.
    Tec. Then comes our torment now the fit is o'er.
    Ch. How mean'st thou by that word ?   I fail to see.
    Tec. He in his rage had rapture of delight
And knew not how he grieved us who stood near
And saw the madding tempest ruining him.
But now 'tis over and he breathes anew,

The counterblast of sorrow shakes his soul,
Whilst our affliction vexeth as before.
Have we not double for our single woe?
   Ch. I feel thy reasoning move me, and I fear
Some heavenly stroke hath fallen.   How else, when the end
Of stormy sickness brings no cheering ray?
   Tec. Our state is certain.   Dream not but 'tis so.
   Ch. How first began the assault of misery?
Tell us the trouble, for we share the pain.
   Tec. It touches you indeed, and ye shall hear
All from the first.   'Twas midnight, and the lamp
Of eve had died, when, seizing his sharp blade,
He sought on causeless errand to creep forth.
I broke in with my word : "Aias, what now?
Why thus uncalled for salliest thou?   No voice
Of herald summoned thee.   No trumpet blew.
What wouldst thou when the camp is hushed in sleep?"
He with few words well known to women's ears
Checked me : " The silent partner is the best."
I saw how 'twas and ceased.   Forth then he went
Alone.—What horror passed upon the plain
This night, I know not.   But he drags within,
Tied in a throng, bulls, shepherd-dogs, and spoil
Of cattle and sheep.   Anon he butchers them,
Felling or piercing, hacking or tearing wide,
Ribs from breast, limb from limb.   Others he seized
Dartingly, and bound, and tortured brutes for men.
Last, out he rushed before the doors, and there
Whirled forth wild language to some shadowy form,

Flouting the generals and Laërtes' son
With torrent laughter and loud triumphing
What in his raid he had wreaked to their despite.
Then diving back within—the fitful storm
Slowly assuaging left his spirit clear.
And when his eye had lightened through the room
Cumbered with ruin, smiting on his brow
He roared ; and, dropping down amidst the wreck
Of woolly carnage that himself had made,
Sate with clenched hand tight twisted in his hair.
Long stayed he so in silence.   Then flashed forth
Those frightful words of threatening vehemence,
That bade me show him all the night's mishap,
And whither he was fallen.   I, dear my friends,
Prevailed on through my fear, told all I knew.
And all at once he raised a bitter cry,
Which heretofore I ne'er had heard ; for still
He made us think such doleful utterance
Betokened the dull craven spirit, and still
Dumb to shrill wailings, he would inly moan
With half-heard muttering, like an angry bull.
But now, by such dark fortune overthrown,
Foodless and dry, amidst the quivering heap
His steel hath quelled, all quietly he broods ;
And out of doubt his mind intends some harm :
Such words, such groanings, burst from him. O friends,—
Therefore I hastened,—enter and give aid
If aught ye can ! Men thus foregone will oft
Grow milder through the counsel of a friend.

  Ch. Teleutas' child ! we shudder at thy tale

That fatal frenzy wastes our hero's soul.

Aias (*within*). Woe's me, me, me!

Tec. More cause anon!   Hear ye not Aias there,
How sharp the cry that shrills from him?

Ai.   Woe! woe!

Ch. Madly it sounds.—Or springs it of deep grief
For proofs of madness harrowing to his eye?

Ai. Boy, boy!

Tec.   What means he?   Oh Eurysakes!
He cries on thee.   Where art thou?   O my heart!

Ai. Teucer I call!   Where's Teucer?   Will he ne'er
Come from the chase, but leave me to my doom?

Ch. Not madness now.   Disclose him.   Let us look.
Haply the sight of us may calm his thought.

Tec. There, then; I open to your view the form
Of Aias, and his fortunes as they are.   [AIAS *is disclosed.*

Ai. Dear comrades of the deep, whose truth and love
Stand forth alone unbroken in my woe,
     Behold what gory sea
     Of storm-lashed agony
Doth round and round me flow!

Ch. (*to* TEC.) Too   true   thy   witness: for   the   fact
     cries out
Wild thoughts were here and Reason's spark extinct.

Ai. Strong helpers of sea-speed, whose nimble hand
Plied hither the salt oar with circling stroke,
     No shepherd there was found
     To give the avenging wound.
Come, lay me with the flock!

Ch. Speak no rash word ! nor curing ill with ill
Augment the plague of this calamity.

Ai.　　　　Mark ye the brave and bold,
　　　　　　Whom none could turn of old,
　　When once he set his face to the fierce fight ?
　　　　　　Now beasts that meant no harm
　　　　　　Have feared this puissant arm.
　　O laughter of my foes ! O mockery of my might !
Tec. Aias, my lord ! I entreat thee, speak not so !
Ai. Thou here ?　Away ! begone, and trouble me not !
　　O ! O !
Tec.　　Be softened ! bear a steadier mind !
Ai. O heaven-accursèd hand
　　　　That let the ruffians go,
　　But falling 'midst the horn'd and bleating band,
　　　　Made darkling blood-streams flow !
Ch. Why vex thy heart with what is past and done ?
Do what we may, this ne'er will alter now.

Ai.　　　　Child of Laërtes old,
　　　　　　Thou that dost still behold
　　And still contrive all shapes of monstrous ill,
　　　　　　Winding in foulest ways
　　　　　　Through the army's sinful maze,—
　　Now even for pleasure thou mayst laugh thy fill.
Ch. Laughter and tears are in the gift of God.
Ai. Ay, might I see him, though thus broken,—ay me !
Even yet—
　　Ch.　　　Nay, vaunt not. Look where thou art fallen.

Ai. Source whence my life-blood springs,
　　　O Zeus, might I but slay
　　That crafty plague, with those twin-sceptered kings,
　　　Then breathe my life away !
Tec. Pray thus, and pray that I too be no more !
If thou wert gone, what were my life to me ?

Ai. Darkness ! my light !
O nether gloom, to me
Brighter than morning to the wakeful eye !
Take me to dwell with thee.
Take me ! What help ? Zeus' daughter with fell might
Torments me sore.　I may not look on high,
Nor to the tribe of momentary men.—
Oh, whither, then,
Should it avail to fly ?
Where should I go and stay ?
All here is ruin.　This my foolish prey
Confounds me : shame is mine for evermore :
Yea, all the Achæan host, with armèd hand,
Is ready at command
To slay me o'er and o'er.

Tec. Woe's me ! to hear from one so good and true,
Words he had scorned to utter in past days.

Ai. Grey firths of foaming brine,
And ye, deep groves, that crown
The sea-caves and long cliffs upon the shore,
Too long did ye confine

My life about the walls of Troia's town :
But no more now ! a breathing man, no more !
The wise may learn that lore.
Ay, let the waters of Scamander know,
That neighbouring flow,
And kindly minister to Argive men :
One man they ne'er shall see again ;
One, I will vaunt it forth !
Highest in warlike worth
Of all Greek forms that Troia's towers have eyed :
Now, shorn of all that pride,
I lie thus low.

Ch. I know not how to let thee speak, nor how
To silence thee.　　Such evils hem thee round.
　　Ai. Ay me !
　　　　　　　　Could human thought have prophesied
My name would thus give echo to my woe ?
" Ai " now for Aias, doubly, trebly said,
Sorts all too well to note my misery ;
Whose father from this land of Troy, as noblest
Of all the host, carrying the fairest prize,
Came girt about with glory to his home.
But I his son, not less of might than he,
Nor poorer in the achievements of my hand,
To this same region following in my prime,
Am scouted by the Achæans and destroyed.
Yet know I one thing well.　　Had Peleus' child,
Living, adjudged his armour as a meed
Of tested bravery, no grasp save mine

Had clutched it.   But the Atridæ with mean craft
Conveyed his heirloom to a wit-proud knave,
Whilst Aias' peerless prowess was despised.
And had not this mine eye and mind distraught
Glanced from my purpose, ne'er again had they
Perverted judgment.   But the invincible
Stern daughter of the Highest, with baneful eye,
Even as mine arm descended, baffled me,
And hurled upon my soul a frenzied plague,
To stain my hand with these dumb victims' blood.
And those mine enemies exult in safety,—
Not with my will; but where a God misguides,
Strong arms are thwarted, and the weakling lives.
    Now, what remains?   Heaven hates me, 'tis too clear:
The Grecian host abhors me: Troy, with all
This country round our camp, is my sworn foe.
Shall I, across the Ægean sailing home,
Leave these Atridæ and their fleet forlorn?
How shall I dare to front my father's eye?
How will he once endure to look on me,
Denuded of the prize of high renown,
Whose coronal stood sparkling on his brow?
No! 'twere too dreadful.   Then shall I advance
Before the Trojan battlements, and there
In single conflict doing valiantly
Last die upon their spears?   Nay, for by this
I might perchance make Atreus' offspring glad.
That may not be imagined.   I must find
Some act to let my grey-haired father feel
No heartless recreant once called him sire.

Shame on the wight who when beset with ill
Cares to live on in misery unreprieved.
Can hour outlasting hour make less or more
Of death ?   Whereby then can it furnish joy ?
That mortal weighs for nothing-worth with me,
Whom Hope can comfort with her fruitless fire.
Honour in life or honour in the grave
Befits the noble heart.   You hear my will.

   Ch. From thine own spirit, Aias, all may tell,
That utterance came, and none have prompted thee.
Yet stay thy hurrying thought, and by thy friends
Be ruled to loose this burden from thy mind.

   Tec. O my great master ! heaviest of all woe
Is theirs whose life is crushed beyond recall.
I, born of one the mightiest of the free
And wealthiest in the Phrygian land, am now
A captive.   So Heaven willed, and thy strong arm
Determined.   Therefore, since the hour that made
My being one with thine, I breathe for thee ;
And I beseech thee by the sacred fire
Of home, and by the sweetness of the night
When from my captor thou becam'st my friend
Leave me not guardless to the unworthy touch
And cruel taunting of thine enemies !
For, shouldst thou die and leave us, then shall I
Borne off by Argive violence with thy boy
Eat from that day the bread of slavery.
And some one of our lords shall smite me there
With galling speech : Behold the concubine
Of Aias, first of all the Greeks for might,

How envied once, worn with what service now !
So will they speak ; and while my quailing heart
Shall sink beneath its burden, clouds of shame
Will dim thy glory and degrade thy race.
Oh ! think but of thy father, left to pine
In doleful age, and let thy mother's grief,—
Who, long bowed down with many a careful year,
Prays oftentimes thou mayst return alive,—
O'er-awe thee.　　Yea and pity thine own son,
Unsheltered in his boyhood, reft of thee,
With bitter foes to tend his orphanhood,
Think, O my lord, what sorrow in thy death
Thou send'st on him and me.　For I have nought
To lean to but thy life.　My fatherland
Thy spear hath ruined.　Fate,—not thou,—hath sent
My sire and mother to the home of death.
What wealth have I to comfort me for thee ?
What land of refuge ?　Thou art all my stay.
Oh, of me too take thought !　Shall men have joy,
And not remember ?　Or shall kindness fade ?
Say, can the mind be noble, where the stream
Of gratitude is withered from the spring ?

　　Ch. Aias, I would thy heart were touched like mine
With pity ; then her words would win thy praise.

　　Ai. My praise she shall not miss, if she perform
My bidding with firm heart, and fail not here.

　　Tec. Dear Aias, I will fail in nought thou bidst me.

　　Ai. Bring me my boy, that I may see his face.

　　Tec. Oh, in my terror I conveyed him hence !

　　Ai. Clear of this mischief, mean'st thou ? or for what ?

Tec. Lest he might run to thee, poor child, and die.
Ai. That issue had been worthy of my fate!
Tec. But I kept watch to fence his life from harm.
Ai. 'Twas wisely done.   I praise thy foresight there.
Tec. Well, since 'tis so, how can I help thee now?
Ai. Give me to speak to him and see him near.
Tec. He stands close by with servants watching him.
Ai. Then why doth he not come, but still delay?
Tec. Boy, father calls for thee.   Come, lead him
    hither,
Whichever of you holds him by the hand.
Ai. Moves he? or do thine accents idly fall?
Tec. See, where thy people bring him to thine eye.
Ai. Lift him to me: lift him!   He will not fear
At sight of this fresh havoc of the sword,
If by a true descent he is my son.
Like some young colt he must be trained and taught
To run fierce courses with his warrior sire.
Be luckier than thy father, boy! but else
Be like him, and thy life will not be low.
One thing even now I envy thee, that none
Of all this misery pierces to thy mind.
For life is sweetest in the void of sense,
Ere thou know joy or sorrow.   But when this
Finds thee, then make thy father's enemies
Feel the great parent in the valiant child.
Meantime grow on in tender youthfulness,
Nursed by light breezes, gladdening this thy mother
No Greek shall trample thee with brutal harm,
That I know well, though I shall not be near—

So stout a warder to protect thy life
I leave in Teucer.　He'll not fail, though now
He follow far the chase upon his foes.
My trusty warriors, people of the sea,
To you I give this charge no less,—and tell
To him my message, that he take this boy
Home to my fatherland, and make him known
To Telamon, and Eribœa too,
My mother.　Let him tend them in their age.
And, for mine armour, let not that be made
The award of Grecian umpires or of him
Who ruined me.　But thou, named of the shield,*
Eurysakes, hold mine, the unpierceable
Seven-hided buckler, and by the well-stitched thong
Grasp firm and wield it mightily.—The rest
Shall lie where I am buried.—Take him now,
Quickly, and close the door.　No tears!　What! weep
For all to see?　How women crave for pity!
Make fast, I say.　No wise practitioner
Chants dirges o'er a knife-demanding wound.

　　Ch. There sounds a vehement ardour in thy words
That likes me not.　I fear thy sharpened tongue.

　　Tec. Aias, my lord, what act is in thy mind?

　　Ai. Inquire not, question not; be wise, thou'rt best.

　　Tec. How my heart sinks!　Oh, by thy child, by
　　　　Heaven,
I pray thee on my knees, forsake us not!

　　Ai. Thou troublest me.　What! know'st thou not
　　　　that Heaven

　　　　　　* Eurysakes means *Broad-shield.*

Has ceased to be my debtor from to-day ?
   Tec. Hush ! Speak not so.
   Ai.   Speak thou to those that hear.
   Tec. Will you not hear me ?
   Ai.   Canst thou not be still ?
   Tec. My fears, my fears !
   Ai. (*to the* Attendants).   Come, shut me in, I say.
   Tec. Oh, yet be softened !
   Ai.   'Tis a foolish hope,
If thou deem'st now to mould me to thy will.
         [AIAS *is withdrawn. Exit* TECMESSA.

CHORUS.

Island of glory ! whom the glowing eyes
Of all the wondering world immortalise,
Thou, Salamis, art planted evermore,
Happy amidst the wandering billows' roar ;
While I—ah, woe the while !—this weary time,
  By the green wold where flocks from Ida stray,
Lie worn with countless hours of wasted prime,
    Hoping—ah, cheerless hope !—to win my way
    Where Hades' horrid gloom shall hide me from the day.

Aias is with me, yea but crouching low,
Where Heaven-sent madness haunts his overthrow,
Beyond my cure or tendance : woful plight !
Whom thou, erewhile, to head the impetuous fight,
Sent'st forth, thy conquering champion.   Now he feeds
  His spirit on lone paths, and on us brings
Deep sorrow ; and all his former peerless deeds

Of prowess drop like unremembered things
From Atreus' loveless brood, this caitiff brace of kings.

Ah! when his mother, full of days and bowed
With hoary eld, shall hear his ruined mind,
How will she mourn aloud!
Not like the warbler of the dale,
The bird of piteous wail,
But in shrill strains far borne upon the wind,
While on the withered breast and thin white hair
Falls the resounding blow, the rending of despair.

Best hid in death were he whom madness drives
Without redress; if, through his father's race
      Born to the noblest place
Among the war-worn Greeks, he lives
      By his own light no more,
Self-aliened from the self he knew before.
Oh, hapless sire, what woe thine ear shall wound!
One that of all thy line no life save this hath found.

Enter AIAS *with a bright sword, and* TECMESSA, *severally.*

Ai. What changes will interminable Time
Not roll to light, what hide not from the day?
What chance shall win men's marvel?   Mightiest oaths
Fall frustrate, and the steely-tempered will.
Ay, and even mine, that stood so diamond-keen
Since bathed in yonder surge, droops now dis-edged
And weakened by this woman, whom to leave
A widow with her orphan to my foes,

Dulls me with pity.   I will go to the baths
And meadows near the cliff, and purging there
My dark pollution, I will screen my soul
From reach of Pallas' grievous wrath.   I will find
Some place untrodden, and digging of the soil
Where none shall see, will bury this my sword,
Weapon of hate! for Death and Night to hold
Evermore underground.   For, since my hand
Had this from Hector mine arch-enemy,
No kindness have I known from Argive men.
So true that saying of the bygone world,
" A foe's gift is no gift, and brings no good."
     Well, we will learn of Time.   Henceforth I'll bow
To heavenly ordinance and give homage due
To Atreus' sons.   Who rules, must be obeyed.
Since naught so fierce and terrible but yields
Place to Authority.   Wild Winter's snows
Make way for bounteous Summer's flowery tread,
And Night's sad orb retires for lightsome Day
With his white steeds to illumine the glad sky.
The furious storm-blast leaves the groaning sea
Gently to rest.   Yea the all-subduer Sleep
Frees whom he binds, nor holds enchained for aye.
And shall not men be taught the temperate will?
Yea, for I now know surely that my foe
Must be so hated, as being like enough
To prove a friend hereafter, and my friend
With friendship I will so far serve, as one
Not always to be with me.   Men have found
But treacherous harbour in companionship.

Our ending, then, is peaceful. Thou, my child,
Go in and pray the Gods my heart's desire
Be all fulfilled.   My comrades, join her here,
Honouring my wishes; and if Teucer come,
Bid him toward us be mindful, kind toward you.
I must go—whither I must go.   Do ye
But keep my word, and ye may learn, though now
Be my dark hour, that all with me is well.

    [*Exit towards the country.*   TECMESSA *retires.*

CHORUS.

A shudder of love thrills through me.   Joy ! I soar.
      O Pan, wild Pan !   [*They dance.*
      Come from Cyllene hoar—
Come from the snowdrift, the rock-ridge, the glen !
      Leaving the mountain bare'
      Fleet through the salt sea-air,
Mover of dances to Gods and to men.
Whirl me in Cnossian ways—thrid me the Nysian maze !
Come, while the joy of the dance is my care !
      Thou too, Apollo, come
      Bright from thy Delian home,
        Bringer of day,
      Fly o'er the southward main
      Here in our hearts to reign,
Loved to repose there and kindly to stay.

Horror is past.   Our eyes have rest from pain.
      O Lord of Heaven !   [*They dance.*

> Now blithesome day again
Purely may smile on our swift-sailing fleet,
> Since, all his woe forgot,
> Aias now faileth not
Aught that of prayer and Heaven-worship is meet.
Time bringeth mighty aid—nought but in time doth
>> fade :
Nothing shall move me as strange to my thought.
> Aias our lord hath now
> Cleared his wrath-burdened brow
>> Long our despair,
> Ceased from his angry feud
> And with mild heart renewed
Peace and goodwill to the high-sceptred pair.

Enter Messenger.

Messenger. Friends, my first news is Teucer's presence
> here,
Fresh from the Mysian heights ; who, as he came
Right towards the generals' quarter, was assailed
With curses from the Argives in a throng :
For when they knew his motion from afar
They swarmed around him, and with cries of blame
From each side one and all assaulted him
As brother to the man who had gone mad
And plotted 'gainst the host,—threatening aloud,
Strive as he would, with stones to pound him dead.
—So far strife ran, that swords unscabbarded
Crossed blades, till as it mounted to the height

Age interposed with counsel and it fell.
　　But where is Aias to receive my word?
Tidings are best told to the rightful ear.
　　Ch. Not in the hut, but just gone forth, preparing
New plans to suit his newly altered mind.
　　Mess. Alas!
Too tardy then was he who sped me forth
This way; or I too slow a messenger?
　　Ch. Wherein? what point is lacking for this need?
　　Mess. Teucer was resolute the man should bide
Close held within-doors till himself should come.
　　Ch. Why, sure his going took the happiest turn
And wisest, to propitiate Heaven's high wrath.
　　Mess. The height of folly lives in such discourse,
If Calchas have the wisdom of a seer.
　　Ch. What knows he of our state? What saith he? Tell.
　　Mess. I can tell only what I heard and saw.
Whilst all the chieftains and the Atridæ twain
Were seated in a ring, Calchas alone
Rose up and left them, and in Teucer's palm
Laid his right hand full friendly; then out-spake
With strict injunction by all means i' the world
To keep beneath yon covert this one day
Your hero, and not suffer him to rove,
If he would see him any more alive.
For through this present light—and ne'er again—
Holy Athena, so he said, will drive him
Before her anger.　Such calamitous woe
Strikes down the unprofitable growth that mounts
Beyond his measure and provokes the sky.

" Thus ever," said the prophet, " must he fall
Who in man's mould hath thoughts beyond a man.
And Aias, ere he left his father's door,
Made foolish answer to his prudent sire.
' My son,' said Telamon, ' choose victory
Always, but victory with an aid from Heaven.'
How loftily, how madly, he replied !
' Father, with heavenly help men nothing worth
May win success.   But I am confident
Without the Gods to pluck this glory down.'
So huge the boast he vaunted !   And again
When holy Pallas urged him with her voice
To hurl his deadly spear against the foe,
He turned on her with speech of awful sound :
' Goddess, by other Greeks take thou thy stand ;
Where I keep rank, the battle ne'er shall break.'
Such words of pride beyond the mortal scope
Have won him Pallas' wrath, unlovely meed.
But yet, perchance, so be it he live to-day,
We, with Heaven's succour, may restore his peace."—
Thus far the prophet, when immediately
Teucer despatched me, ere the assembly rose,
Bearing to thee this missive to be kept
With all thy care.   But if my speed be lost,
And Calchas word have power, the man is dead.

   Ch. O trouble-tost Tecmessa, born to woe,
Come forth and see what messenger is here !
This news bites near the bone, a death to joy.

Enter TECMESSA.

Tec. Wherefore again, when sorrow's cruel storm
Was just abating, break ye my repose ?

   Ch. (*pointing to the* Messenger). Hear what he saith,
      and how he comes to bring
News of our Aias that hath torn my heart.

   Tec. Oh me ! what is it, man? Am I undone?

   Mess. Thy case I know not ; but of Aias this,
That if he roam abroad, 'tis dangerous.

   Tec. He is, indeed, abroad.   Oh ! tell me quickly !

   Mess. 'Tis Teucer's strong command to close him fast
Beneath this roof, nor let him range alone.

   Tec. But where is Teucer? and what means his word?

   Mess. Even now at hand, and eager to make known
That Aias, if he thus go forth, must fall.

   Tec. Alas ! my misery !   Whence learned he this?

   Mess. From Thestor's prophet-offspring, who to-day
Holds forth to Aias choice of life or death.

   Tec. Woe's me !   O friends, this desolating blow
Descends !   Oh, stand ye forward to prevent !
And some bring Teucer with more haste, while some
Explore the western bays and others search
Eastward to find your hero's fatal path !
For well I see I am cheated and cast forth
From the old favour.   Child, what shall I do?

[Looking at EURYSAKES.

We must not stay.   I too will fare along,
So far as I have power.   Come, let us go.
Bestir ye !   'Tis no moment to sit still,

If we would save him who now speeds to die.
   Ch. I am ready.   Come!   Fidelity of foot,
And swift performance, shall approve me true.

[Exeunt omnes.

The scene changes to a lonely wooded spot.

AIAS (discovered alone).

The executioner stands prepared,—and when
More keen?   Let me take time for thinking too!
This gift of Hector, whom of foreign men
I hated most with heart and eyes, is set
In hostile Trojan soil, with grinding hone
New-edged, and here embedded by my care
Thus firm, to give me swift and friendly death.
Fine instrument, so much for thee!   Then, first,
Thou, for 'tis meet, great Father, give thine aid.
No lofty boon I crave of thee.   Send one
To carry Teucer the ill news, that he
May first uplift me freshly fallen in death
Upon my bleeding sword, ere I be spied
By some of those who hate me, and be flung
To dogs and vultures for an outcast prey.
So far I sue thee, Lord of Heaven.   And thou,
Guide Hermes of the shadowy world below,
Speed me to rest, and when with this sharp steel
I have cleft a sudden passage to my heart,
At one swift bound waft me to painless slumber!
But most be ye my helpers, awful Powers,
Who know no blandishments, but still perceive
All wicked deeds i' the world—strong, swift, and sure,

Avenging Furies, understand my wrong,
See how my life is ruined, and by whom.
Come, ravin on Achæan flesh—spare none ;
Rage through the camp ! Last, thou that driv'st thy
    course
Up yon steep Heaven, thou Sun, when thou behold'st
My fatherland, checking thy golden rein,
Report my fall, and this my fatal end,
To my old sire, and the poor soul who tends him.
Ah, hapless one ! when she shall hear this word,
How she will make the city ring with woe !
  'Twere from the business idly to condole.
To work, then, and despatch.   O Death ! O Death !
Now come, and welcome !   Yet with thee, hereafter,
I shall find close communion where I go.
But unto thee, fresh beam of shining Day,
And thee, thou travelling Sun-god, I may speak
Now, and no more for ever.   O fair light !
O sacred fields of Salamis my home !
Thou, firm-set natal hearth : Athens renowned,
And ye her people whom I love ; O rivers,
Brooks, fountains here—yea, even the Trojan plain
I now invoke !—kind fosterers, farewell !
This one last word from Aias peals to you :
Henceforth my speech will be with souls unseen.

                        [Falls on his sword.

        Chorus (*re-entering severally*).

Ch. a. Toil upon toil brings toil,
      And what save trouble have I ?

Which path have I not tried?
And never a place stops me to learn its tale.
Hark! lo, again a sound!
Ch. b. 'Tis we, the comrades of your good ship's crew.
Ch. a. Well, sirs?
Ch. b. We have trodden all the westward curve o' the
      bay.
Ch. a. Well, have ye found?
Ch. b. Trouble enow, but nought for eyes to hold.
Ch. a. Nor yet along the road that fronts the dawn
      Is any sign of Aias to be seen.

Ch. Who then will tell me, who? What hard sea-liver,
   What toiling fisher in his sleepless quest,
What heaven-born nymph, what oozy Thracian river,
   Hath seen our wanderer of the tameless breast?
      Where? tell me where!
     'Tis hard that I, far-toiling voyager,
       Crossed by some evil wind,
       Cannot the haven find,
Nor catch his form that flies me, where? ah! where?
Tec. (*behind*). Oh, woe is me! woe, woe!
Ch. a. Who cries there from the covert of the grove?
Tec. O boundless misery!
Ch. b. Steeped in this audible sorrow I behold
Tecmessa, poor fate-burdened bride of war.
Tec. Friends, I am spoiled, lost, ruined, overthrown!
Ch. What ails thee now?
Tec. See where our Aias lies, but newly slain,
Fallen on his sword concealed within the ground.

Ch.	Woe for my hopes of home !
	Aias, my lord, thou hast slain
	Thy comrades on the salt sea foam.
		Alas for us, and thee,
		Child of calamity !

Tec. So lies our fortune.   Well mayst thou com-
	plain.

Ch. Whose hand employed he for the deed of blood ?

Tec. His own, 'tis manifest.   This planted steel,
Fixed by his hand, gives verdict from his breast.

Ch. Woe for my fault, my loss !
		Thou hast fallen in blood alone,
	And not a friend to cross
		Or guard thee. I, deaf, senseless as a stone,
Left all undone.   Oh, where, then, lies the stern ·
Aias, of saddest name, whose purpose none might
	turn ?

Tec. No eye shall see him.   I will veil him round
With this all-covering mantle, since no heart
That loved him could endure to view him there,
With ghastly expiration spouting forth
From mouth and nostrils, and the deadly wound,
The gore of his self-slaughter.   Ah, my lord !
What shall I do ?   What friend will carry thee ?
Oh, where is Teucer !   Timely were his hand,
Might he come now to smooth his brother's corse.
O thou most noble, here ignobly laid,
Even enemies methinks must mourn thy fate !

Ch. Ah ! 'twas too clear thy firm-knit thoughts would
    fashion,
  Early or late, an end of boundless woe !
Such heaving groans, such bursts of heart-bruised
    passion,
  Midnight and morn, bewrayed the fire below.
    "The Atridæ might beware !"
A plenteous fount of pain was opened there,
    What time the strife was set,
    Wherein the noblest met,
  Grappling the golden prize that kindled thy despair !

Tec. Woe, woe is me !
Ch. Deep sorrow wrings thy soul, I know it well.
Tec. O woe, woe, woe !
Ch. Thou mayst prolong thy moan, and be believed,
Thou that hast lately lost so true a friend.
Tec. Thou mayst imagine ; 'tis for me to know.
Ch. Ay, ay, 'tis true.
Tec. Alas, my child ! what slavish tasks and hard
We are drifting to !   What eyes control our will !

Ch. Ay me !   Through thy complaint
    I hear the wordless blow
Of two high-throned, who rule without restraint
    Of Pity.   Heaven forefend
    What evil they intend !

Tec. The work of heaven hath brought our life thus low.
Ch. 'Tis a sore burden to be laid on men.

Tec. Yet such the mischief Zeus' resistless maid,
Pallas, hath planned to make Odysseus glad.

Ch. O'er that dark-featured soul
　　　What waves of pride shall roll,
　　　What floods of laughter flow,
　　To greet this madness-prompted woe,
Alas! from him who all things dares endure,
And from that lordly pair, who hear, and seat them sure!

Tec. Ay, let them laugh and revel o'er his fall.
Perchance albeit in life they missed him not
Dead they will cry for him in straits of war.
For dullards know not goodness in their hand,
Nor prize the jewel till 'tis cast away.
To me more bitter than to them 'twas sweet,
His death to him was gladsome, for he found
The lot he longed for, his self-chosen doom.
What cause have they to laugh? Heaven, not their crew,
Hath glory by his death. Then let Odysseus
Insult with empty pride. To him and his
Aias is nothing; but to me, to me,
He leaves distress and sorrow in his room!
　　Teucer (*within*). Alas, undone!
　　Ch. Hush! that was Teucer's cry. Methought I heard
His voice salute this object of dire woe.

Enter TEUCER.

Teu. Aias, dear brother, comfort of mine eye,
Hast thou then done even as the rumour holds?

Ch. Be sure of that, Teucer.   He lives no more.

Teu. Oh, then how heavy is the lot I bear !

Ch. Yes ; thou hast cause—

Teu.   O destiny of woe !—

Ch. To mourn full loud.

Teu.   Ay me ! and where, oh where
On Trojan earth, tell me, is this man's child ?

Ch. Beside the huts, untended.

Teu. (*to* TEC.).   Oh, with haste
Go bring him hither, lest some enemy's hand
Snatch him, as from the lion's widowed mate
The lion-whelp is taken.   Spare not speed.
All soon combine in mockery o'er the dead.

                              [*Exit* TECMESSA.

Ch. Even such commands he left thee ere he died
As thou fulfillest by this timely care.

Teu. O sorest spectacle mine eyes e'er saw !
Woe for my journey of to-day ! that most
Hath pained my heart, here speeding since I knew
Thy fate, dear Aias, and pursued and tracked
Thy footsteps.   For there darted through the host
As from some God a swift report of thee
That thou wert lost in death.   I, hapless, heard,
And mourned even then for that whose presence kills me.
Ay me !   But come,
Unveil.   Let me behold my misery.

                              [*The corpse of* AIAS *is uncovered.*

O sight unbearable !   Cruelly brave !
Dying, what store of griefs thou sow'st for me !
Where, amongst whom of mortals, can I go,

That stood not near thee in thy troublous hour?
Will Telamon, my sire and thine, receive me
With radiant countenance and favouring brow
Returning without thee?   Most like! as one
Who smiles no more, yield Fortune what she may
Will he hide aught or soften any word,
Rating the bastard of his spear-won thrall,
Whose cowardice and dastardy betrayed
Thy life, dear Aias,—or my murderous guile,
To rob thee of thy lordship and thy home?
Such greeting waits me from the man of wrath,
Whose testy age even without cause would storm.
Last, I shall leave my land a castaway
Thrust forth, no freeman, but a slave proclaimed;
So should I fare at home.   And here in Troy
My foes are many and my comforts few.
All these things are my portion through thy death.
Woe's me, my heart! how shall I bear to draw thee,
O thou ill-starred! from this discoloured blade,
Thy self-shown slayer?   Didst thou then perceive
Dead Hector was at length to be thine end?—
I pray you all, consider these two men.
Hector, whose gift from Aias was a girdle,
Tight-braced therewith to the car's rim, was dragged
And scarified till he breathed forth his life.
And Aias with this present from his foe
Finds through such means his death-fall and his doom.
Say then what cruel workman forged the gifts,
But Fury this sharp sword, Hell that bright band?
In this, and all that touches men, I find

Gods are the artificers. . My thought is said.
And if there be who cares not for my thought,
Let him hold fast his faith and leave me mine.

　Ch. Spare longer speech, and think how to secure
Thy brother's burial, and what plea will serve;
Since one comes here hath no good will to us
And like a villain comes perchance in scorn.

　Teu. What man of all the host hath caught thine eye?
　Ch. The cause for whom we sailed, the Spartan King.
　Teu. Yes; I discern him, now he moves more near.

Enter MENELAUS.

Menelaus. Fellow, give o'er.　Cease tending yon dead
　　man!
Obey my voice, and leave him where he lies.
　Teu. Thy potent cause for spending so much breath?
　Men. My will, and his whose word is sovereign here.
　Teu. May we not know the reasons of your will?
　Men. Because he, whom we trusted to have brought
To lend us loyal help with heart and hand,
Proved in the trial a worse than Phrygian foe,
Who lay in wait for all the host by night,
And sallied forth in arms to shed our blood;
That, had not one in Heaven crushed this attempt,
Our lot had been to lie as he doth here
Dead and disgraced for ever, while full life.
Were his.　But Heaven hath turned this turbulence
To fall instead upon the harmless flock.
Wherefore no strength of man shall once avail
To case his body with a seemly tomb,

But outcast on the wide and watery sand,
He'll feed the birds that batten on the shore.
Nor let thy towering spirit therefore rise
In threatening wrath.   Wilt thou or not, our hand
Shall rule him dead, howe'er he braved us living,
And that by force; for never would he yield,
Even while he lived, to words from me.   And yet
It shows base metal when the subject-wight
Deigns not to hearken to the chief in power.
Since without settled awe, neither in states
Can laws have rightful sway, nor can a host
Be governed with due wisdom, if no fear
Or wholesome shame be there to shield its safety.
And though a man be great in thews and bulk,
He should reflect how small a wound may slay him.
Whoever knows respect and honour both
Stands free from risk of dark vicissitude.
But whereso pride and licence have their fling,
Be sure that state will one day lose her course
And founder in the abysm.   Let fear have place
Still where it ought, say I, nor let men think
To do their pleasure and not bide the pain.
That wheel comes surely round.   Once Aias raged
With turbulent fierceness.   Now I mount in pride,
And loudly bid thee bury him not, lest burying
Thy brother thou be burrowing thine own grave.

   Ch. Menelaüs, make not thy philosophy
A platform whence to insult the valiant dead.

   Teu. I nevermore will marvel, sirs, when one
Of humblest parentage is prone to sin,

Since those reputed men of noble strain
Stoop to such phrase of prating frowardness.
Come, tell it o'er again,—said you ye brought
My brother bound to aid you with his power?
Sailed he not forth of his own sovereign will?
Where is thy voucher of command o'er him?
Where of thy right o'er those that followed him?
Sparta, not we, shall buckle to thy sway.
'Twas written nowhere in the bond of rule
That thou shouldst check him rather than he thee.
Thou sailedst under orders, not in charge
Of all, much less of Aias.   Then pursue
Thy limited direction, and chastise,
In haughty phrase, the men who fear thy nod.
But I will bury Aias, whether thou
Or the other general give consent or no.
'Tis not for me to tremble at thy word.
Not to reclaim thy wife, like those poor souls
Thou fill'st with labour, issued this man forth,
But caring for his oath, and not for thee,
Or any other nobody.   Then come
With heralds all arow, and bring the man
Called king of men with thee!   For thy sole noise
I budge not, wert thou twenty times thy name.

 Men. Our bowman carries no small pride, I see.
 Teu. No mere mechanic's menial craft is mine.
 Men. How wouldst thou vaunt it hadst thou but a shield!
 Teu. Unarmed I fear not thee in panoply.
 Men. Redoubted is the wrath lives on thy tongue.
 Teu. Whose cause is just hath licence to be proud.

Men. Just, that my murderer have a peaceful end?

Teu. Thy murderer?　Strange, to have been slain and
　　live!

Men. Yea, through Heaven's mercy.　By his will, I
　　am dead.

Teu. If Heaven have saved thee, give the Gods their
　　due.

Men. Am I the man to thwart Heaven's ordinance?

Teu. Thou dost, to come and frustrate burial.

Men. Honour forbids to yield my foes a tomb.

Teu. And Aias was thy foeman?　Where and when?

Men. Hate lived betwixt us; that thou know'st full
　　well.

Teu. For thy proved knavery, coining votes i' the
　　court.

Men. The judges voted.　He ne'er lost through me.

Teu. Guilt-hiding guile wears often fairest front.

Men. I know whom pain shall harass for that word.

Teu. Not without giving equal pain, 'tis clear.

Men. No more, but this.　No burial for this man!

Teu. Yea, this much more.　He shall have instant
　　burial.

Men. I have seen ere now a man of doughty tongue
Urge sailors in foul weather to unmoor,
Who, caught in the sea-misery by-and-by,
Lay voiceless, muffled in his cloak, and suffered
Who would of the sailors over-trample him.
Even so methinks thy truculent mouth ere long
Shall quench its outcry when this little cloud
Breaks forth on thee with the full tempest's might.

Teu. I too have seen a man whose windy pride
Poured forth loud insults o'er a neighbour's fall,
Till one whose cause and temper showed like mine
Spake to him in my hearing this plain word:
"Man, do the dead no wrong; but, if thou dost,
Be sure thou shalt have sorrow."   Thus he warned
The infatuate one: ay, one whom I behold;
For all may read my riddle—thou art he.

Men. I will be gone.   'Twere shame to me, if known,
To chide when I have power to crush by force.

Teu. Off with you, then!   'Twere triple shame in me
To list the vain talk of a blustering fool.

[Exit MENELAUS.

CHORUS.

High the quarrel rears his head!
  Haste thee, Teucer, trebly haste,
Grave-room for the valiant dead
  Furnish with what speed thou may'st,
Hollowed deep within the ground,
Where beneath his mouldering mound
Aias aye shall be renowned.

Re-enter TECMESSA *with* EURYSAKES.

Teu. Lo! where the hero's housemate and his child,
Hitting the moment's need, appear at hand,
To tend the burial of the ill-fated dead.
Come, child, take thou thy station close beside:
Kneel and embrace the author of thy life,
In solemn suppliant fashion holding forth

This lock of thine own hair and hers and mine
With threefold consecration, that if one
Of the army force thee from thy father's corse,
My curse may banish him from holy ground,
Far from his home, unburied, and cut off
From all his race, even as I cut this curl.
There, hold him, child, and guard him; let no hand
Stir thee, but lean to the calm breast and cling.
(*To* Chorus) And ye, be not like women in this scene,
Nor let your manhoods falter; stand true men
To this defence, till I return prepared,
Though all cry No, to give him burial.　　　　　*[Exit.*

CHORUS.

When shall the tale of wandering years be done?
When shall arise our exile's latest sun?
Oh, where shall end the incessant woe
Of troublous spear-encounter with the foe,
　　Through this vast Troïan plain,
Of Grecian arms the lamentable stain?

Would he had gone to inhabit the wide sky,
Or that deep home of death where millions lie,
Who taught our Grecian world the way
To use vile swords and knit the dense array!
　　His toil gave birth to toil
In endless line.　He made mankind his spoil.

He forced me to forego
The garland, and the goblet's bounteous flow.

Yea, and the flute's dear noise,
And night's more tranquil joys;
Ay me! nor only these,
The fruits of golden ease,
But Love, but Love—O crowning sorrow!—
Hath ceased for me.   I may not borrow
Sweet thoughts from him to smooth my dreary bed,
Where dank night-dews fall ever on my head,
Lest once I might forget the sadness of the morrow.

Even here in Troy, Aias was erst my rock,
From darkling fears and 'midst the battle-shock
        To screen me with huge might;
        Now he is sunk in night
        And horror.   Where again
        Shall gladness heal my pain?
Ah! were I where the waters hoary,
Beneath wild Sunium's upland vale,
Plash the pine-shadowed seaward promontory;
That holiest Athens once more I might hail!

Enter TEUCER.

Teu. My steps were hastened, brethren, when I saw
Great Agamemnon hitherward afoot.
He means to talk perversely, I can tell.

Enter AGAMEMNON.

Ag. And so I hear thou'lt stretch thy mouth agape
With big bold words against us undismayed—
Thou, the she-captive's offspring!   High would scale

Thy speech, and pert would be thy strutting gait,
Were but thy mother noble; since, being naught,
So stiff thou stand'st for him who is nothing now,
And swear'st we came not as commanders here
Of all the Achæan navy, nor of thee,
But Aias sailed, thou say'st, with absolute right.
Must we endure detraction from a slave?
What was the man thou noisest here so proudly?
Have I not set my foot as firm and far?
Or stood his valour unaccompanied
In all this host?   High cause have we to rue
That prize-encounter for Pelides' arms,
Seeing Teucer's sentence stamps our knavery
For all to know it; and nought will serve but ye,
Being vanquished, kick at the award that passed
By voice of the majority in the court,
And either pelt us with rude calumnies,
Or stab at us, ye laggards! with base guile.
Howbeit, these ways will never help to build
The wholesome order of established law,
If men shall hustle victors from their right,
And mix the hindmost rabble with the van.
This must be curbed.   'Tis not by bulky size,
Or shoulder's breadth, the perfect man is known;
But wisdom gives chief power in all the world.
The ox hath a huge broadside, yet is held
Straight in the furrow by a slender goad;
Which remedy, I perceive, will pass thy way
Ere long, unless thy gains in wisdom grow;
Who hast uttered forth such daring insolence

For the pale shadow of a vanished man.
Learn modestly to know thy place and birth,
And bring with thee some freeborn advocate
To plead thy cause before us in thy room.
I understand not in the barbarous tongue,
And all thy speech is nonsense to mine ear.

Ch. Would ye might both have sense to curb your ire!
No better wish for either can I speak.

Teu. Fie! How doth gratitude when men are dead
Prove renegade and swiftly fall away!
This Agamemnon hath no slightest word
Of kind remembrance any more for thee,
Aias, who oftentimes for his behoof
Hast jeoparded thy iife in labour of war.
Now all is clean forgotten and cast away.
Thou who hast multiplied words void of sense,
Hast thou no faintest memory of the time
When who but Aias came and rescued you
Already locked within the toils,—all lost,
The rout begun : when close abaft the ships
The torches flared, and o'er the bootless trench
Hector was bounding high to board our fleet?
Who stayed that onset?   Was not Aias he?
Whom thou deny'st to have once set foot by thine.
Find ye no merit in this deed?   And then
When he met Hector singly, man to man,
Not by your bidding, but the lottery's choice,
His lot, that skulked not low adown i' the heap,
A moist earth-clod, but sure to spring in air,
And first to clear the plumy helmet's brim.

Yes, Aias was the man, and I too there
Kept rank, the " barbarous mother's servile son."
I pity thee the blindness of that word.
Who was thy father's sire, but a barbarian,
Pelops, the Phrygian, if you trace him far ?
And what was Atreus, thine own sire, but one
Who served his brother with the abominable
Dire feast of his own flesh ?   And thou thyself
Camest from a Cretan mother, whom her sire
Caught with a man who had no right in her
And gave dumb fishes the polluted prey.
Such was thy race.   What is the race thou spurnest ?
My father, Telamon, of all the host
Being foremost proved in valour, took as prize
My mother for his mate : a princess she,
Born of Laomedon ; Alcmena's son
Endowed him with her as a glorious boon.
Thus royally descended and thus brave,
Shall I disgrace the brother of my blood,
Or suffer thee to thrust him in his woes
Far from all burial, shameless as thou art ?
Be sure that, if ye cast him forth, ye'll cast
Three bodies more beside him in one spot ;
For nobler should I find it here to die
In open quarrel for my kinsman's weal,
Than for thy wife—or Menelaüs', was't ?
Consider then, not my case, but your own.
For if you harm me, you will wish some day
To have been a coward rather than dare me.

   Ch. Hail, Lord Odysseus ! thou art come in time
Not to begin, but help to end, a fray.

Enter ODYSSEUS.

Od. What quarrel, sirs?   I well perceived from far
The kings high-voicing o'er the valiant dead.
   Ag. Yea, Lord Odysseus, for our ears are full,
Even now, with this man's heart-offending talk.
   Od. What words have passed?   I cannot blame the
        man
Who meets foul speech with bitterness of tongue.
   Ag. My speech was bitter, for his deeds were foul.
   Od. What deed of his could harm thy sovereign head?
   Ag. He boldly says this corse shall not be left
Unburied, but he'll bury it in our spite.
   Od. May I then speak true counsel to my friend,
And pull with thee in policy as of yore?
   Ag. Speak.   I were else a madman; for no friend
Of all the Argeians do I count thy peer.
   Od. Then hear me in Heaven's name!   Be not so
        hard
Thus without ruth tombless to cast him forth;
Nor be so vanquished by a vehement will,
That to thy hate even Justice' self must bow.
I, too, had him for my worst enemy,
Since I gained mastery o'er Pelides' arms.
But though he used me so, I ne'er will grudge
For his proud scorn to yield him thus much honour,
That, save Achilles' self, I have not seen
So noble an Argive on the fields of Troy.
Then 'twere not just in thee to slight him now;
Nor would thy treatment wound him, but confound

The laws of Heaven.   No hatred should have scope
To offend the noble spirits of the dead.

    Ag. Wilt thou thus fight against me on his side?

    Od. Yea, though I hated him, while hate was noble.

    Ag. Why, thou shouldst trample him the more, being
        dead.

    Od. Rejoice not, King, in feats that soil thy fame!

    Ag. 'Tis hard for power to observe each pious rule.

    Od. Not hard to grace the good words of a friend.

    Ag. The " noble spirit " should hearken to command.

    Od. No more !   'Tis conquest to be ruled by love.

    Ag. Remember what he was thou gracest so.

    Od. A noisome enemy ; but his life was great.

    Ag. And wilt thou honour such a pestilent corse?

    Od. Unkindness yields to nobleness of thought.

    Ag. With addle-pated fools.

    Od.   Full many are found
Friends for an hour, yet bitter in the end.

    Ag. And wouldst thou have us gentle to such friends?

    Od. I would not praise ungentleness in aught.

    Ag. We shall be known for weaklings through thy
        counsel.

    Od. Not so, but righteous in all Grecian eyes.

    Ag. Thou bidst me then let bury this dead man ?

    Od. I urge thee to the course myself shall follow.

    Ag. Ay, every man for his own line !   That holds.

    Od. Why not for my own line ?   What else were
        natural ?

    Ag. 'Twill be thy doing then, ne'er owned by me.

    Od. Own it or not, the kindness is the same.

Ag. Well, for thy sake I'd grant a greater boon ;
Then why not this ?   However, rest assured
That in the grave or out of it, Aias still
Shall have my hatred. ·Do thou what thou wilt.   [*Exit.*
    Ch. Whoso would sneer at thy philosophy,
While such thy ways, Odysseus, were a fool.
    Od. And now let Teucer know that from this hour
I am more his friend than I was once his foe,
And fain would help him in this burial-rite
And service ·to his brother, nor would fail
In aught that mortals owe their noblest dead.
    Teu. Odysseus, best of men, thine every word
Hath my heart's praise, and my worst thought of thee
Is foiled by thy staunch kindness to the man
Who was thy rancorous foe.   Thou wast not keen
To insult in presence of his corse, like these,
The insensate general and his brother-king,
Who came with proud intent to cast him forth
Foully debarred from lawful obsequy.
Wherefore may he who rules in yon wide heaven,
And the unforgetting Fury-spirit, and she,
Justice, who crowns the right, so ruin them
With cruellest destruction, even as they
Meant heartlessly to rob him of his tomb !
For thee, revered Laërtes' lineal seed,
I fear to admit thy hand unto this rite,
Lest we offend the spirit that is gone.
But for the rest, I hail thy proffered aid ;
And bring whom else thou wilt, I'll ne'er resent it.
This work shall be my single care ; but thou,

Be sure I love thee for thy generous heart.

Od. I had gladly done it ; but, since thou declinest,
I bow to thy decision, and depart.   *[Exit.*

 Teu. Speed we, for the hour grows late :
   Some to scoop his earthy cell,
  Others by the cauldron wait,
   Plenished from the purest well.
  Hoist it, comrades, here at hand,
  High upon the three-foot stand !
  Let the cleansing waters flow ;
  Brightly flame the fire below !
  Others in a stalwart throng
  From his chamber bear along
  All the arms he wont to wield,
  But alone the mantling shield.
  Thou with me thy strength employ,
  Lifting this thy father, boy ;
  Hold his frame with tender heed—
  Still the gashed veins darkly bleed.
  Who professes here to love him ?
  Ply your busy cares above him.
  Come and labour for the man,
  Nobler none since time began,
  Aias, while his life-blood ran.

 Ch. Oft we know not till we see.
  Weak is human prophecy.
  Judge not, till the hour have taught thee
  What the destinies have brought thee.

ELECTRA.

———————

THE PERSONS.

Aᴺ Oʟᴅ Mᴀɴ, *formerly one of the retainers of Agamemnon.*

Oʀᴇꜱᴛᴇꜱ, *son of Agamemnon and Clytemnestra.*

Eʟᴇᴄᴛʀᴀ, *sister of Orestes.*

Cʜᴏʀᴜꜱ *of Argive Women.*

Cʜʀʏꜱᴏᴛʜᴇᴍɪꜱ, *sister of Orestes and Electra.*

Cʟʏᴛᴇᴍɴᴇꜱᴛʀᴀ.

Æɢɪꜱᴛʜᴜꜱ.

Pʏʟᴀᴅᴇꜱ *appears with* Oʀᴇꜱᴛᴇꜱ, *but does not speak.*

AGAMEMNON, on his return from Troy, had been murdered by his wife Clytemnestra and her paramour Ægisthus. Orestes, then a child, had been rescued by his sister Electra, and sent into Phocis with the one servant who remained faithful to his old master. He now returns, being of a full age, with this same attendant and his friend Pylades, with whom he has already concerted a plan for taking vengeance on his father's murderers.

The SCENE is laid in Argos, before the Palace of the Pelopidæ.

ELECTRA.

ORESTES *and the* Old Man—PYLADES *is present.*

Old Man. Son of the king who ruled the army at Troy,
See now around thee what through many a year
Thy forward spirit hath sighed for.   Argolis
Lies here before us, hallowed as the scene
Of Io's wildering pain : yonder, the mart
Named from the wolf-slaying God,* and there, to our
   left,
Stands Hera's temple.   For we reach the bourne
Of far-renowned Mycenæ, rich in gold.
And Pelops' fatal roofs before us rise,
Haunted with many horrors, whence my hand,
Thy murdered sire then lying in his gore,
Received thee from thy sister, and removed
Where I have kept thee safe and nourished thee
To this bright manhood thou dost bear, to be
The avenger of thy father's bloody death.

 * Agora Lyceius (sacred to Apollo Lyceius—from Lycos, a wolf).

R

Wherefore, Orestes, and thou, Pylades,
Dearest of friends, though from a foreign soil,
Prepare this enterprise with speed.   Dark night
Is vanished with her stars, and day's bright orb
Hath waked the birds of morn into full song.
Now, then, ere foot of man go forth, ye two
Knit counsels.   'Tis no time for shy delay :
The very moment of our act is come.

   Or. Kind faithful friend, how well thou mak'st appear
Thy constancy in service to our house !
As some good steed, aged, but nobly bred,
Slacks not his spirit in the day of war,
But points his ears to the fray, even so dost thou
Press on and urge thy master in the van.
Hear, then, our purpose, and if aught thy mind,
Keenly attent, discerns of weak or crude
In this I now set forth, admonish me.

   I, when I visited the Pythian shrine
Oracular, that I might learn whereby
To punish home the murderers of my sire,
Had word from Phœbus which you straight shall hear.
" No shielded host, but thine own craft, O King !
The righteous death-blow to thine arm shall bring."
Then, since the will of Heaven is so revealed,
Go thou within, when opportunity
Shall marshal thee the way, and gathering all
Their business, bring us certain cognisance.
Age and long absence are a safe disguise ;
They never will suspect thee who thou art.
And let thy tale be that another land,

Phocis, hath sent thee forth, and Phanoteus,
Than whom they have no mightier help in war.
Then, prefaced with an oath, declare thy news,
Orestes' death by dire mischance, down-rolled
From wheel-borne chariot in the Pythian course.
So let the fable be devised ; while we
In firm obedience to the God, with curls
Shorn from our brows, and fair libations, crown
Our father's sepulchre, and then return
Bearing aloft the shapely vase of bronze
That's hidden hard by in brushwood, as thou knowest,
And bring them welcome tidings, that my form
Is fallen ere now to ashes in the fire.

  How should this pain me, in pretence being dead,
Really to save myself and win renown ?
No saying bodes men ill, that brings them gain.
Oft have I known the wise, dying in word,
Return with glorious salutation home.
So lightened by this rumour shall mine eye
Blaze yet like bale-star on mine enemies.
O native earth ! and Gods that hold the land,
Accept me here, and prosper this my way !
Thou, too, paternal hearth ! To thee I come,
Justly to cleanse thee by behest from heaven.
Send me not bootless, Gods, but let me found
A wealthy line of fair posterity !

  I have spoken. To thy charge ! and with good speed
Perform it. We go forth. The Occasion calls,
Great taskmaster of enterprise to men.

  Electra (*within*). Woe for my hapless lot !

Old M. Hark! from the doors, my son, methought
    there came
A moaning cry, as of some maid within.
  Or. Can it be poor Electra?   Shall we stay,
And list again the lamentable sound?
  Old M. Not so.   Let nothing come before the attempt
To obey at once Apollo's sovereign will,
And pour libation to thy sire: this makes
Victory ours, and our success assured.   [*Exeunt.*

Enter ELECTRA.

  El. O purest light!
And air by earth alone
Measured and limitable, how oft have ye
Heard many a piercing moan,
Many a blow fall on my bleeding breast,
When gloomy night
  Hath slackened pace and yielded to the day!
And through the hours of rest,
Ah! well 'tis known
To my sad pillow in yon house of woe,
What vigil of scant joyance keeping,
Whiles all within are sleeping,
For my dear father without stint I groan,
Whom not in bloody fray
The War-god in the stranger-land
Received with hospitable hand
But she that is my mother, and her groom,
As woodmen fell the oak,
Cleft through the skull with murdering stroke.

And o'er this gloom
No ray of pity, save from only me,
Goes forth on thee,
My father, who didst die
A cruel death of piteous agony.
But ne'er will I
Cease from my crying and sad mourning lay,
While I behold the sky,
Glancing with myriad fires, or this fair day.
But, like some brood-bereavèd nightingale,
With far-heard wail,
Here at my father's door my voice shall sound.
O home beneath the ground!
Hades unseen, and dread Persephone,
And darkling Hermes, and the Curse revered,
And ye, Erinyes, of mortals feared,
Daughters of Heaven, that ever see
Who die unjustly, who are wronged i' the bed
Of those they wed,
Avenge our father's murder on his foe!
Aid us, and send my brother to my side;
Alone I cannot longer bide
The oppressive strain of strength o'ermastering woe.

CHORUS (*entering*).

Electra, child!
Child of a mother hardened to her own!
Wherefore so wild
Pour'st thou thy plaint, thus pining in thy moan,
For him who of long time

Was taken by thy mother's subtlety,
And darkly butcher'd with base hands of crime—
Great Agamemnon?   Let me pray,
If thus I may,
That they who caused this grief may perish utterly.

   El. O daughters of a noble line,
Ye come to soothe me from my troublous woe.
I see, I know:
Your love is not unrecognized of mine.
But yet I will not seem as I forgot,
Or cease to mourn my hapless father's lot.
Oh, of all love
That ever may you move,
This only boon I crave—
Leave me to rave!

   Ch. Lament, nor praying breath
Will make thy father rise
From yon dim gulf of death,
Where with the multitude of men he lies.
But thou with desperate excess of pain,
Immoderate in thy mourning strain,
Wilt waste thy life in woes without relief.
Why thus in love with grief?

   El. Devoid of sense were he
That could forget
A parent lost so piteously.
My heart is set
On her, divinely taught,
Poor bird, distraught,
For "Itys," "Itys," ever heard to pine.

O thou, of sorrows queen !
With tearful mien,
I hold thee all-divine,
Sad Niobe, whose moan
Is muffled in thy sepulchre of stone.
 Ch. Daughter, not thou alone
Hast found calamity, that thou so far
Shouldst urge thy groan
Beyond those, who of thine own kindred are,
And trace one source with thee.
What life hath she,
Chrysothemis, and Iphianassa bright,
And he whose light
Is hidden afar from taste of horrid doom,
Youthful Orestes, who shall come
To fair Mycenæ's glorious town,
Welcomed as worthy of his sire's renown,
Sped by great Zeus with kindly thought,
And to this land with happiest omens brought?
 El. Whom I,
Ever awaiting, inly sigh :
Patient, unwed, and childless still I go,
With tears in constant flow ;
Girt round with misery that hath no cure.
So I endure :
While he forgets his wrong and all my teaching.
What message have I sent beseeching,
But baffled flies back idly home ?
Ever he longs, but, longing, will not come.
 Ch. Fear not, my child ; still mighty in the sky

Is Zeus, who ruleth all things and surveys.
Commit to him thy wrath that surgeth high,
And walk in safer ways,
Not all forgetting, but not hating sore :—
Time hath heart's ease in store :—
Both he that dwells on Crisa's pastoral shore
Shall turn again unto his own,
And he who reigns upon his Stygian throne.

El. Ah ! but the flower of my life is flown
Without one gleam of hope.   My spirit falls.
Orphan'd I pine without protecting care,
And like a sojourner that hath no share,
I do mean service in my father's halls,
With raiment ragged thus and bare,
And meagre is the board at which I stand.

Ch. Sad was thy greeting when he touched the strand,
Piteous thy crying where thy father lay
On that fell day
When the bronze edge with deadly stroke was driven.
By craft 'twas planned,
By lust the blow was given.
Mother and father of a monstrous birth,
Whether a God there wrought or mortal of the Earth.

El. O day beyond all days that yet have rolled
Accursed to my sight !
O horror of that night !
O hideous feast, abhorr'd, not to be told !
How could I bear it, when my father's eye
Saw death advancing from the ruthless pair,
Conjoint in cruel villainy,

By whom my life was plunged in dark despair ?
Oh, to the workers of such deeds as these
May great Olympus' Lord
Dire penalty of sorrow still afford,
Nor let them wear the gloss of sovran ease !
   Ch. Take thought thy voice to rule,
And make thy recent suffering thy school.
Hast thou not sense to see
Why all unworthily
Even now thou fall'st on self-procurèd woe ?
Thou mak'st thine evil proudly overflow,
Still breeding angry strife
Unto thy sullen life.
But he who strives against the strong
Prevails not long.
   El. 'Tis dire oppression wrings from me this cry,
I am well aware my passion surges high.
But no dominion shall subdue this fire,
No cruelties, however dire
Shall check my lamentation while I live.
Say, who can give,
Kind souls, what tongue can give me timely rede,
Or counsel suited to my need ?
No comfort more ! ah ! leave,
And let me grieve.
Beyond all cure shall this my plaint be known,
Nor will I cease from pain, unmeasured in my moan.
   Ch. With kind intent
Full tenderly my words are meant ;
Like a true mother pressing heart to heart,

I pray thee, do not aggravate thy smart.

 El. But have my miseries a measure? Tell.
Is it so well
To pour forgetfulness upon the dead?
Hath mortal head
Conceived a wickedness so bold?
O never may such brightness shine for me,
Nor let me peaceful be
With aught of good my life may still enfold,
If from wide echoing of my father's name
The wings of keen lament I must withhold.
Sure holy shame
And pious care would vanish from 'mongst men,
If he mere earth and nothingness must lie
In darkness, and his foes shall not again
Render him blood for blood in ample penalty.

 Ch. Less from our own desires, my child, we care,
Than for thy sake. But, if we speak amiss,
Take thine own course. We still will side with thee
 El. Full well I feel that too impatiently
I seem to multiply the sounds of woe.
Yet suffer me, my women; for strong force
Compels me. Who that had a noble heart
And saw her father's cause, as I have done,
By day and night more outraged, could refrain?
Are my woes lessening? Are they not in bloom?—
My mother full of hate and hateful proved,
Whilst I in my own home must dwell with these,
My father's murderers, and by them be ruled,

Dependent on their mercy even for bread.
And then what days suppose you I must pass,
When I behold Ægisthus on the throne
That was my father's ; when I see him wear
Such robes, and pour libations by the hearth
Where he destroyed him ; lastly, when I see
Their crowning insolence,—our regicide
Laid in my father's chamber beside her
My mother—if she still must bear the name
When resting in those arms ?   Her shame is dead.
She harbours with blood-guiltiness, and fears
No vengeance, but, as laughing at the wrong,
She watches for the day on which with guile
She killed our sire, and orders dance and mirth
That day o' the month, and joyful sacrifice
Of thanksgiving.   But I within the house
See this, and weep and pine, and mourn that feast
Of infamy, called by my father's name,
All to myself ; for not even grief may flow
As largely as my spirit would desire.
That so-called princess of a noble line,
O'ercrows my sorrow with her loud reproach :
" Hilding ! are you alone in grief?   Are none
Mourning for loss of fathers but yourself?
'Fore the blest Gods I ill may you thrive, and ne'er
Find cure of sorrow from the powers below !"
So she insults : unless she hear one say
Orestes will be here : then, standing close,
She shouts like one possessed into mine ear,
" These are your doings, this your work, I trow.

I live to vex them :—though my life be poor,
Yet this suffices, for I honour him,
My sire, if any kindness touch the dead.
You say you hate them, but belie your word,
Consorting with your father's murderers.
I then, were all the gifts in which you glory
Brought to my feet, will never more obey
This power.   I leave you your rich board and life
Of luxury !   My food shall be to feel
A single heart and uncorrupted will.
I care not for such honour as thou hast.
Nor wouldst thou care if thou wert wise.   But now,
Having the noblest of all men for sire,
Be called thy mother's offspring, so shall most
Discern thine infamy and traitorous mind
To thy dead father and thy dearest kin.
   Ch. No anger, we entreat.   Both have said well,
If each would learn of other, and so do.
   Chr.   For my part, women, use hath seasoned me
To her discourse.   Nor had I spoken of this,
Had I not heard a horror coming on.
That will restrain her from her endless moan.
   El. Come speak it forth, this terror ! I will yield,
If thou canst tell me worse than I endure.
   Chr. I'll tell thee all I know.   If thou persist
In these thy wailings, they will send thee far
From thine own land, and close thee from the day,
Where in a rock-hewn chamber thou may'st chant
Thine evil orisons in darkness drear.
Think of it, while there's leisure to reflect ;

Or, if thou suffer, henceforth blame me not.

 El. And have they so determined on my life?

 Chr. 'Tis sure; whene'er Ægisthus shall return.

 El. If that be all, let him return with speed!

 Chr. Unhappy! why this curse upon thyself?

 El. If this be their intent, why, let him come!

 Chr. To work such harm on thee! What thought is
  this?

 El. Far from mine eye to banish all your brood.

 Chr. Art not more tender of the life thou hast?

 El. Fair, to a marvel, is my life, I trow!

 Chr. It would be, couldst thou be advised for good.

 El. Never advise me to forsake my kin.

 Chr. I do not: only to give place to power.

 El. Thine be such flattery. 'Tis not my way.

 Chr. Sure, to be wrecked by rashness is not well.

 El. Let me be wrecked in 'venging my own sire.

 Chr. I trust his pardon for my helplessness.

 El. Such talk hath commendation from the vile.

 Chr. Wilt thou not listen? Wilt thou ne'er be ruled?

 El. No; not by thee! Let me not sink so low.

 Chr. Then I will hie me to mine errand straight.

 El. Stay; whither art bound? For whom to burn
  those gifts?

 Chr. Sent by my mother to my father's tomb
To pour libations to him.

 El.   How? To him?
Most hostile to her of all souls that are?

 Chr. Who perished by her hand—so thou wouldst
  say.

El. What friend hath moved her? Who hath cared
　for this?
Chr. Methinks 'twas some dread vision, seen by night.
El. Gods of my father, O be with me now!
Chr. What? art thou hopeful from the fear I spake of?
El. Tell me the dream, and I will answer thee.
Chr. I know but little of it.
El.　　　　　　　　　　　　　Speak but that.
A little word hath ofttimes been the cause
Of ruin or salvation unto men.
　　Chr. 'Tis said she saw our father's spirit come
Once more to visit the abodes of light;
Then take and firmly plant upon the hearth
The sceptre which he bore of old, and now
Ægisthus bears: and out of this upsprang
A burgeoned shoot, that shadowed all the ground
Of loved Mycenæ. So I heard the tale
Told by a maid who listened when the Queen
Made known her vision to the God of Day.
But more than this I know not, save that I
Am sent by her through terror of the dream.
And I beseech thee by the Gods we serve
To take my counsel and not rashly fall.
If thou repel me now, the time may come
When suffering shall have brought thee to my side.
　　El. Now, dear Chrysothemis, of what thou bearest
Let nothing touch his tomb. 'Tis impious
And criminal to offer to thy sire
Rites and libations from a hateful wife.
Then cast them to the winds, or deep in dust

Conceal them, where no particle may reach
His resting-place : but lie in store for her
When she goes underground.   Sure, were she not
Most hardened of all women that have been,
She ne'er had sent this loveless drink-offering
To grace the sepulchre of him she slew.
For think how likely is the buried king
To take such present kindly from her hand,
Who slew him like an alien enemy,
Dishonoured even in death, and mangled him,
And wiped the death-stain with his flowing locks—
Sinful purgation ! Think you that you bear
In those cold gifts atonement for her guilt ?
It is not possible.   Wherefore let be.
But take a ringlet from thy comely head,
And this from mine *—a scanty gift, I know,
Unmeet for offering.   Ah ! but give it to him,
All I can give, and this my maiden-zone,
Not glistening with the smoothness of delight.
Then, falling prostrate, pray that from the ground
He would arise to help us 'gainst his foes,
And grant his son Orestes with high hand
Strongly to trample on his enemies ;
That in our time to come from ampler stores
We may endow him, than are ours to-day.
I cannot but imagine that his will
Hath part in visiting her sleep with fears.

* *Or,*
           " that lingers on my brow
    Longing to shade his tomb. Ah, give it to him,"

But howsoe'er, I pray thee, sister mine,
Do me this service, and thyself, and him,
Dearest of all the world to me and thee,
The father of us both, who rests below.

Ch. She counsels piously; and thou, dear maid,
If thou art wise, wilt do her bidding here.

Chr. Yea, when a thing is right, it is not well
Idly to wrangle, but to act with speed.
Only, dear friends, in this my enterprise,
Let me have silence from your lips, I pray;
For should my mother know of it, sharp pain
Will follow yet my bold adventurous feat.

                    [*Exit* CHRYSOTHEMIS.

CHORUS.

    An erring seer am I,
Of sense and wisdom lorn,
If this presaging Justice come not nigh,
O'ertaking sin ere many an hour be born.
My daughter, I am bold,
Since to my heart was told
Yon soft-breathed vision of the night.
For ne'er doth he,
King, father, Hellas' lord,
Grow dull of memory,
Nor that bronze-griding axe-tooth, dark with time,
Keen as a two-edged sword,
That dealt him cruel death with foul inhuman crime.
    From ambush deep and dread
With many feet and many a hand shall spring
The Fury of the adamantine tread,

Swift recompense to bring
For wicked speed unhallowed and unwed,
For blood-stained dalliance of a lawless pair.
No omen fair,—
Their impious course hath fixed this in my soul,—
Nought but black portents full of blame shall roll
Before their guilty eyes that wrought or aided there.
Small force of divination would there seem
In prophecy or solemn dream,
Should not this vision of the night
Land in reality aright.

O chariot-course of Pelops,* full of toil !
How wearisome and sore
Hath been thine issue to our native soil !—
Since, from his golden car
Hurled to the deep afar,
Myrtilus sank and slept,
Cruelly plucked from that fell chariot-floor,
This house unceasingly hath kept
Crime and misfortune gathering evermore

Enter CLYTEMNESTRA.

Clytemnestra. Again you are let loose and range at will.
Ay, for Ægisthus is not here, who kept
Your rashness from defaming your own kin
Beyond the gates.   But now he's gone, you care

---

* Pelops won his race (and his bride Hippodameia) by throwing
Myrtilus into the sea. This was the first of the long series of crimes
that ruined the Pelopidæ.

No whit for me : though you have noised abroad
That I am cruel and unjust, and rule
'Tyrannically, to oppress thy life.
I am no tyrant, but I speak thee ill,
For thou art ever speaking ill of me—
Still holding forth thy father's death, that I
Have done it.   So I did : I know it well :
That I deny not : for not I alone
But Justice slew him ; and if you had sense,
To side with Justice ought to be your part.
For who but he of all the Greeks, your sire,
For whom you whine and cry, who else but he
Took heart to sacrifice unto the Gods
Thy sister,—having less of pain I trow
In getting her, than I, her mother, knew ?
Come, let me question thee !   To pay what debt
Slew he my child ?   To help the Argive host ?
What right had they to traffic in my flesh ?—
Menelaus was his brother.   Wilt thou say
He slew my daughter for his brother's sake ?
Then how should he escape my wrath ?   Had he,
Menelaus, not two children, born of those
On whose behalf that army sailed to Troy ?
Was Death then so enamoured of my seed,
That he must feast thereon and let theirs be ?
Or was the God-abandoned father's heart
Tender toward them and cruel to my child ?
Doth this not show a dull and senseless sire ?
I think so, though your wisdom may demur.
And could my lost one speak, she would confirm it.

For my part, I can dwell upon the past
Without remorse. You, if you disapprove,
Bring reasons forth and blame me to my face !

 El. Thou canst not say this time that I began
And brought this on me by some taunting word.
But, so you'd suffer me, I would declare
The right both for my sister and my sire.

 Cly. Thou hast my sufferance. Nor would hearing vex,
If ever thus you tuned your speech to me.

 El. Then I will speak. You say you slew him. Where
Could there be found confession more depraved,
Even though the cause were righteous? But I'll show
No rightful vengeance drew thee to the deed,
But the vile bands of him you dwell with now.
Or ask the huntress Artemis, what sin
Was punished by the raging winds that swept
On Aulis.—I will tell thee, for her voice
Thou ne'er may'st hear ! 'Tis rumoured that my sire
Sporting within the precincts of the Queen,
His foot disturbed a dappled hart, whose death
Drew from his lips some rash and boastful word.
Wherefore Latona's daughter in fell wrath
Stayed the army, that in quittance for the deer
My sire should slay at the altar his own child.
So came the occasion of her death. The fleet
Had else no hope of being launched to Troy
Nor to their homes. Wherefore, with much constraint,
And painful urging of his backward will,
Hardly he yielded ;—not for his brother's sake.
But grant it were so, grant thy speech were sooth,

And Menelaus were the cause, for this
Was he to perish by thy hand ?   What law
Ordaining ?   See to it, in establishing
Such precedent, thou dost not lay in store
Remorse and sorrow for thyself.   For if
One die for one, thou first wilt be destroyed
If justice find thee.—But again beware
Lest this be after all a vain pretence.
For tell me, I beseech, what wrong you wreak
In doing now the basest deeds of all,
Chambered with the blood-guilty one, with whom
You slew our father in that day.   For him
You now bear children—driving from their right
The pious offspring of a holy sire.
What sanction shall I urge for this ? Wilt say
Thus thou dost 'venge thy daughter's injury ?
O shameful plea !   Where is the thought of honour,
If foes are married for a daughter's sake ?—
Enough.   I may not counsel thee.   Thy tongue
With checkless clamour cries that we revile
Our mother.   Nay, no mother, but the chief
Of tyrants to us !   For my life is full
Of weariness and misery from thee
And from thy paramour.   Whilst he abroad,
Orestes, our one brother, who escaped
Hardly from thy attempt, unhappy boy !
Wears out his life, victim of cross mischance.
Oft hast thou taunted me with fostering him
To be thy punisher.   And this, be sure,
Had I but strength, I had done.   Now for this word,

Proclaim me what thou wilt,—evil in soul,
Or loud in curses, or devoid of shame :
For if I am infected with such guilt,
Methinks my nature is not fallen from thine.

   Ch. (*looking at* CLYTEMNESTRA). I see her fuming with
      fresh wrath : the thought
Of justice enters not her bosom now.

   Cly. What thought of justice should be mine for her,
Who at her age can so insult a mother ?
Will shame withhold her from the wildest deed ?

   El. Not unashamed, assure thee, I stand here,
Little as thou mayest deem it. Well I feel
My words unseemly and my deeds unfit.
But your hostility and treatment force me
Against my disposition to this course.
Shameful behaviour still is taught by shames.

   Cly. O brazen impudence ! Too much in truth
Is taught thee by my conduct and my speech.

   El. The deeds are yours ; therefore the shame is yours:
They only find expression through my tongue.

   Cly. By sovereign Artemis, whom still I serve,
You'll rue this boldness when Ægisthus comes.

   El. See now, your anger bears you off, and ne'er
Will let you listen, though you gave me leave.

   Cly. Must I not even sacrifice in peace
From your harsh clamour, when you've had your say ?

   El. I have done. I check thee not. Go, sacrifice !
Accuse not me of hindering piety.

   Cly. (*to an attendant*). Then lift for me those fruitful
      offerings,

While to Apollo, before whom we stand,
I raise my supplication for release
From doubts and fears that shake my bosom now.
And, O defender of our house ! attend
My secret utterance.   No friendly ear
Is that which hearkens for my voice.   My thought
Must not be blazoned while she standeth by,
Lest with her envy and wide-babbling tongue
She fill the city full of wild surmise.
List, then, as I shall speak : and grant the dreams
Whose two-fold apparition I to-night
Have seen, if good their bodement, be fulfilled ;
If hostile, turn their influence on my foes.
And yield not them their wish that would by guile
Depose me from my fortune, but vouchsafe
That ever thus exempt from harms I rule
The palace and the kingdom, in full life,
Partaking with the friends I live with now
All fair prosperity, and with my children,
Save those who hate and vex me bitterly.
Lyceian Phœbus, favourably hear
My prayer, and grant to all of us our need !
More is there, which, though I be silent here,
Methinks a God should know.   No secret thing
Is hidden from the all-seeing sons of Heaven.

Enter the Old Man.

Old M. Kind dames and damsels, may I clearly know
If these be King Ægisthus' palace-halls ?
　　Ch. They are, sir ; you yourself have guessed aright.

Old M. And am I right in my surmise that here
I see his wife ?   She wears a royal mien.

 Ch. Right to a wish.   She is present to your sight.

 Old. M. Princess, all hail !   To thee and to thy spouse
I come with words of gladness from a friend.

 Cly. That auspice I accept.   But I would first
Learn from thee who of men hath sent thee forth ?

 Old M. Phanoteus the Phocian, with a charge of weight.

 Cly. Declare it, stranger.   Coming from a friend,
Thou bring'st us friendly tidings, I feel sure.

 Old M. Orestes' death.   Ye have the sum in brief.

 El. Ah me ! undone !   This day hath ruined me.

 Cly. What?   Let me hear again.   Regard her not.

 Old M. Again I say, Orestes is no more.

 El. Undone ! undone !   Farewell to life and hope !

 Cly. (*to* ELECTRA). See thou to thine own case ! (*To*
  Old Man) Now, stranger, tell me
In true discourse the manner of his death.

 Old M. Therefore I came, and I will tell the whole.
He, coming to the great arena famed
As Hellas' pride, to win a Delphian prize,
Heard the loud proclamation of the man
Calling the foot-race, which hath trial first,
And entered, glorious, worshipped of the throng.
And when his prowess in the course fulfilled
The promise of his form, he issued forth
Dowered with the splendid meed of victory.—
To tell a few out of the many feats
Of such a hero were beyond my power.
Know then, in brief, that of the brilliant crowns

For every customary course proclaimed
By order of the judges, the whole sum
Victoriously he gathered, happy deemed
By all ; declared an Argive, and his name
Orestes, son of him who levied once
The mighty armament of Greeks for Troy.
So fared he then : but when a God inclines
To hinder happiness, not even the strong
May 'scape.   So, on another day, when came
At sunrise the swift race of charioteers,
He entered there with many a rival car :—
One from Achaia, one from Sparta, two
Libyan directors of the chariot-yoke ;
And he amongst them as the fifth, with steeds
From Thessaly ;—the sixth Ætolia sent
With chestnut mares ; the seventh a Magnete man ;
The eighth with milk-white steeds from Œta's vale ;
The ninth from god-built Athens ; and the tenth
Bœotia gave to make the number full.
Then stood they where the judges of the course
Had posted them by lot, each with his team ;
And sprang forth at the brazen trumpet's clang.
Shouting together to their steeds, they shook
The reins, and all the course was filled with noise
Of rattling chariots, and the dust arose
To heaven.   Now all in a confusèd throng
Spared not the goad, when one before the rest
Drew his hot axle and his snorting team ;
But all at once about his circling wheels
And stooping sides fell flakes of panted foam.

Orestes, ever nearest at the turn,
With whirling axle seemed to graze the stone,
And loosing with free rein the right-hand steed
That pulled the side-rope, held the near one in.
 So for a time all chariots upright moved.
But soon the Œtæan's hard-mouthed horses broke
From all control, and wheeling as they passed
From the sixth course to enter on the seventh,*
Smote front to front against the Barcan car.
And now, when that one mischief had befallen,
Each dashed against his neighbour and was thrown,
Till the whole plain was strewn with chariot-wreck. ·
Then the Athenian, skilled to ply the rein,
Drew on one side, and heaving to, let pass
The rider-crested surge that rolled i' the midst.
Meanwhile Orestes, trusting to the end,
Was driving hindmost with tight rein ; but now,
Seeing him left the sole competitor,
Hurling fierce clamour through his steeds, pursued :
So drave they yoke by yoke—now this, now that
Pushing ahead with car and team. Orestes,
Ill-fated one, each previous course had driven
Safely without a check, but after this,
In letting go the horse that made the turn,
He struck the edge of the stone before he knew,
And stove the axle's end, and tumbled prone,
Caught in the reins,† that dragged him with sharp thongs.

* They had to go twelve times round.

† In an ancient chariot-race the reins were often passed round
the body of the charioteer, so as to give more purchase.

Then as he fell to the earth, the horses swerved,
And roamed the field.   And when the people saw
That he was fallen from out the car, they cried,
Lamenting the fair youth, who had achieved
So gloriously, and now had found such woe,—
Dashed on the ground, then tossed with legs aloft
In air,—until the drivers of the cars,
Hardly restraining the impetuous team,
Released him covered so with blood that none,—
No friend who saw,—had known his hapless form.
Which then we duly burned upon the pyre ;
And straightway men appointed to the task
From all the Phocians bear his mighty frame—
Poor ashes ! narrowed in a brazen urn,—
That he may find in his own fatherland
His share of sepulture.—Such our report,
Painful to hear, but unto us, who saw,
The mightiest horror that e'er met mine eye.

   Ch. Alas ! the stock of our old masters, then,
Is utterly uprooted and destroyed.

   Cly. O heavens ! what shall I say?   That this is
     well ?
Or terrible, but gainful?   Hard my lot,
To save my life through my calamity !

   Old M. Lady, why hath my speech disheartened thee?

   Cly. To be a mother hath a marvellous power.
No injury can make one hate one's child.

   Old M. Then it should seem our coming was in vain.

   Cly. In vain ?   Nay, verily ; thou, that hast brought
Clear evidences of his fate, who, sprung

From my life's essence, severed from my breast
And nurture, was estranged in banishment,
And never saw me from the day he went
Out from this land, but for his father's blood
Threatened me still with accusation dire;
That sleep nor soothed at night nor sweetly stole
My senses from the day, but all my time
Each instant led me on the way to death!—
This moment hath released me from all fear
Of him,—and of this maid : who being at home
Troubled me more, and with unmeasured thirst
Kept draining my life's blood; but now her threats
Will leave us quiet days, methinks, and peace
Unbroken.—How then shouldst thou come in vain ?

   El. O misery !   'Tis time to wail thy fate,
Orestes, when, in thy calamity,
Thy mother thus insults thee.   Is it well ?

    Cly. 'Tis well that he is dead, not that you live.

    El. Hear, 'venging spirits of the lately dead !

    Cly. The avenging spirits have heard and answered
      well.

    El. Insult us now, for thou art fortunate !

    Cly. You and Orestes are to quench my pride.

    El. Our pride is quenched.   No hope of quenching
      thee !

    Cly. A world of good is in thy coming, stranger,
Since thou hast silenced this so clamorous tongue.

    Old M. Then I may go my way, since all is well.

    Cly. Nay, go not yet ! That would disgrace alike
Me and the friend who sent you to our land.

But come thou in, and leave her out of door
To wail her own and loved ones' evil case.

　　　　　　　[*Exeunt* CLYTEMNESTRA *and* Old Man.

El. Think you the wretch in heartfelt agony
Weeps inconsolably her perished son?
She left us with a laugh! O misery!
How thou hast ruined me, dear brother mine,
By dying! Thou hast torn out of my heart
The only hope I cherished still, that thou
Living wouldst come hereafter to avenge
Thy father's woes and mine.   Where must I go?
Since I am left of thee and of my sire
Bereaved and lonely, and once more must be
The drudge and servant of my bitterest foes,
My father's murderers.   Say, is it well?
Nay, never more will I consort with these,
But dropping here before the palace-gate,
Thus, friendless, I will wither out my life.
At this if any in the house be vexed,
Let him destroy me ; for to take my life—
Were kindness, and to live is only pain
Life hath not kindled my desires with joy.

　　　　Ch. O burning sun !
　　O lightnings of the Sire !
　　Can ye behold this done
　　And tamely hide your fire?
　　　　El. Ah me !
　　　　Ch. My daughter, why these tears ?
　　　　El. Woe ! woe !

Ch. Nay cry not ! Calm thy fears.

El. Oh, you will kill me !

Ch. How ?

El. To breathe a hope for those
So manifestly sunk in long repose,
'Tis to afflict me more,
Already pining sore.

Ch. Was not Amphíareus tangled in the toils
Of women, buried by their glittering coils ?
Who now beneath ——

El. Ah woe !

Ch. Rules with a spirit unimpaired and strong.

El. Oh, dreadful !

Ch. Dreadful truly was the wrong.

El. But she was quelled?

Ch. Yea, so.

El. I know, I know !
For one there came to show some piety
Towards him they mourned. But I
Have no man now. The one
I had, is gone, is gone !
Swept into nothingness.

Ch. Thou art wrung with sore distress.

El. Thou tell'st me what I know :
Yes, I in chief !
Taught by a life of woe
Where horror ever dwells without relief.

Ch. Our eyes have seen thy grief.

El. Then comfort not again——

Ch. Where turns thy strain ?

El. One utterly bereft ;
Seeing no hope is left,
Of help from kindred hands owning the same great sire.
   Ch. 'Tis nature's debt——
   El.   To expire
On sharp-cut dragging thongs,
'Mid swiftly trampling throngs
Of racing hoofs, like him,
Poor hapless one?
   Ch.   Vast, dim,
And boundless was the harm !
   El. Yea, severed from mine arm,
By strangers kept——
   Ch.   O cruel pain !
   El. Hidden he must remain,
Of me unsepulchred, unmourned, unwept.

Enter CHRYSOTHEMIS.

   Chr. Driven by delight, dear sister, I am come,
Reckless of dignity, with headlong speed.
For news I bear of joy and sweet relief
From ills that bruised from thee thy ceaseless moan.
   El. Whence couldst thou hear of succour for my woes,
That close in darkness without hope of dawn ?
   Chr. Here is Orestes, learn it from my mouth,
As certainly as you now look on me.
   El. What ?   Art thou mad, unhappy one, to laugh
Over thine own calamity and mine ?
   Chr. No, by our father's hearth, I say not this
In mockery.   I tell you he is come.

El. Me miserable ! Who hath given thine ear
The word that so hath wrought on thy belief?
   Chr. Myself am the eyewitness ; no one else
Gained my belief, but proofs I clearly saw.
   El. What sign hath so engrossed thine eye, poor girl ?
What sight hath fired thee with this quenchless glow ?
   Chr. But list to me, I pray thee, that henceforth
Thou mayest pronounce me clear-eyed, or a fool !
   El. By all means, if it pleasure thee, say on.
   Chr. Well, I will tell thee all I saw :—I came
Unto the ancient tomb that holds our sire,
And from the topmost mound I marked a stream
Of milk fresh-flowing, and his resting-place
Ringed round with garlands of all flowers that blow.
I marvelled at the sight, and peered about,
Lest some one might be nearer that we knew.
But finding all was quiet in the spot,
I ventured closer to the tomb, and there,
Close by the limit, I beheld a curl
Of hair new-shorn, with all the gloss of youth.
And straight it struck my heart, as with a sense
Of something seen, ah me ! long, long ago,
And told me that my sight encountered here
The token of Orestes, dearest soul.
Then, clasping it, I did not cry aloud,
But straight mine eyes were filled with tears of joy.
And now as much as then I feel assured
He and none else bestowed this ornament.
To whom beyond thyself and me belongs
Such consecration ? And I know this well,

T

I did it not,—nor thou.   Impossible!
Thou canst not worship even the blessed Gods
Forth of this roof, unpunished.   And, most sure,
Our mother's heart inclines not to perform
Such deeds, nor had she done it unperceived.
This offering comes then of Orestes' hand.
Take courage, dear one.   Not one fate pursues
One house continually, but changeth still.
Ours was a sullen Genius, but perchance
This day begins the assurance of much good.

 El. Oh how I pity thy infatuate mind!

 Chr. Why?   Dost thou find no pleasure in my news?

 El. You know not where you roam.   Far wide! far
  wide!

 Chr. Not know? when I have seen it with mine eyes?

 El. Dear, he is dead.   Look not to him, poor girl!
Salvation comes to thee no more from him.

 Chr. Oh me, unfortunate!   Who told thee this?

 El. He who stood by and saw his life destroyed.

 Chr. Amazement seizes me.   Where is this man?

 El. Right welcome to the mother there within.

 Chr. Me miserable!   Who then can have decked
With all those ceremonies our father's tomb?

 El. I cannot but suppose some hand hath brought
These gifts in memory of Orestes dead.

 Chr. O cruel fate!   While I in ecstasy
Sped with such news, all ignorant, it seems,
Of our dire fortune; and, arriving, find
Fresh sorrows added to the former woe.

 El. It is so, sister; yet if thou wilt list

To me, thou mayest disperse this heaviness.
  Chr. What?   Shall I raise the dead again to life?
  El. I did not mean so.   I am not so fond.
  Chr. What bid you then that I have power to do?
  El. To endure courageously what I enjoin.
  Chr. If it make profit, I will not refuse.
  El. Remember, without toil no plan may thrive!
  Chr. I know that, and will aid thee to my power.
  El. Then hearken my resolve.   Thou seëst now,
We have no friendly succour in the world;
But death has taken all, and we are left
Two only.   I, so long as I could hear
My brother lived and flourished, still had hope
He would arise to wreak his father's blood.
But now that he is gone, to thee I turn,
To help thy sister boldly to destroy
The guilty author of our father's death,
Ægisthus.—Wherefore hide it from thee now?
—Yea, sister!   Till what time wilt thou remain
Inactive?   To what end?   What hope is still
Left standing?   Surely thou hast cause to grieve,
Robbed of thy father's opulent heritage,
And feeling bitterly the creeping years
That find thee still a maiden and unwed.
Nay, nor imagine thou shalt ever know
That comfort.   Not so careless of his life
Is King Ægisthus, as to risk the birth
Of sons from us, to his most certain fall.
But if thou wilt but follow my resolve,
First thou shalt win renown of piety

From our dead father, and our brother too,
Who rést beneath the ground, and shalt be free
For evermore in station as in birth,
And nobly matched in marriage, for the good
Draw gazers to them still.　Then seest thou not
What meed of honour, if thou dost my will,
Thou shalt apportion to thyself and me?
For who, beholding us, what citizen,
What foreigner, will not extend the hand
Of admiration, and exclaim, " See, friends,
These scions of one stock, these noble twain,
These that have saved their father's house from woe,
Who once when foes were mighty, set their life
Upon a cast, and stood forth to avenge
The stain of blood!　Who will not love the pair
And do them reverence?　Who will not give
Honour at festivals, and in the throng
Of populous resort, to these in chief,
For their high courage and their bold emprise?"
Such fame will follow us in all the world,
Living or dying, still to be renowned.
Ah, then, comply, dear sister; give thy sire
This toil—this labour to thy brother give,
End these my sufferings, end thine own regret:
The well-born cannot bear to live in shame.

　　Ch. In such affairs, for those who speak and hear
Wise thoughtfulness is still the best ally.

　　Chr. True, noble women, and before she spake
Sound thought should have prevented the rash talk
That now has proved her reckless.　What wild aim

Beckons thee forth in arming this design
Whereto thou wouldst demand my ministry ?
Dost not perceive, thou art not man but woman,
Of strength inferior to thine enemies,—
Their Genius daily prospering more and more,
While ours is dwindling into nothingness ?
Who then that plots against a life so strong
Shall rid him of the danger without harm ?
Take heed that in our evil case we do not
Get us worse evils, if this plan be told.
Sorry release and scanty boon were this,
To win brief praise, and then inglorious die.
Nay, death is not so hateful as when one
Desiring death, is balked of that desire.
And I beseech thee, ere in utter ruin
We perish and make desolate our race,
Restrain thy rage.   And I will guard for thee
In silence these thy words unrealized ;
If thou wilt learn this wisdom from long time,
Having no strength, to bow before the strong.

   Ch. Comply.   Than prudence and a heedful mind,
No fairer treasure can be found for men.

   El. Thy words have not surprised me.   Well I knew
The good I offered would come back with scorn.
I, all alone and with a single hand,
Must do this.   For it shall not rest undone.

   Chr. Oh that such reasons had been thine, when he,
Our sire, was dying !   Thou hadst compassed all.

   El. My spirit was the same : my mind was less.

   Chr. Be such the life-long temper of thy mind !

El. Thine admonition augurs little help.

Chr. Yea. For the attempt would bring me certain
woe.

El. I envy thee thy prudence, hate thy fear.

Chr. Even when thou speak'st me fair, I will endure it.

El. Take heart. That never will be thine from me.

Chr. Long time remains to settle that account.

El. I find no profit in thee. Go thy way.

Chr. Profit there is, hadst thou a mind to learn.

El. Go to thy mother and declare all this !

Chr. I am not so in hatred of thy life.

El. Yet know the shame thou wouldst prepare for me.

Chr. No, no. Not shame, but care for thine estate.

El. Must I still follow as thou thinkest good ?

Chr. When thou hast wisdom, thou shalt be the guide.

El. 'Tis hard when error wears the garb of sense.

Chr. Right. That is the misfortune of your case.

El. Why ? Feel you not the justice of my speech ?

Chr. Justice may chance to bring me injury.

El. I care not, I, to live by such a rule.

Chr. Well, if you do this, you will find me wise.

El. Well, I will do it, nought dismayed by you.

Chr. Speak you plain sooth ? and will you not be
counselled ?

El. No, for bad counsel is of all most hateful.

Chr. You take the sense of nothing that I say.

El. Long since, not newly, my resolve is firm.

Chr. Then I will go. Thy heart will ne'er be brought
To praise my words, nor I thine action here.

El. Then go within ! I will not follow thee,

Though thou desire it vehemently.   None
But foolish souls would hunt an empty trail.
　　Chr. If this seem wisdom to thee, then be wise
Thy way : but in the hour of misery,
When it hath found thee, thou wilt praise my words.

　　　　　　　　　　　　[*Exit* CHRYSOTHEMIS.

CHORUS.

Wise are the birds of air,
That with due care
Provide convenient food
For those who gave them birth, who wrought their good.
Why do not men beholding them
The like perfection prove?
But, by the lightning flash of Jove
And heavenly Rectitude,
Fierce recompense they shall not long elude.

O human voice
That piercest to the shades beneath the ground !
To Atreus' son cry out with mournful sound
Of sad reproach, not bidding him rejoice.
Stained is the honour of his father's hall,
And broken is the battle-call,
That heretofore his children twain
In loving concord did sustain.
Alone, deserted, vexed, Electra sails,
Storm-tossed with rugged gales,
Like Philomel lamenting evermore,
And wailing sore

For her lost father, caring not for death,
 But ready to resign her breath,
Might she but quell
This twofold progeny of Hell.

What soul so worthy of a noble race ?
For none, my child, my child !
Born high in place
As thou, will let their glory be defiled,
Living in misery and base renown.
Yet thou hast chosen to come down
And have thy portion with the tearful crowd,
So to take arms against the proud*
And conquering evil, win a two-fold prize,
Known as the noblest maiden and most wise.

May thy life soar above thy foes as far
In wealth and might, as they now sovereign are
Since I have found thee, not in bright estate,
Nor blest by fate,
But in the noblest cause
Of piety to Heaven, wearing the crown
Of perfectest renown,
And dowered by the mightiest laws.

> * *Or*, What maid more worthy of her father's fame ?
> For none of noble race
> Will let their glory be defiled,
> Descending to things base.
> Even so hast thou, my child,
> Chosen to partake the doom that all men mourn,
> If thou may'st purge thy father's name
> From overwhelming scorn,
> And conquering, etc.

Enter ORESTES *and* PYLADES, *with the urn.*

Or. Say, dames and damsels, have we heard aright,
And speed we to the goal of our desire?
 Ch. And what desire or quest hath brought thee
  hither?
 Or. I seek Ægisthus' dwelling all this while.
 Ch. Welcome. The tongue that told thee hath no
  blame.
 Or. Which of you all will intimate within
We two are present here with kind intent?
 Ch. This maiden, if the nearest should report.
 Or. Mistress, wilt thou go in and signify
That certain Phocians on Ægisthus wait?
 El. Oh! can it be that you are come to bring
Clear proofs of the sad rumour we have heard?
 Or. I know not thy report. Old Strophius
Charged me with tidings of Orestes' fate.
 El. What, stranger? How this terror steals on me!
 Or. Bearing scant remnants of his body dead
In this small vase thou seest, we come therewith.
 El. O sorrow! thou art here: I see full well
That burden of my heart in present view.
 Or. If thou hast tears for aught Orestes suffered,
Know that he lies within this vessel's room.
 El. Ah, sir! by all in Heaven, if yonder urn
Hide him, ah! give it once into mine hand,
That o'er that dust I may lament and mourn
Myself and mine own house and all our woe!
 Or. Bring it and give her, whosoe'er she be.

For not an enemy—this petition shows it—
But of his friends or kindred, is this maid.

> [*The urn is given into* ELECTRA'S *hands.*

El. O monument of him whom o'er all else
I loved ! sole relic of Orestes' life,
How cold in this thy welcome is the hope
Wherein I decked thee as I sent thee forth !
Then, brilliant was thy going, whom I now
Bear lightly, a mere nothing, in my hands.
Would I had passed from life, ere I despatched
Thee from these arms that saved thee to a land
Of strangers, stealing thee from death ! For then
Thou hadst been quiet on that far-off day,
And had thy portion in our father's tomb.
Now thou hast perished miserably, afar
From home and from thy sister, in exile.
And I, O wretchedness ! neither have bathed
And laid thee forth, nor from the blazing fire
Collected the sad burden, as was meet :
But thou, when foreign hands have tended thee,
Com'st a small handful in a narrow shell.
Woe for the constant care I spent on thee
Of old all vainly, with sweet toil ! For never
Wast thou thy mother's darling, nay, but mine,
And I of all the household most thy nurse,
While " sister, sister," was thy voice to me.
But now all this is vanished in one day,
Dying in thy death. Thou hast carried all away
As with a whirlwind, and art gone. No more
My father lives : myself am dead in thee.

Thyself art lost in death.   Our enemies
Triumph, and she is maddened with her joy,
Our mother most unmotherly, of whom
Thy secret missives often told me, thou
Wouldst rise to be the punisher.   But this
The hapless Genius of thy lot and mine
Has reft away, and sends thee thus to me,—
For thy loved form thy dust and fruitless shade.
O bitterness !   O piteous sight !   Woe ! woe !
O sent on thy dire journey, dearest one,
How thou hast ruined me !   Thou hast indeed,
Dear brother !   Then receive me to thyself,
Hide me in this thy covering, there to dwell,
Me who am nothing, with thy nothingness,
For ever !   Yea, when thou wast here above,
I ever shared with thee in all, and now
I would not have thee shut me from thy tomb.
O let me die and follow thee ! the dead,
My mind assures me now, have no more pain.

   Ch. Electra, think !   Thou hadst a mortal sire,
And mortal was thy brother.   Grieve not far.

   Or. O me !   What shall I speak, or which way turn
The desperate word ?   I cannot hold my tongue.

   El. Wherefore?   What trouble overcomes thee so ?

   Or. Can this be famed Electra I behold?

   El. No other.   In sad case, as you may see.

   Or. Ah ! deep indeed was this calamity !

   El. Is't possible that thou shouldst grieve for me ?

   Or. O ruined form ! abandoned to disgrace !

   El. 'Tis me you mean, stranger, I feel it now.

Or. Woe's me! Untrimmed for bridal, hapless maid!

El. Why this fixed gaze, O stranger! that deep groan?

Or. How all unknowing was I of mine ill!

El. What thing hath passed to bring this cognisance?

Or. The sight of thee attired with boundless woe.

El. And yet thine eye sees little of my pain.

Or. Can aught be still more hateful to be seen?

El. I have my dwelling with the murderers—

Or. Of whom? What evil would thy words disclose?

El. Of him who gave me birth. I am their slave.

Or. Whose power compels thee to this sufferance?

El. One called my mother, most unmotherly.

Or. How? by main force, or by degrading shames?

El. By force and shames, and every kind of evil.

Or. And is there none to succour or prevent?

El. None. Him I had, you give me here in dust.

Or. How mine eye pities thee this while, poor maid!

El. Know now, none ever pitied me but you.

Or. None ever came whose heart like sorrow wrung.

El. Is't possible we have some kinsman here?

Or. I would disclose it, if these maids be friendly.

El. They are. They may be trusted. Only speak.

Or. Let go yon vase, that thou may'st learn the whole.

El. Nay, by the Gods! be not so cruel, sir!

Or. Comply, and thou wilt never come to harm.

El. Ah, never rob me of what most I love!

Or. You must not keep it.

El.   O me miserable

For thee, Orestes, if I lose thy tomb !

  Or. Speak no rash word. Thou hast no right to
    mourn.

  El. No right to mourn my brother who is gone ?

  Or. Such utterance belongs not to thy tongue.

  El. Oh, am I thus dishonoured of the dead ?

  Or. Far from dishonour. But this ne'er was thine.

  El. Is't not Orestes' body that I bear ?

  Or. Nay, but the idle dressing of a tale.

  El. And where is his poor body's resting-place ?

  Or. Nowhere. Seek not the living with the dead.

  El. My son, what saidst thou ?

  Or.   Nought but what is true.

  El. Doth he yet live ?

  Or.   If I have life in me.

  El. Art thou Orestes ?

  Or.   Let my signet here,

That was our father's, tell thine eyes, I am.

  El. O day of days !

  Or.   Time hath no happier hour.

  El. Is it thy voice ?

  Or.   Hearken not otherwhere.

  El. Have my arms caught thee ?

  Or.   Hold me so for aye !

  El. O dearest women, Argives of my home !

Ye see Orestes, dead in craft, but now

By that same craft delivered and preserved.

  Ch. We see, dear daughter, and the gladsome tear

Steals from our eye to greet the bright event.

El. Offspring of him I loved beyond all telling,
Ah ! thou art come.
Even now thou camest, foundest, sawest those
Thou didst desire to see.

    Or. True, I am here.   But bide in silence still.
    El. What?
    Or.   Hush. 'Tis best, lest some within should know.
    El. By ever-virgin Artemis, ne'er will I
Think worthy of my fear
This useless mass of woman-cowardice
Not peering out of door.

    Or. Yet know that women too have might in war.
Of this methinks thou hast the proof.

    El.   O ! O !
Thou hast unveiled and thrust before my gaze
That fiery grief of ours
No time will ever heal.

    Or. I know.   But when their presence calls to mind
Their evil, then let this remembrance work.

    El. All times alike are fit with instant pain
Justly to mind me of that dreadful day ;
Even now but hardly hath my tongue been free.

    Or. Yes, that is it.   Therefore preserve this boon.
    El. Whereby?
    Or. Put limits to unseasonable talk.
    El. Ah ! who, when thou art come,
Could find it meet to change
Language for silence, as thou bidst me do?
Since beyond hope or thought
Was this thy sight to me.

Or. God gave me to your sight when so he willed.

El. O heaven of grace beyond
The joy I knew but now!
If God hath brought thee to our roof,
A miracle of bounty then is here.

Or. I hate to curb the gladness of thy spirit
But yet I fear this ecstasy of joy.

El. O! after all these years,
Now thou at length hast sped
Thy dearest advent on the wished-for way, ·
Do not, in all this woe
Thou seest surrounding me——

Or. What means this prayer?

El.   Forbid me not my joy,
Nor make me lose the brightness of thy face!

Or. Deep were my wrath at him who should attempt it.

El. Is my prayer heard?

Or.   Why doubt it?

El.   Friends, I learned
A tale beyond my thought; and hearing I restrained
My passion, voiceless in my misery,
Uttering no cry.   But now
I have thee safe; now, dearest, thou art come,
With thy blest countenance, which I
Could ne'er forget, even at the worst of woe.

Or. A truce now to unnecessary words.
My mother's vileness and Ægisthus' waste,
Draining and squandering with spendthrift hand
Our patrimony, tell me not anew.
Such talk might stifle opportunity.

But teach me, as befits the present need,
What place may serve by lurking vigilance
Or sudden apparition to o'erwhelm
Our foes in the adventure of to-day.
And, when we pass within, take heedful care
Bright looks betray thee not unto our mother.
But groan as for the dire calamity
Vainly reported : let's achieve success,
Then with free hearts we may rejoice and laugh.

 El. Dear brother, wheresoe'er thy pleasure leads,
My will shall follow, since the joys I know,
Not from myself I took them, but from thee.
And ne'er would I consent thy slightest grief
Should win for me great gain. Ill should I then
Serve the divinity of this high hour !
Thou knowest how matters in the palace stand.
Sure, thou hast heard, Ægisthus is from home,
And she, our mother, is within. Nor fear
She should behold me with a smiling face.
Mine ancient hate of her hath sunk too deep.
And from the time I saw thee, tears of joy
Will cease not. Wherefore should I stint their flow?
I, who in this thy coming have beheld
Thee dead and living. Strangely hast thou wrought
On me ;—that should my father come alive,
I would not think the sight were miracle,
But sober truth. Since such thy presence, then,
Lead us the way thy spirit prompts. For I
Alone, of two things had achievèd one,
Noble deliverance or a noble death.

Or. Be silent ; for I hear within the house
A footstep coming forth.

El. (loudly).　　　　　Strangers, go in !
For none within the palace will reject
Your burden, nor be gladdened by the event.

Enter the Old Man.

Old M. O lost in folly and bereft of soul !
Is't that your care for life hath ebbed away,
Or were you born without intelligence,
When fallen, not near, but in the midst of ill,
And that the greatest, ye perceive it not?
Had I not watched the doors this while, your deeds
Had come within the palace ere yourselves.
But, as it is, my care hath fenced you round.
Now, then, have done with long-protracted talk,
And this insatiable outburst of joy,
And enter, for in such attempts as these
Delay is hurtful : and 'tis more than time.

Or. But how shall I find matters here within ?
Old M. Well. You are shielded by their ignorance.
Or. That means you have delivered me as dead.
Old M. Alone of shadows thou art here above.
Or. Doth this delight them, or how went the talk ?
Old M. I will report, when all is done. Meanwhile,
Know, all is well with them, even what is evil.

El. Who is this, brother ? I beseech thee, tell.
Or. Dost not perceive ?
El.　　　　　　　　I cannot call to mind.
Or. Know'st not the hand to whom thou gav'st me once?

El. Whose hand?   How say you?

Or.   His, who through thy care
Conveyed me secretly to Phocis' plain.

El. What ! is this he, whom I, of all the band,
Found singly faithful in our father's death ?   .

Or. He is that man.   No more !

El.   Light of mine eye !
Dear only saviour of our father's house !
How cam'st thou hither ? Art thou he indeed,
That did preserve Orestes and myself
From many troubles ? O dear hands, kind feet,
Swift in our service,—how couldst thou so long
Be near, nor showone gleam, but didst destroy
My heart with words, hiding the loveliest deeds ?
Father !—in thee methinks I see my father.
O welcome ! thou of all the world to me
Most hated and most loved in one short hour.

Old M. Enough, dear maiden ! Many nights and days
Are circling hitherward, that shall reveal
In clear recountment all that was between.

But to you two that stand beside I tell,
Now is your moment, with the Queen alone,
And none of men within ; but if you pause,
Know that with others of profounder wit
You'll have to strive, beside your present foes.

Or. Then, Pylades, we need no more to dwell
On words, but enter on this act with speed,
First worshipping the altars of the Gods
That were my father's, harbouring at the gate.

> [*They pass within.* ELECTRA *remains in an
> attitude of prayer.*

El. O King Apollo ! hear them graciously,
And hear me too, that with incessant hand
Honoured thee richly from my scanty store !
And now, fierce slayer, I importune thee,
And woo thee with such gifts as I can give,
Be kindly aidant to this enterprise,
And make the world take note, what meed of bane
Heaven still bestows on man's impiety.

　　　　　　　　　　　　　　[ELECTRA *goes within.*

Ch. See where the War-god moves
On, on to his design
Breathing hot slaughter of an evil feud !
Even now the inevitable hounds that track
Dark deeds of crime
Are gone beneath the covert of the domes.
Not long shall hang
Doubtful the dreaming presage of my soul.

For lo ! within is led
With crafty tread the avenger of the shades,
Even to his father's throne of ancient power,
And in his hand the bright new-sharpened death !
And Hermes, Maia's son,
Is leading him, and hath concealed the guile
Even to the fatal end in clouds of night.
His time of weary waiting all is o'er.

　　　　　　　Re-enter ELECTRA.

El. O dearest women ! they are even now
About it.　 Only bide in silence still.

Ch. What is the present scene?

El. She decks the vase
For burial, and the twain are standing by.

Ch. And wherefore hast thou darted forth?

El. To watch
Ægisthus' coming, that he enter not
At unawares.

Cly. (*within*). Ah! ah! Woe for the house,
Desert of friends, and filled with hands of death!

El. A cry within! Did ye not hear it, friends?

Ch. Would I had not! I heard, and shivered through.

Cly. (*within*). Oh me! Alas, Ægisthus! where art thou?

El. Hark! yet again that sound.

Cly. (*within*). O son, have pity!
Pity the womb that bare thee.

El. Thou hadst none
For him, nor for his father, in that day.

Ch. Poor city! hapless race!
Thy destiny to-day
Wears thee away, away.
What morn shall see thy face?

Cly. (*within*). Oh, I am smitten!

El. Give a second stroke,
If thou hast power.

Cly. (*within*). Oh me! again, again!

El. Would thou wert shrieking for Ægisthus too!

Ch. The curse hath found, and they in earth who lie
Are living powers to-day.
Long dead, they drain away
The streaming blood of those who made them die

Enter ORESTES *and* PYLADES.

Behold, they come, they come !
His red hand dripping as he moves
With drops of sacrifice the War-god loves.
My 'wildered heart is dumb.
  El. How is it with you, boy ?
  Or.   If Phœbus' word
Was rightly given, the state within is well.
  El. Wretched one, is she dead ?
  Or.   No more have fear
Thou shalt be slighted by thy mother's will.
  Ch. Cease, for I see Ægisthus near in view.
  El. In, in again, boys !
  Or.   Where do ye behold
The man ?
  El.   Here to our hand from yonder gate
He comes with beaming look.
  Ch. Haste, with what speed ye may,
Stand on the doorway stone,
That, having thus much done,
Ye may do all to-day.
  Or. Fear not : we will perform it.
  El.   Speed ye now :
Follow your thought.
  Or.   We are already there.
  El. Leave matters here to me.   All shall go well.
                   [*Exit* ORESTES *with* PYLADES.
  Ch. Few words, as if in gentleness, 'twere best

You spake to him, that, eager and unware,
One step may launch him on the field of doom.

Enter ÆGISTHUS.

Ægisthus. Which of you know where are the Phocian
　　men.
Who brought the news I hear, Orestes' life
Hath suffered shipwreck in a chariot-race ?
You, you I question, you in former time
So fearless !　You methinks most feelingly
Can tell us, for it touches you most near.
　El. I know : assure thee.　Else had I not heard
The dearest of all fortunes to my heart.
　Æg. Where are the strangers then ?　Enlighten me.
　El. Where they found kind reception from a friend.
　Æg. And did they certainly report him dead ?
　El. Not only so.　They showed him to our sight.
　Æg. May this clear evidence be mine to see ?
　El. I envy not the sight that waits you there.
　Æg. Against their wont thy words have given me
　　joy.
　El. Much joy be thine, if this be joy to thee !
　Æg. Silence, I say !　Wide let the gates be flung !
For all the Myceneans to behold
And all in Argolis, that if but one
Hath heretofore been buoyed on empty hopes
Fixed in Orestes, seeing him now dead,
He may accept my manage, and not wait
For our stern chastisement to teach him sense.

El. My lesson is already learnt : at length
I am schooled to labour with the stronger will.

> [*The body of* CLYTEMNESTRA *is disclosed under a
> veil :* ORESTES *standing by.*

Æg. Zeus ! Divine envy surely hath laid low
The form I here behold.   But if the truth
Provoke Heaven's wrath, be it unexpressed.—Unveil !
Off with all hindrance, that mine eyes may see,
And I may mourn my kinsman as I should.

Or. Thyself put forth thy hand.   Not mine but
    thine
To look and speak with kindness to this corse.

Æg. I will, for thou advisest well ; but thou,
Call Clytemnestra, if she be within.

>   [ÆGISTHUS *lifts the shroud.*

Or. She is beside thee, gaze not otherwhere.

Æg. What do I see ! oh !

Or.   Why so strange ? Whom fear you ?

Æg. Who are the men into whose midmost toils
All hapless I am fallen ?

Or.   Ha ! knowest thou not
Thou hast been taking living men for dead ?

Æg. I understand that saying.   Woe is me !
I know, Orestes' voice addresseth me.

Or. A prophet !   How wast thou so long deceived ?

Æg. Undone, undone !   Yet let me speak one word.

El. Brother, by Heaven, no more ! Let him not
    speak.
When death is certain, what do men in woe
Gain from a little time ?   Kill him at once !

And, killed, expose him to such burial
From dogs and vultures, as beseemeth such,
Far from our view.   Nought less will solace me
For the remembrance of a life of woe.
  Or. Go in and tarry not.   No contest this
Of verbal question, but of life or death.
  Æg. Why drive you me within?   If this you do
Be noble, why must darkness hide the deed?
Why not destroy me out of hand?
  Or.   Command not!
Enter, and in the place where ye cut down
My father, thou shalt yield thy life to me.
  Æg. Is there no help but this abode must see
The past and future ills of Pelops' race?
  Or. Thine anyhow.   That I can prophesy
With perfect inspiration to thine ear.
  Æg. The skill you boast belonged not to your sire.
  Or. You question and delay.   Go in !
  Æg.   Lead on.
  Or. Nay, go thou first.
  Æg.   That I may not escape thee ?
  Or. No, that thou may'st not have thy wish in death.
I may not stint one drop of bitterness.
And would this doom were given without reprieve,
If any try to act beyond the law,
To kill them.   Then the wicked would be few.
  Ch. O seed of Atreus ! how triumphantly
Through grief and hardness thou hast freedom found,
With full achievement in this onset crowned !

THE TRACHINIAN MAIDENS.

THE PERSONS.

DEIANIRA, *Wife of Heracles.*

An Attendant.

HYLLUS, *son of Heracles and Deianira.*

CHORUS *of Trachinian Maidens.*

A Messenger.

LICHAS, *the Herald.*

A Nurse.

An Old Man.

HERACLES.

IOLE, *who does not speak.*

THIS tragedy is named from the Chorus. From the subject it might have been called, Deianira or the Death of Heracles.

The Centaur Nessus, in dying by the arrow of Heracles, which had been dipped in the venom of the Hydra, had persuaded the bride Deianira, whose beauty was the cause of his death, to keep some of the blood from the wound as a love-charm for her husband. Many years afterwards, when Heracles was returning from his last exploit of sacking Œchalia, in Eubœa, he sent before him Iŏlè, the king's daughter, whom he had espoused. Then Deianira sent him a robe anointed with the charm, hoping by this means to regain his affection. But the poison of the Hydra did its work, and he died in agony, Deianira having already killed herself on discovering what she had done. The action takes place in Trachis, near the Maliac Gulf, where Heracles and Deianira have been living in exile. At the close of the drama, Heracles, while yet alive, is carried towards his pyre on Mount Œta.

The scene is before the temporary abode of Heracles at Trachis.

THE TRACHINIAN MAIDENS.

———•———

Deianira. Men oft repeat the word pronounced of old,
" No life of mortal, ere he die, can once
Be known for good or evil."   But I know,
Before I come to the dark dwelling-place,
Mine is a lot, adverse and hard and sore.
Who even at Pleuron, in my father's home,
Of all Ætolian women had most cause
To shrink from bridal.   For a river-god,
Swift Acheloüs, was my suitor there
And sought me from my father in three forms ;
Now in his own bull-likeness, now a serpent
Of coiling sheen, and now in manly shape
Bull-crowned, while from the forest of his beard
Sprang fountain-waters with perpetual spray.
Looking for such a husband, I, poor girl !
Still prayed that Death might find me, ere I knew
This nuptial.—Later, to my glad relief,
Zeus' and Alcmena's glorious offspring came,
And closed with him in conflict, and released
My heart from torment.   How the fight was won,

I could not tell.   If any were who saw
Unshaken of dread foreboding, such may speak.
But I sate quailing with an anguished fear,
Lest beauty might procure me nought but pain,
Till He that holds the issues of all strife,
Gave fortunate end—if fortunate !   For since,
Assigned by that day's conquest, I have known
The couch of Heracles, my life is spent
In one continual terror for his fate.
Night brings him, and, ere morning, some fresh toil
Drives him afar.   And I have borne him seed ;
Which he, like some strange husbandman, that farms
A distant field, finds but at sowing time
And once in harvest.   Such a weary life
Still tossed him to and fro,—no sooner home
But forth again, serving I know not whom.

  And when his glorious life had risen beyond
These labours, came the strongest of my fear.
For since he quelled the might of Iphitus,
We here in Trachis dwell, far from our home,
Dependent on a stranger, but where he
Is gone, none knoweth.   Only this I know,
His going pierced my heart with pangs for him,
And now I am all but sure he bears some woe.
These fifteen months he hath sent me not one word.
And I have cause for fear.   Ere he set forth
He left a scroll with me, whose dark intent
I oft pray Heaven may bring no sorrow down.

  Attendant. Queen Deianira, many a time ere now
Have I beheld thee with all-tearful moan

Bewailing the departure of thy lord.
But, if it be not rashness in a slave
To tender counsel to the free, sure I
May venture this.   Of thy strong band of sons
Why is not one commissioned to explore
For Heracles? and why not Hyllus first,
Whom most it would beseem to show regard
For tidings of his father's happiness?
Ah! here I see him bounding home, with light
And nimble footstep! If you count me wise,
He and my counsels wait upon your will.

Enter HYLLUS.

Dei. Dear child, dear boy! even from the lowliest
          head
Right words, it seems, may fall.   This woman here,
Though a bond-maiden, hath a free-born tongue.
Hyl. What word is spoken, mother? May I know?
Dei. That, with thy father lost to us so long,
'Tis shame thou dost not learn his dwelling-place.
Hyl. Yea, I have learnt, if one may trust report.
Dei. Where art thou told his seat is fixed, my son?
Hyl. 'Tis said that through the length of this past year
He wrought as bondman to a Lydian girl.
Dei. Hath he borne that? Then nothing can be
          strange!
Hyl. Well, that is over, I am told.   He is free.
Dei. Where is he rumoured then, alive or dead?
Hyl. In rich Euboea, besieging, as they tell,
The town of Eurytus, or offering siege.

Dei. Child, hast thou heard, what holy oracles
He left with me, touching that very land?

Hyl. What were they, mother, for I never knew?

Dei. That either he must end his being there,
Or, this one feat performed, his following time
Should grace his life with fair prosperity.
Wilt thou not then, my child, when he is held
In such a crisis of uncertain peril,
Run to his aid?—since we must perish with him,
Or owe our lasting safety to his life.

Hyl. I will go, mother.   Had I heard this voice
Of prophecy, long since I had been there.
Fear is unwonted for our father's lot.
But now I know, my strength shall all be spent
To learn the course of these affairs in full.

Dei. Go then, my son.   Though late, to learn and do
What wisdom bids, hath certainty of gain.

[Exit HYLLUS.   DEIANIRA withdraws.

CHORUS (*entering and turning toward the East*).

Born of the starry night in her undoing,
Lulled in her bosom at thy parting glow,
   O Sun ! I bid thee show,
What journey is Alcmena's child pursuing?
   What region holds him now,
'Mongst winding channels of the deep,
Or Asian plains, or rugged Western steep?
   Declare it, thou
Peerless in vision of thy flashing ray!

For ah ! I learn that she alway,
 Poor Deianira, with an aching breast,
Sad bride of strife and queen of sore unrest,
 Like some lorn bird,
With sorrows ever freshly stirred,
Ne'er giveth slumber to her wistful eye,
 Nor lets her tears be dry,
But ever mindful of her husband's way,
 With panic night and day
Pines on her widowed couch of ceaseless thought,
By fear of evil destiny distraught.

   [*They turn towards the house.* DEIANIRA
     advances.

For many as are billows of the South
Blowing unweariedly, or Northern gale,
One going and another coming on
Incessantly, baffling the gazer's eye,·
Such Cretan ocean of unending toil
Cradles our Cadmus-born, and swells his fame.
 But still some power doth his foot recall
  From stumbling down to gloomy Hades' hall.

Wherefore, in censure of thy mood, I bring
Glad, though opposing, counsel. Let not hope
Grow weary. Never hath a painless life
Been cast on mortals by the power supreme
Of the All-disposer, Cronos' son. But joy
And sorrow visit in perpetual round
 All mortals, even as circleth still on high
  The constellation of the Northern sky.

What lasteth in the world ?   Not starry night,
Nor wealth, nor tribulation ; but is gone
All suddenly, and in its stead there comes
New joy or new privation to the soul.
    These hopes I bid thee also, O my Queen !
    Hold fast continually, for who hath seen
    Zeus so forgetful of his own ?
    How can his providence forsake his son ?

Dei. I see you have been told of my distress,
And that hath brought you.   But my inward woe,
Be it evermore unknown to you, as now !
Such the fair garden of untrammeled ease
When the young life grows safely.   No fierce heat,
No rain, no wind disturbs it, but unharmed
It rises amid airs of peace and joy,
Till maiden turn to matron, and one night
Bring years of care for husband or for child.
Then, imaged through her own calamity,
Some one may guess the burden of my life.
    Full many have been the sorrows I have wept,
But one above the rest I tell to-day.
When my great husband parted last from home,
He left within the house an ancient scroll
Inscribed with characters of mystic note,
Which Heracles had never heretofore,
In former labours, cared to let me see,—
As bound for bright achievement, not for death.
But now, as though his life had end, he told
What marriage-portion I must keep, what shares

He left his sons out of their father's ground :
And set a time, when fifteen moons were spent,
Counted from his departure, that even then
Or he must die, or if that date were out
And he had run beyond it, he should live
Thenceforth a painless and untroubled life.
Such by Heaven's fiat was the promised end
Of Heracles' long labours, as he said ;
So once the ancient oak-tree had proclaimed
In high Dodona through the sacred doves.
Of which prediction on this present hour
In destined order of accomplishment
The veritable issue doth depend.
And I, dear friends, while taking rest, will oft
Start from sweet slumbers with a sudden fear,
Scared by the thought, my life may be bereft
Of the best husband in the world of men.
  Ch. Hush ! For I see approaching one in haste,
Garlanded, as if laden with good news.

Enter Messenger.

Messenger. Queen Deianira, mine shall be the tongue
To free thee first from fear. Alcmena's child
Is living, be assured, and triumphing,
And bringing to our Gods the fruits of war.
  Dei. What mean'st thou, aged sir, by what thou sayest ?
  Mess. That soon thy husband, envied all around,
Will come, distinguished with victorious might.
  Dei. What citizen or stranger told thee this ?
  Mess. Your herald Lichas, where the oxen graze

x

The summer meadow, cries this to a crowd.
I, hearing, flew off hither, that being first
To bring thee word thereof, I might be sure
To win reward and gratitude from thee.
 Dei. And how is he not here, if all be well?
 Mess. He is crossed by no light hindrance, O my
   Queen.
For all the Maliac people, gathering round,
Throng him with questions, that he cannot move.
But he must still the travail of each soul,
And none will be dismissed unsatisfied.
Such willing audience he unwillingly
Harangues, but soon himself will come in sight.
 Dei. O Zeus! who rulest Œta's virgin wold,
At last, though late, thou hast vouchsafed us joy.
Lift up your voices, O my women! ye
Within the halls, and ye beyond the gate!
For now we reap the gladness of a ray,
That dawns unhoped for in this rumour's sound.

 Ch. With a shout by the hearth let the palace-roof
   ring
From those that are dreaming of bridal; and ye,
Young men, let your voices in harmony sing
To the God of the quiver, the Lord of the free!
And the Pæan withal from the maiden band
To Artemis, huntress of many a land,
Let it rise o'er the glad roof-tree,
To Phœbus' own sister, with fire in each hand,
And the Nymphs that her co-mates be!

My spirit soars.   O sovereign of my soul !
I will accept the thrilling flute's control.   [*They dance.*
　The ivy-crownèd thyrsus, see !
　With Bacchic fire is kindling me,
　And turns my emulous tread
　Where'er the mazy dance may lead.
Euoï !   Euoï !
O Pœan ! send us joy.
See, dearest Queen, behold !
Before thy gaze the event will now unfold.

Dei. Think not mine eye hath kept such careless
　　guard,
Dear maids, that I could miss this moving train.
Herald, I bid thee hail, although so late
Appearing, if thou bringest health with thee !

Enter LICHAS, *with* Captive Maidens.

Lichas. A happy welcome on a happy way,
As prosperous our achievement.   Meet it is
Good words should greet bright actions, mistress mine !
　Dei. Kind friend, first tell me what I first would
　　know—
Shall I receive my Heracles alive?
　Lich. I left him certainly alive and strong :
Blooming in health, not with disease oppressed.
　Dei. At home, or in a savage country?   Tell !
　Lich. Eubœa's island hath a promontory,
Where to Cenæan Zeus he consecrates
Rich altars and the tribute of the ground.

Dei. Moved by an oracle, or by some vow?

Lich. So vowed he when he conquered with the spear
The country of these women whom you see.

Dei. And who, by Heaven, are they?   Who was their
    sire?
Their case is piteous, or eludes my thought.

Lich. He took them for the service of the Gods
And his own house, when high Œchalia fell.

Dei. Was't then before that city he was kept
Those endless ages of uncounted time?

Lich. Not so. · The greater while he was detained
Among the Lydians, sold, as he declares,
To bondage.   Nor be jealous of the word,
Since Heaven, my Queen, was author of the deed.
Enthrallèd so to Asian Omphale,
He, as himself avers, fulfilled his year.
The felt reproach whereof so chafed his soul,
He bound fierce curses on himself and sware
That,—children, wife and all,—he yet would bring
In captive chains the mover of this harm.
Nor did this perish like an idle word,
But, when the stain was off him, straight he drew
Allied battalions to assault the town
Of Eurytus, whom, sole of earthly powers,
He had noted as the source of his annoy,
Because, having received him in his hall
A guest of ancient days, he burst on him
With outrage of loud voice and villanous mind,
Saying, "with his hand upon the unerring bow,
Œchalia's princes could o'ershoot his skill":

And how that, like a serf, his spirit was quelled
Beneath a freeman,—and, to crown this cry,
When at a banquet he was filled with wine,
He flung him out of door.   Whereat being wroth,
When Iphitus to Tiryns' upland came,
Tracking the footmarks of his ranging steeds,
He, while the thought and eye of the man by chance
Were sundered, threw him from the towering cliff.
In anger for which deed the Olympian King,
Father of Gods and men, delivered him
To be a bond-slave, nor could brook the offence,
That of all lives he vanquished, this alone
Should have been ta'en by guile.   For had he wrought
In open quittance of the wrong, even Zeus
Had surely granted that his cause was just.
The braggart hath no favour even in Heaven.
Whence they, o'erweening with their evil tongue,
Now dwell in darkness one and all, and leave
Their city to captivity;—but these
Whom thou beholdest, from their blest estate
Brought suddenly to taste of piteous woe,
Come to thy care.   This task thy wedded lord
Ordained, and I, his faithful minister,
Seek to perform.   But, for his noble self,
When with pure hands he hath done sacrifice
To his Great Father for the victory given,
Look for his coming, lady.   This last word
Of all my happy speech is far most sweet.
   Ch. Now surety of delight is thine, my Queen,
Part by report and part before thine eye.

Dei. Yea, now I learn this triumph of my lord,
Joy reigns without a rival in my breast.
This needs must run with that in fellowship.
Yet wise consideration even of good
Is flecked with fear of what reverse may come.
And I, dear friends, when I behold these maids,
Am visited with sadness deep and strange.
Poor friendless beings, in a foreign land
Wandering forlorn in homeless orphanhood !
Erewhile, free daughters of a freeborn race,
Now, snared in strong captivity for life.
O Zeus of battles, breaker of the war,
Ne'er may I see thee turn against my seed
So cruelly ; or, if thou meanest so,
Let me be spared that sorrow by my death !
Such fear in me the sight of these hath wrought.
Who art thou, of all damsels most distressed ?
Single or child-bearing ? Thy form would say,
Untouched of this, as noble. Lichas, tell,
Who is the stranger-nymph ? Who gave her birth ?
Who was her sire ? Mine eye hath pitied her
O'er all, as she o'er all hath sense of woe.
   Lich. What know I ?   Why wouldst thou demand ?
      Perchance
Not lowest in the list of souls there born.
   Dei. How if a princess, offspring of their King ?
   Lich. I cannot tell. I did not question far.
   Dei. Have none of her companions breathed her name ?
   Lich. I brought them silently. I did not hear.
   Dei. Yet speak it to us of thyself, poor maid !

'Tis sorrow not to know thee who thou art.

Lich. She'll ne'er untie her tongue, if she maintain
An even tenor, since nor more nor less
Would she disclose; but, poor unfortunate !
With agonizing sobs and tears she mourns
This crushing sorrow, from the day she left
Her war-swept home.   Her case is cruel, sure,—
And claims a privilege from all who feel.

Dei. Well, let her go, and pass beneath the roof
In peace, as she desires; nor let fresh pain
From me be added to her previous woe.
She hath enough already.   Come, away !
Let's all within at once, that thou mayest speed
Thy path, and I may order all things here.

       [*Exit* Lichas, *with* Captives, *into the house.*
       Deianira *is about to follow them.*

Re-enter Messenger.

Mess. Pause first there on the threshold, till you learn
(Apart from those) who 'tis you take within,
And more besides that you yet know not of,
Which deeply imports your knowing.   Of all this
I throughly am informed.

Dei.   What cause hast thou
Thus to arrest my going?

Mess.   Stand, and hear.
Not idle was my former speech, nor this.

Dei. Say, must we call them back in presence here,
Or wouldst thou tell thy news to these and me ?

Mess. To thee and these I may, but let those be.

Dei. Well, they are gone.   Let words declare thy drift.
Mess. That man, in all that he hath lately said,
Hath sinned against the truth : or now he's false,
Or else unfaithful in his first report.
Dei. What?   Tell me thy full meaning clearly forth.
That thou hast uttered is all mystery.
Mess. I heard this herald say, while many thronged
To hearken, that this maiden was the cause,
Why lofty-towered Œchalia and her lord
Fell before Heracles, whom Love alone
Of heavenly powers had warmed to this emprise,
And not the Lydian thraldom or the tasks
Of rigorous Omphale, nor that wild fate
Of rock-thrown Iphitus,—though now he swerves
From the first tale and wrongs his former word.
   When he that was her sire could not be brought
To yield the maid for Heracles to hold
In love unrecognized, he framed erelong
A quarrel on some trifling cause, and marched
In arms against this damsel's fatherland
(Where Eurytus, the herald said, was king)
And slew the chief her father ; yea, and sacked
Their town.   And now returning, as you see,
He sends her hither to his halls, no slave,
Nor unregarded, lady,—dream not so !
Since all his heart is kindled with desire.
I, O my Queen ! thought right to show thee all
The tale I chanced to gather from his mouth,
Which many heard as well as I, i' the midst
Of our Trachinian market-place, and sure

Would certify.—It pains me if my speech
Sound harshly, but the honest truth I tell.

   Dei. Ah me!   Where am I?   Whither am I fallen?
What hidden woe have I unwarily
Taken beneath my roof?   O misery!
Was she then nameless, as her convoy sware?

   Mess. Nay, most distinguished both in birth and mien;
Called in her day of freedom Iole,
Eurytus' daughter,—of whose parentage,
Forsooth as ignorant, he ne'er would speak.

   Ch. I curse not all the wicked, but the man
Whose secret practices deform his life.

   Dei. Say, maidens, how must I proceed?   The words
Now spoken have bewildered all my mind.

   Ch. Go in and question Lichas, who perchance
Will tell the truth if you but tax him home.

   Dei. I will; you counsel reasonably.
   Mess.   And I,
Shall I bide here till thou com'st forth?   Or how?

   Dei. Remain.   For see, without my sending for him,
He issueth from the palace of himself.

Enter LICHAS.

   Lich. What message must I carry to my lord?
Tell me, my Queen.   I am going, as thou seëst.

   Dei. So slow in coming, and so quickly flown,
Ere one have time to talk with thee anew!

   Lich. What wouldst thou ask me?   I am bent to
       hear.

   Dei. And art thou bent on truth in the reply?

Lich. By Heaven ! in all that I have knowledge of.

Dei. Then tell me, who is she thou brought'st with
  thee ?

Lich. An islander.   I cannot trace her stock.

Mess. Look hither, man. Who is't to whom thou
  speakest ?

Lich. Why such a question ? What is thine intent ?

Mess. Nay, start not, but make answer if thou knowest.

Lich. To Deianira, Œneus' queenly child,   .
Heracles' wife,—if these mine eyes be true,—
My mistress.

Mess.   Ay, that is the very word
I longed to hear thee speak.   Thy mistress, sayest ?

Lich. To whom I am bound.

Mess.   Hold there ! What punishment
Wilt thou accept, if thou art found to be
Faithless to her ?

Lich.   I faithless ! What dark speech
Hast thou contrived ?

Mess.   Not I at all.   'Tis thou
Dost wrap thy thoughts i' the dark.

Lich.   Well, I will go.
'Tis folly to have heard thee for so long.

Mess. You go not till you answer one word more.

Lich. One, or a thousand ! You'll not stint, I see.

Mess. Thou knowest the captive maid thou leddest
  home ?

Lich. I do.   But wherefore ask ?

Mess.   Did you not say
That she, on whom you look with ignorant eye,

Was Iole, the daughter of the King,
Committed to your charge ?

Lich.   Where ?   Among whom ?
What witness of such words will bear thee out ?

Mess. Many and sound.   A goodly company
In Trachis' market-place heard thee speak this.

Lich. Ay.
I said 'twas rumoured.   But I could not give
My vague impression for advised report.

Mess. Impression, quotha !   Did you not on oath,
Proclaim your captive for your master's bride ?

Lich. My master's bride !   Dear lady, by the Gods,
Who is the stranger ? for I know him not.

Mess. One who was present where he heard thee tell,
How that whole city was subdued and ta'en,
Not for the bondage to the Lydian girl,
But through the longing passion for this maid.

Lich. Dear lady, let the fellow be removed.
To prate with madmen is mere foolishness.

Dei. Nay, I entreat thee by his name, whose fire
Lightens down Œta's topmost glen, be not
A niggard of the truth.   Thou tell'st thy tale
To no weak woman, but to one who knows
Mankind is never constant to one joy.
Whoso would rise to buffet Love, his thought
Is vain.   For Love leads Heaven and Earth at will,
And me.   Then how not others, like to me ?
'Twere madness, sure, in me to blame my lord
When this hath caught him, or the woman there,
His innocent accomplice in a thing,

No shame to either, and no harm to me.
It is not so.   But if from him thou learnest
To deal in falsehood, it were best unlearnt ;·
Or if the lesson be thine own, the claim
Of kindness will but aggravate thy wrong.
Then tell me all the truth.   To one free-born
The name of liar is a hateful lot.
And thou canst not be hid.   Thy news was heard
By many, who will tell me.   If thou fearest,
Thou hast no cause—for doubtfulness is pain,
But to know all, what hurts it?   Many a love
Hath fettered him ere now, and none hath borne
Reproach or· evil word from me.   She shall not,
Though his new passion were as strong as death.
Since most mine eye hath pitied her, because
Her beauty was the ruin of her life,
And all unweeting, she her own bright land,
Poor hapless one ! hath ravaged and enslaved.—
Well, this must pass, as Heaven hath willed.   But thou
Though false to others, be still true to me.

    Ch. 'Tis fairly said.   Comply.   Thou ne'er wilt blame
Her promise, and thou wilt deserve our loves.

    Lich. Yea, dear my Queen, now I have seen thee hold
Thy mortal wishes within mortal bound
So meekly, I will freely tell thee all.
It is as he avers.   This maiden's love,
Piercing through Heracles, was the sole cause,
Why her Œchalia, land of plenteous woe,
Was made the conquest of his spear.   And he—
For I dare so far clear him—never bade

Concealment or denial.   But myself,
Fearing the word might wound thy queenly heart,
Sinned, if thou count such tenderness a sin.
But now that all is known, for both your sakes,
His, and thine own no less, look favouringly
Upon the woman, and confirm the word
Thou here hast spoken in regard to her :—
For he, whose might is in all else supreme,
Is wholly overmastered by her love.

   Dei. Yea, so my mind is bent.   I will do so.
I will not, in a bootless strife 'gainst Heaven,
Drive off this foreign mischief from my door.
Cóme, go we in, that thou may'st bear from me
Such message as is meet, and also carry
Gifts, such as are befitting to return
For gifts new-given.   Thou ought'st not to depart
Unladen, having brought so much with thee.   [*Exeunt.*

CHORUS.

   Triumphant in her might,
      The Queen of soft delight
Still ranges onward with resistless sway.
      What she from Cronos' son
      And strong Poseidon won,
And Pluto, King of Night, I durst not say.

      But who, to earn this bride,
      Came forth in sinewy pride
To strive, or e'er the nuptial might be known,

Leaving the Gods, I tell,
What heroes wrestled well,
With showering blows, and dust in clouds upthrown.

One was a river bold,
Horn-crowned, with tramp fourfold,
Bull Achelôüs from the isles o' the main :
And one from Bacchus' town,
Own son of Zeus, came down,
With brandished mace, bent bow, and lances twain.

Who then in battle brunt,
Together, front to front,
Hurled, eager both to win the beauteous prize ;
And Cypris 'mid the fray
Alone, that dreadful day,
Sate umpire, holding promise in her eyes.

Then clashed the fist, then clanged the bow ;
Then horns gave crashing blow for blow,
Whilst, as they clung,
The twining hip-throw both essay
And hurtling foreheads' fearful play,
And groans from each were wrung.

But the tender fair one far away
Sate watching with an eye of piteous cheer,
(A mother's heart will heed the thing I say),
Till claimed by him who freed her from her fear.

Sudden she leaves her mother's gentle side,
Borne through the waste, a hero's tender bride.

Enter DEIANIRA.

Dei. Dear friends, while yonder herald in the house
Holds converse with the captives ere he go,
I have stol'n forth to you, partly to tell
The craft my hand hath compassed, and in part,
To crave your pity for my wretchedness.
For I have taken to my hearth a maid,
And yet, methinks, no maiden any more,
But married, as some merchant might receive
A cargo, fraught with treason to his soul.
And now we two are closed in one embrace
Beneath one coverlet.   Such generous meed
For faith in guarding home this dreary while
Hath the kind Heracles, our trusty spouse,
Sent in return !   Yet, oft as he hath caught
This same distemperature, I know not how
To harbour indignation against him.
But who that is a woman could endure
To dwell with her, both married to one man ?
One bloom is still advancing, one doth fade.
The budding flower is plucked ; the full-blown head
Is left to wither, while love passeth by
On the other side.   My fear is simply this :
He will be called my husband, but her mate,
For she is younger.   Yet no prudent wife
Would take this angerly, as I have said.
But, dear ones, I will tell you of a way,

Whereof I have bethought me, to prevent
This heart-break.   I had hidden of long time
In a bronze urn the ancient Centaur's gift,
Which I, when a mere girl, culled from the wound
Of hairy-breasted Nessus in his death.
He o'er Evenus' rolling depths, for hire,
Conveyed men with his hands, not plying the oar
Of the ferryman, or canvas-wingèd bark.
Who, when with Heracles, a new-made bride,
I followed by my father's sending forth,
Shouldering me too, in the mid-stream, annoyed
With wanton touch.   And I cried out ; and he,
Zeus' son, turned suddenly, and from his bow
Sent a wing'd shaft, that whizzed into his chest
To the lungs.   Then the weird creature spake so much
In dying.   Child of aged Œneüs,
Since thee I last have ferried o'er, this boon
Be thine, proceeding from mine act, if thou
Wilt do my bidding.   With a careful hand
Collect and bear away the clotted gore
That clogs my wound, e'en where the monster snake
Had dyed the arrow with dark tinct of gall ;
And thou shalt have this as a charm of soul
For Heracles, that never through the eye
Shall he receive another love than thine.
Bethinking me of this, for since his death
I kept it in a closet locked with care,
I have applied it to this robe, with such
Addition as his living voice ordained.—
The thing is done.   No criminal attempts

Could e'er be mine.   Far be they from my thought,
As I abhor the woman who conceives them !
But if by any means through gentle spells
And bonds on Heracles' affection, we
May triumph o'er this maiden in his heart,
My scheme is perfected.   Unless you deem
My action wild.   If so, I will desist.

Ch. If any ground of confidence approve
Thine act, we cannot check thy counsel here.

Dei. My confidence is grounded on belief,
Though hitherto experience bides aloof.

Ch. Then be thou 'ware that, till experience come,
Thou hast no surety, though thou hast belief.

Dei. The truth will soon be known, for lo ! he comes
Already forth, and quickly will be there.
Screen ye but well my counsel.   Doubtful deeds,
Wrapt close, will not deliver us to shame.

Enter LICHAS.

Lich. Daughter of Œneus, tell me thy commands.
Already time rebukes our tardiness.

Dei. For that I have been busied, while thy tongue,
Indoors, was talking to the stranger-maids,
Lichas, that thou shouldst bear this spacious web,
A present from these fingers to my lord.
And when thou giv'st it, say that none of men
Must wear it on his shoulders before him ;
And neither light of sun may look upon it,
Nor holy temple-court, nor household flame,
Till he in open station 'fore the Gods

Y

Display it on a day of hecatombs.
So once I vowed, that should I ever see
Or hear his safe return, I would enfold
His glorious person in this robe, and show
To all the Gods in doing sacrifice
Him a fresh worshipper in fresh array.—
The truth hereof he will with ease descry
Betokened on this treasure-guarding seal.—
Now go, and be advised, of this in chief,
To act within thine office ; then of this,
To bear thee so, that from his thanks and mine
Meeting in one, a twofold grace may spring.

    Lich. If this my Hermes-craft be firm and sure,
Then never will I fail thee, O my Queen !
But I will show this vessel as it is
To whom I bear it, and in faithfulness
Add all the words thou sendest in fit place.

    Dei. Go, then, at once.   Thou hast full cognizance
How things within the palace are preserved ?

    Lich. I know, and will declare.   There is no flaw.

    Dei. Methinks thou knowest too, for thou hast seen,
My kind reception of the stranger-maid ?

    Lich. I saw, and was amazed with heart-struck joy.

    Dei. What more is there to tell?—Too rash, I fear,
Were thy report of longing on my part,
Till we can learn if we are longed for there.

                     [*Exeunt severally*

CHORUS.

      O ye that haunt the strand
      Where ships in quiet land

Near Œta's height and the warm rock-drawn well,
And ye round Melis' inland gulf who dwell,
Worshipping her who wields the golden wand,—
(There Hellas' wisest meet in council strong) :
  Soon shall the flute arise
  With sound of glad surprise,
Thrilling your sense with no unwelcome song,
But tones that to the harp of Heavenly Muse belong.

  Zeus' and Alcmena's son,—
  All deeds of glory done,—
Speeds now triumphant to his home, whom we
Twelve weary months of blind expectancy
Lost in vast distance, from our country gone.
While, sadly languishing, his loving wife,
  Still flowing down with tears,
  Pined with unnumbered fears.
But Ares, lately stung to furious strife,
Frees him for ever from the toilsome life.*

  O let him come to-day !
  Ne'er may his vessel stay,
But glide with feathery sweep of many an oar,
Till from his altar by yon island shore
Even to our town he wind his prosperous way,
  In mien returning mild,
  And inly reconciled,
With that anointing in his heart ingrained,
Which the dark Centaur's wizard lips ordained.

  * His last contest has brought him final deliverance.

Enter DEIANIRA.

Dei. O how I fear, my friends, lest all too far
I have ventured in my action of to-day !
    Ch. What ails thee, Deianira, Œneus' child ?
    Dei. I know not, but am haunted by a dread,
Lest quickly I be found to have performed
A mighty mischief, through bright hopes betrayed.
    Ch. Thóu dost not mean thy gift to Heracles ?
    Dei. Indeed I do.   Now I perceive how fond
Is eagerness, where actions are obscure.
    Ch. Tell, if it may be told, thy cause of fear.
    Dei. A thing is come to pass, which should I tell,
Will strike you with strange wonder when you learn.
For, O my friends, the stuff wherewith I dressed
That robe, a flock of soft and milkwhite wool,
Is shrivelled out of sight, not gnawn by tooth
Of any creature here, but, self-consumed,
Frittered and wasting on the courtyard-stones.

    To let you know the circumstance at full,
I will speak on.   Of all the Centaur-Thing,
When labouring in his side with the fell point
O' the shaft, enjoined me, I had nothing lost,
But his vaticination in my heart
Remained indelible, as though engraved
With pen of iron upon brass.   'Twas thus :—
I was to keep this unguent closely hid
In dark recesses, where no heat of fire
Or warming ray might reach it, till with fresh
Anointing I addressed it to an end.

So I had done.   And now this was to do,
Within my chamber covertly I spread
The ointment with a piece of wool, a tuft
Pulled from a home-bred sheep ; and, as ye saw,
I folded up my gift and packed it close
In hollow casket from the glaring Sun.
But, entering in, a fact encounters me
Past human wit to fathom with surmise.
For, as it happened, I had tossed aside
The bit of wool I worked with, carelessly,
Into the open daylight, 'mid the blaze
Of Helios' beam.   And, as it kindled warm,
It fell away to nothing, crumbled small,
Like dust in severing wood by sawyers strewn.
So, on the point of vanishing, it lay.
But, from the place where it had lain, brake forth
A frothy scum in clots of seething foam,
As when in bloomy vintage Earth receives
Rich liquor running o'er from Bacchus' vine.
And I, unhappy, know not toward what thought
To turn me, but I see mine act is dire.
For wherefore should the Centaur, for what end,
Show kindness to the cause for whom he died ?
That cannot be.   But seeking to destroy
His slayer, he cajoled me.   This I learn
Too late, by sad experience, for no good.
And, if I err not now, my hapless fate
Is all alone to be his murderess.
For, well I know, the shaft that made the wound
Gave pain to Chiron, who was more than man ;

And wheresoe'er it falls, it ravageth
All the wild creatures of the world.   And now
This gory venom blackly spreading bane
From Nessus' angry wound, must it not cause
The death of Heracles ?   I think it must.

  And yet of this I am resolved, if aught
Harm him, my life shall follow at a bound.
She cannot bear to live in evil fame,
Who cares to have a nature pure from ill.

  Ch. Horrid mischance must needs occasion fear.
But Hope is not condemned before the event.

  Dei. In ill-devised proceeding not even Hope
Remains to minister a cheerful mind.

  Ch. Yet to have erred unwittingly abates
The fire of wrath ; and thou art in this case.

  Dei. So speaks not he who hath a share of sin,
But who is clear of all offence at home.

  Ch. 'Twere well to silence further speech, unless
Thou hast aught for thine own son : for he is here,
Who went erewhile to find his father forth.

HYLLUS (re-entering).

O mother, mother !
I would to Heaven one of three things were true :
Either that thou wert dead, or, living, wert
No mother to me, or hadst found a mind
Furnished with better thoughts than thou hast now !

  Dei. My son ! what canst thou so mislike in me ?

  Hyl. I tell thee thou this day hast been the death
Of him that was thy husband and my sire.

Dei. What word hath passed thy lips? my child, my child!

Hyl. A word that must be verified.   For who
Can make the accomplished fact as things undone?

Dei Alas, my son! what saidst thou? Who hath told
That I have' wrought a deed so full of woe?

Hyl. 'Twas I myself that saw with these mine eyes
My father's heavy state :—no hearsay word.

Dei. And where didst thou come near him and stand by?

Hyl. Art thou to hear it?   On, then, with my tale!
When he came triumphing with fruits of war
From sacking Eurytus' world-famous town,—
There is a headland, last of long Eubœa,
Surf-beat Cenæum,—where to his father Zeus
He dedicates high altars and a grove.
There first I saw him, gladdened from desire.
And when he now addressed him to the work
Of various sacrifice, the herald Lichas
Arrived from home, bearing thy fatal gift,
The deadly robe : wherewith invested straight,
As thou hadst given charge, he sacrificed
The firstlings of the spoil, twelve bulls entire,
Each after each.   But the full count he brought
Was a clear hundred of all kinds of head.
  Then the all-hapless one commenced his prayer
In solemn gladness for the bright array.
But presently, when from the holy things,
And from the richness of the oak-tree core,
There issued flame mingled with blood, a sweat
Rose on his flesh, and close to every limb
Clung, like stone-drapery from the craftsman's hand,

The garment, glued unto his side.   Then came
The tearing pangs within his bones, and then
The poison feasted like the venomed tooth
Of deadly basilisk.—When this began,
He shouted on poor Lichas, none to blame
For thy sole crime, " What guile is here, thou knave ?
What was thy fraud in bringing me this robe ? "
He, all-unknowing, hapless man, declared
His message, that the gift was wholly thine.
Whereat the hero, while the shooting spasm
Had fastened on the lungs, seized him by the foot
Where the ankle turns i' the socket, and, with a thought,
Hurl'd on a surf-vex'd reef that showed i' the sea :
And rained the grey pulp from the hair, the brain
Being scattered with the blood.   Then the great throng
Saddened their festival with piteous wail
For one in death and one in agony.
And none had courage to approach my sire,—
Convulsed upon the ground, then thrown i' the air
With horrid yells and crying, till the cliffs
Echoed around, the mountain-promontories
Of Locris, and the forelands of Eubœa.
Wearied at length with flinging on the earth,
.And shrieking oft with lamentable cry,
Cursing the fatal marriage with thyself
The all-wretched, and the bond to Œneus' house,
That prize that was the poisoner of his peace,
He lifted a wild glance above the smoke
That hung around, and 'midst the crowd of mèn
Saw me in tears, and looked on me and said,

"O son, come near ; fly not from my distress,
Though thou shouldst be consumèd in my death,
But lift and bear me forth ; and, if thou mayest,
Set me where no one of mankind shall see me.
But if thy heart withhold thee, yet convey me
Out of this land as quickly as ye may.
Let me not die where I am now."   We then,
Thus urgently commanded, laid him down
Within our bark, and hardly to this shore
Rowed him convulsed and roaring.—Presently,
He will appear, alive or lately dead.

Such, mother, is the crime thou hast devised
And done against our sire, wherefore let Right
And Vengeance punish thee !—May I pray so ?
I may : for thou absolv'st me by thy deed,
Thou that hast slain the noblest of the Earth,
Thy spouse, whose like thou ne'er wilt see again.

[Exit DEIANIRA.

Ch. Why steal'st thou off in silence ? Know'st thou not
Thy silence argues thine accuser's plea ?

Hyl. Let her go off.   Would that a sudden flood
Might sweep her far and swiftly from mine eye !
Why fondle vainly the fair-sounding name
Of mother, when her acts are all unmotherly ?
Let her begone for me : and may such joy
Be hers, as she hath rendered to my sire ! [*Exit* HYLLUS.

CHORUS.

See where falls the doom, of old
By the unerring Voice foretold,—

" When twelve troublous years have rolled,
Toil on toil no more shall tire
The offspring of the Eternal Sire."
Lo ! the destined Hour is come !
Lo ! it brings its burden home.
For when eyes have looked their last
    How can labour vex again ?
How, when will and thought are past,
    Shall the life be thralled to pain ?

And if Nessus' withering shroud,
    Wrought by destiny and craft,
Steep him in a poisonous cloud
    Steaming from the venomed shaft,
Which to Death in hideous lair
The many-wreathèd Hydra bare,
How shall he another day
Feel the glad warmth of Helios' ray ?
Enfolding him I see the Monster-Thing
Of Lerna's water, and the cruel sting
Of the shagg'd Centaur's murderous-guileful tongue
Breaks forth withal to do him painful wrong.

While she, poor innocent, who saw
Checkless advancing to the gate
A mighty harm unto her state,—
This rash young bridal without fear of law,—
Gave not her will to * aught that caused this woe,

* *Or*, Received no hint of.

But since it came through that strange mind's con-
    ceiving,—
That ruined her in meeting,—deeply grieving,
She mourns with dewy tears in tender flow.
And sure some secret dread doth coming Fate foreshow.

    The springs of sorrow are unbound,
      And such an agony disclose,
As never from the hands of foes
To afflict the life of Heracles was found.
O dark with battle-stains, world-champion spear,
That from Œchalia's highland leddest then
This bride that followed swiftly in thy train !
How fatally overshadowing was thy fear !
But these wild sorrows all too clearly come
From Love's dread minister, disguised and dumb.*

    Half-chorus 1. Am I a fool, or do I truly hear
Lament new-arising from our master's home.?
Tell !

    H-ch. 2. Clearly from within a wailing voice
Peals piteously.   The house hath some fresh woe.

    H-ch. 1. Mark !
How strangely, with what cloud upon her brow,
Yon aged matron with her tidings moves !

            Enter Nurse.

Nurse. Ah ! mighty, O my daughters ! was the grief
Sprung from the gift to Heracles conveyed !

* *I.e.* from Aphrodite, working through the concealed and silent
captive maiden.

Ch. What new thing is befallen? What dost thou
  mean?
Nur. Our Queen hath found her latest journey's end,
Even now departing, without stirring foot.
Ch. Not dead?
Nur.   You know the whole.
Ch.   Dead! hapless Queen!
Nur. The truth hath twice been told.
Ch.   O tell us how!
What was her death, poor victim of dire woe?
Nur. Most ruthless was the deed.
Ch.   Say, woman, say!
What was the sudden end?
Nur.   Herself she slew.
Ch. What rage, what madness, clutched
The mischief-working brand?
How could her single thought
Contrive accomplishment of death on death?
Nur. Chill iron stopped the sources of her breath.
Ch. And thou, poor helpless crone, didst see this done?
Nur. Yea, I stood near and saw.
Ch.   How was it? Tell!
Nur. With her own hand this violence was given.
Ch. What do I hear?
Nur.   The certainty of truth.
Ch. A child is come,
From this new bridal that hath rushed within,
A fresh-born Fury of woe!
Nur. Too true.   But hadst thou been at hand to see
Her action, pity would have wrung thy soul.

Ch. Could this be ventured by a woman's hand ?
Nur. Ay, and in dreadful wise, as thou shalt hear
When she had entered all alone within
The house, and in the court beheld her boy
Spreading the couch that should receive his sire,
Ere he returned to meet him,—out of sight
She hid herself, and fell at the altar's foot,
And loudly cried that she was left forlorn ;
And, taking in her touch each household thing
That formerly she used, poor lady, wept
O'er all ; and then went ranging through the rooms,
Where, if there caught her eye the well-loved form
Of any of her household, she would gaze
And weep aloud, accusing her own fate
And her abandoned lot, childless henceforth !
When this was ended, suddenly I see her
Fly to the hero's room of genial rest.
With unsuspected gaze o'ershadowed near,
I watched, and saw her casting on the bed
The finest sheets of all, and when 'twas done,
She leapt upon the couch where they had lain
And sat there in the midst.   And the hot flood
Burst from her eyes before she spake :—" Farewell,
My bridal bed, for never more shalt thou
Give me the comfort I have known thee give."
Then with tight fingers she undid her robe,
Where the brooch lay before the breast, and bared
All her left arm and side.   I, with what speed
Strength ministered, ran forth to tell her son
The act she was preparing.   But meanwhile,

Ere we could come again, the fatal blow
Fell, and we saw the wound.   And he, her boy,
Seeing, wept aloud.   For now the hapless youth
Knew that himself had done this in his wrath,
'Told all too late i' the house, how she had wrought
Most innocently, from the Centaur's wit.
So now the unhappy one, with passionate words
And cries and wild embracings of the dead,
Groaned forth that he had slain her with false breath
Of evil accusation, and was left
Orphaned of both, his mother and his sire.
    Such is the state within.   What fool is he
That counts one day, or two, or more to come !
To-morrow is not, till the present day
Have passed with unalloyed prosperity.   [*Exit.*

CHORUS.

Which shall come first in my wail,
Which shall be last to prevail,
Is a doubt that will never be done.

Trouble at home may be seen,
Trouble is looked for with teen ;
And to have and to look for are one.

Would some fair wind
But waft me forth to roam
Far from the region of my home,
Ere death me find
Oppressed with wild affright

Even at the sudden sight
Of him, the valiant son of Zeus most High !
Before the house, they tell, he fareth nigh,
A wonder beyond thought,
With torment unapproachable distraught.

Hark ! . . . .   .
The cause then of my cry
Was all too nigh :
(Doth the clear nightingale lament for nought ?)
Some step of stranger folk is this way brought.
    As for a friend they love
Heavy and slow with noiseless feet they move.
Which way ? which way ?
Ah me ! behold him come.
His lips are dumb.
Dead, or at rest in sleep ? What shall I say ?
    [HERACLES *is brought in on a litter, accompanied*
        by HYLLUS *and an* Old Man.

Hyl. Oh, woe is me !
My father, piteous woe for thee !
Oh, whither shall I turn my thought ! Ah me !
    Old M. Hush ! speak not, O my child,
Lest torment fierce and wild
Rekindle in thy father's rugged breast,
And break this rest
Where now his life is held at point to fall.
With firm lips clenched refrain thy voice through all.
    Hyl. Yet tell me, doth he live,
Old sir ?

Old M. Wake not the slumberer,
Nor kindle and revive
The terrible recurrent power of pain,
My son!
Hyl. My foolish words are done,
But my full heart sinks 'neath the heavy strain.

Heracles. O Father, who are these?
What countrymen? Where am I? What far land
Holds me in pain that ceaseth not? Ah me!
Again that pest is rending me.   Pain, pain!
Old M. Now thou may'st know
'Twas better to have lurked in silent shade
And not thus widely throw
The slumber from his eyelids and his head.
Hyl. I could not brook
All speechless on his misery to look.

Her. O altar on the Eubœan strand,
High-heaped with offerings from my hand,
What meed for lavish gifts bestowed
From thy new sanctuary hath flowed!
Father of Gods! thy cruel power
Hath foiled me with an evil blight.
Ah! would mine eyes have closed in night
Ere madness in a fatal hour
Had burst upon them with a blaze,
No help or soothing once allays!
What hand to heal, what voice to charm,
Can e'er dispel this hideous harm?

Whose skill save thine,
Monarch Divine?
Mine eyes, if such I saw,
Would hail him from afar with trembling awe.

Ah! ah!
O vex me not, touch me not, leave me to rest,
To sleep my last sleep on Earth's gentle breast.
You touch me, you press me, you turn me again,
You break me, you kill me! O pain! O pain!
You have kindled the pang that had slumbered still.
It comes, it hath seized me with tyrannous will!

Where are ye, men, whom over Hellas wide
This arm hath freed, and o'er the ocean-tide,
And through rough brakes, from every monstrous
     thing;
But now in my misfortune none will bring
A sword to aid, a fire to quell this fire,
O most unrighteous! nor to my desire
Will come and quench the hateful life I hold
With mortal stroke! Ah! is there none so bold?

  Old M. Son of our hero, this hath mounted past
  My feeble force to cope with. Take him thou!
Fresher thine eye and more the hope thou hast
  Than mine to save him.
  Hyl.   I support him now
Thus with mine arm : but neither fleshly vest
Nor inmost spirit can I lull to rest

From torture.   None may dream
To wield this power, save he, the King supreme.

Her. Son !
Where art thou to lift me and hold me aright ?
It tears me, it kills me, it rushes in might,
This cruel, devouring, unconquered pain
Shoots forth to consume me.   Again ! again !
O Fate !   O Athena !—O son, at my word
Have pity and slay me with merciful sword !

Pity thy father, boy, with sharp relief
Smite on my breast, and heal the wrathful grief
Wherewith thy mother, God-abandoned wife,
Hath wrought this ruin on her husband's life.
O may I see her falling, even so
As she hath thrown me, to like depth of woe !
Sweet Hades, with swift death,
Brother of Zeus, release my suffering breath !

Ch. Horror hath caught me as I hear this woe,
Racking our mighty one with mightier pain.
Her. Many hot toils and hard beyond report,
With hands and struggling shoulders have I borne.
But no such labour hath the Thunderer's wife
Or sour Eurystheus ever given, as this,
Which Œneus' daughter of the treacherous eye
Hath fastened on my back, this amply-woven
Net of the Furies, that is breaking me.
For, glued unto my side, it hath devoured

Thy flesh to the bone, and helping to the lungs
It frozen the vital channels, and hath drunk
The fresh lifeblood, and wastes all my frame,
Felled in the might of a resistless bond.
Nor me, nor Typhon, nor Earth's giant brood,
Nor Centaur's murderous violence could subdue,
Nor Hellas, nor the Stranger, nor all lands
Where I have gone, cleansing the world from harm;
But a sick woman without manhood's strain
Alone and unprotected hath conquered me.
Son, let me know that mine wert born, nor rate
Thy mother's claim beyond thy sire's, but bring
Thyself from out the chambers to my hand
Her body that hath borne thee, that my heart
May be assured, if kinder than my pain
I will discover that to behold her face
With righteous vengeance agonized and torn.
Stay, shrink not, son, but pity me, when all
They pity—me, who, like a tender girl,
Am bound to weep aloud!   This none could say
He knew in me of old; for, murmuring not,
I went with evil fortune, silent still.
Now, such a foe hath found the woman in me!

Ay, but come near; stand by me, and behold
What cause I have for crying.   Look but here!
Here is the mystery unveiled.   O see!
Ye people, gaze on this poor quivering flesh,
Look with compassion on my misery!
Ah me!
Ah! ah! Again!

Even now the hot convulsion of disease
Shoots through my side, and will not let me rest
From this fierce exercise of wearing woe.
Take me, O King of Night!
O sudden thunderstroke,
Smite me! O sire, transfix me with the dart
Of thy swift lightning! Yet again that fang
Is tearing; it hath blossomed forth anew,
It soareth to the height! O breast and back,
O hands and arms of mine, ye are the same
That crushed the dweller of the Némean wild,
The lion unapproachable and rude,
The oxherd's plague, and Hydra of the lake
Of Lerna, and the twy-form prancing throng
Of Centaurs,—insolent, unsociable,
Lawless, ungovernable;—the monster huge
Of Erymanthus, and the three-necked whelp
Of Pluto underground, a perilous fear
Born from the monster-worm; and, on the verge
Of Earth, the dragon, guarding fruits of gold.
These toils and others countless I have tried,
And none hath triumphed on my strength. But now
Jointless and riven to tatters, I am wrecked
Thus utterly by imperceptible woe;
I, proudly named Alcmena's child, and his
Who reigns in highest heaven, the King supreme!
    Ay, but even yet, I tell ye, even from here,
Where I am nothingness and cannot move,
She who hath done this thing shall feel my power.
Let her come near, that, mastered by my might,

She may have this to tell the world, that, dying,
As living, I gave punishment to wrong.

Ch. O Hellas, how I grieve for thy distress!
How thou wilt mourn in losing him we see!

Hyl. My father, since thy silence gives me leave,
Still hear me patiently, though in thy pain!
For my request is just.   Lend me thy mind
Less wrathfully distempered than 'tis now;
Else thou canst never know, where thou art keen
With vain resentment and with vain desire.

Her. Speak what thou wilt and cease, for I in pain
Catch not the sense of thy mysterious talk.

Hyl. I come to tell thee of my mother's case,
And her involuntary unconscious fault.

Her. Base villain! hast thou breathed thy mother's name,
Thy father's murderess, in my hearing too!

Hyl. Her state requires not silence, but full speech.

Her. Her faults in former time might well be told.

Hyl. So might her fault to-day, couldst thou but know.

Her. Speak, but beware base words disgrace thee not.

Hyl. List! She is dead even now with new-given wound.

Her. By whom?   Thy words flash wonder through my
    woe.

Hyl. Her own hand slaughtered her; no foreign stroke.

Her. Wretch! to have reft this office from my hands.

Hyl. Even your rash spirit were softened, if you knew.

Her. This bodes some knavery.   But pronounce thy
    thought!

Hyl. She erred with good intent.   The whole is said.

Her. Good, O thou villain, to destroy thy sire!

Hyl. When she perceived that marriage in her home,
She erred, supposing to enchain thy love.

Her. Hath Trachis a magician of such might?

Hyl. Long since the Centaur Nessus moved her mind
To work this charm for heightening thy desire.

Her. O horror, thou art here!   I am no more.
My day is darkened, boy!   Undone, undone!
I see our plight too plainly: woe is me!
Come, O my son!—thou hast no more a father,—
Call to me all the brethren of thy blood,
And poor Alcmena, wedded all in vain
Unto the Highest, that ye may hear me tell
With my last breath what prophecies I know.

Hyl. Thy mother is not here, but by the shore
Of Tiryns hath obtained a dwelling-place;
And of thy sons, some she hath living with her,
And some, my sire, inhabit Thebe's town.
But all we who are here, if there be aught
That may by us be done, will hear, and do.

Her. Then hearken thou unto this task, and show
If worthily thou art reputed mine.
The time to prove thee is at hand.   My sire
Forewarned me long ago that I should die
By none who lived and breathed, but from the will
Of one now dwelling in the house of death.
And so this Centaur, as the voice Divine
Then prophesied, in death hath slain me living.
Yea, and consenting with that ancient word,
Fresh oracles I will disclose, which I
Took note of when I came within the grove

Of the hill-roving and earth-couching Selli,—
Dictated to me by the mystic tongue
Innumerous, of my Father's sacred tree ;
Declaring that my ever instant toils
Should in the time that now hath being and life
End and release me.   And I looked for joy.
But the true meaning plainly was my death.—
No labour is appointed for the dead.—
Then, since all argues one event, my child,
Once more thou must befriend me, and not wait
For my voice goading thee, but of thyself
Submit and second my resolve, and know
Filial obedience for thy noblest rule.

Hyl. I will obey thee, father, though my heart
Sinks heavily in approaching such a theme.

Her. Before aught else, lay thy right hand in mine.

Hyl. Why so intent on this assurance, sire ?

Her. Give it at once and be not froward, boy.

Hyl. There is my hand : I will gainsay thee nought.

Her. Swear by the head of him who gave me life.

Hyl. Tell me the oath, and I will utter it.

Her. Swear thou wilt do the thing I bid thee do.

Hyl. I swear, and make Zeus witness of my troth.

Her. But if you swerve, pray that the curse may come.

Hyl. It will not come for swerving :—but I pray.

Her. Now, dost thou know on Œta's topmost height
The crag of Zeus ?

Hyl.   I know it, and full oft
Have stood there sacrificing.

Her.   Then even there,

With thine own hand uplifting this my body,
Taking what friends thou wilt, and having lopped
Much wood from the deep-rooted oak, and rough
Wild olive, lay me on the gathered pile,
And burn all with the touch of pine-wood flame.
And let no tear of mourning dim thine eye ;
But silent, with dry gaze, if thou art mine,
Perform it.   Else my curse awaits thee still
To weigh thee down when I am lost in night.

Hyl. How cruel, O my father, is thy tongue !

Her. 'Tis peremptory.   Else, if thou refuse,
Be called another's and be no more mine.

Hyl. Alas that thou shouldst challenge me to this,
To be thy murderer, guilty of thy blood !

Her. Not I, in sooth : but healer of my life,
And sole preserver from my present woe.

Hyl. How can it heal to burn thee on the pyre ?

Her. If this act frighten thee, perform the rest.

Hyl. Mine arms shall not refuse to carry thee.

Her. And wilt thou gather the appointed wood ?

Hyl. So my hand touch it not.   In all but this,
Not scanting labour, I will do my part.

Her. Enough.   'Tis well.   And having thus much given,
Add one small kindness to a list so full.

Hyl. How great soe'er it were, it should be done.

Her. The maid of Eurytus thou knowest, I ween.

Hyl. Of Iole thou speak'st, or I mistake.

Her. Of her.   This then is all I urge, my son.
When I am dead, if thou wouldst show thy duty,
Think of thine oath to me, and, at my word,

Make her thy wife : nor let another man
Take her, but only thou ; since she hath lain
So near this heart.   Obey me, O my boy !
And be thyself the maker of this bond.
To spurn at trifles after great things given,
Were to confound the meed already won.

Hyl. Oh, anger is not right, when men are ill !
But who could bear to see thee in this mind ?

Her. You murmur, as you meant to disobey.

Hyl. How can I do it, when my mother's death
And thy sad state sprang solely from this girl ?   '
Who, not possessed with furies, could choose this ?
Far better, father, for me too to die,
Then to live still with my worst enemy.

Her. This youth withdraws his reverence in my death.
But; if thou yield'st not to thy father's word,
The curse from Heaven shall dog thy footsteps still.

Hyl. Ah ! thou wilt tell me that thy pain is come.

Her. Yea, for thou wak'st the torment that had slept.

Hyl. Ay me ! how cross and doubtful is my way !

Her. Because you will reject your father's word.

Hyl. Must I be taught impiety from thee ?

Her. It is not impious to content my heart.

Hyl. Then you require this with an absolute will ?

Her. And bid Heaven witness to my strong command.

Hyl. Then I will do it, for the act is thine.
I will not cast it off.   Obeying thee,
My sire, the Gods will ne'er reprove my deed.

Her. Thou endest fairly.   Now, then, O my son,
Add the performance swiftly, that, before

Some spasm or furious onset of my pain
Have seized me, ye may place me on the pyre.
Come, loiter not, but lift me.   Now my end
Is near, the last cessation of my woe.
    Hyl. Since thy command is urgent, O my sire !
We tarry not, but bear thee to the pyre.
    Her.   Stubborn heart, ere yet again
          Wakes the fierce rebound of pain,
          While the evil holds aloof,
          Thou, with bit of iron proof,
          Curb thy cry, with forcèd will
          Seeming to do gladly still !
    Hyl.   Lift him, men, and hate not me
          For the evil deeds ye see,
          Since the Heavens' relentless sway
          Recks not of the righteous way.
          He who gave life and doth claim
          From his seed a father's name
          Can behold this hour of blame.
          Though the future none can tell,
         Yet the present is not well :
          Sore for him who bears the blow,
          Sad for us who feel his woe,
          Shameful to the Gods, we trow.
    Ch.   Maidens from the palace-hall,
          Come ye forth, too, at our call !
          Mighty deaths beyond belief,
          Many an unknown form of grief,
          Ye have seen to-day ; and nought
          But the power of Zeus hath wrought.

PHILOCTETES.

THE PERSONS.

ODYSSEUS.

NEOPTOLEMUS.

CHORUS *of Mariners*.

PHILOCTETES.

Messenger, disguised as a Merchantman.

HERACLES, *appearing from the sky.*

IT was fated that Troy should be taken by Neoptolemus, the son of Achilles, assisted by the bow of Heracles in the hands of Philoctetes.

Now Philoctetes had been rejected by the army because of a trouble in his foot, which made his presence with them insufferable ; and had been cast away by Odysseus on the island of Lemnos.

But when the decree of fate was revealed by prophecy, Odysseus undertook to bring Philoctetes back, and took with him Neoptolemus, whose ambition could only be gratified through the return of Philoctetes with his bow.

Philoctetes was resolutely set against returning, and at the opening of the drama Neoptolemus is persuaded by Odysseus to take him with guile.

But when Philoctetes appears, the youth's ingenuous nature is so wrought upon through pity and remorse, that his sympathy and native truthfulness at length overcome his ambition.

When the inward sacrifice is complete, Heracles appears from heaven, and by a few words changes the mind of Philoctetes, so that all ends well.

SCENE—Lemnos,—a rocky shore.

PHILOCTETES.

Odysseus—Neoptolemus.

Odysseus. This coast of sea-girt Lemnos, where we
    stand,
Is uninhabited, untrodden of men.
And here, O noblest son of noblest sire,
Achilles-born Neoptolemus, I erewhile,—
Ordered by those who had command,—cast forth
Trachinian Philoctetes, Pœas' son,
His foot dark-dripping with the festering plague ;
When with his cries, that frighted holy rest,
Filling the camp, he troubled every rite
Of sacrifice and drink-offering, that none
Might touch them, but his noise disturbed our peace.
    But why these words ?   No moment this for talk
Lest he discern my coming, and I lose
The scheme, wherewith I think to catch him soon.
Now most behoves thy service, to explore
This headland for a cave with double mouth,

Whose perforated structure, in cold days,
Gives choice of sunshine, and in summer noons
The breeze wafts slumber through the airy cell.
Then, something lower down, upon the left,
Unless 'tis dried, thine eye may note a spring.
Go near now silently, and make me know
If still he persevere and hold this spot,
Or have roamed elsewhere, that informed of this
I may proceed with what remains to say,
And we may act in concert.

  Neoptolemus.   Lord Odysseus,
Thy foremost errand will not task me far.
Methinks I see the cave whereof thou speakest.

 Od. Where? let me see it. Above there, or below?

 Neo. Yonder, above. And yet I hear no tread.

      [NEOPTOLEMUS *climbs up to the cave.*

 Od. Look if he be not lodged in slumber there.

 Neo. I find no inmate, but an empty room.

 Od. What? no provision for a dwelling-place?

 Neo. A bed of leaves for some one harbouring here.

 Od. Nought else beneath the roof? Is all forlorn?

 Neo. A cup of wood, some feeble craftsman's skill,
And, close at hand, these embers of a fire.

 Od. That store is his. I read the token clear.

 Neo. Oh! and these festering rags give evidence,
Steeped as with dressing some malignant sore.

 Od. The man inhabits here: I know it now.
And sure he's not far off. How can he range,
Whose limb drags heavy with an ancient harm?
But he's gone, either to bring forage home,

Or where he hath found some plant of healing power.
Send therefore thine attendant to look forth,
Lest unawares he find me.　All our host
Were not so fair a·prize for him as I.

　Neo. My man is going, and shall watch the path.
What more dost thou desire of me?　Say on.

　Od. Son of Achilles, know that thou art come
To serve us nobly, not with strength alone,
But, faithful to thy mission, if so be,
To do things strange, unwonted to thine ear.

　Neo. What dost thou bid me?

　Od.　　　　　　　　　　　　'Tis thy duty now
To entrap the mind of Pœas' son with words.
When he shall ask thee, who and whence thou art,
Tell thy true name and parentage.　Not this
I charge thee to conceal.　But for thy voyage,
'Tis homeward, leaving the Achean host,
With perfect hatred hating them, because
They who had drawn thee with strong prayers from home
Their only hope for taking Troy, refused
Thy just demand to have thy father's arms,
But, ere thy coming, wrongly gave them o'er
Unto Odysseus : and on this launch forth
With boundless execration against me.
That will not pain me : but if thou reject
This counsel, thou wilt trouble all our host,
Since, if his bow shall not be ta'en, thy life
Will ne'er be crowned through Troy's discomfiture.

　Now let me show, why thine approach to him
Is safe and hopeful as mine cannot be.

Thou didst sail forth, not to redeem thine oath,
Nor by constraint, nor with the foremost band.
All which reproaches I must bear : and he,
But seeing me, while master of his bow,
Will slay me, and my ruin will be thine.
This point then craves our cunning, to acquire
By subtle means the irresistible bow.—
Thy nature was not framed, I know it well,
For speaking falsehood, or contriving harm.
Yet, since the prize of victory is so dear,
Endure it.—We'll be just another day.
But now, for one brief hour, devote thyself
To serve me without shame, and then for aye
Hereafter be the pearl of righteousness.

Neo. The thing whose name is painful to mine ear,
Son of Laërtes, I abhor to do.
'Tis not my nature, no, nor, as they tell,
My father's, to work aught by craft and guile.
I'll undertake to bring him in by force,
Not by deceit.   For, sure, with his one foot,
He cannot be a match for all our crew.
Being sent, my lord, to serve thee, I am loth
To be called traitor.   But I rather choose
To offend with honour, than to win by wrong.

Od. Son of a valiant sire, I, too, in youth,
Had once a slow tongue and an active hand.
But since I have proved the world, I clearly see
Words and not deeds are masters among men.

Neo. What then is thy command?   To lie?   No
        more ?

Od. To entangle Philoctetes by deceit.

Neo. Why through deceit? May not persuasion fetch
 him?

Od. Never. And force as certainly will fail.

Neo. What lends him such assurance of defence?

Od. Arrows, the unerring harbingers of Death.

Neo. Then to go near him is a perilous thing.

Od. Unless with subtlety, as I have said.

Neo. And is not lying shameful to thy soul?

Od. Not if by lying I can save my soul.

Neo. How must one look in speaking such a word?

Od. Where gain invites, this shrinking is not good.

Neo. What gain I through his coming back to Troy?

Od. His arms alone have power to take Troy-town.

Neo. Then am not I the spoiler, as was said?

Od. Thou without them, they without thee, are power-
 less.

Neo. If it be so, they must be sought and won.

Od. Yea, for in this two prizes will be thine.

Neo. What? When I learn them, I will not refuse.

Od. Wisdom and virtue joined in one good name.

Neo. Shame, to the winds! Come, I will do this
 thing.

Od. Say, dost thou keep my bidding full in mind?

Neo. Doubt not, since once for all I have embraced it.

Od. Thou, then, wait here till he return, but I

Will go, for fear my presence should be seen,

And take back our attendant to the ship.

And then once more, should ye appear to waste

The time unduly, I will send again

This same man hither in disguise, transformed
To the strange semblance of a merchantman ;
From dark suggestions of whose crafty tongue,
Thou, O my son, shalt gather timely counsel.
  Now to my ship.   This charge I leave to thee.
May secret Hermes guide us to our end,
And civic Pallas, named of victory,
The sure defender of my devious way.

The CHORUS *enter.*

Chorus 1. Strange in a stranger land,
      What shall I speak ?   What hide
      From a heart suspicious of ill ?
      Tell me, O master mine !
      Wise above all is the man,
      Peerless in searching thought,
      Who with the Zeus-given wand
      Wieldeth a Heaven-sent power.
      This unto thee, my child,
      Fraught with ancestral might,
      This to thy life hath come.
      Wherefore I bid thee declare,
      What must I do for thy need ?

Neo. Even now methinks thou longest to espy
Near ocean's verge the place where he doth lie.
Gaze without fear.   But when the traveller stern,
Who from this roof is parted, shall return,
Advancing still as I the signal give,
To do each moment's errand thou shalt strive.
  Ch. 2.   That, O my son, from of old

Hath been my care, to observe
What by thy beck'ning is told;
Still thy'chief business to serve.
But first, O tell me, what home
He dwells in, or where doth he roam?
This for my need thóu must say,
Lest unawares I be ta'en,
Where doth he move or remain,
Here lodging, or wandering away?

Neo. Thou seëst yon double doorway of his lair,
Poor habitation of the rock.

Ch. 2.   But where
Is the pain-withered wight himself abroad?

Neo. To me 'tis clear, that, in his quest for food,
Here, not far off, he trails this furrowed path.
For, as they tell, such mode the sufferer hath
Of sustenance, O hardness! bringing low
Wild creatures with wing'd arrows from his bow;
Nor findeth healer for his troublous woe.

Ch. 3.   I feel his misery.
With no responding eye,
Far from all human care,
He pines with fierce disease;
Each want he hourly sees
Awakening new despair.
How can he bear it still?
O cruel Heavens!   O pain
Of that sad mortal train
Whose life sharp sorrows fill!

Ch. 4.   Born in a princely hall,

Highest, perchance, of all,
Now lies he comfortless
Alone in deep distress,
'Mongst rough and dappled brutes,
With pangs and hunger worn ;
While from far distance shoots,
On airy pinion borne,
The unbridled Echo, still replying
To his most bitter crying.

Neo. At nought of this I marvel—for if I
Judge rightly, there assailed him from on high
That former plague through Chrysa's * cruel sting :
And if to-day he suffer anything
With none to soothe, it must be from the will
Of some great God, who careth to fulfil
The word of prophecy, lest he should bend
On Troy the shaft no mortal may forefend,
Before the arrival of Troy's destined hour,
When she must fall, o'er-mastered by their power.

Ch. 1. Hush, my son !
Neo.   Why so ?
Ch. 1.   A sound
Fostered of some mortal woe,
Started from the neighbouring ground.
Here, or there ?   Ah ! now I know.

---

* Chrysa is an island near the Troad, sacred to a Goddess of
the name, whose precinct was guarded by a serpent. The serpent,
whose fang left an incurable wound, had bitten Philoctetes in the
foot.

Hark ! 'tis the voice of one in pain,
Moving hardly, the deep strain
Of human anguish, all too clear,
That strikes my heart, that wounds mine ear.
Ch. 2. From far it peals.   But thou, my son !
Neo. What ?
Ch. 2.   Think again.   He cometh nigh :
He holds the region : not with tone
Of piping shepherd's rural minstrelsy,
But belloweth his far cry,
Stumbling perchance with mortal pain,
Or else in wild amaze,
As he our ship surveys
Unwonted on the inhospitable main.

Enter PHILOCTETES.

Philoctetes. Ho !
What men are ye that to this desert shore,
Harbourless, uninhabited, are come
On shipboard?   Of what country or what race
Shall I pronounce ye?   For your outward garb
Is Grecian, ever dearest to this heart
That hungers now to hear your voices' tune.
Ah ! do not fear me, do not shrink away
From my wild looks : but, pitying one so poor,
Forlorn and desolate in nameless woe,
Speak, if with friendly purpose ye are come.
O answer !   'Tis not meet that I should lose
This kindness from your lips, or ye from mine.

Neo. Then know this first, O stranger, as thou wouldst,
That we are Greeks.

　　Phi.　　　　　　　　O dear, dear name!　Ah me!
In all these years, once, only once, I hear it!
My son, what fairest gale hath wafted thee?
What need hath brought thee to the shore?　What
　　mission?
Declare all this, that I may know thee well.

　　Neo. The sea-girt Scyros is my native home.
Thitherward I make voyage :—Achilles' son,
Named Neoptolemus.—I have told thee all.

　　Phi. Dear is that shore to me, dear is thy father.
O ancient Lycomedes' foster-child,
Whence cam'st thou hither?　How didst thou set forth?

　　Neo. Troy was the port we left with this convoy.

　　Phi. How?　Sure thou wast not with us, when at first
We launched our vessels on the Troyward course?

　　Neo. Hadst thou a share in that adventurous toil?

　　Phi. And know'st thou not whom thou behold'st in me,
Young boy?

　　Neo.　　　　　How should I know him whom I ne'er
Set eye on?

　　Phi.　　　　Hast not even heard my name,
Nor sounding rumour of my ruinous woe?

　　Neo. Nay, I know nought of all thy questioning.

　　Phi. How full of sorrows, how abhorred of Heaven,
Am I, when of my state no faintest word
Hath reached my home, or any Grecian land!
But they, who pitilessly cast me forth,
Keep silence and are glad, while this my plague

Blooms ever, and is strengthened more and more.
Boy, great Achilles' offspring, in this form
Thou seest the man, of whom erewhile, methinks,
Thou hast been told, to whom the Herculean bow
Descended, Philoctetes, Pœas' son;
Whom the two generals and the Ithacan king
Cast out thus shamefully forlorn, distressed
With the fierce malady and desperate wound
Caused by the cruel basilisk's murderous tooth.
With this for company they left me, child!
Exposed upon this shore, deserted, lone.

   From seaward Chrysa came they with their fleet
And touched at Lemnos. I had fallen to rest
From the long tossing, in a shadowy cave
On yonder cliff by the shore. Gladly they saw,
And left me, having set forth for my need,
Poor man! some scanty rags, and a thin store
Of provender. Such food be theirs, I pray!
Imagine, oh my son, when they were gone,
What wakening, what arising, then was mine;
What weeping, what lamenting of my woe!
When I beheld the ships, wherewith I sailed,
Gone, one and all! and no man in the place,
None to bestead me, none to comfort me
In my sore sickness. And where'er I looked,
Nought but distress was present with me still.
No lack of that, for one thing!—Ah! my son,
Time passed, and there I found myself, alone,
Within my narrow lodging, forced to serve
Each pressing need. For body's sustenance

This bow supplied me with sufficient store,
Wounding the feathered doves, and when the shaft,
From the tight string, had struck, myself, ay me!
Dragging this foot, would crawl to my swift prey.
Then water must be fetched, and in sharp frost
Wood must be found and broken,—all by me.
Nor would fire come unbidden, but with flint
From flints striking dim sparks, I hammered forth
The struggling flame that keeps the life in me.
For houseroom with the single help of fire
Gives all I need, save healing for my sore.

Now learn, my son, the nature of this isle.
No mariner puts in here willingly.
For it hath neither moorage, nor sea-port,
For traffic or kind shelter or good cheer.
Not hitherward do prudent men make voyage.
Perchance one may have touched against his will.
Many strange things may happen in long time.
These, when they come, in words have pitied me,
And given me food, or raiment, in compassion.
But none is willing, when I speak thereof,
To take me safely home.   Wherefore I pine
Now this tenth year, in famine and distress,
Feeding the hunger of my ravenous plague.

Such deeds, my son, the Atridæ, and the might
Of wise Odysseus, have performed on me.
Wherefore may all the Olympian gods, one day,
Plague them with sharp requital for my wrong!

Ch. Methinks my feeling for thee, Pœas' child,
Is like that of thy former visitants.

Neo. I, too, a witness to confirm his words,
Know them for verities, since I have found
The Atridæ and Odysseus evil men.
   Phi. Art thou, too, wrath with the all-pestilent sons
Of Atreus ?   Have they given thee cause to grieve ?
   Neo. Would that my hand might ease the wrath I
       feel !
Then Sparta and Mycenæ should be ware
That Scyros too breeds valiant sons for war.
   Phi. Brave youth ! I love thee.   Tell me the great
       cause
Why thou inveighest against them with such heat ?
   Neo. O son of Pœas, hardly shall I tell
What outrage I endured when I had come ;
Yet I will speak it.   When the fate of death
O'ertook Achilles——
   Phi.   Out, alas ! no more !
Hold, till thou first hast made me clearly know,
Is Peleus' offspring dead ?
   Neo.   Alas ! he is,
Slain by no mortal, felled by Phœbus' shaft :
So men reported.
   Phi.   Well, right noble was he !
And noble is he who slew him.   Shall I mourn
Him first, or wait till I have heard thy tale ?
   Neo. Methinks thou hast enough to mourn, poor man !
Without the burden of another's woe.
   Phi. Well said.   Renew thy speech then, and declare
Once more the act wherewith they insulted thee.
   Neo. There came to fetch me, in a gallant ship,

Odysseus and the fosterer of my sire,*
Saying, whether soothly, or in idle show,
That, since my father perished, it was known,
None else but I should take Troy's citadel.
Such words from them, my friend, thou may'st believe,
Held me not long from making voyage with speed,
Chiefly through longing for my father's corse,
To see him yet unburied,—for I ne'er
Had seen him.   Then, besides, 'twas a fair cause,
If, by my going, I should vanquish Troy.
One day I had sailed, and on the second came
To sad Sigeum with wind-favoured speed,
When straightway all the host, surrounding me
As I set foot on shore, saluted me,
And swore the dead Achilles was in life,
Their eyes being witness, when they looked on me.
He lay there in his shroud : but I, unhappy,
Soon ending lamentation for the dead,
Went near to those Atridæ, as to friends,
To ask my father's armour and all else
That had been his.   And then,—alas the while,
That men should be so hard !—they spake this word :
" Seed of Achilles, thou may'st freely take
All else thy father owned, but for those arms,
Another wields them now, Laërtes' son."
Tears rushed into mine eyes, and in hot wrath
I straightway rose, and bitterly outspake :

* Phœnix, the tutor of Achilles.
† The legend which makes Achilles go to Troy from Scyros is
probably ignored.

"O miscreant ! What ? And have ye dared to give
Mine arms to some man else, unknown to me ?"
Then said Odysseus, for he chanced to be near,
"Yea, child, and justly have they given me these. ·
I saved them and their master in the field."
Then in fierce anger all at once I launched
All terms of execration at his head,
Bating no word, as maddened by the thought
That I should lose this heirloom,—and to him !
He, at this pass, though not of wrathful mood,
Stung by such utterance, made rejoinder thus :·
"Thou wast not with us here, but wrongfully
Didst bide afar. And, since thou mak'st so bold,
I tell thee, never shall thou, as thou sayest,
Sail with these arms to Scyros."—Thus reviled,
With such an evil echo in mine ear,
I voyage homeward, rifled of mine own
By that vile offset of an evil tree.*
Yet less I blame him than the men in power.
For every multitude, be it host or state,
Takes tone from those who rule it, and all taint
Of disobedience from bad counsel springs.
I have spoken. May the Atridæ's enemy
Be dear to Heaven, as he is loved by me !

   Ch. 1. Mother of mightiest Zeus,
       Feeder of all that live,
       Who from thy mountainous breast

* Odysseus was said by his enemies to be the son, not really of
Laërtes, but of Sisyphus.

Rivers of gold dost give!
To thee, O Earth, I cried that shameful day,
When insolence from Atreus' sons went forth
Full on our lord : when they bestowed away
His father's arms to crown Odysseus' worth ;
Thou, whom bull-slaughtering lions yokèd bear,
O mighty mother, hear!

Phi. Your coming is commended by a grief
That makes you kindly welcome.   For I feel
A chord that vibrates to your voice, and tells,
Thus have Odysseus and the Atridæ wrought.
Full well I know, Odysseus' poisoned tongue
Shrinks from no mischief nor no guileful word,
That leads to bad achievement in the end.
This moveth not my marvel, but if one
Saw this and bore it,—Aias the elder-born.
　Neo. Ah, friend, he was no more.   Had he but lived,
This robbery had ne'er been wrought on me.
　Phi. What?   Is he too departed?
　Neo.　　　　　　　　　　　He is dead.
The light no more beholds him.
　Phi.　　　　　　　　　Oh! alas!
But Tydeus' offspring, and the rascal birth
Laërtes bought of Sisyphus, they live :
I know it.   For their death were to be wished.
　Neo. Yea, be assured, they live and flourish high,
Exalted in the host of Argive men.
　Phi. And Nestor, my old friend, good aged man,
Is he yet living?   Oft he would prevent

Their evils, by the wisdom of his thought.

   Neo. He too is now in trouble, having lost
Antilochus, the son he had at Troy.

   Phi. There, there! In one brief word thou hast re-
        vealed
The mournful case of twain, whom I would last
Have chosen to hear of as undone.   Ah me !
Where must one look ? when these are dead, and he,
Odysseus, lives,—and in a time like this,
That craves their presence, and his death for theirs.

   Neo. He wrestles cleverly ; but, O my friend,
Even clever wits are ofttimes snared at last.

   Phi. Tell me, I pray, what was become of him,
Patroclus, whom thy father loved so well ?

   Neo. He, too, was gone.   I'll teach thee in a word
One truth for all.   War doth not willingly
Snatch off the wicked, but still takes the good.

   Phi. True, and to prove thy saying, I will inquire
The fate of a poor dastard, of mean worth,
But ever shrewd and nimble with his tongue.

   Neo. Whom but Odysseus canst thou mean by this ?

   Phi. I meant not him.   But there was one Thersites,
Who ne'er made conscience to stint speech, where all
Cried "Silence !"   Is he living, dost thou know ?

   Neo. I saw him not, but knew he was alive.

   Phi. He must be : for no evil yet was crushed.
The Heavens will ever shield it.   'Tis their sport
To turn back all things rancorous and malign
From going down to the grave, and send instead
The good and true.   Oh, how shall we commend

Such acts, how construe them?   When I extol
Things god-like, I find evil in the Gods.
  Neo. I, O thou child of a Trachinian sire,
Henceforth will take good care, from far away
To look on Troy and Atreus' children twain.
Yea, where the worse man lords it o'er the just,
And goodness languishes and rascals rule,
—Such courses I will nevermore endure.
But rock-bound Scyros henceforth shall suffice
To yield me full contentment in my home.
Now, to my vessel!   And thou, Pœas' child,
Farewell, most heartily farewell!   May Heaven
Grant thy desire, and rid thee of thy plague!
Let us be going, that when God shall give
Fair voyage, that moment we may launch away.
  Phi. My son, are ye now setting forth?
  Neo.   Our time
Bids us go near and look to sail erelong.
  Phi. Now by thy father, by thy mother,—nay,
By all thy love e'er cherished in thy home,
Suppliant I beg thee, leave me not thus lone,
Forlorn in all my misery. which thou seest,
In all thou hast heard of here surrounding me!
But take me by the way.   Such freight, I know,
Is full of trouble and vexatious care.
Yet venture!   Surely to the noble mind
All shame is hateful and all kindness blest.
And shame would be thy meed, didst thou fail here,
But, in thus doing, thou shalt have glorious fame,
When I return alive to Œta's vale.

Come, 'tis the labour not of one whole day.
So thou durst take me, fling me where thou wilt
O' the ship, in hold, prow, stern, or wheresoe'er
I may least trouble those on board with me.
Ah! by great Zeus, the suppliant's friend, comply,
My son, be softened! See, where I am fall'n
Thus on my knees before thee, though so weak,
Crippled and powerless. Ah! forsake me not
Thus far from human footstep. Take me, take me!
If only to thy home, or to the stalls
Of old Chalcodon * in Eubœa.—From thence
I have not far to Œta, and the ridge
Of Trachis, and Spercheius flowing mild.
So thou shalt bless my father with my sight.
And yet I fear he may be long since gone.
For oft I sent him suppliant prayers by men
Who touched this isle, entreating him to fetch
And bear me safely home with his own crew.
But either he is dead, or else, methinks,
It well may be, my messengers made light
Of my concerns, and hastened onward home.
But now in thee I find both messenger
And convoy, thou wilt pity me and save.
For, well thou knowest, danger never sleeps,
And fear of dark reverse is always nigh.
Mortals, when free, should look where mischief lurks,
And in their happiest hour consider well
Their life, lest ruin unsuspected come.

* Chalcodon was a friend and neighbour of Pœas, the father of
Philoctetes.

Ch. 2.   Pity him, O my king !
                 Many a crushing woe
                 He telleth, such as I pray
                 None of my friends may know.
          And if, dear master, thou mislikest sore
          Yon cruel-hearted lordly pair, I would,
          Turning their plan of evil to his good,
          On swift ship bear him to his native shore,
          Meeting his heart's desire ; and free thy path
                 From fear of heavenly wrath.

Neo. Thou mak'st small scruple here ; but be advised :
Lest, when this plague on board shall weary thee,
Thy voice should alter from this liberal tone.
     Ch. No, truly !   Fear not thou shalt ever have
Just cause to utter this reproach on me.
     Neo. Then sure 'twere shame, should I more backward prove
          prove
Than thou, to labour for the stranger's need.
Come, if thou wilt, let us make voyage, and he,
Let him set forth with speed.   Our ship shall take him.
He shall not be refused.   Only may Heaven
Lead safely hence and to our destined port !
     Phi. O morning full of brightness !   Kindest friend,
Sweet mariners, how can I make you feel,
In act, how dearly from my heart I love you !
Ye have won my soul.   Let us be gone, my son,—
First having said farewell to this poor cave,
My homeless dwelling-place, that thou may'st know,
How barely I have lived, how firm my heart !

Methinks another could not have endured
The very sight of what I bore.   But I
Through strong necessity have conquered pain.
    Ch. Stay : let us understand.   There come two men,
A stranger, with a shipmate of thy crew.
When ye have heard them, ye may then go in.

Enter Messenger, *disguised as a merchantman.*

Merchantman. Son of Achilles, my companion here,
Who with two more remained to guard thy ship,
Agreed to show me where thou wert, since I
Most unexpectedly, through fortune's will,
Have met thee, mooring by the self-same shore.
For like a merchantman, with no great sail,
Making my course from Ilion to my home,
Grape-clustered Peparethos, when I heard
The mariners declare that one and all
Were of thy crew, I would not launch again,
Without a word, till we had told our news.—
Methinks thou knowest nought of thine own case,
What new devices of the Argive chiefs
Surround thee ; nor devices only now,
But active deeds, no longer unperformed.
    Neo. Well, stranger, for the kindness thou hast shown,—
Else were I base,—my heart must thank thee still.
But tell me what thou meanest, that I may learn
What new-laid plot thou bring'st me from the camp.
    Mer. Old Phœnix, Acamas and Demophon
Are gone in thy pursuit with ships and men.
    Neo. To bring me back with reasons or perforce ?

Mer. I know not.   What I heard, I am here to tell.

Neo. How?   And is this in act?   Are they set forth
To please the Atridæ, Phœnix and his men?

Mer. The thing is not to do, but doing now.

Neo. What kept Odysseus back, if this be so,
From going himself?   Had he some cause for fear?

Mer. He and the son of Tydeus, when our ship
Hoist sail, were gone to fetch another man.

Neo. For whom could he himself be sailing forth?

Mer. For one,—but tell me first, and whisper low
Whate'er thou speakest,—who is this I see?

Neo. (*speaking aloud*). This, sir, is Philoctetes the re-
      nowned.

Mer. (*aside to* NEOPTOLEMUS). Without more question,
      snatch thyself away
And sail forth from this land.

Phi.   What saith he, boy?
Through what dark traffic is the mariner
Betraying me with whispering in thine ear?

Neo. I have not caught it, but whate'er he speaks
He must speak openly to us and thee.

Mer. Seed of Achilles, let me not offend
The army by my words! Full many a boon,
Being poor, I reap from them for service done.

Neo. The Atridæ are my foes; the man you see
Is my fast friend, because he hates them sore.
Then, if you come as friendly, you must hide
Nothing from him or me of all thou hast heard.

Mer. See what thou doest, my son!

Neo.   I see it well.

Mer. Thou shalt be answerable.

Neo.   Content : but speak.

Mer. Then hear me.   These two men whom I have
   named,
Diomedes and Odysseus, are set forth
Engaged on oath to bring this man by force
If reasons fail.   The Achæans every one
Have heard this plainly from Odysseus' mouth.
He was the louder and more confident.

Neo. Say, for what cause, after so long a time,
Can Atreus' sons have turned their thoughts on him,
Whom so long since they had cast forth?   What touch
Of conscience moved them, or what stroke from Heaven,
Whose wrath requites all wicked deeds of men ?

Mer. Methinks thou hast not heard what I will now
Unfold to thee.   There was a princely seer,
A son of Priam, Helenus by name,
Whom he for whom no word is bad enough,
Crafty Odysseus, sallying forth alone
One night, had taken, and in bonds displayed
'Fore all the Achæans, a right noble prey,
He, 'mid his other prophecies, foretold,
No Grecian force should sack Troy's citadel,
Till with fair reasons they had brought this man
From off this isle, his lonely dwelling-place.

When thus the prophet spake, Laërtes' son
Straight undertook to bring and show this man
To all the camp :—he hoped, with fair consent :
But else, perforce.—And, if he failed in this,
Whoever would might smite him on the head.

My tale is told, dear youth.   I counsel speed
To thee and to the man for whom thou carest.
   Phi. Ah me, unhappy ! has that rascal knave
Sworn to fetch me with reasons to their camp?
As likely might his reasons bring me back,
Like his begetter, from the house of death.
   Mer. You talk of what I know not.   I will go
Shipward.   May God be with you for all good.   [*Exit.*

   Phi. Is not this terrible, Laërtes' son
Should ever think to bring me with soft words
And show me from his deck to all the host ?
No ! Sooner will I listen to the tongue
Of the curs'd basilisk that thus hath maim'd me.
   Ay, but he'll venture anything in word
Or deed.   And now I know he will be here.
Come, O my son, let us be gone, while seas
And winds divide us from Odysseus' ship.
Let us depart.   Sure timely haste brings rest
And quiet slumber when the toil is done.
   Neo. Shall we not sail when this south-western wind
Hath fallen, that now is adverse to our course?
   Phi. All winds are fair to him who flies from woe.
   Neo. Nay, but this head-wind hinders them no less.
   Phi. No head-wind hinders pirates on their way,
When violence and rapine lead them on.
   Neo. Well, then, let us be going, if you will;
When you have taken from within the cave
What most you need and value.
   Phi.   Though my all

Be little, there is that I must not lose.

 Neo. What can there be that we have not on board?

 Phi. A leaf I have found, wherewith I still the rage
Of my sore plague, and lull it quite to rest.

 Neo. Well, bring it forth.—-What?   Is there something
  more?

 Phi. If any of these arrows here are fallen,
I would not leave them for a casual prey.

 Neo. How?   Do I see thee with the marvellous bow?

 Phi. Here in my hand.   The world has only one.

 Neo. And may one touch and handle it, and gaze
With reverence, as on a thing from Heaven?

 Phi. Thou mayest, my son.   This and whate'er of
  mine
May stead thee, 'tis thy privilege to enjoy.

 Neo. In very truth I long for it, but so,
That longing waits on leave.   Am I permitted?

 Phi. Thou art, my son,—and well thou speakest,—
  thou art.
Thou, that hast given me life and light, the joy
Of seeing Mount Œta and my father's home,
With all I love there, and his aged head,—
Thou that hast raised my head above my foes
Who triumphed!   Thou may'st take it in thine hand,
And,—when thou hast given it back to me,—may'st
  vaunt
Alone of mortals for thine excellence
To have held this in thy touch.   I, too, at first,
Received it as a boon for kindness done.

 Neo. Well, go within.

Phi.   Nay, I must take thee too.
My sickness craves thee for its comforter.

  [PHILOCTETES *and* NEOPTOLEMUS *go into the cave.*

CHORUS.

In fable I have heard,
Though sight hath ne'er confirmed the word,
That he, who pressed the couch of the Most High,
Was cast by the All-father on a wheel,
Tied head and heel,
Still bound,
Ever around
To fly.
None else I have known by hearsay nor by sight,
Whose hateful plight
Could be compared with his I see !
O depth of misery,
For one who did no theft or violent deed,
But rather earned the meed
Of justice, had he dwelt among the just !
Who now is thrust
Away in solitude to hear the billows roar,
That break around the shore !
How could a life so sad remain in light ?

Where neighbour there was none,
Saving himself alone,
No arm to stay his faltering steps and sore,
No echo to his moan

From hearts to whom his pangs he might deplore !
   None, who whene'er the bloody flow
Came o'er him, and the issue from his wound
Was rushing hot, might healing herbs bestow,
Or pluck them from the grassy ground,
To soothe the sharpness of his hideous woe !
  Like infant whom the nurse lets go,
With tottering footsteps here and there
He crawled for comfort, whensoe'er
His soul-consuming torment left him free :—

Not fed on produce of boon earth, which we
Find to sustain us, ever-toiling men,
   But only now and then
With wingèd things, by his wing'd shafts brought low,
He stayed his hunger from his bow.
Poor soul, that never once in ten years' space
   Brightened his face
   With the fruit of the vine,
  But still returning to some standing pool,
  Nor clear nor cool,
   Drank it for wine !

But now, consorted with the hero's child,
He winneth greatness and a joyful change
From that low state : over the water wild
Borne by the friendly bark beneath the range
Of Œta, where Spercheius fills
Calm basins between lovely hills
Haunted of Melian nymphs, till he espies

The roof-tree of his father's hall,
 And high o'er all
Gleams the majestic form, whose home is in the skies.*
 [NEOPTOLEMUS *comes out of the cave, followed*
  by PHILOCTETES *in pain.*

Neo. Prithee, come on ! Why dost thou stand aghast,
Voiceless, and thus astonied in thine air ?
Phi. Oh ! oh !
Neo.   What ?
Phi.   Nothing. Come my son, fear nought.
Neo. Is pain upon thee? Has thy trouble come ?
Phi. No pain, no pain ! 'Tis past ; I am easy now.
Ye heavenly powers !
Neo.   Why dost thou groan aloud,
And cry to Heaven ?
Phi.   To come and save. Kind Heaven!
Oh, oh !
Neo. What is't ? Why silent ? Wilt not speak ?
I see thy misery.
Phi.   Oh ! I am lost my son !
I cannot hide it from you. Oh ! it shoots,
It pierces. Oh unhappy ! Oh ! my woe !
I am lost, my son, I am devoured. Oh me !
O ! O ! O ! O ! Pain ! pain ! Oh pain ! oh pain !
Child, if a sword be to thine hand, smite hard,
Shear off my foot ! heed not my life ! Quick, come !
Neo. What hath so suddenly arisen, that thus
Thou makest ado and groanest o'er thyself ?

* Heracles, imagined as standing transfigured upon Mount Œta.

Phi. Thou knowest.

Neo. What know I?

Phi. O! thou knowest, my son!

Neo. I know not.

Phi. How? Not know? Ah me! Pain, pain!

Neo. Thy plague is a sore burden, heavy and sore.

Phi. Sore? 'Tis unutterable. Have pity on me!

Neo. What shall I do?

Phi. Do not in fear forsake me.
This wandering evil comes in force again,
Hungry as ere it fed.

Neo. O hapless one!
Thrice hapless in thy manifold distress!
What wilt thou? Shall I raise thee on mine arm?

Phi. Nay, but receiving from my hand the bow,
As late thou didst desire me, keep it safe
And guard it, till this fury of my pain
Pass over me and cease. For when 'tis spent,
Slumber will seize me, else it ne'er would end.
I must sleep undisturbed. But if meanwhile
They come,—by Heaven I charge thee, in no wise,
Willingly nor perforce, let them have this!
Else thou wilt be the slayer of us both;
Of me thy suppliant, and of thyself.

Neo. Fear not my care. No hand shall hold these
    arms
But thine and mine. Give, and Heaven bless the deed!

Phi. I give them; there, my son! But look to
    Heaven
And pray no envy smite thee, nor such bane

In having them, as fell on me and him
Who bore them formerly.

 Neo.   O grant it, Gods !
And grant us fair and happy voyage, where'er
Our course is shaped and righteous Heaven shall guide.

 Phi. Ah ! but I fear, my son, thy prayer is vain :
For welling yet again from depths within,
This gory ooze is dripping. It will come !
I know it will. Oh, foot, torn helpless thing,
What wilt thou do to me ? Ah ! ah ! It comes,
It is at hand. 'Tis here ! Woe's me, undone !
I have shown you all Stay near me. Go not far.
Ah ! ah !
O island king, I would this agony
Might cleave thy bosom through and through ! Woe,
   woe,
Woe ! Ah ! ye two commanders of the host,
Agamemnon, Menelaus, oh that ye,
Another ten years' durance in my room
Might nurse this malady ! O Death, Death, Death !
I call thee daily—wilt thou never come ?
Will it not be ?—My son, thou noble boy,
If thou art noble, take and burn me there
Aloft in yonder worshipped Lemnian fire.
Yea, when that bow was my reward, I once
Performed like service for the son of Zeus.
How now, my son?
What say'st ? Art silent ? Where—where art thou,
   boy ?

 Neo. My heart is full, and groaning o'er thy woes.

Phi. Nay, yet have comfort.   This affliction oft
Goes no less swiftly than it came.   I pray thee,
Stand fast and leave me not alone !

Neo.   Fear nought :
We will not stir.

Phi.   Wilt thou remain ?

Neo.   Be sure of it.

Phi. I'll not degrade thee with an oath, my son.

Neo. Rest satisfied.   I may not go without thee.

Phi. Thy hand, to pledge me that !

Neo.   There, I will stay.

Phi. Now, now, aloft !

Neo.   Where mean'st thou ?

Phi.   Yonder aloft !

Neo. Whither ?   Thou rav'st.   Why starest thou at
     the sky ?

Phi. Now, let me go.

Neo.   Where ?

Phi.   Let me go, I say !

Neo. I will not.

Phi.   You will kill me.   Let me go !

Neo. Well, thou know'st best.   I hold thee not.

Phi.   O Earth,
I die : receive me to thy breast !   This pain
Subdues me utterly ; I cannot stand.

Neo. Methinks he will be fast in slumber soon.
This head sinks backward, and a clammy sweat
Bathes all his limbs, while from his foot hath burst
A vein, dark-bleeding.   Let us leave him, friends,
In quietness, till he hath fallen to sleep.

CHORUS.

Lord of the happiest life,
Sleep, thou that know'st not strife,
    That know'st not grief,
Still wafting sure relief,
    Come, saviour, now !
Thy healing light is spread .
Over this pain-worn head ;
Quench not the light * that gives calm to his brow.

Look, O my lord, to thy path,
Either to go or to stay :
How is my thought to proceed ?
What is our cause for delay ?
Look !   Opportunity's power,
Fitting the task to the hour,
Giveth the race to the swift.

Neo. He hears not.   But I see that to have ta'en
His bow without him were a bootless gain.
He must sail with us.   So the god hath said.
Heaven hath decreed this garland for his head :
And to have failed with falsehood were a meed
Of shameful soilure for a shameless deed.

Ch.   God shall determine the end :—
      But for thine answer, O friend,
          Waft soft words low !
      All sick men's sleep, we know,

* *Or,* Loose not the band.

> Hath open eye ; .
> Their quickly ruffling mind
> Quivers in lightest wind,
> Sleepless in slumber new danger to spy.

> Think, O my lord, of thy path,
> Secretly look forth afar,
> What wilt thou do for thy need ?
> How with the wise wilt thou care ?
> If toward the nameless thy heart
> Chooseth this merciful part,
> Huge are the dangers that drift.

The wind is fair, my son, the wind is fair,
The man is dark and helpless, stretched in night.
(O kind warm sleep that calmest human care !)
Powerless of hand and foot and ear and sight,
Blind, as one lying in the house of death :
(Think well if here thou utterest timely breath.)
This, O my son, is all my thought can find,
Best are the toils that without frightening bind.

  Neo. Hush ! One word more were madness. He
    revives.
His eye hath motion. He uplifts his head.
  Phi. Fair daylight following sleep, and ye, dear
    friends,
Faithful beyond all hope in tending me !
I never could have dreamed that thou, dear youth,
Couldst thus have borne my sufferings and stood near

So full of pity to relieve my pain.
Not so the worthy generals of the host ;—
This princely patience was not theirs to show.
Only thy noble nature, nobly sprung,
Made light of all the trouble, though oppressed
With fetid odours and unceasing cries.
And now, since this my plague would seem to yield
Some pause and brief forgetfulness of pain,
With thine own hand, my son, upraise me here,
And set me on my feet, that, when my strength
After exhaustion shall return again,
We may move shoreward and launch forth with speed.

   Neo. I feel unhoped for gladness when I see
Thy painless gaze, and hear thy living breath,
For thine appearance and surroundings both
Were deathlike.   But arise !   Or, if thou wilt,
These men shall raise thee.   For they will not shrink
From toil, where thy command and mine are one.

   Phi. Right, right, my son ! But lift me thine own self,
As I am sure thou meanest.   Let these be,
Lest they be burdened with the noisome smell
Too soon.   Enough for them the task on board
Of living near me.

   Neo.   Well, stand up, endure !
   Phi. Fear not.   Old custom will enable me.

   Neo. Oh me !
What shall I do ?   Now 'tis my turn to exclaim !
   Phi. What can the matter be ?   What change is here,
My son ?

Neo.   I know not how to shift the word.
'Tis hopeless.

Phi.   What is hopeless?   Speak not so,
Dear child !

Neo.   But so my wretched lot hath fallen.

Phi. Ah ! Can it be, the offence of my disease
Hath moved thee not to take me now on board ?

Neo. All is offence to one who hath forced himself
From the true bent to an unbecoming deed.

Phi. Nought misbecoming to thyself or sire
Doest thou or speak'st, befriending a good man.

Neo. My baseness will appear.   That wrings my soul.

Phi. Not in thy deeds.   But for thy words, I fear me !

Neo. O Heaven ! Must double vileness then be mine,
Both shameful silence and most shameful speech ?

Phi. Or my discernment is at fault, or thou
Mean'st to betray me and make voyage without me.

Neo. Nay, not without thee, there is my distress !
Lest I convey thee to thy bitter grief.

Phi. How ? how, dear son ?   I do not comprehend.

Neo. Here I unveil it.   Thou art to sail to Troy,
To join the chieftains and the Achæan host.

Phi. What do I hear ?   Ah !

Neo.   Grieve not till you learn.

Phi. Learn what ? What wilt thou make of me ? What
        mean'st thou ?

Neo. First to release thee from this plague, and then
With thee to go and take the realm of Troy.

Phi. And is this thine intent ?

Neo.   'Tis so ordained

Unchangeably.   Be not dismayed !   'Tis so.
  Phi. Me miserable !   I am betrayed, undone !
What guile is here ?   My bow ! give back my bow !
  Neo. I may not.   Interest, and duty too,
Force me to obey commandment.
  Phi.   O thou fire,
Thou terror of the world !   Dark instrument
Of ever-hateful guile !—What hast thou done ?
How hast thou cheated me !   Art not ashamed
To look on him that sued to thee for shelter ?
O heart of stone, thou hast stolen my life away
With yonder bow !—Ah, yet I beg of thee,
Give it me back, my son, I entreat thee, give !
By all thy father worshipped, rob me not
Of life !   Ah me !   Now he will speak no more,
But turns away, obdúrate to retain it.
O ye, my comrades in this wilderness,
Rude creatures of the rocks, O promontories,
Creeks, precipices of the hills, to you
And your familiar presence I complain
Of this foul trespass of Achilles' son.
Sworn to convey me home, to Troy he bears me.
And under pledge of his right hand hath ta'en
And holds from me perforce my wondrous bow,
The sacred gift of Zeus-born Heracles,
Thinking to wave it midst the Achæan host
Triumphantly for his.   In conquering me
He vaunts as of some valorous feat, and knows not
He is spoiling a mere corse, an empty dream,
The shadow of a vapour.   In my strength

He ne'er had vanquished me.   Even as I am,
He could not, but by guile.   Now, all forlorn,
I am abused, deceived.   What must I do?
Nay, give it me.   Nay, yet be thy true self!
Thou art silent.   I am lost.   O misery!
Rude face of rock, back I return to thee
And thy twin gateway, robbed of arms and food,
To wither in thy cave companionless :——
No more with these mine arrows to destroy
Or flying bird or mountain-roving beast.
But, all unhappy!   I myself must be
The feast of those on whom I fed, the chase
Of that I hunted, and shall dearly pay
In bloody quittance for their death, through one
Who seemed all ignorant of sinful guile.
Perish,—not till I am certain if thy heart
Will change once more,—if not, my curse on thee!

 Ch. What shall we do, my lord?   We wait thy word
Or to sail now, or yield to his desire.

 Neo. My heart is pressed with a strange pity for him,
Not now commencing, but continued long.

 Phi. Ay, pity me, my son! by all above,
Make not thy name a scorn by wronging me!

 Neo. O! I am troubled sore.   What must I do?
Would I had never left mine island home!

 Phi. Thou art not base, but seemest to have learnt
Some baseness from base men.   Now, as 'tis meet,
Be better guided—leave me mine arms, and go.

 Neo. (to Chorus). What shall we do?

Enter ODYSSEUS.

Odysseus.   What art thou doing, knave ?
Give me that bow, and haste thee back again.

  Phi. Alas !   What do I hear ?   Odysseus' voice ?

  Od. Be sure of that.   Odysseus, whom thou seest.

  Phi. Oh, I am bought and sold, undone !   'Twas he,
That kidnapped me, and robbed me of my bow.

  Od. Yea.   I deny it not.   Be sure, 'twas I.

  Phi. Give back, my son, the bow, release it !

  Od.   That,
Though he desire it, he shall never do.
Thou too shalt march along, or these shall force thee.

  Phi. They force me !   O thou boldest of bad men !
They force me ?

  Od.   If thou com'st not willingly.

  Phi. O Lemnian earth and thou almighty flame,
Hephæstos' workmanship, shall this be borne,
That he by force must drag me from your care ?

  Od. 'Tis Zeus, I tell thee, monarch of this isle,
Who thus hath willed.   I am his minister.

  Phi. Wretch, what vile words thy wit hath power to
       say !
The gods are liars when called in by thee.

  Od. Nay, 'tis their truth compels thee to this voyage.

  Phi. I will not have it so.

  Od.   I will.   Thou shalt.

  Phi. Woe for my wretchedness !   My father, then,
Begat no freeman, but a slave in me.

  Od. Nay, but the peer of noblest men, with whom

Thou art to take and ravage Troy with might.
 Phi. Never,—though I must suffer direst woe,—
While this steep Lemnian ground is mine to tread !
 Od. What now is thine intent ?
 Phi.   Down from the crag
This head shall plunge and stain the crag beneath.
 Od. Ay, seize and bind him. Baffle him in this.
 Phi. Poor hands, for lack of your beloved string,
Caught by this craven ! O corrupted soul !
How thou hast undermined me, having ta'en
To screen thy quest this youth to me unknown,
Far worthier of my friendship than of thine,
Who knew no better than to obey command.
Even now 'tis manifest he burns within
With pain for his own error and my wrong.
But, though unwilling and inapt for ill,
Thy crafty, mean, and cranny-spying soul
Too well hath lessoned him in sinful lore.
Now thou hast bound me, O thou wretch, and thinkest
To take me from this coast, where thou didst cast me
Outlawed and desolate, a corse 'mong men.
 Oh !
I curse thee now, as ofttimes in the past :
But since Heaven yields me nought but bitterness,
Thou livest and art blithe, while 'tis my pain
To live on in my misery, laughed to scorn
By thee and Atreus' sons, those generals twain
Whom thou art serving in this chase. But thou
With strong compulsion and deceit was driven
Troyward, whilst I, poor victim, of free will

Took my seven ships and sailed there, yet was thrown
Far from all honour,—as thou sayest, by them,
But, as they turn the tale, by thee.—And now
Why fetch me hence and take me?   To what end?
I am nothing, dead to you this many a year.
How, O thou Heaven-abhorred! am I not now
Lame and of evil smell? how shall ye vaunt
Before the gods drink-offering or the fat
Of victims, if I sail among your crew?
For this, as ye professed, was the chief cause
Why ye disowned me.   Perish!—So ye shall,
For the wrong done me, if the Heavens be just.
And that they are, I know.   Else had ye ne'er
Sailed on this errand for an outcast wretch,
Had they not pricked your heart with thoughts of me.
Oh, if ye pity me, chastising powers,
And thou, the genius of my land, revenge,
Revenge this crime on all their heads at once!
My life is pitiable; but if I saw
Their ruin, I would think me well and strong.
   Ch. How full of bitterness is his resolve,
Sullenly spoken with unbending will!
   Od. I might speak long in answer, did the time
Give scope, but now one thing is mine to say.
I am known to vary with the varying need;
And when 'tis tried, who can be just and good,
My peer will not be found for piety.
But though on all occasions covetous
Of victory, this once I yield to thee,
And willingly.   Unhand him there.   Let go!

Leave him to stay.   What further need of thee,
When we have ta'en these arms?   Have we not Teucer,
Skilled in this mystery?   Yea, I may boast
Myself thine equal both in strength and aim
To wield them.   Fare thee well then !   Thou art free
To roam thy barren isle.   We need thee not.
Let us be going | And perchance thy gift
May bring thy destined glory to my brow.

 Phi. What shall I do?   Alas, shalt thou be seen
Graced with mine arms amongst Achæan men ?·

 Od. No more !   I am going.
 Phi.   O Achilles' child !
Wilt thou, too, vanish?   Must I lose thy voice ?

 Od. Come on and look not, noble as thou art,
Lest thou undo our fortune.   [*Exit.*

 Phi.   Mariners,
Must ye, too, leave me thus disconsolate ?
Will ye not pity me ?

 Ch.   Our captain's here.
Whate'er he saith to thee, that we too speak.

 Neo. My chief will call me weakling, soft of heart,
But go not yet, since our friend bids you stay,
Till we have prayed, and all be ready on board.
Meanwhile, perchance, he may conceive some thought
That favours our design.   We two will start ;
And ye, be swift to speed forth at our call.   [*Exit.*

 Phi. O cavern of the hollow rock
Frosty and stifling in the seasons' change !
How I seem fated never more to range

From thy sad covert, that hath felt the shock
Of pain on pain, steeped with my wretchedness.
Now thou shalt be my comforter in death !
O grief-worn covert, filled with my distress !
Tell me, what hope is mine of daily food,
Who will be careful for my good ?
I fail.   Ye cowering creatures of the sky,
   Oh as ye fly,
Seize me, descending on the blast's sharp breath !
 Ch. 1. Thou child of misery !
   No mightier power hath this decreed,
   But thine own will and deed
   Hath bound thee thus in grief,
Since, when kind Heaven had sent relief
And shown the path of wisdom firm and sure,
Thou still hast chosen this evil to endure.
 Phi. Oh hapless life, sore bruised with pain !
No more with living mortal may I dwell,
But ever pining in this desert cell
In lonely grief, all famished must remain
And perish, for what food is mine to share,
When this strong arm no longer wields my bow,
Whose fleet shafts flew to smite the birds of air ?
I was o'erthrown by words, words dark and blind,
Low-creeping from a traitorous mind !
O might I see him, whose unrighteous thought
   This ruin wrought,
Plagued for no less a period with like woe !
 Ch. 2.   I cannot find
   That thou wast caught by craft of mine,

But destiny divine
Hath thus o'erta'en thee.   Turn away
Thy dreadful curse from us, we pray,
To fall on others ! We shall grieve
If thou wilt not our love receive.

Phi. Now, seated by the shore
Of heaving ocean hoar,
He mocks me, waving high
The sole support of my precarious being,
The bow which none e'er held but I.
O treasure of my heart, torn from this hand,
That loved thy touch,—if thou canst understand,
How sad must be thy look in seeing
Thy master destined now no more,
Like Heracles of yore,
To wield thee with an archer's might !
But in the grasp of an all-scheming wight,
O bitter change ! thou art plied ;
And swaying ever by his side,
Shalt view his life of dark malignity,
Teeming with guileful shames, like those he wrought
    on me.

Ch. 3.   Nobly to speak for the right
Is manly and strong ;
But not with an envious blight
To envenom the tongue ;
And he, as the host had decreed
With a many-voiced word,
Gave help to his nation at need
By commanding our lord.

Phi. Come, legions of the wild,
Fowl from the fields of air,
And beasts, that know not care,
Of aspect fierce or mild,
That walk these savage ways
With bright untroubled gaze,
Come near my cave and stay!
Why should ye flee away?
The might I had, alas! is no more mine,
Stolen with those arms divine.
This fortress hath but feeble guard,
No longer to be fear'd.
Now is your time to swarm
And glut your vengeance on these tainted limbs,
Quivering and warm!
Already death bedims
My fainting sense.   Who thus can live on air,
Tasting no gift of earth that breathing mortals share?
   Ch. 4. Ah! do not shrink from thy friend,
       If love thou reverest,
       But know 'tis for thee to forfend
       The fate which thou fearest.
       The lot thou hast here to deplore,
       Is sad to maintain,
       And hardship in sickness is sore,
       But sorest in pain.
  Phi. Kindest of all that e'er before
Have trod this shore,
Again thou mind'st me of mine ancient woe!
Why wilt thou ruin me?   What wouldst thou do?

Ch. 5. How mean'st thou?

Phi.   If to Troy, of me abhorred,
Thou e'er hast hoped to lead me with thy lord.

Ch. 6. So I judge best.

Phi.   Begone at once, begone!

Ch. 7. Sweet is that word, and swiftly shall be done!
Let us be gone, each to his place on board.

                    [*The Chorus make as if they were going.*

Phi. Nay, by dear Zeus, to whom all suppliants moan,
Leave me not yet!

Ch. 8.   Keep measure in thy word.

Phi. Stay, by Heaven, stay!

Ch. 9. .What wilt thou say?

Phi. O, misery! O, cruel power
That rul'st this hour!
I am destroyed.   Ah me!
O poor torn limb, what shall I do with thee
Through all my days to be?
Ah, strangers, come, return, return!

Ch. 10. What new command are we to learn
Crossing thy former mind?

Phi. Ah! yet be kind.
Reprove not him, whose tongue, with grief distraught,
Obeys not, in dark storms, the helm of thought!

Ch. 11. Come, poor friend, the way we call.

Phi. Never, know it once for all!
Not though he, whom Heaven obeys,
Burn me with fierce lightning's blaze!
Perish Troy, and all your host,

That have chosen, to their cost,
To despise and cast me forth,
Since my plague obscured my worth !
Ah, but, strangers, if your sense
Hath o'er-mastered this offence,
Yield but one thing to my prayer !

 Ch. 12. What wouldst thou have?

 Phi.   Some weapon bare,
Axe or sword or sharpened dart,
Bring it to content my heart.

 Ch. 13. What is thy new intent?

 Phi. To sever point by point
This body, joint from joint.
On bloody death my mind is bent.

 Ch. 14. Wherefore?

 Phi.   To see my father's face.

 Ch. 15. Where upon earth ?

 Phi.   He hath no place
Where sun doth shine, but in the halls of night.
O native country, land of my delight,
Would I were blest one moment with thy sight !
Why did I leave thy sacred dew
And loose my vessels from thy shore,
To join the hateful Danaän crew
And lend them succour ?   Oh, I am no more !

 Ch. 1. Long since thou hadst seen me nearing yonder
   ship,
Had I not spied Odysseus and the son
Of great Achilles hastening to our side.

Od. Wilt thou not tell me why thou art hurrying
This backward journey with reverted speed?

Neo. To undo what I have wrongly done to-day.

Od. Thy words appal me. What is wrongly done?

Neo. When in obeying thee and all the host——

Od. Thou didst what deed that misbecame thy life?

Neo. I conquered with base stratagem and fraud——

Od. Whom? What new plan is rising in thy mind?

Neo. Not new. But to the child of Pœas here——

Od. What wilt thou do? I quake with strange alarm.

Neo. From whom I took these weapons, back
     again——

Od. O Heaven! thou wilt not give them! Mean'st
     thou this?

Neo. Yea, for I have them through base sinful means.

Od. I pray thee, speak'st thou thus to anger me?

Neo. If the truth anger thee, the truth is said.

Od. Achilles' son! What word is fallen from thee?

Neo. Must the same syllables be thrice thrown forth?

Od. Once was too much. Would they might rest
     unsaid!

Neo. Enough. Thou hast heard my purpose clearly
     told.

Od. I know what power shall thwart thee in the deed.

Neo. Whose will shall hinder me?

Od.   The Achæan host,
And I among them.

Neo.   Thou'rt sharp-witted, sure!
But little wit or wisdom show'st thou here.

Od. Neither thy words nor thy design is wise.

Neo. But if 'tis righteous, that is better far.

Od. How, righteous, to release what thou hast ta'en
By my device?

Neo.   I sinned a shameful sin,
And I will do mine utmost to retrieve it.

Od. How! Fear'st thou not the Achæans in this act?

Neo. In doing right I fear not them nor thee.

Od. I call thy power in question.

Neo.   Then I'll fight,
Not with Troy's legions, but with thee.

Od.   Come on !
Let fortune arbitrate.

Neo.   Thou seest mine hand
Feeling the hilt.

Od.   And me thou soon shalt see
Doing the like and dallying not !—And yet
I will not touch thee, but will go and tell
The army, that shall wreak this on thy head.   [*Exit.*

Neo. Thou show'st discretion : which if thou preservest
Hereafter, thou may'st walk exempt from pain.
Ho ! son of Pœas, Philoctetes, come
Forth from thy habitation in the rock.

Phi. What noise again is troubling my poor cave ?
Why do ye summon me ? What crave ye, sirs ?
Ha ! 'tis some knavery. Are ye come to add
Some monster evil to my mountainous woe ?

Neo. Fear not, but hearken to what now I speak.

Phi. I needs must fear thee, whose fair words erewhile
Drew me to bitter fortune.

Neo.   May not men

Repent and change?

Phi.   Such wast thou in thy talk,
When thou didst rob me of my bow,—so bright
Without, so black within.

Neo.   Ah, but not now,
Assure thee! Only let me hear thy will,
Is't constant to remain here and endure,
Or to make voyage with us?

Phi.   Stop, speak no more!
Idle and vain will all thine utterance be.

Neo. Thou art so resolved?

Phi.   More firmly than I say.

Neo. I would I might have brought thee to my mind,
But since my words are out of tune, I have done.

Phi. Thou wert best. No word of thine can touch my
    soul
Or win me to thy love, who by deceit
Hast reft my life away. And then thou com'st
To school me,—of noblest father, basest son!
Perish, the Atridæ first of all, and then
Laërtes' child, and thou!

Neo.   Curse me no more,
But take this hallowed weapon from mine hand.

Phi. What words are these? Am I again deceived?

Neo. No, by the holiest name of Zeus on high!

Phi. O voice of gladness, if thy speech be true!

Neo. The deed shall prove it. Only reach thy hand,
And be again sole master of thy bow.

                    [ODYSSEUS *appears behind.*

Od. But I make protest, in the sight of Heaven,

For Atreus' sons and all the Achæan host.

   Phi. Dear son, whose voice disturbs us ? Do I hear
Odysseus ?

   Od.   Ay, and thou behold'st him nigh,
And he shall force thee to the Trojan plain,
Howe'er Achilles' offspring make or mar.

   Phi. This shaft shall bear thee sorrow for that boast.

   Neo. Let it not fly, by Heaven !

   Phi.   Dear child, let go
Mine arm !

   Neo.   I will not.

   Phi.   Ah ! Why hast thou robbed
My bow of bringing down mine enemy ?

   Neo. This were ignoble both for thee and me.

   Phi. One thing is manifest, the first o' the host,
Lying forerunners of the Achæan band,
Are brave with words, but cowards with the steel.

   Neo. Well, now the bow is thine. Hast thou still cause
Of anger or resentment against me ?

   Phi. None. Thou hast proved thy birthright, dearest
      boy.
Not from the loins of Sisyphus thou camest,
But from Achilles, who in life was held
Noblest of men alive, and now o' the dead.

   Neo. It gladdens me to hear thee bless my sire
And me. But listen, till I show thee once
The boon for which I sue thee.—Mortal men
Must bear such evils as high Heaven ordains,
But those whom self-inflicted troubles find,
Like thine to-day, receive not from just men

Or kind indulgence or compassionate thought.
And thou art restive grown, and wilt not hear;
And if one counsel thee with kind'st intent,
Dost take him for a dark malignant foe.
But, calling Zeus to witness for my soul,
I yet will speak.   Know this, and mark it well.
Thou bear'st this sickness by a heavenly doom,
Through coming near to Chrysa's sentinel,
The lurking snake, that guards the sky-roofed fold.*
And from this plague thou ne'er shall find reprieve
While the same Sun-god rears him from the east
And droops to west again, till thou be come
Of thine own willing mind to Troia's plain,
Where our physicians, sons of Phœbus' child,†
Shall soothe thee from thy sore, and thou with me
And with this bow shalt take Troy's citadel.
How do I know this? I will tell thee straight.
We have a Trojan captive, Helenus,
Both prince and prophet, who hath clearly told .
This must be so; yea, and ere harvest-time
This year, great Troy must fall; else if his words
Be falsified, he bids who will destroy him.
Now, since thou know'st of this, yield thy consent;
For glorious is the gain, being singled forth
From all the Greeks as noblest, first to come
To healing hands, and then to win renown
Unrivalled, vanquishing all-tearful Troy.

  * *I.e.* The open precinct, that was sacred to the goddess, merely
surrounded by a wall.
  † Asclepius.

Phi. O how I hate my life ! Why must it keep
This breathing form from sinking to the shades ?
How can I prove a rebel to his mind
Who thus exhorts me with affectionate heart ?
And yet, O misery ! must I give way ?
Then how could I endure the light of heaven ?
With whom could I exchange a word ? Ay me !
Eyes that have seen each act of my sad life,
How could ye bear it, to behold the sons
Of Atreus, who destroyed me, comrades now
And friends ! Laërtes' wicked son, my friend !
And less I feel the grief of former wrong
Than shudder with expectance of fresh harm
They yet may work on me.   For when the mind
Hath once been mother of an evil brood,
It nurses nought but evils.   Yea, at thee
I marvel.   Thou should'st ne'er return to Troy,
Nor suffer me to go, when thou remember'st
What insult they have done thee, ravishing
Thy father's rights from thee.   And wilt thou then
Sail to befriend them, pressing me in aid ?
Nay, do not, son ; but, even as thou hast sworn,
Convey me home, and thou, in Scyros dwelling,
Leave to their evil doom those evil men.
So thou shalt win a twofold gratitude
From me and from my father, and not seem,
Helping vile men, to be as vile as they.

Neo. 'Tis fairly spoken.   Yet I would that thou,
Relying on my word and on Heaven's aid,
Would'st voyage forth from Lemnos with thy friend.

Phi. Mean'st thou to Troy, and to the hateful sons
Of Atreus, me, with this distressful limb?

Neo. Nay, but to those that will relieve the pain
Of thy torn foot and heal thee of thy plague.

Phi. Thy words are horrible.　What mean'st thou,
　　boy?

Neo. The act I deem the noblest for us both.

Phi. Wilt thou say so? Where is thy fear of Heaven?

Neo. Why should I fear, when I see certain gain?

Phi. How? gain for the Atridæ, or for me?

Neo. Methinks a friend should give thee friendly
　　counsel.

Phi. Friendly, to hand me over to my foes?

Neo. Ah, be not hardened in thy misery!

Phi. I know thou wilt ruin me by what thou speakest.

Neo. Not I.　The case is dark to thee, I see.

Phi. I know the Atridæ cast me on this rock.

Neo. But how, if they should save thee afterward?

Phi. They ne'er shall make me see Troy with my will.

Neo. Hard is my fortune, then, if by no sleight
Of reasoning I can draw thee to my mind.
For me, 'twere easiest to end speech, that thou
Might'st live on as thou livest in hopeless pain.

Phi. Then leave me to my fate!—But thou hast touched
My right hand with thine own, and given consent
To bear me to my home.　Do this, dear son!
And do not linger to take thought of Troy.
Enough that name hath sounded in my groans.

Neo. If thou wilt, let us be going.

Phi.   Nobly hast thou said the word.

Neo. Lean thy steps on mine.

Phi.   As firmly as my foot will strength afford.

Neo. Ah ! but how shall I escape Achæan anger ?

Phi.   Do not care !

Neo. Ah ! but if they spoil my country !

Phi.   I to shield thee will be there.

Neo. How to shield me, how to aid me ?

Phi.   With the shafts of Heracles
I will scare them.

Neo. Give thy blessing to this isle, and come in peace.

HERACLES *appears from above.*

Heracles. First, son of Pœas, wait till thou hast heard
The voice of Heracles, and weighed his word.
Him thou beholdest from the Heavenly seat
Come down, for thee leaving the blest retreat,
To tell thee what high Zeus intends, and stay
Thy purpose in the journey of to-day.

  Then hear me, first how after all my toils
By strange adventure I have found and won
Immortal glory, which thine eyes perceive.
And the like lot, I tell thee, shall be thine,
After these pains to rise to glorious fame.
Sailing with this thy comrade to Troy-town,
First thou shalt heal thee from thy grievous sore,
And then, being singled forth from all the host
As noblest, thou shalt conquer with that bow
Paris, prime author of these years of harm,
And capture Troy, and bear back to thine hall

The choicest guerdon, for thy valour's meed,
To Œta's vale and thine own father's home.
But every prize thou tak'st be sure thou bear
Unto my pyre, in memory of my bow.
    This word, Achilles' offspring, is for thee
No less.   For, as thou could'st not without him,
So, without thee, he cannot conquer Troy.
Then, like twin lions hunting the same hill,
Guard thou him, and he thee ! and I will send
Asclepius Troyward to relieve thy pain.
For Ilion a second time must fall
Before the Herculean bow.   But, take good heed,
Midst all your spoil to hold the gods in awe.
For our great Father counteth piety
Far above all.   This follows men in death,
And fails them not when they resign their breath.

    Phi. Thou whom I have longed to see,
Thy dear voice is law to me.
    Neo. I obey with gladdened heart.
    Her. Lose no time : at once depart !
Bright occasion and fair wind
Urge your vessel from behind.

    Phi. Come, let me bless the region ere I go.
Poor house, sad comrade of my watch, farewell !
Ye nymphs of meadows where soft waters flow,
Thou ocean headland, pealing thy deep knell,
Where oft within my cavern as I lay
My hair was moist with dashing south-wind's spray,

And ofttimes came from Hermes' foreland high
Sad replication of my storm-vext cry;
Ye fountains and thou Lycian water sweet,—
I never thought to leave you, yet my feet
Are turning from your paths,—we part for aye.
Farewell! and send me kindly on my way,
O Lemnian earth enclosed by circling seas,
To sail, where mighty Fate my course decrees,
And friendly voices point me, and the will
Of that heroic power, who doth this act fulfil.

Ch. Come now all in one strong band;
Then, ere loosing from the land,
Pray we to the nymphs of sea
Kind protectresses to be,
Till we touch the Trojan strand.

THE END.

PRINTED BY WILLIAM CLOWES AND SONS, LIMITED, LONDON AND BECCLES.

A LIST OF

KEGAN PAUL, TRENCH & CO.'S

PUBLICATIONS.

3.89

1, *Paternoster Square,*
London.

A LIST OF
KEGAN PAUL, TRENCH & CO.'S
PUBLICATIONS.

CONTENTS.

	PAGE			PAGE
GENERAL LITERATURE.	2	MILITARY WORKS.		33
PARCHMENT LIBRARY	18	POETRY.		34
PULPIT COMMENTARY	20	NOVELS AND TALES		39
INTERNATIONAL SCIENTIFIC		BOOKS FOR THE YOUNG		41
SERIES	29			

GENERAL LITERATURE.

AINSWORTH, W. F.—Personal Narrative of the Euphrates Expedition. 2 vols. Demy 8vo, 32*s.*

A. K. H. B.—From a Quiet Place. A Volume of Sermons. Crown 8vo, 5*s.*

ALEXANDER, William, D.D., Bishop of Derry.—The Great Question, and other Sermons. Crown 8vo, 6*s.*

ALLIES, T. W., M.A.—Per Crucem ad Lucem. The Result of a Life. 2 vols. Demy 8vo, 25*s.*

A Life's Decision. Crown 8vo, 7*s.* 6*d.*

AMHERST, Rev. W. J.—The History of Catholic Emancipation and the Progress of the Catholic Church in the British Isles (chiefly in England) from 1771-1820. 2 vols. Demy 8vo, 24*s.*

AMOS, Professor Sheldon.—The History and Principles of the Civil Law of Rome. An aid to the Study of Scientific and Comparative Jurisprudence. Demy 8vo, 16*s.*

Are Foreign Missions doing any Good? An Enquiry into their Social Effects. Crown 8vo, 1*s.*

ARISTOTLE.—The Nicomachean Ethics of Aristotle. Translated by F. H. Peters, M.A. Third Edition. Crown 8vo, 6*s.*

AUBERTIN, J. J.—A Flight to Mexico. With 7 full-page Illustrations and a Railway Map of Mexico. Crown 8vo, 7s. 6d.

Six Months in Cape Colony and Natal. With Illustrations and Map. Crown 8vo, 6s.

A Fight with Distances. Illustrations and Maps. Crown 8vo, 7s. 6d.

Aucassin and Nicolette. Edited in Old French and rendered in Modern English by F. W. BOURDILLON. Fcap 8vo, 7s. 6d.

BADGER, George Percy, D.C.L.—An English-Arabic Lexicon. In which the equivalent for English Words and Idiomatic Sentences are rendered into literary and colloquial Arabic. Royal 4to, 80s.

BAGEHOT, Walter.—The English Constitution. Fifth Edition. Crown 8vo, 7s. 6d.

Lombard Street. A Description of the Money Market. Ninth Edition. Crown 8vo, 7s. 6d.

Essays on Parliamentary Reform. Crown 8vo, 5s.

Some Articles on the Depreciation of Silver, and Topics connected with it. Second Edition. Demy 8vo, 5s.

BAGOT, Alan, C.E.—Accidents in Mines: their Causes and Prevention. Crown 8vo, 6s.

The Principles of Colliery Ventilation. Second Edition, greatly enlarged. Crown 8vo, 5s.

The Principles of Civil Engineering as applied to Agriculture and Estate Management. Crown 8vo, 7s. 6d.

BAKER, Ella.—Kingscote Essays and Poems. Fcap 8vo. 2s. 6d.

BALDWIN, Capt. J. H.—The Large and Small Game of Bengal and the North-Western Provinces of India. With 20 Illustrations. New and Cheaper Edition. Small 4to, 10s. 6d.

BALL, John, F.R.S.—Notes of a Naturalist in South America. With Map. Crown 8vo, 8s. 6d.

BALLIN, Ada S. and F. L.—A Hebrew Grammar. With Exercises selected from the Bible. Crown 8vo, 7s. 6d.

BASU, K. P., M.A.—Students' Mathematical Companion. Containing problems in Arithmetic, Algebra, Geometry, and Mensuration, for Students of the Indian Universities. Crown 8vo, 6s.

BAUR, Ferdinand, Dr. Ph.—A Philological Introduction to Greek and Latin for Students. Translated and adapted from the German, by C. KEGAN PAUL, M.A., and E. D. STONE, M.A. Third Edition. Crown 8vo, 6s.

Becket, Thomas, Martyr Patriot. By R. A. THOMPSON, M.A. Crown 8vo. 6*s.*

BENSON, A. C.—**William Laud, sometime Archbishop of Canterbury.** A Study. With Portrait. Crown 8vo, 6*s.*

BLOOMFIELD, The Lady.—**Reminiscences of Court and Diplomatic Life.** New and Cheaper Edition. With Frontispiece. Crown 8vo, 6*s.*

BLUNT, The Ven. Archdeacon. — **The Divine Patriot,** and other Sermons. Preached in Scarborough and in Cannes. New and Cheaper Edition. Crown 8vo, 4*s.* 6*d.*

BLUNT, Wilfrid S.—**The Future of Islam.** Crown 8vo, 6*s.*

Ideas about India. Crown 8vo. Cloth, 6*s.*

BOWEN, H. C., M.A.—**Studies in English.** For the use of Modern Schools. Tenth Thousand. Small crown 8vo, 1*s.* 6*d.*

English Grammar for Beginners. Fcap. 8vo, 1*s.*

Simple English Poems. English Literature for Junior Classes. In four parts. Parts I., II., and III., 6*d.* each. Part IV., 1*s.* Complete, 3*s.*

BRADLEY, F. H.—**The Principles of Logic.** Demy 8vo, 16*s.*

Bradshaw, Henry: Memoir. By G. W. PROTHERO. With Portrait and Facsmile. Demy 8vo. 16*s.*

BRIDGETT, Rev. T. E.—**History of the Holy Eucharist in Great Britain.** 2 vols. Demy 8vo, 18*s.*

BROOKE, Rev. Stopford A.—**The Fight of Faith.** Sermons preached on various occasions. Fifth Edition. Crown 8vo, 7*s.* 6*d.*

The Spirit of the Christian Life. Third Edition. Crown 8vo, 5*s.*

Theology in the English Poets.—Cowper, Coleridge, Wordsworth, and Burns. Sixth Edition. Post 8vo, 5*s.*

Christ in Modern Life. Seventeenth Edition. Crown 8vo, 5*s.*

Sermons. First Series. Thirteenth Edition. Crown 8vo, 5*s.*

Sermons. Second Series. Sixth Edition. Crown 8vo, 5*s.*

BROWN, Horatio F.—**Life on the Lagoons.** With 2 Illustrations and Map. Crown 8vo, 6*s.*

Venetian Studies. Crown 8vo, 7*s.* 6*d.*

BROWN, Rev. J. Baldwin.—**The Higher Life.** Its Reality, Experience, and Destiny. Seventh Edition. Crown 8vo, 5*s.*

Doctrine of Annihilation in the Light of the Gospel of Love. Five Discourses. Fourth Edition. Crown 8vo, 2*s.* 6*d.*

The Christian Policy of Life. A Book for Young Men of Business. Third Edition. Crown 8vo, 3*s.* 6*d.*

BURKE, The Late Very Rev. T. N.—His Life. By W. J. Fitz-
   patrick. 2 vols. With Portrait. Demy 8vo, 30*s*.

BURTON, Lady.—The Inner Life of Syria, Palestine, and
   the Holy Land. Post 8vo, 6*s*.

BURY, Richard de.—Philobiblon. Edited by E. C. Thomas. Crown
   8vo. 10*s*. 6*d*.

CANDLER, C.—The Prevention of Consumption. A Mode of
   Prevention founded on a New Theory of the Nature of the
   Tubercle-Bacillus. Demy 8vo, 10*s*. 6*d*.

CARPENTER, W. B.—The Principles of Mental Physiology.
   With their Applications to the Training and Discipline of the
   Mind, and the Study of its Morbid Conditions. Illustrated.
   Sixth Edition. 8vo, 12*s*.

   Nature and Man. With a Memorial Sketch by the Rev. J.
   Estlin Carpenter. Portrait. Large crown 8vo, 8*s*. 6*d*.

Catholic Dictionary. Containing some Account of the Doctrine,
   Discipline, Rites, Ceremonies, Councils, and Religious Orders of
   the Catholic Church. Edited by Thomas Arnold, M.A. Third
   Edition. Demy 8vo, 21*s*.

Charlemagne. A History of Charles the Great. By J. I. Mombert,
   D.D. Medium 8vo. 15*s*.

CHARLES, Rev. R. H.—Forgiveness, and other Sermons. Crown
   8vo, 4*s*. 6*d*.

CHEYNE, Canon.—The Prophecies of Isaiah. Translated with
   Critical Notes and Dissertations. 2 vols. Fifth Edition. Demy
   8vo, 25*s*.

   Job and Solomon; or, the Wisdom of the Old Testament.
   Demy 8vo, 12*s*. 6*d*.

   The Psalms; or, Book of The Praises of Israel. Translated
   with Commentary. Demy 8vo. 16*s*.

Churgress, The. By "The Prig." Fcap. 8vo, 3*s*. 6*d*.

CLAIRAUT.—Elements of Geometry. Translated by Dr.
   Kaines. With 145 Figures. Crown 8vo, 4*s*. 6*d*.

CLAPPERTON, Jane Hume.—Scientific Meliorism and the
   Evolution of Happiness. Large crown 8vo, 8*s*. 6*d*.

CLODD, Edward, F.R.A.S.—The Childhood of the World: a
   Simple Account of Man in Early Times. Eighth Edition.
   Crown 8vo, 3*s*.
      A Special Edition for Schools. 1*s*.

   The Childhood of Religions. Including a Simple Account of
   the Birth and Growth of Myths and Legends. Eighth Thousand.
   Crown 8vo, 5*s*.
      A Special Edition for Schools. 1*s*. 6*d*.

CLODD, Edward, F.R.A.S.—continued.

Jesus of Nazareth. With a brief sketch of Jewish History to the Time of His Birth. Second Edition. Small crown 8vo, 6s.
A Special Edition for Schools. In 2 parts. Each 1s. 6d.

COGHLAN, J. Cole, D.D.—The Modern Pharisee, and other Sermons. Edited by the Very Rev. H. H. DICKINSON, D.D., Dean of Chapel Royal, Dublin. New and Cheaper Edition. Crown 8vo, 7s. 6d.

COLERIDGE, The Hon. Stephen.—Demetrius. Crown 8vo, 5s.

CONNELL, A. K.—Discontent and Danger in India. Small crown 8vo, 3s. 6d.

The Economic Revolution of India. Crown 8vo, 4s. 6d.

CORR, the late Rev. T. J., M.A.—Favilla : Tales, Essays, and Poems. Crown 8vo, 5s.

CORY, William.—A Guide to Modern English History. Part I. —MDCCCXV.-MDCCCXXX. Demy 8vo, 9s. Part II.— MDCCCXXX.-MDCCCXXXV., 15s.

COTTON, H. J. S.—New India, or India in Transition. Third Edition. Crown 8vo, 4s. 6d.; Cheap Edition, paper covers, 1s.

COWIE, Right Rev. W. G.—Our Last Year in New Zealand. 1887. Crown 8vo, 7s. 6d.

COX, Rev. Sir George W., M.A., Bart.—The Mythology of the Aryan Nations. New Edition. Demy 8vo, 16s.

Tales of Ancient Greece. New Edition. Small crown 8vo, 6s.

A Manual of Mythology in the form of Question and Answer. New Edition. Fcap. 8vo, 3s.

An Introduction to the Science of Comparative Mythology and Folk-Lore. Second Edition. Crown 8vo. 7s. 6d.

COX, Rev. Sir G. W., M.A., Bart., and JONES, Eustace Hinton.— Popular Romances of the Middle Ages. Third Edition, in 1 vol. Crown 8vo, 6s.

COX, Rev. Samuel, D.D.—A Commentary on the Book of Job. With a Translation. Second Edition. Demy 8vo, 15s.

Salvator Mundi ; or, Is Christ the Saviour of all Men ? Twelfth Edition. Crown 8vo, 2s. 6d.

The Larger Hope. A Sequel to "Salvator Mundi." Second Edition. 16mo, 1s.

The Genesis of Evil, and other Sermons, mainly expository. Third Edition. Crown 8vo, 6s.

Balaam. An Exposition and a Study. Crown 8vo, 5s.

Miracles. An Argument and a Challenge. Crown 8vo, 2s. 6d.

CRAVEN, Mrs.—A Year's Meditations. Crown 8vo, 6*s.*

CRAWFURD, Oswald.—Portugal, Old and New. With Illustrations and Maps. New and Cheaper Edition. Crown 8vo, 6*s.*

Cross Lights. Crown 8vo. 5*s.*

CRUISE, Francis Richard, M.D.—Thomas à Kempis. Notes of a Visit to the Scenes in which his Life was spent. With Portraits and Illustrations. Demy 8vo, 12*s.*

Dante: The Banquet (Il Convito). Translated by KATHARINE HILLARD. Crown 8vo. 7*s.* 6*d.*

DARMESTETER, Arsene.—The Life of Words as the Symbols of Ideas. Crown 8vo, 4*s.* 6*d.*

DAVIDSON, Rev. Samuel, D.D., LL.D.—Canon of the Bible: Its Formation, History, and Fluctuations. Third and Revised Edition. Small crown 8vo, 5*s.*

The Doctrine of Last Things contained in the New Testament compared with the Notions of the Jews and the Statements of Church Creeds. Small crown 8vo, 3*s.* 6*d.*

DAWSON, Geo., M.A. Prayers, with a Discourse on Prayer. Edited by his Wife. First Series. Tenth Edition. Small Crown 8vo, 3*s.* 6*d.*

Prayers, with a Discourse on Prayer. Edited by GEORGE ST. CLAIR, F.G.S. Second Series. Small Crown 8vo, 3*s.* 6*d.*

Sermons on Disputed Points and Special Occasions. Edited by his Wife. Fourth Edition. Crown 8vo, 6*s.*

Sermons on Daily Life and Duty. Edited by his Wife. Fifth Edition. Small Crown 8vo, 3*s.* 6*d.*

The Authentic Gospel, and other Sermons. Edited by GEORGE ST. CLAIR, F.G.S. Third Edition. Crown 8vo, 6*s.*

Every-day Counsels. Edited by GEORGE ST. CLAIR, F.G.S. Crown 8vo, 6*s.*

Biographical Lectures. Edited by GEORGE ST. CLAIR, F.G.S. Third Edition. Large crown 8vo, 7*s.* 6*d.*

Shakespeare, and other Lectures. Edited by GEORGE ST. CLAIR, F.G.S. Large crown 8vo, 7*s.* 6*d.*

DE JONCOURT, Madame Marie.—Wholesome Cookery. Fifth Edition. Crown 8vo, cloth, 1*s.* 6*d*; paper covers, 1*s.*

DENT, H. C.—A Year in Brazil. With Notes on Religion, Meteorology, Natural History, etc. Maps and Illustrations. Demy 8vo, 18*s.*

DOWDEN, Edward, LL.D.—Shakspere: a Critical Study of his Mind and Art. Ninth Edition. Post 8vo, 12*s.*

DOWDEN, Edward, LL.D.—continued.

Studies in Literature, 1789-1877. Fourth Edition. Large post 8vo, 6s.

Transcripts and Studies. Large post 8vo. 12s.

Drummond, Thomas, Under Secretary in Ireland, 1835-40. Life and Letters. By R. BARRY O'BRIEN. Demy 8vo. 14s.

Dulce Domum. Fcap. 8vo, 5s.

DU MONCEL, Count.—The Telephone, the Microphone, and the Phonograph. With 74 Illustrations. Third Edition. Small crown 8vo, 5s.

DUNN, H. Percy.—Infant Health. The Physiology and Hygiene of Early Life. Crown 8vo. 3s. 6d.

DURUY, Victor.—History of Rome and the Roman People. Edited by Prof. MAHAFFY. With nearly 3000 Illustrations. 4to. 6 vols. in 12 parts, 30s. each vol.

Education Library. Edited by Sir PHILIP MAGNUS :—

An Introduction to the History of Educational Theories. By OSCAR BROWNING, M.A. Second Edition. 3s. 6d.

Industrial Education. By Sir PHILIP MAGNUS. 6s.

Old Greek Education. By the Rev. Prof. MAHAFFY, M.A. Second Edition. 3s. 6d.

School Management. Including a general view of the work of Education, Organization, and Discipline. By JOSEPH LANDON. Seventh Edition. 6s.

EDWARDES, Major-General Sir Herbert B.—Memorials of his Life and Letters. By his Wife. With Portrait and Illustrations. 2 vols. Demy 8vo, 36s.

Eighteenth Century Essays. Selected and Edited by AUSTIN DOBSON. Cheap Edition. Cloth 1s. 6d.

ELSDALE, Henry.—Studies in Tennyson's Idylls. Crown 8vo, 5s.

Emerson's (Ralph Waldo) Life. By OLIVER WENDELL HOLMES. English Copyright Edition. With Portrait. Crown 8vo, 6s.

EYTON, Rev. Robert.—The True Life, and other Sermons. Crown 8vo, 7s. 6d.

Five o'clock Tea. Containing Receipts for Cakes, Savoury Sandwiches, etc. Seventh Thousand. Fcap. 8vo, cloth, 1s. 6d. ; paper covers, 1s.

FLINN, D. Edgar.—Ireland : its Health-Resorts and Watering-Places. With Frontispiece and Maps. Demy 8vo, 5s.

Forbes, Bishop : A Memoir. By the Rev. DONALD J. MACKAY. With Portrait and Map. Crown 8vo, 7*s*. 6*d*.

FOTHERINGHAM, James.—**Studies in the Poetry of Robert Browning.** Second Edition. Crown 8vo, 6*s*.

Franklin (Benjamin) as a Man of Letters. By J. B. MAC-MASTER. Crown 8vo, 5*s*.

FREWEN, Moreton.—**The Economic Crisis.** Crown 8vo, 2*s*. 6*d*.

From World to Cloister; or, My Novitiate. By BERNARD. Crown 8vo, 5*s*.

FULLER, Rev. Morris.—**Pan-Anglicanism : What is it ?** or, The Church of the Reconciliation. Crown 8vo. 5*s*.

GARDINER, Samuel R., and J. BASS MULLINGER, M.A.—**Introduction to the Study of English History.** Second Edition. Large crown 8vo, 9*s*.

GEORGE, Henry.—**Progress and Poverty.** An Inquiry into the Causes of Industrial Depressions, and of Increase of Want with Increase of Wealth. The Remedy. Fifth Library Edition. Post 8vo, 7*s*. 6*d*. Cabinet Edition. Crown 8vo, 2*s*. 6*d*. Also a Cheap Edition. Limp cloth, 1*s*. 6*d*. ; paper covers, 1*s*.

> **Protection, or Free Trade.** An Examination of the Tariff Question, with especial regard to the Interests of Labour. Second Edition. Crown 8vo, 5*s*. Cheap Edition, limp cloth, 1*s*. 6*d*. ; paper covers, 1*s*.

> **Social Problems.** Fourth Thousand. Crown 8vo, 5*s*. Cheap Edition, paper covers, 1*s*. ; cloth, 1*s*. 6*d*.

GILBERT, Mrs. — **Autobiography, and other Memorials.** Edited by JOSIAH GILBERT. Fifth Edition. Crown 8vo, 7*s*. 6*d*.

GILLMORE, Parker.—**Days and Nights by the Desert.** Illustrated. Demy 8vo, 10*s*. 6*d*.

GLANVILL, Joseph.—**Scepsis Scientifica ;** or, Confest Ignorance, the Way to Science ; in an Essay of the Vanity of Dogmatizing and Confident Opinion. Edited, with Introductory Essay, by JOHN OWEN. Elzevir 8vo, printed on hand-made paper, 6*s*.

GLASS, H. A.—**The Story of the Psalters.** A History of the Metrical Versions from 1549 to 1885. Crown 8vo, 5*s*.

Glossary of Terms and Phrases. Edited by the Rev. H. PERCY SMITH and others. Second and Cheaper Edition. Medium 8vo, 7*s*. 6*d*.

GLOVER, F., M.A.—**Exempla Latina.** A First Construing Book, with Short Notes, Lexicon, and an Introduction to the Analysis of Sentences. Second Edition. Fcap. 8vo, 2*s*.

GOODCHILD, John A. **Chats at St. Ampelio.** Crown 8vo. 5*s*.

GOODENOUGH, Commodore J. G.—Memoir of, with Extracts from his Letters and Journals. Edited by his Widow. With Steel Engraved Portrait. Third Edition. Crown 8vo, 5*s*.

GORDON, Major-General C. G.—His Journals at Kartoum. Printed from the original MS. With Introduction and Notes by A. EGMONT HAKE. Portrait, 2 Maps, and 30 Illustrations. Two vols., demy 8vo, 21*s*. Also a Cheap Edition in 1 vol., 6*s*.

Gordon's (General) Last Journal. A Facsimile of the last Journal received in England from GENERAL GORDON. Reproduced by Photo-lithography. Imperial 4to, £3 3*s*.

Events in his Life. From the Day of his Birth to the Day of his Death. By Sir H. W. GORDON. With Maps and Illustrations. Second Edition. Demy 8vo, 7*s*. 6*d*.

GOSSE, Edmund.—Seventeenth Century Studies. A Contribution to the History of English Poetry. Demy 8vo, 10*s*. 6*d*.

GOUGH, E.—The Bible True from the Beginning. Vol. I. Demy 8vo, 16*s*.

GOULD, Rev. S. Baring, M.A.—Germany, Present and Past. New and Cheaper Edition. Large crown 8vo, 7*s*. 6*d*.

GOWAN, Major Walter E.—A. Ivanoff's Russian Grammar. (16th Edition.) Translated, enlarged, and arranged for use of Students of the Russian Language. Demy 8vo, 6*s*.

GOWER, Lord Ronald. My Reminiscences. MINIATURE EDITION, printed on hand-made paper, limp parchment antique, 10*s*. 6*d*.

Bric-à-Brac. Being some Photoprints illustrating art objects at Gower Lodge, Windsor. With descriptions. Super royal 8vo. 15*s*. ; extra binding, 21*s*.

Last Days of Mary Antoinette. An Historical Sketch. With Portrait and Facsimiles. Fcap. 4to, 10*s*. 6*d*.

Notes of a Tour from Brindisi to Yokohama, 1883-1884. Fcap. 8vo, 2*s*. 6*d*.

GRAHAM, William, M.A.—The Creed of Science, Religious, Moral, and Social. Second Edition, Revised. Crown 8vo, 6*s*.

The Social Problem, in its Economic, Moral, and Political Aspects. Demy 8vo, 14*s*.

GRIMLEY, Rev. H. N., M.A.—Tremadoc Sermons, chiefly on the Spiritual Body, the Unseen World, and the Divine Humanity. Fourth Edition. Crown 8vo, 6*s*.

The Temple of Humanity, and other Sermons. Crown 8vo, 6*s*.

GURNEY, Alfred.—Our Catholic Inheritance in the Larger Hope. Crown 8vo, 1*s*. 6*d*.

Wagner's Parsifal. A Study. Fcap. 8vo, 1*s*. 6*d*.

HADDON, Caroline.—The Larger Life, Studies in Hinton's Ethics. Crown 8vo, 5*s.*

HAECKEL, Prof. Ernst.—The History of Creation. Translation revised by Professor E. RAY LANKESTER, M.A., F.R.S. With Coloured Plates and Genealogical Trees of the various groups of both Plants and Animals. 2 vols. Third Edition. Post 8vo, 32*s.*

The History of the Evolution of Man. With numerous Illustrations. 2 vols. Post 8vo, 32*s.*

A Visit to Ceylon. Post 8vo, 7*s.* 6*d.*

Freedom in Science and Teaching. With a Prefatory Note by T. H. HUXLEY, F.R.S. Crown 8vo, 5*s.*

Hamilton, Memoirs of Arthur, B.A., of Trinity College, Cambridge. Crown 8vo, 6*s.*

Handbook of Home Rule, being Articles on the Irish Question by Various Writers. Edited by JAMES BRYCE, M.P. Second Edition. Crown 8vo, 1*s.* sewed, or 1*s.* 6*d.* cloth.

HAWEIS, Rev. H. R., M.A.—Current Coin. Materialism—The Devil—Crime—Drunkenness—Pauperism—Emotion—Recreation —The Sabbath. Fifth Edition. Crown 8vo, 5*s.*

Arrows in the Air. Fifth Edition. Crown 8vo, 5*s.*

Speech in Season. Sixth Edition. Crown 8vo, 5*s.*

Thoughts for the Times. Fourteenth Edition. Crown 8vo, 5*s.*

Unsectarian Family Prayers. New Edition. Fcap. 8vo, 1*s.* 6*d.*

HAWTHORNE, Nathaniel.—Works. Complete in Twelve Volumes. Large post 8vo, 7*s.* 6*d.* each volume.

HEIDENHAIN, Rudolph, M.D.—Hypnotism, or Animal Magnetism. With Preface by G. J. ROMANES. Second Edition. Small crown 8vo, 2*s.* 6*d.*

HENDRIKS, Dom Lawrence.—The London Charterhouse : its Monks and its Martyrs. Illustrated. Demy 8vo, 14*s.*

HINTON, J.—Life and Letters. With an Introduction by Sir W. W. GULL, Bart., and Portrait engraved on Steel by C. H. Jeens. Sixth Edition. Crown 8vo, 8*s.* 6*d.*

Philosophy and Religion. Selections from the Manuscripts of the late James Hinton. Edited by CAROLINE HADDON. Second Edition. Crown 8vo, 5*s.*

The Law Breaker, and The Coming of the Law. Edited by MARGARET HINTON. Crown 8vo, 6*s.*

The Mystery of Pain. New Edition. Fcap. 8vo, 1*s.*

Homer's Iliad. Greek text, with a Translation by J. G. CORDERY. 2 vols. Demy 8vo, 24*s.*

HOOPER, Mary.—Little Dinners: How to Serve them with Elegance and Economy. Twenty-first Edition. Crown 8vo, 2s. 6d.

Cookery for Invalids, Persons of Delicate Digestion, and Children. Fifth Edition. Crown 8vo, 2s. 6d.

Every-day Meals. Being Economical and Wholesome Recipes for Breakfast, Luncheon, and Supper. Seventh Edition. Crown 8vo, 2s. 6d.

HOPKINS, Ellice.—Work amongst Working Men. Sixth Edition. Crown 8vo, 3s. 6d.

HORNADAY, W. T.—Two Years in a Jungle. With Illustrations. Demy 8vo, 21s.

HOSPITALIER, E.—The Modern Applications of Electricity. Translated and Enlarged by JULIUS MAIER, Ph.D. 2 vols. Second Edition, Revised, with many additions and numerous Illustrations. Demy 8vo, 25s.

HOWARD, Robert, M.A.—The Church of England and other Religious Communions. A course of Lectures delivered in the Parish Church of Clapham. Crown 8vo, 7s. 6d.

HYNDMAN, H. M.—The Historical Basis of Socialism in England. Large crown 8vo, 8s. 6d.

IDDESLEIGH, Earl of.—The Pleasures, Dangers, and Uses of Desultory Reading. Fcap. 8vo, 2s. 6d.

IM THURN, Everard F.—Among the Indians of Guiana. Being Sketches, chiefly anthropologic, from the Interior of British Guiana. With 53 Illustrations and a Map. Demy 8vo, 18s.

JEAFFRESON, Herbert H.—The Divine Unity and Trinity. Demy 8vo, 12s.

JENKINS, E., and RAYMOND, J.—The Architect's Legal Handbook. Fourth Edition, revised. Crown 8vo, 6s.

JENKINS, Rev. Canon R. C.—Heraldry. English and Foreign. With a Dictionary of Heraldic Terms and 156 Illustrations. Small crown 8vo, 3s. 6d.

Jerome, St., Life. By M. J. MARTIN. Crown 8vo, 6s.

JOEL, L.—A Consul's Manual and Shipowner's and Shipmaster's Practical Guide in their Transactions Abroad. With Definitions of Nautical, Mercantile, and Legal Terms; a Glossary of Mercantile Terms in English, French, German, Italian, and Spanish; Tables of the Money, Weights, and Measures of the Principal Commercial Nations and their Equivalents in British Standards; and Forms of Consular and Notarial Acts. Demy 8vo, 12s.

JOHNSTON, H. H., F.Z.S.—**The Kilima-njaro Expedition.** A Record of Scientific Exploration in Eastern Equatorial Africa, and a General Description of the Natural History, Languages, and Commerce of the Kilima-njaro District. With 6 Maps, and over 80 Illustrations by the Author. Demy 8vo, 21*s.*

KAUFMANN, Rev. M., M.A.—**Socialism** its Nature, its Dangers, and its Remedies considered. Crown 8vo, 7*s.* 6*d.*

Utopias ; or, Schemes of Social Improvement, from Sir Thomas More to Karl Marx. Crown 8vo, 5*s.*

Christian Socialism. Crown 8vo, 4*s.* 6*d.*

KAY, David, F.R.G.S.—**Education and Educators.** Crown 8vo. 7*s.* 6*d.*

Memory : what it is and how to improve it. Crown 8vo, 6*s.*

KAY, Joseph.—**Free Trade in Land.** Edited by his Widow. With Preface by the Right Hon. JOHN BRIGHT, M.P. Seventh Edition. Crown 8vo, 5*s.*

**** Also a cheaper edition, without the Appendix, but with a Review of Recent Changes in the Land Laws of England, by the RIGHT HON. G. OSBORNE MORGAN, Q.C., M.P. Cloth, 1*s.* 6*d.* ; paper covers, 1*s.*

KELKE, W. H. H.—**An Epitome of English Grammar for the Use of Students.** Adapted to the London Matriculation Course and Similar Examinations. Crown 8vo, 4*s.* 6*d.*

KEMPIS, Thomas à.—**Of the Imitation of Christ.** Parchment Library Edition.—Parchment or cloth, 6*s.* ; vellum, 7*s.* 6*d.* The Red Line Edition, fcap. 8vo, cloth extra, 2*s.* 6*d.* The Cabinet Edition, small 8vo, cloth limp, 1*s.* ; cloth boards, 1*s.* 6*d.* The Miniature Edition, cloth limp, 32mo, 1*s.* ; or with red lines, 1*s.* 6*d.*

**** All the above Editions may be had in various extra bindings.

Notes of a Visit to the Scenes in which his Life was spent. With numerous Illustrations. By F. R. CRUISE, M.D. Demy 8vo, 12*s.*

KENDALL, Henry.—**The Kinship of Men.** An argument from Pedigrees, or Genealogy viewed as a Science. With Diagrams. Crown 8vo, 5*s.*

KENNARD, Rev. R. B.—**A Manual of Confirmation.** 18mo. Sewed, 3*d.* ; cloth, 1*s.*

KIDD, Joseph, M.D.—**The Laws of Therapeutics ;** or, the Science and Art of Medicine. Second Edition. Crown 8vo, 6*s.*

KINGSFORD, Anna, M.D.—**The Perfect Way in Diet.** A Treatise advocating a Return to the Natural and Ancient Food of our Race. Third Edition. Small crown 8vo, 2*s.*

KINGSLEY, Charles, M.A.—**Letters and Memories of his Life.** Edited by his Wife. With two Steel Engraved Portraits, and Vignettes on Wood. Sixteenth Cabinet Edition. 2 vols. Crown 8vo, 12*s.*

*** Also a People's Edition, in one volume. With Portrait. Crown 8vo, 6*s.*

All Saints' Day, and other Sermons. Edited by the Rev. W. HARRISON. Third Edition. Crown 8vo, 7*s.* 6*d.*

True Words for Brave Men. A Book for Soldiers' and Sailors' Libraries. Sixteenth Thousand. Crown 8vo, 2*s.* 6*d.*

KNOX, Alexander A.—**The New Playground ;** or, Wanderings in Algeria. New and Cheaper Edition. Large crown 8vo, 6*s.*

Lamartine, Alphonse de, Life. By Lady MARGARET DOMVILE. Large crown 8vo, 7*s.* 6*d.*

Land Concentration and Irresponsibility of Political Power, as causing the Anomaly of a Widespread State of Want by the Side of the Vast Supplies of Nature. Crown 8vo, 5*s.*

LANDON, Joseph.—**School Management ;** Including a General View of the Work of Education, Organization, and Discipline. Seventh Edition. Crown 8vo, 6*s.*

LANG, Andrew.—**Lost Leaders.** Crown 8vo, 5*s.*

LAURIE, S. S.—**The Rise and Early Constitution of Universities.** With a Survey of Mediæval Education. Crown 8vo, 6*s.*

LEFEVRE, Right Hon. G. Shaw.—**Peel and O'Connell.** Demy 8vo, 10*s.* 6*d.*

Incidents of Coercion. A Journal of visits to Ireland. Third Edition. Crown 8vo, limp cloth, 1*s.* 6*d.* ; paper covers, 1*s.*

Letters from an Unknown Friend. By the Author of " Charles Lowder." With a Preface by the Rev. W. H. CLEAVER. Fcap. 8vo, 1*s.*

LILLIE, Arthur, M.R.A.S.—**The Popular Life of Buddha.** Containing an Answer to the Hibbert Lectures of 1881. With Illustrations. Crown 8vo, 6*s.*

Buddhism in Christendom ; or, Jesus the Essene. With Illustrations. Demy 8vo, 15*s.*

LITTLE, E. A.—**Log-Book Notes through Life.** Oblong. Illustrated. 6*s.*

LOCHER, Carl.—**An Explanation of Organ Stops,** with Hints for Effective Combinations. Demy 8vo, 5*s.*

LONGFELLOW, H. Wadsworth.—**Life.** By his Brother, SAMUEL LONGFELLOW. With Portraits and Illustrations. 3 vols. Demy 8vo, 42*s.*

LONSDALE, Margaret.—Sister Dora : a Biography. With Portrait. Thirtieth Edition. Small crown 8vo, 2s. 6d.

George Eliot : Thoughts upon her Life, her Books, and Herself. Second Edition. Small crown 8vo, 1s. 6d.

LOUNSBURY, Thomas R.—James Fenimore Cooper. With Portrait. Crown 8vo, 5s.

LOWDER, Charles.—A Biography. By the Author of " St. Teresa." Twelfth Edition. Crown 8vo. With Portrait. 3s. 6d.

LÜCKES, Eva C. E.—Lectures on General Nursing, delivered to the Probationers of the London Hospital Training School for Nurses. Third Edition. Crown 8vo, 2s. 6d.

LYTTON, Edward Bulwer, Lord.—Life, Letters and Literary Remains. By his Son, the EARL OF LYTTON. With Portraits, Illustrations and Facsimiles. Demy 8vo. Vols. I. and II., 32s.

MACHIAVELLI, Niccolò. — Life and Times. By Prof. VILLARI. Translated by LINDA VILLARI. 4 vols. Large post 8vo, 48s.

Discourses on the First Decade of Titus Livius. Translated from the Italian by NINIAN HILL THOMSON, M.A. Large crown 8vo, 12s.

The Prince. Translated from the Italian by N. H. T. Small crown 8vo, printed on hand-made paper, bevelled boards, 6s.

MACNEILL, J. G. Swift.—How the Union was carried. Crown 8vo, cloth, 1s. 6d. ; paper covers, 1s.

MAGNUS, Lady.—About the Jews since Bible Times. From the Babylonian Exile till the English Exodus. Small crown 8vo, 6s.

MAGNUS, Sir Philip.—Industrial Education. Crown 8vo, 6s.

Maintenon, Madame de. By EMILY BOWLES. With Portrait, Large crown 8vo, 7s. 6d.

Many Voices. A volume of Extracts from the Religious Writers of Christendom from the First to the Sixteenth Century. With Biographical Sketches. Crown 8vo, cloth extra, red edges, 6s.

MARKHAM, Capt. Albert Hastings, R.N.—The Great Frozen Sea : A Personal Narrative of the Voyage of the *Alert* during the Arctic Expedition of 1875-6. With 6 full-page Illustrations, 2 Maps, and 27 Woodcuts. Sixth and Cheaper Edition. Crown 8vo, 6s.

MARTINEAU, Gertrude.—Outline Lessons on Morals. Small crown 8vo, 3s. 6d.

MASON, Charlotte M.—Home Education : a Course of Lectures to Ladies. Crown 8vo, 3s. 6d.

MASSEY, Gerald. — The Secret Drama of Shakspeare's Sonnets. 4to. 12s. 6d.

Matter and Energy: An Examination of the Fundamental Concepceptions of Physical Force. By B. L. L. Small crown 8vo, 2*s.*

MATUCE, H. Ogram. **A Wanderer.** Crown 8vo, 5*s.*

MAUDSLEY, H., M.D.—**Body and Will.** Being an Essay concerning Will, in its Metaphysical, Physiological, and Pathological Aspects. 8vo, 12*s.*

   Natural Causes and Supernatural Seemings. Second Edition. Crown 8vo, 6*s.*

McGRATH, Terence.—**Pictures from Ireland.** New and Cheaper Edition. Crown 8vo, 2*s.*

McKINNEY, S. B. G.—**Science and Art of Religion.** Crown 8vo, 8*s.* 6*d.*

MILLER, Edward.—**The History and Doctrines of Irvingism ;** or, The so-called Catholic and Apostolic Church. 2 vols. Large post 8vo, 15*s.*

MILLS, Herbert.—**Poverty and the State ;** or, Work for the Unemployed. An Inquiry into the Causes and Extent of Enforced Idleness, with a Statement of a Remedy. Crown 8vo, 6*s.* Cheap Edition, limp cloth, 1*s.* 6*d.* ; paper covers, 1*s.*

MINTON, Rev. Francis.—**Capital and Wages.** 8vo, 15*s.*

Mitchel, John, Life. By WILLIAM DILLON. 2 vols. 8vo. With Portrait. 21*s.*

MITCHELL, Lucy M.—**A History of Ancient Sculpture.** With numerous Illustrations, including 6 Plates in Phototype. Super-royal 8vo, 42*s.*

MIVART, St. George.—**On Truth.** Demy 8vo, 16*s.*

MOCKLER, E.—**A Grammar of the Baloochee Language,** as it is spoken in Makran (Ancient Gedrosia), in the Persia-Arabic and Roman characters. Fcap. 8vo, 5*s.*

MOHL, Julius and Mary.—**Letters and Recollections of.** By M. C. M. SIMPSON. With Portraits and Two Illustrations. Demy 8vo, 15*s.*

MOLESWORTH, Rev. W. Nassau, M.A.—**History of the Church of England from 1660.** Large crown 8vo, 7*s.* 6*d.*

MOORE, Aubrey L.—**Science and the Faith :** Essays on Apologetic Subjects. Crown 8vo, 6*s.*

MORELL, J. R.—**Euclid Simplified in Method and Language.** Being a Manual of Geometry. Compiled from the most important French Works, approved by the University of Paris and the Minister of Public Instruction. Fcap. 8vo, 2*s.* 6*d.*

MORISON, J. Cotter.—**The Service of Man :** an Essay towards the Religion of the Future. Crown 8vo, 5*s.*

MORRIS, Gouverneur, U.S. Minister to France.—**Diary and Letters.** 2 vols. Demy 8vo, 30*s.*

MORSE, E. S., Ph.D.—**First Book of Zoology.** With numerous Illustrations. New and Cheaper Edition. Crown 8vo, 2s. 6d.

My Lawyer : A Concise Abridgment of the Laws of England. By a Barrister-at-Law. Crown 8vo, 6s. 6d.

Natural History. "Riverside" Edition. Edited by J. S. KINGSLEY. 6 vols. 4to. 2200 Illustrations. £6 6s.

NELSON, J. H., M.A.—**A Prospectus of the Scientific Study of the Hindû Law.** Demy 8vo, 9s.

Indian Usage and Judge-made Law in Madras. Demy 8vo, 12s.

NEVILL, F.—**The Service of God.** Small 4to, 3s. 6d.

NEWMAN, Cardinal.—**Characteristics from the Writings of.** Being Selections from his various Works. Arranged with the Author's personal Approval. Eighth Edition. With Portrait. Crown 8vo, 6s.

*** A Portrait of Cardinal Newman, mounted for framing, can be had, 2s. 6d.

NEWMAN, Francis William.—**Essays on Diet.** Small crown 8vo, cloth limp, 2s.

Miscellanies. Vol. II. Essays, Tracts, and Addresses, Moral and Religious. Demy 8vo, 12s.

Reminiscences of Two Exiles and Two Wars. Crown 8vo, 3s. 6d.

New Social Teachings. By POLITICUS. Small crown 8vo, 5s.

NICOLS, Arthur, F.G.S., F.R.G.S.—**Chapters from the Physical History of the Earth :** an Introduction to Geology and Palæontology. With numerous Illustrations. Crown 8vo, 5s.

NOEL, The Hon. Roden.—**Essays on Poetry and Poets.** Demy 8vo, 12s.

NOPS, Marianne.—**Class Lessons on Euclid.** Part I. containing the First Two Books of the Elements. Crown 8vo, 2s. 6d.

Nuces : EXERCISES ON THE SYNTAX OF THE PUBLIC SCHOOL LATIN PRIMER. New Edition in Three Parts. Crown 8vo, each 1s.

*** The Three Parts can also be had bound together, 3s.

OATES, Frank, F.R.G.S.—**Matabele Land and the Victoria Falls.** A Naturalist's Wanderings in the Interior of South Africa. Edited by C. G. OATES, B.A. With numerous Illustrations and 4 Maps. Demy 8vo, 21s.

O'BRIEN, R. Barry.—**Irish Wrongs and English Remedies,** with other Essays. Crown 8vo, 5s.

OLIVER, Robert.—**Unnoticed Analogies.** A Talk on the Irish Question. Crown 8vo, 3s. 6d.

C

O'MEARA, *Kathleen.*—Henri Perreyve and his Counsels to the Sick. Small crown 8vo, 5s.

One and a Half in Norway. A Chronicle of Small Beer. By Either and Both. Small crown 8vo, 3s. 6d.

OTTLEY, *H. Bickersteth.*—The Great Dilemma. Christ His Own Witness or His Own Accuser. Six Lectures. Second Edition. Crown 8vo, 3s. 6d.

Our Priests and their Tithes. By a Priest of the Province of Canterbury. Crown 8vo, 5s.

Our Public Schools—Eton, Harrow, Winchester, Rugby, Westminster, Marlborough, The Charterhouse. Crown 8vo, 6s.

OWEN, *F. M.*—Across the Hills. Small crown 8vo, 1s. 6d.

PALMER, *the late William.*—Notes of a Visit to Russia in 1840-1841. Selected and arranged by JOHN H. CARDINAL NEWMAN, with Portrait. Crown 8vo, 8s. 6d.

Early Christian Symbolism. A Series of Compositions from Fresco Paintings, Glasses, and Sculptured Sarcophagi. Edited by the Rev. Provost NORTHCOTE, D.D., and the Rev. Canon BROWNLOW, M.A. With Coloured Plates, folio, 42s., or with Plain Plates, folio, 25s.

Parchment Library. Choicely Printed on hand-made paper, limp parchment antique or cloth, 6s. ; vellum, 7s. 6d. each volume.

Sartor Resartus. By THOMAS CARLYLE.

The Poetical Works of John Milton. 2 vols.

Chaucer's Canterbury Tales. Edited by A. W. POLLARD. 2 vols.

Letters and Journals of Jonathan Swift. Selected and edited, with a Commentary and Notes, by STANLEY LANE-POOLE.

De Quincey's Confessions of an English Opium Eater. Reprinted from the First Edition. Edited by RICHARD GARNETT.

The Gospel according to Matthew, Mark, and Luke.

Selections from the Prose Writings of Jonathan Swift. With a Preface and Notes by STANLEY LANE-POOLE and Portrait.

English Sacred Lyrics.

Sir Joshua Reynolds's Discourses. Edited by EDMUND GOSSE.

Selections from Milton's Prose Writings. Edited by ERNEST MYERS.

Parchment Library—*continued.*

The Book of Psalms. Translated by the Rev. Canon T. K. CHEYNE, M.A., D.D.

The Vicar of Wakefield. With Preface and Notes by AUSTIN DOBSON.

English Comic Dramatists. Edited by OSWALD CRAWFURD.

English Lyrics.

The Sonnets of John Milton. Edited by MARK PATTISON. With Portrait after Vertue.

French Lyrics. Selected and Annotated by GEORGE SAINTS-BURY. With a Miniature Frontispiece designed and etched by H. G. Glindoni.

Fables by Mr. John Gay. With Memoir by AUSTIN DOBSON, and an Etched Portrait from an unfinished Oil Sketch by Sir Godfrey Kneller.

Select Letters of Percy Bysshe Shelley. Edited, with an Introduction, by RICHARD GARNETT.

The Christian Year. Thoughts in Verse for the Sundays and Holy Days throughout the Year. With Miniature Portrait of the Rev. J. Keble, after a Drawing by G. Richmond, R.A.

Shakspere's Works. Complete in Twelve Volumes.

Eighteenth Century Essays. Selected and Edited by AUSTIN DOBSON. With a Miniature Frontispiece by R. Caldecott.

Q. Horati Flacci Opera. Edited by F. A. CORNISH, Assistant Master at Eton. With a Frontispiece after a design by L. Alma Tadema, etched by Leopold Lowenstam.

Edgar Allan Poe's Poems. With an Essay on his Poetry by ANDREW LANG, and a Frontispiece by Linley Sambourne.

Shakspere's Sonnets. Edited by EDWARD DOWDEN. With a Frontispiece etched by Leopold Lowenstam, after the Death Mask.

English Odes. Selected by EDMUND GOSSE. With Frontis-piece on India paper by Hamo Thornycroft, A.R.A.

Of the Imitation of Christ. By THOMAS À KEMPIS. A revised Translation. With Frontispiece on India paper, from a Design by W. B. Richmond.

Poems : Selected from PERCY BYSSHE SHELLEY. Dedicated to Lady Shelley. With a Preface by RICHARD GARNETT and a Miniature Frontispiece.

PARSLOE, Joseph.—**Our Railways.** Sketches, Historical and Descriptive. With Practical Information as to Fares and Rates, etc., and a Chapter on Railway Reform. Crown 8vo, 6s.

PASCAL, Blaise.—The Thoughts of. Translated from the Text of Auguste Molinier, by C. KEGAN PAUL. Large crown 8vo, with Frontispiece, printed on hand-made paper, parchment antique, or cloth, 12s. ; vellum, 15s. New Edition. Crown 8vo, 6s.

PATON, W. A.—Down the Islands. A Voyage to the Caribbees. With Illustration. Medium 8vo, 16s.

PAUL, C. Kegan.—Biographical Sketches. Printed on hand-made paper, bound in buckram. Second Edition. Crown 8vo, 7s. 6d.

PEARSON, Rev. S.—Week-day Living. A Book for Young Men and Women. Second Edition. Crown 8vo, 5s.

PENRICE, Major J.—Arabic and English Dictionary of the Koran. 4to, 21s.

PESCHEL, Dr. Oscar.—The Races of Man and their Geographical Distribution. Second Edition. Large crown 8vo, 9s.

PIDGEON, D.—An Engineer's Holiday ; or, Notes of a Round Trip from Long. 0° to 0°. New and Cheaper Edition. Large crown 8vo, 7s. 6d. ·

Old World Questions and New World Answers. Second Edition. Large crown 8vo, 7s. 6d.

Plain Thoughts for Men. Eight Lectures delivered at Forester's Hall, Clerkenwell, during the London Mission, 1884. Crown 8vo, cloth, 1s. 6d ; paper covers, 1s.

PLOWRIGHT, C. B.—The British Uredineæ and Ustilagineæ. With Illustrations. Demy 8vo, 12s.

PRICE, Prof. Bonamy. — Chapters on Practical Political Economy. Being the Substance of Lectures delivered before the University of Oxford. New and Cheaper Edition. Crown 8vo, 5s. ·

Prigment, The. "The Life of a Prig," "Prig's Bede," "How to Make a Saint," "The Churgress." In 1 vol. Crown 8vo, 6s.

Prig's Bede : the Venerable Bede, Expurgated, Expounded, and Exposed. By "THE PRIG." Second Edition. Fcap. 8vo, 3s. 6d.

Pulpit Commentary, The. (*Old Testament Series.*) Edited by the Rev. J. S. EXELL, M.A., and the Very Rev. Dean H. D. M. SPENCE, M.A., D.D.

Genesis. By the Rev. T. WHITELAW, D.D. With Homilies by the Very Rev. J. F. MONTGOMERY, D.D., Rev. Prof. R. A. REDFORD, M.A., LL.B., Rev. F. HASTINGS, Rev. W. ROBERTS, M.A. An Introduction to the Study of the Old Testament by the Venerable Archdeacon FARRAR, D.D., F.R.S.; and Introductions to the Pentateuch by the Right Rev. H. COTTERILL, D.D., and Rev. T. WHITELAW, M.A. Ninth Edition. 1 vol., 15s.

Pulpit Commentary, The—*continued.*

Exodus. By the Rev. Canon RAWLINSON. With Homilies by Rev. J. ORR, D.D., Rev. D. YOUNG, B.A., Rev. C. A. GOODHART, Rev. J. URQUHART, and the Rev. H. T. ROBJOHNS. Fourth Edition. 2 vols., 9*s.* each.

Leviticus. By the Rev. Prebendary MEYRICK, M.A. With Introductions by the Rev. R. COLLINS, Rev. Professor A. CAVE, and Homilies by Rev. Prof. REDFORD, LL.B., Rev. J. A. MACDONALD, Rev. W. CLARKSON, B.A., Rev. S. R. ALDRIDGE, LL.B., and Rev. MCCHEYNE EDGAR. Fourth Edition. 15*s.*

Numbers. By the Rev. R. WINTERBOTHAM, LL.B. With Homilies by the Rev. Professor W. BINNIE, D.D., Rev. E. S. PROUT, M.A., Rev. D. YOUNG, Rev. J. WAITE, and an Introduction by the Rev. THOMAS WHITELAW, M.A. Fifth Edition. 15*s.*

Deuteronomy. By the Rev. W. L. ALEXANDER, D.D. With Homilies by Rev. C. CLEMANCE, D.D., Rev. J. ORR, D.D., Rev. R. M. EDGAR, M.A., Rev. D. DAVIES, M.A. Fourth edition. 15*s.*

Joshua. By Rev. J. J. LIAS, M.A. With Homilies by Rev. S. R. ALDRIDGE, LL.B., Rev. R. GLOVER, REV. E. DE PRESSENSÉ, D.D., Rev. J. WAITE, B.A., Rev. W. F. ADENEY, M.A.; and an Introduction by the Rev. A. PLUMMER, M.A. Fifth Edition. 12*s.* 6*d.*

Judges and Ruth. By the Bishop of BATH and WELLS, and Rev. J. MORISON, D.D. With Homilies by Rev. A. F. MUIR, M.A., Rev. W. F. ADENEY, M.A., Rev. W. M. STATHAM, and Rev. Professor J. THOMSON, M.A. Fifth Edition. 10*s.* 6*d.*

1 and 2 Samuel. By the Very Rev. R. P. SMITH, D.D. With Homilies by Rev. DONALD FRASER, D.D., Rev. Prof. CHAPMAN, and Rev. B. DALE. Seventh Edition. 15*s.* each.

1 Kings. By the Rev. JOSEPH HAMMOND, LL.B. With Homilies by the Rev. E. DE PRESSENSÉ, D.D., Rev. J. WAITE, B.A., Rev. A. ROWLAND, LL.B., Rev. J. A. MACDONALD, and Rev. J. URQUHART. Fifth Edition. 15*s.*

1 Chronicles. By the Rev. Prof. P. C. BARKER, M.A., LL.B. With Homilies by Rev. Prof. J. R. THOMSON, M.A., Rev. R. TUCK, B.A., Rev. W. CLARKSON, B.A., Rev. F. WHITFIELD, M.A., and Rev. RICHARD GLOVER. 15*s.*

Ezra, Nehemiah, and Esther. By Rev. Canon G. RAWLINSON, M.A. With Homilies by Rev. Prof. J. R. THOMSON, M.A., Rev. Prof. R. A. REDFORD, LL.B., M.A., Rev. W. S. LEWIS, M.A., Rev. J. A. MACDONALD, Rev. A. MACKENNAL, B.A., Rev. W. CLARKSON, B.A., Rev. F. HASTINGS, Rev. W. DINWIDDIE, LL.B., Rev. Prof. ROWLANDS, B.A., Rev. G. WOOD, B.A., Rev. Prof. P. C. BARKER, M.A., LL.B., and the Rev. J. S. EXELL, M.A. Seventh Edition. 1 vol., 12*s.* 6*d.*

Pulpit Commentary, The—*continued.*

> **Isaiah.** By the Rev. Canon G. RAWLINSON, M.A. With Homilies by Rev. Prof. E. JOHNSON, M.A., Rev. W. CLARKSON, B.A., Rev. W. M. STATHAM, and Rev. R. TUCK, B.A. Second Edition. 2 vols., 15*s.* each.

> **Jeremiah.** (Vol. I.) By the Rev. Canon T. K. CHEYNE, D.D. With Homilies by the Rev. W. F. ADENEY, M.A., Rev. A. F. MUIR, M.A., Rev. S. CONWAY, B.A., Rev. J. WAITE, B.A., and Rev. D. YOUNG, B.A. Third Edition. 15*s.*

> **Jeremiah (Vol. II.) and Lamentations.** By Rev. Canon T. K. CHEYNE, D.D. With Homilies by Rev. Prof. J. R. THOMSON, M.A., Rev. W. F. ADENEY, M.A., Rev. A. F. MUIR, M.A., Rev. S. CONWAY, B.A., Rev. D. YOUNG, B.A. 15*s.*

> **Hosea and Joel.** By the Rev. Prof. J. J. GIVEN, Ph.D., D.D. With Homilies by the Rev. Prof. J. R. THOMSON, M.A., Rev. A. ROWLAND, B.A., LL.B., Rev. C. JERDAN, M.A., LL.B., Rev. J. ORR, D.D., and Rev. D. THOMAS, D.D. 15*s.*

Pulpit Commentary, The. (*New Testament Series.*)

> **St. Mark.** By Very Rev. E. BICKERSTETH, D.D., Dean of Lichfield. With Homilies by Rev. Prof. THOMSON, M.A., Rev. Prof. J. J. GIVEN, Ph.D., D.D., Rev. Prof. JOHNSON, M.A., Rev. A. ROWLAND, B.A., LL.B., Rev. A. MUIR, and Rev. R. GREEN. Fifth Edition. 2 vols., 10*s.* 6*d.* each.

> **St. Luke.** By the Very Rev. H. D. M. SPENCE. With Homilies by the Rev. J. MARSHALL LANG, D.D., Rev. W. CLARKSON, and Rev. R. M. EDGAR. Vol. I., 10*s.* 6*d.*

> **St. John.** By Rev. Prof. H. R. REYNOLDS, D.D. With Homilies by Rev. Prof. T. CROSKERY, D.D., Rev. Prof. J. R. THOMSON, M.A., Rev. D. YOUNG, B.A., Rev. B. THOMAS, Rev. G. BROWN. Second Edition. 2 vols., 15*s.* each.

> **The Acts of the Apostles.** By the Bishop of BATH and WELLS. With Homilies by Rev. Prof. P. C. BARKER, M.A., LL.B., Rev. Prof. E. JOHNSON, M.A., Rev. Prof. R. A. REDFORD, LL.B., Rev. R. TUCK, B.A., Rev. W. CLARKSON, B.A. Fourth Edition. 2 vols., 10*s.* 6*d.* each.

> **1 Corinthians.** By the Ven. Archdeacon FARRAR, D.D. With Homilies by Rev. Ex-Chancellor LIPSCOMB, LL.D., Rev. DAVID THOMAS, D.D., Rev. D. FRASER, D.D., Rev. Prof. J. R. THOMSON, M.A., Rev. J. WAITE, B.A., Rev. R. TUCK, B.A., Rev. E. HURNDALL, M.A., and Rev. H. BREMNER, B.D. Fourth Edition. 15*s.*

> **2 Corinthians and Galatians.** By the Ven. Archdeacon FARRAR, D.D., and Rev. Prebendary E. HUXTABLE. With Homilies by Rev. Ex-Chancellor LIPSCOMB, LL.D., Rev. DAVID THOMAS, D.D., Rev. DONALD FRASER, D.D., Rev. R. TUCK, B.A., Rev. E. HURNDALL, M.A., Rev. Prof. J. R. THOMSON, M.A., Rev. R. FINLAYSON, B.A., Rev. W. F. ADENEY, M.A., Rev. R. M. EDGAR, M.A., and Rev. T. CROSKERY, D.D. Second Edition. 21*s.*

Pulpit Commentary, The—*continued.*

Ephesians, Philippians, and Colossians. By the Rev. Prof. W. G. BLAIKIE, D.D., Rev. B. C. CAFFIN, M.A., and Rev. G. G. FINDLAY, B.A. With Homilies by Rev. D. THOMAS, D.D., Rev. R. M. EDGAR, M.A., Rev. R. FINLAYSON, B.A., Rev. W. F. ADENEY, M.A., Rev. Prof. T. CROSKERY, D.D., Rev. E. S. PROUT, M.A., Rev. Canon VERNON HUTTON, and Rev. U. R. THOMAS, D.D. Second Edition. 21*s.*

Thessalonians, Timothy, Titus, and Philemon. By the Bishop of Bath and Wells, Rev. Dr. GLOAG, and Rev. Dr. EALES. With Homilies by the Rev. B. C. CAFFIN, M.A., Rev. R. FINLAYSON, B.A., Rev. Prof. T. CROSKERY, D.D., Rev. W. F. ADENEY, M.A., Rev. W. M. STATHAM, and Rev. D. THOMAS, D.D. 15*s.*

Hebrews and James. By the Rev. J. BARMBY, D.D., and Rev. Prebendary E. C. S. GIBSON, M.A. With Homiletics by the Rev. C. JERDAN, M.A., LL.B., and Rev. Prebendary E. C. S. GIBSON. And Homilies by the Rev. W. JONES, Rev. C. NEW, Rev. D. YOUNG, B.A., Rev. J. S. BRIGHT, Rev. T. F. LOCKYER, B.A., and Rev. C. JERDAN, M.A., LL.B. Second Edition. 15*s.*

PUSEY, Dr.—**Sermons for the Church's Seasons from Advent to Trinity.** Selected from the Published Sermons of the late EDWARD BOUVERIE PUSEY, D.D. Crown 8vo, 5*s.*

QUEKETT, Rev. W.—**My Sayings and Doings.** With Reminiscences of my Life. With Illustrations. Demy 8vo, 18*s.*

RANKE, Leopold von.—**Universal History.** The oldest Historical Group of Nations and the Greeks. Edited by G. W. PROTHERO. Demy 8vo, 16*s.*

Remedy (The) for Landlordism ; or, Free Land Tenure. Small crown 8vo, 2*s.* 6*d.*

RENDELL, J. M.—**Concise Handbook of the Island of Madeira.** With Plan of Funchal and Map of the Island. Fcap. 8vo, 1*s.* 6*d.*

REYNOLDS, Rev. J. W.—**The Supernatural in Nature.** A Verification by Free Use of Science. Third Edition, Revised and Enlarged. Demy 8vo, 14*s.*

The Mystery of Miracles. Third and Enlarged Edition. Crown 8vo, 6*s.*

The Mystery of the Universe our Common Faith. Demy 8vo, 14*s.*

The World to Come: Immortality a Physical Fact. Crown 8vo, 6*s.*

RIBOT, Prof. Th.—**Heredity:** A Psychological Study of its Phenomena, its Laws, its Causes, and its Consequences. Second Edition. Large crown 8vo, 9*s.*

RICHARDSON, Austin.—"What are the Catholic Claims?" With Introduction by Rev. LUKE RIVINGTON. Crown 8vo, 3*s.* 6*d.*

RIVINGTON, Luke.—Authority, or a Plain Reason for joining the Church of Rome. Fifth Edition. Crown 8vo., 3*s.* 6*d.*

ROBERTSON, The late Rev. F. W., M.A.—Life and Letters of. Edited by the Rev. STOPFORD BROOKE, M.A.
    I. Two vols., uniform with the Sermons. With Steel Portrait. Crown 8vo, 7*s.* 6*d.*
    II. Library Edition, in Demy 8vo, with Portrait. 12*s.*
    III. A Popular Edition, in 1 vol. Crown 8vo, 6*s.*
Sermons. Five Series. Small crown 8vo, 3*s.* 6*d.* each.

Notes on Genesis. New and Cheaper Edition. Small crown 8vo, 3*s.* 6*d.*

Expository Lectures on St. Paul's Epistles to the Corinthians. A New Edition. Small crown 8vo, 5*s.*

Lectures and Addresses, with other Literary Remains. A New Edition. Small crown 8vo, 5*s.*

An Analysis of Tennyson's "In Memoriam." (Dedicated by Permission to the Poet-Laureate.) Fcap. 8vo, 2*s.*

The Education of the Human Race. Translated from the German of GOTTHOLD EPHRAIM LESSING. Fcap. 8vo, 2*s.* 6*d.*

⁎⁎⁎ A Portrait of the late Rev. F. W. Robertson, mounted for framing, can be had, 2*s.* 6*d.*

ROGERS, William.—Reminiscences. Compiled by R. H. HADDEN. With Portrait. Crown 8vo, 6*s.* Cheap Edition, 2*s.* 6*d.*

ROMANES, G. J.—Mental Evolution in Animals. With a Posthumous Essay on Instinct by CHARLES DARWIN, F.R.S. Demy 8vo, 12*s.*

Mental Evolution in Man : Origin of Human Faculty. Demy 8vo, 14*s.*

ROSMINI SERBATI, Antonio.—Life. By the REV. W. LOCKHART. 2 vols. With Portraits. Crown 8vo, 12*s.*

ROSS, Janet.—Italian Sketches. With 14 full-page Illustrations. Crown 8vo, 7*s.* 6*d.*

RULE, Martin, M.A.—The Life and Times of St. Anselm, Archbishop of Canterbury and Primate of the Britains. 2 vols. Demy 8vo, 32*s.*

SANTIAGOE, Daniel.—The Curry Cook's Assistant. Fcap. 8vo, cloth. 1*s.* 6*d.* ; paper covers, 1*s.*

SAVERY, C. E.—The Church of England ; an Historical Sketch. Crown 8vo, 1*s.* 6*d.*

SAYCE, Rev. Archibald Henry.—Introduction to the Science of Language. 2 vols. Second Edition. Large post 8vo, 21*s.*

SCOONES, W. Baptiste.—Four Centuries of English Letters: A Selection of 350 Letters by 150 Writers, from the Period of the Paston Letters to the Present Time. Third Edition. Large crown 8vo, 6*s.*

Selwyn, Bishop, *of New Zealand and of Lichfield.* A Sketch of his Life and Work, with Further Gleanings from his Letters, Sermons, and Speeches. By the Rev. Canon CURTEIS. Large crown 8vo, 7*s.* 6*d.*

SEYMOUR, W. Digby, Q.C.,—Home Rule and State Supremacy. Crown 8vo, 3*s.* 6*d.*

Shakspere's Macbeth. With Preface, Notes, and New Renderings. By MATTHIAS MULL. Demy 8vo, 6*s.*

Shakspere's Works. The Avon Edition, 12 vols., fcap. 8vo, cloth, 18*s.* ; in cloth box, 21*s.* ; bound in 6 vols., cloth, 15*s.*

Shakspere's Works, an Index to. By EVANGELINE O'CONNOR. Crown 8vo, 5*s.*

SHELLEY, Percy Bysshe.—Life. By EDWARD DOWDEN, LL.D. 2 vols. With Portraits. Demy 8vo, 36*s.*

SHILLITO, Rev. Joseph.—Womanhood: its Duties, Temptations, and Privileges. A Book for Young Women. Third Edition. Crown 8vo, 3*s.* 6*d.*

Shooting, Practical Hints on. Being a Treatise on the Shot Gun and its Management. By "20 Bore." With 55 Illustrations. Demy 8vo, 12*s.*

Sister Augustine, Superior of the Sisters of Charity at the St. Johannis Hospital at Bonn. Authorized Translation by HANS THARAU, from the German "Memorials of AMALIE VON LASAULX." Cheap Edition. Large crown 8vo, 4*s.* 6*d.*

SKINNER, James.—A Memoir. By the Author of "Charles Lowder." With a Preface by the Rev. Canon CARTER, and Portrait. Large crown, 7*s.* 6*d.*

   **** Also a cheap Edition. With Portrait. Fourth Edition. Crown 8vo, 3*s.* 6*d.*

SMITH, L, A.—The Music of the Waters: Sailor's Chanties and Working Songs of the Sea. Demy 8vo, 12*s.*

Spanish Mystics. By the Editor of "Many Voices." Crown 8vo, 5*s.*

Specimens of English Prose Style from Malory to Macaulay. Selected and Annotated, with an Introductory Essay, by GEORGE SAINTSBURY. Large crown 8vo, printed on hand-made paper, parchment antique or cloth, 12*s.* ; vellum, 15*s.*

STRACHEY, Sir John, G.C.S.I.—India. With Map. Demy 8vo, 15*s.*

Stray Papers on Education, and Scenes from School Life. By B. H. Second Edition. Small crown 8vo, 3*s.* 6*d.*

STRECKER-WISLICENUS.—**Organic Chemistry.** Translated and Edited, with Extensive Additions, by W. R. HODGKINSON, Ph.D., and A. J. GREENAWAY, F.I.C. Second and cheaper Edition. Demy 8vo, 12*s.* 6*d.*

Suakin, 1885: being a Sketch of the Campaign of this year. By an Officer who was there. Second Edition. Crown 8vo, 2*s.* 6*d.*

SULLY, James, M.A.—**Pessimism:** a History and a Criticism. Second Edition. Demy 8vo, 14*s.*

SWEDENBORG, Eman.—**De Cultu et Amore Dei ubi Agitur de Telluris ortu, Paradiso et Vivario, tum de Primogeniti Seu Adami Nativitate Infantia, et Amore.** Crown 8vo, 6*s.*

On the Worship and Love of God. Treating of the Birth of the Earth, Paradise, and the Abode of Living Creatures. Translated from the original Latin. Crown 8vo, 7*s.* 6*d.*

Prodromus Philosophiæ Ratiocinantis de Infinito, et Causa Finali Creationis: deque Mechanismo Operationis Animæ et Corporis. Edidit THOMAS MURRAY GORMAN, M.A. Crown 8vo, 7*s.* 6*d.*

TARRING, C. J.—**A Practical Elementary Turkish Grammar.** Crown 8vo, 6*s.*

TAYLOR, Rev. Canon Isaac, LL.D.—**The Alphabet.** An Account of the Origin and Development of Letters. With numerous Tables and Facsimiles. 2 vols. Demy 8vo, 36*s.*

Leaves from an Egyptian Note-book. Crown 8vo, 5*s.*

TAYLOR, Reynell, C.B., C.S.I. **A Biography.** By E. GAMBIER PARRY. With Portait and Map. Demy 8vo, 14*s.*

TAYLOR, Sir Henry.—**The Statesman.** Fcap. 8vo, 3*s.* 6*d.*

THOM, J. Hamilton.—**Laws of Life after the Mind of Christ.** Two Series. Crown 8vo, 7*s.* 6*d.* each.

THOMPSON, Sir H.—**Diet in Relation to Age and Activity.** Fcap. 8vo, cloth, 1*s.* 6*d.* ; paper covers, 1*s.*

Modern Cremation. Crown 8vo, 2*s.* 6*d.*

TODHUNTER, Dr. J.—**A Study of Shelley.** Crown 8vo, 7*s.*

TOLSTOI, Count Leo.—**Christ's Christianity.** Translated from the Russian. Large crown 8vo, 7*s.* 6*d.* .

TRANT, William.—**Trade Unions: Their Origin, Objects, and Efficacy.** Small crown 8vo, 1*s.* 6*d.* ; paper covers, 1*s.*

TRENCH, The late R. C., Archbishop.—**Letters and Memorials.** By the Author of "Charles Lowder." With two Portraits. 2 vols. 8vo, 21*s.*

Notes on the Parables of Our Lord. 8vo, 12*s.* Cheap Edition. Fifty-sixth Thousand. 7*s. 6d.*

Notes on the Miracles of Our Lord. 8vo, 12*s.* Cheap Edition. Forty-eighth Thousand. 7*s. 6d.*

Studies in the Gospels. Fifth Edition, Revised. 8vo, 10*s. 6d.*

Brief Thoughts and Meditations on Some Passages in Holy Scripture. Third Edition. Crown 8vo, 3*s. 6d.*

Synonyms of the New Testament. Tenth Edition, Enlarged. 8vo, 12*s.*

Sermons New and Old. Crown 8vo, 6*s.*

Westminster and other Sermons. Crown 8vo, 6*s.*

On the Authorized Version of the New Testament. Second Edition. 8vo, 7*s.*

Commentary on the Epistles to the Seven Churches in Asia. Fourth Edition, Revised. 8vo, 8*s. 6d.*

The Sermon on the Mount. An Exposition drawn from the Writings of St. Augustine, with an Essay on his Merits as an Interpreter of Holy Scripture. Fourth Edition, Enlarged. 8vo, 10*s. 6d.*

Shipwrecks of Faith. Three Sermons preached before the University of Cambridge in May, 1867. Fcap. 8vo, 2*s. 6d.*

Lectures on Mediæval Church History. Being the Substance of Lectures delivered at Queen's College, London. Second Edition. 8vo, 12*s.*

English, Past and Present. Thirteenth Edition, Revised and Improved. Fcap. 8vo, 5*s.*

On the Study of Words. Twentieth Edition, Revised. Fcap. 8vo, 5*s.*

Select Glossary of English Words used Formerly in Senses Different from the Present. Sixth Edition, Revised and Enlarged. Fcap. 8vo, 5*s.*

Proverbs and Their Lessons. Seventh Edition, Enlarged. Fcap. 8vo, 4*s.*

Poems. Collected and Arranged anew. Tenth Edition. Fcap. 8vo, 7*s. 6d.*

Poems. Library Edition. 2 vols. Small crown 8vo, 10*s.*

Sacred Latin Poetry. Chiefly Lyrical, Selected and Arranged for Use. Third Edition, Corrected and Improved. Fcap. 8vo, 7*s.*

TRENCH, The late R. C., Archbishop—continued.

A Household Book of English Poetry. Selected and Arranged, with Notes. Fourth Edition, Revised. Extra fcap. 8vo, 5s. 6d.

An Essay on the Life and Genius of Calderon. With Translations from his "Life's a Dream" and "Great Theatre of the World." Second Edition, Revised and Improved. Extra fcap. 8vo, 5s. 6d.

Gustavus Adolphus in Germany, and other Lectures on the Thirty Years' War. Third Edition, Enlarged. Fcap. 8vo, 4s.

Plutarch : his Life, his Lives, and his Morals. Second Edition, Enlarged. Fcap. 8vo, 3s. 6d.

Remains of the late Mrs. Richard Trench. Being Selections from her Journals, Letters, and other Papers. New and Cheaper Issue. With Portrait. 8vo, 6s.

TUTHILL, C. A. H.—Origin and Development of Christian Dogma. Crown 8vo, 3s. 6d.

Two Centuries of Irish History. By various Writers. Edited by Prof. J. BRYCE. Demy 8vo, 16s.

UMLAUFT, Prof. F.—The Alps. Illustrations and Maps. 8vo, 25s.

VAL d'EREMAO, Rev. J. P.—The Serpent of Eden. A Philological and Critical Essay. Crown 8vo, 4s. 6d.

VOLCKXSOM, E. W. v.—Catechism of Elementary Modern Chemistry. Small crown 8vo, 3s.

WALLER, C. B.—Unfoldings of Christian Hope. Second Edition. Crown 8vo, 3s. 6d.

WALPOLE, Chas. George.—A Short History of Ireland from the Earliest Times to the Union with Great Britain. With 5 Maps and Appendices. Third Edition. Crown 8vo, 6s.

WARD, Wilfrid.—The Wish to Believe. A Discussion Concerning the Temper of Mind in which a reasonable Man should undertake Religious Inquiry. Small crown 8vo, 5s.

WARD, William George, Ph.D.—Essays on the Philosophy of Theism. Edited, with an Introduction, by WILFRID WARD. 2 vols. Demy 8vo, 21s.

WARTER, J. W.—An Old Shropshire Oak. 2 vols. Demy 8vo, 28s.

WEDMORE, Frederick.—The Masters of Genre Painting. With Sixteen Illustrations. Post 8vo, 7s. 6d.

WHIBLEY, Charles.—In Cap and Gown. Crown 8vo.

WHITMAN, Sidney.—Conventional Cant: its Results and Remedy. Crown 8vo, 6s.

WHITNEY, Prof. William Dwight.—Essentials of English Grammar, for the Use of Schools. Second Edition. Crown 8vo, 3s. 6d.

WHITWORTH, George Clifford.—An Anglo-Indian Dictionary : a Glossary of Indian Terms used in English, and of such English or other Non-Indian Terms as have obtained special meanings in India. Demy 8vo, cloth, 12s.

Wilberforce, Bishop, *of Oxford and Winchester*. Life. By his Son REGINALD WILBERFORCE. Crown 8vo, 6s.

WILSON, Mrs. R. F.—The Christian Brothers. Their Origin and Work. With a Sketch of the Life of their Founder, the Ven. JEAN BAPTISTE, de la Salle. Crown 8vo, 6s.

WOLTMANN, Dr. Alfred, and WOERMANN, Dr. Karl.—History of Painting. With numerous Illustrations. Medium 8vo. Vol. I. Painting in Antiquity and the Middle Ages. 28s. ; bevelled boards, gilt leaves, 30s. Vol. II. The Painting of the Renascence. 42s. ; bevelled boards, gilt leaves, 45s.

Words of Jesus Christ taken from the Gospels. Small crown 8vo, 2s. 6d.

YOUMANS, Edward L., M.D.—A Class Book of Chemistry, on the Basis of the New System. With 200 Illustrations. Crown 8vo, 5s.

YOUMANS, Eliza A.—First Book of Botany. Designed to cultivate the Observing Powers of Children. With 300 Engravings. New and Cheaper Edition. Crown 8vo, 2s. 6d.

THE INTERNATIONAL SCIENTIFIC SERIES.

I. Forms of Water in Clouds and Rivers, Ice and Glaciers. By J. Tyndall, LL.D., F.R.S. With 25 Illustrations. Ninth Edition. 5s.

II. Physics and Politics ; or, Thoughts on the Application of the Principles of " Natural Selection " and " Inheritance " to Political Society. By Walter Bagehot. Eighth Edition. 5s.

III. Foods. By Edward Smith, M.D., LL.B., F.R.S. With numerous Illustrations. Ninth Edition. 5s.

IV. Mind and Body : the Theories of their Relation. By Alexander Bain, LL.D. With Four Illustrations. Eighth Edition. 5s.

V. The Study of Sociology. By Herbert Spencer. Fourteenth Edition. 5s.

VI. **The Conservation of Energy.** By Balfour Stewart, M.A., LL.D., F.R.S. With 14 Illustrations. Seventh Edition. 5*s.*

VII. **Animal Locomotion ;** or, Walking, Swimming, and Flying. By J. B. Pettigrew, M.D., F.R.S., etc. With 130 Illustrations. Third Edition. 5*s.*

VIII. **Responsibility in Mental Disease.** By Henry Maudsley, M.D. Fourth Edition. 5*s.*

IX. **The New Chemistry.** By Professor J. P. Cooke. With 31 Illustrations. Ninth Edition. 5*s.*

X. **The Science of Law.** By Professor Sheldon Amos. Sixth Edition. 5*s.*

XI. **Animal Mechanism :** a Treatise on Terrestrial and Aerial Locomotion. By Professor E. J. Marey. With 117 Illustrations. Third Edition. 5*s.*

XII. **The Doctrine of Descent and Darwinism.** By Professor Oscar Schmidt. With 26 Illustrations. Seventh Edition. 5*s.*

XIII. **The History of the Conflict between Religion and Science.** By J. W. Draper, M.D., LL.D. Twentieth Edition. 5*s.*

XIV. **Fungi : their Nature, Influences, and Uses.** By M. C. Cooke, M.A., LL.D. Edited by the Rev. M. J. Berkeley, M.A., F.L.S. With numerous Illustrations. Fourth Edition. 5*s.*

XV. **The Chemistry of Light and Photography.** By Dr. Hermann Vogel. With 100 Illustrations. Fifth Edition. 5*s.*

XVI. **The Life and Growth of Language.** By Professor William Dwight Whitney. Fifth Edition. 5*s.*

XVII. **Money and the Mechanism of Exchange.** By W. Stanley Jevons, M.A., F.R.S. Eighth Edition. 5*s.*

XVIII. **The Nature of·Light.** With a General Account of Physical Optics. By Dr. Eugene Lommel. With 188 Illustrations and a Table of Spectra in Chromo-lithography. Fifth Edition. 5*s.*

XIX. **Animal Parasites and Messmates.** By P. J. Van Beneden. With 83 Illustrations. Third Edition. 5*s.*

XX. **On Fermentation.** By Professor Schützenberger. With 28 Illustrations. Fourth Edition. 5*s.*

XXI. **The Five Senses of Man.** By Professor Bernstein. With 91 Illustrations. Fifth Edition. 5*s.*

XXII. **The Theory of Sound in its Relation to Music.** By Professor Pietro Blaserna. With numerous Illustrations. Third Edition. 5*s.*

XXIII. **Studies in Spectrum Analysis.** By J. Norman Lockyer, F.R.S. With six photographic Illustrations of Spectra, and numerous engravings on Wood. Fourth Edition. 6*s.* 6*d.*

XXIV. **A History of the Growth of the Steam Engine.** By Professor R. H. Thurston. With numerous Illustrations. Fourth Edition. 5*s.*

XXV. **Education as a Science.** By Alexander Bain, LL.D. Seventh Edition. 5*s.*

XXVI. **The Human Species.** By Professor A. de Quatrefages. Fourth Edition. 5*s.*

XXVII. **Modern Chromatics.** With Applications to Art and Industry. By Ogden N. Rood. With 130 original Illustrations. Second Edition. 5*s.*

XXVIII. **The Crayfish:** an Introduction to the Study of Zoology. By Professor T. H. Huxley. With 82 Illustrations. Fifth Edition, 5*s.*

XXIX. **The Brain as an Organ of Mind.** By H. Charlton Bastian, M.D. With numerous Illustrations. Third Edition. 5*s.*

XXX. **The Atomic Theory.** By Prof. Wurtz. Translated by E. Cleminshaw, F.C.S. Fifth Edition. 5*s.*

XXXI. **The Natural Conditions of Existence as they affect Animal Life.** By Karl Semper. With 2 Maps and 106 Woodcuts. Third Edition. 5*s.*

XXXII. **General Physiology of Muscles and Nerves.** By Prof. J. Rosenthal. Third Edition. With 75 Illustrations. 5*s.*

XXXIII. **Sight:** an Exposition of the Principles of Monocular and Binocular Vision. By Joseph le Conte, LL.D. Second Edition. With 132 Illustrations. 5*s.*

XXXIV. **Illusions:** a Psychological Study. By James Sully. Third Edition. 5*s.*

XXXV. **Volcanoes: what they are and what they teach.** By Professor J. W. Judd, F.R.S. With 96 Illustrations on Wood. Fourth Edition. 5*s.*

XXXVI. **Suicide:** an Essay on Comparative Moral Statistics. By Prof. H. Morselli. Second Edition. With Diagrams. 5*s.*

XXXVII. **The Brain and its Functions.** By J. Luys. With Illustrations. Second Edition. 5*s.*

XXXVIII. **Myth and Science:** an Essay. By Tito Vignoli. Third Edition. With Supplementary Note. 5*s.*

XXXIX. **The Sun.** By Professor Young. With Illustrations. Third Edition. 5*s.*

XL. **Ants, Bees, and Wasps:** a Record of Observations on the Habits of the Social Hymenoptera. By Sir John Lubbock, Bart., M.P. With 5 Chromo-lithographic Illustrations. Ninth Edition. 5*s.*

XLI. **Animal Intelligence.** By G. J. Romanes, LL.D., F.R.S. Fourth Edition. 5*s.*

XLII. **The Concepts and Theories of Modern Physics.** By J. B. Stallo. Third Edition. 5*s.*

XLIII. **Diseases of Memory** : An Essay in the Positive Psychology. By Prof. Th. Ribot. Third Edition. 5*s.*

XLIV. **Man before Metals.** By N. Joly, with 148 Illustrations. Fourth Edition. 5*s.*

XLV. **The Science of Politics.** By Prof. Sheldon Amos. Third Edition. 5*s.*

XLVI. **Elementary Meteorology.** By Robert H. Scott. Fourth Edition. With Numerous Illustrations. 5*s.*

XLVII. **The Organs of Speech and their Application in the Formation of Articulate Sounds.** By Georg Hermann Von Meyer. With 47 Woodcuts. 5*s.*

XLVIII. **Fallacies.** A View of Logic from the Practical Side. By Alfred Sidgwick. Second Edition. 5*s.*

XLIX. **Origin of Cultivated Plants.** By Alphonse de Candolle. Second Edition. 5*s.*

L. **Jelly-Fish, Star-Fish, and Sea-Urchins.** Being a Research on Primitive Nervous Systems. By G. J. Romanes. With Illustrations. 5*s.*

LI. **The Common Sense of the Exact Sciences.** By the late William Kingdon Clifford. Second Edition. With 100 Figures. 5*s.*

LII. **Physical Expression : Its Modes and Principles.** By Francis Warner, M.D., F.R.C.P., Hunterian Professor of Comparative Anatomy and Physiology, R.C.S.E. With 50 Illustrations. 5*s.*

LIII. **Anthropoid Apes.** By Robert Hartmann. With 63 Illustrations. 5*s.*

LIV. **The Mammalia in their Relation to Primeval Times.** By Oscar Schmidt. With 51 Woodcuts. 5*s.*

LV. **Comparative Literature.** By H. Macaulay Posnett, LL.D. 5*s.*

LVI. **Earthquakes and other Earth Movements.** By Prof. John Milne. With 38 Figures. Second Edition. 5*s.*

LVII. **Microbes, Ferments, and Moulds.** By E. L. Trouessart. With 107 Illustrations. 5*s.*

LVIII. **Geographical and Geological Distribution of Animals.** By Professor A. Heilprin. With Frontispiece. 5*s.*

LIX. **Weather.** A Popular Exposition of the Nature of Weather Changes from Day to Day. By the Hon. Ralph Abercromby. Second Edition. With 96 Illustrations. 5*s.*

LX. **Animal Magnetism.** By Alfred Binet and Charles Féré. Second Edition. 5*s.*

LXI. **Manual of British Discomycetes,** with descriptions of all the Species of Fungi hitherto found in Britain included in the Family, and Illustrations of the Genera. By William Phillips, F.L.S. 5*s.*

LXII. **International Law.** With Materials for a Code of International Law. By Professor Leone Levi. 5*s.*

LXIII. **The Geological History of Plants.** By Sir J. William Dawson. With 80 Figures. 5*s.*

LXIV. **The Origin of Floral Structures through Insect and other Agencies.** By Rev. Prof. G. Henslow. With 88 Illustrations. 5*s.*

LXV. **On the Senses, Instincts, and Intelligence of Animals.** With special Reference to Insects. By Sir John Lubbock, Bart., M.P. 100 Illustrations. Second Edition. 5*s.*

LXVI. **The Primitive Family: Its Origin and Development.** By C. N. Starcke.

MILITARY WORKS.

BRACKENBURY, Col. C. B., R.A. — Military Handbooks for Regimental Officers.

I. **Military Sketching and Reconnaissance.** By Col. F. J. Hutchison and Major H. G. MacGregor. Fifth Edition. With 16 Plates. Small crown 8vo, 4*s.*

II. **The Elements of Modern Tactics Practically applied to English Formations.** By Lieut.-Col. Wilkinson Shaw. Sixth Edition. With 25 Plates and Maps. Small crown 8vo, 9*s.*

III. **Field Artillery.** Its Equipment, Organization and Tactics. By Major Sisson C. Pratt, R.A. With 12 Plates. Third Edition. Small crown 8vo, 6*s.*

IV. **The Elements of Military Administration.** First Part: Permanent System of Administration. By Major J. W. Buxton. Small crown 8vo, 7*s. 6d.*

V. **Military Law: Its Procedure and Practice.** By Major Sisson C. Pratt, R.A. Fourth Edition. Revised. Small crown 8vo, 4*s. 6d.*

VI. **Cavalry in Modern War.** By Major-General F. Chenevix Trench. Small crown 8vo, 6*s.*

BRACKENBURY, Col. C. B., R.A.—continued.
 VII. Field Works. Their Technical Construction and Tactical Application. By the Editor, Col. C. B. Brackenbury, R.A. Small crown 8vo, in 2 parts, 12*s.*

BROOKE, Major, C. K.—A System of Field Training. Small crown 8vo, cloth limp, 2*s.*

Campaign of Fredericksburg, November—December, 1862. A Study for Officers of Volunteers. By a Line Officer. With 5 Maps and Plans. Second Edition. Crown 8vo, 5*s.*

CLERY, C. Francis, Col.—Minor Tactics. With 26 Maps and Plans. Eighth Edition, Revised. Crown 8vo, 9*s.*

COLVILE, Lieut.-Col. C. F.—Military Tribunals. Sewed, 2*s.* 6*d.*

CRAUFURD, Capt. H. J.—Suggestions for the Military Training of a Company of Infantry. Crown 8vo, 1*s.* 6*d.*

HAMILTON, Capt. Ian, A.D.C.—The Fighting of the Future. 1*s.*

HARRISON, Col. R.—The Officer's Memorandum Book for Peace and War. Fourth Edition, Revised throughout. Oblong 32mo, red basil, with pencil, 3*s.* 6*d.*

Notes on Cavalry Tactics, Organisation, etc. By a Cavalry Officer. With Diagrams. Demy 8vo, 12*s.*

PARR, Col. H. Hallam, C.M.G.—The Dress, Horses, and Equipment of Infantry and Staff Officers. Crown 8vo, 1*s.*

 Further Training and Equipment of Mounted Infantry. Crown 8vo, 1*s.*

SCHAW, Col. H.—The Defence and Attack of Positions and Localities. Fourth Edition. Crown 8vo, 3*s.* 6*d.*

STONE, Capt. F. Gleadowe, R.A.—Tactical Studies from the Franco-German War of 1870–71. With 22 Lithographic Sketches and Maps. Demy 8vo, 10*s.* 6*d.*

WILKINSON, H. Spenser, Capt. 20th Lancashire R.V.—Citizen Soldiers. Essays towards the Improvement of the Volunteer Force. Crown 8vo, 2*s.* 6*d.*

POETRY.

ALEXANDER, William, D.D., Bishop of Derry.—St. Augustine's Holiday, and other Poems. Crown 8vo, 6*s.*

AUCHMUTY, A. C.—Poems of English Heroism : From Brunanburh to Lucknow ; from Athelstan to Albert. Small crown 8vo, 1*s.* 6*d.*

BARNES, William.—Poems of Rural Life, in the Dorset Dialect. New Edition, complete in one vol. Crown 8vo, 6*s.*

BAYNES, Rev. Canon H. R.—Home Songs for Quiet Hours. Fourth and Cheaper Edition. Fcap. 8vo, cloth, 2*s.* 6*d.*

BEVINGTON, L. S.—Key Notes. Small crown 8vo, 5*s.*

BLUNT, Wilfrid Scawen.—The Wind and the Whirlwind. Demy 8vo, 1*s.* 6*d.*

The Love Sonnets of Proteus. Fifth Edition. Elzevir 8vo, 5*s.*

In Vinculis. With Portrait. Elzevir 8vo, 5*s.*

BOWEN, H. C., M.A.—Simple English Poems. English Literature for Junior Classes. In Four Parts. Parts I., II., and III., 6*d.* each, and Part IV., 1*s.* Complete, 3*s.*

BRYANT, W. C.—Poems. Cheap Edition, with Frontispiece. Small crown 8vo, 3*s.* 6*d.*

Calderon's Dramas : the Wonder-Working Magician — Life is a Dream—the Purgatory of St. Patrick. Translated by DENIS FLORENCE MACCARTHY. Post 8vo, 10*s.*

Camoens' Lusiads. — Portuguese Text, with Translation by J. J. AUBERTIN. Second Edition. 2 vols. Crown 8vo, 12*s.*

CHRISTIE, Albany J.—The End of Man. Fourth Edition. Fcap. 8vo, 2*s.* 6*d.*

COLERIDGE, Hon. Stephen.—Fibulæ. Small crown 8vo, 4*s.* 6*d.*

COXHEAD, Ethel.—Birds and Babies. With 33 Illustrations. Imp. 16mo, 1*s.*

Dante's Divina Commedia. Translated in the *Terza Rima* of Original, by F. K. H. HASELFOOT. Demy 8vo, 16*s.*

DENNIS, J.—English Sonnets. Collected and Arranged by. Small crown 8vo, 2*s.* 6*d.*

DE VERE, Aubrey.—Poetical Works.

    I. THE SEARCH AFTER PROSERPINE, etc. 3*s.* 6*d.*
    II. THE LEGENDS OF ST. PATRICK, etc. 3*s.* 6*d.*
    III. ALEXANDER THE GREAT, etc. 3*s.* 6*d.*

The Foray of Queen Meave, and other Legends of Ireland's Heroic Age. Small crown 8vo, 3*s.* 6*d.*

Legends of the Saxon Saints. Small crown 8vo, 3*s.* 6*d.*

Legends and Records of the Church and the Empire. Small crown 8vo, 3*s.* 6*d.*

DOBSON, Austin.—Old World Idylls, and other Verses. Eighth Edition. Elzevir 8vo, gilt top, 6*s.*

NOEL, The Hon. Roden—continued.

Songs of the Heights and Deeps. Crown 8vo, 6*s.*
A Modern Faust, and other Poems. Small crown 8vo, 5*s.*

O'HAGAN, John.—The Song of Roland. Translated into English Verse. New and Cheaper Edition. Crown 8vo, 5*s.*

Publisher's Playground. Fcap. 8vo, 3*s.* 6*d.*

Rare Poems of the 16th and 17th Centuries. Edited by W. J. LINTON. Crown 8vo, 5*s.*

ROBINSON, A. Mary F.—A Handful of Honeysuckle. Fcap. 8vo, 3*s.* 6*d.*

The Crowned Hippolytus. Translated from Euripides. With New Poems. Small crown 8vo, 5*s.*

SEAL, W. H.—Visions of the Night. Crown 8vo, 4*s.*

SMITH, J. W. Gilbart.—The Loves of Vandyck. A Tale of Genoa. Small crown 8vo, 2*s.* 6*d.*

The Log o' the "Norseman." Small crown 8vo, 5*s.*
Serbelloni. Small crown 8vo, 5*s.*

Sophocles : The Seven Plays in English Verse. Translated by LEWIS CAMPBELL. Crown 8vo, 7*s.* 6*d.*

SYMONDS, John Addington.—Vagabunduli Libellus. Crown 8vo, 6*s.*

TAYLOR, Sir H.—Works. Complete in Five Volumes. Crown 8vo, 30*s.*

Philip Van Artevelde. Fcap. 8vo, 3*s.* 6*d.*
The Virgin Widow, etc. Fcap. 8vo, 3*s.* 6*d.*

TODHUNTER, Dr. J.—Laurella, and other Poems. Crown 8vo, 6*s.* 6*d.*

Forest Songs. Small crown 8vo, 3*s.* 6*d.*
The True Tragedy of Rienzi : a Drama. 3*s.* 6*d.*
Alcestis : a Dramatic Poem. Extra fcap. 8vo, 5*s.*
Helena in Troas. Small crown 8vo, 2*s.* 6*d.*
The Banshee, and other Poems. Small crown 8vo, 3*s.* 6*d.*

TYNAN, Katherine.—Louise de la Valliere, and other Poems. Small crown 8vo, 3*s.* 6*d.*

Shamrocks. Small crown 8vo, 5*s.*

Twilight and Candleshades. By EXUL. With 15 Vignettes. Small crown 8vo, 5*s.*

Victorian Hymns : English Sacred Songs of Fifty Years. Dedicated to the Queen. Large post 8vo, 10*s.* 6*d.*

Wordsworth Birthday Book, The. Edited by ADELAIDE and VIOLET WORDSWORTH. 32mo, limp cloth, 1s. 6d.; cloth extra, 2s.

Wordsworth, Selections from. By WM. KNIGHT and other members of the Wordsworth Society. Large crown 8vo. Printed on hand-made paper. With Portrait. Parchment, 12s; vellum, 15s.

YEATS, W. B.—**The Wanderings of Oisin,** and other Poems. Small crown 8vo, 5s.

NOVELS AND TALES.

BAKER, Ella.—**Kingscote Stories.** Crown 8vo, 5s.
    Bertram de Drumont. Crown 8vo, 5s.

BANKS, Mrs. G. L.—**God's Providence House.** Crown 8vo, 6s.

CRAWFURD, Oswald.—**Sylvia Arden.** With Frontispiece. Crown 8vo, 1s.

GARDINER, Linda.—**His Heritage.** With Frontispiece. Crown 8vo, 6s.

GRAY, Maxwell.—**The Silence of Dean Maitland.** Fifteenth Thousand. With Frontispiece. Crown 8vo, 6s.

GREY, Rowland.—**In Sunny Switzerland.** A Tale of Six Weeks. Second Edition. Small crown 8vo, 5s.
    Lindenblumen and other Stories. Small crown 8vo, 5s.
    By Virtue of his Office. Crown 8vo, 6s.

HUNTER, Hay.—**The Crime of Christmas Day.** A Tale of the Latin Quarter. By the Author of "My Ducats and my Daughter." 1s.

HUNTER, Hay, and WHYTE, Walter.—**My Ducats and My Daughter.** With Frontispiece. Crown 8vo, 6s.

INGELOW, Jean.—**Off the Skelligs.** A Novel. With Frontispiece. Crown 8vo, 6s.

LANG, Andrew.—**In the Wrong Paradise,** and other Stories. Crown 8vo, 6s.

MACDONALD, G.—**Donal Grant.** A Novel. With Frontispiece. Crown 8vo, 6s.
    Home Again. With Frontispiece. Crown 8vo, 6s.
    Castle Warlock. A Novel. With Frontispiece. Crown 8vo, 6s.
    Malcolm. With Portrait of the Author engraved on Steel. Crown 8vo, 6s.

MACDONALD, G.—continued.

The Marquis of Lossie. With Frontispiece. Crown 8vo, 6*s.*

St. George and St. Michael. With Frontispiece. Crown 8vo, 6*s.*

What's Mine's Mine. With Frontispiece. Crown 8vo, 6*s.*

Annals of a Quiet Neighbourhood. With Frontispiece. Crown 8vo, 6*s.*

The Seaboard Parish : a Sequel to " Annals of a Quiet Neighbourhood." With Frontispiece. Crown 8vo, 6*s.*

Wilfred Cumbermede. An Autobiographical Story. With Frontispiece. Crown 8vo, 6*s.*

Thomas Wingfold, Curate. With Frontispiece. Crown 8vo, 6*s.*

Paul Faber, Surgeon. With Frontispiece. Crown 8vo, 6*s.*

The Elect Lady. With Frontispiece. Crown 8vo, 6*s.*

MALET, Lucas.—Colonel Enderby's Wife. A Novel. With Frontispiece. Crown 8vo, 6*s.*

A Counsel of Perfection. With Frontispiece. Crown 8vo, 6*s.*

MULHOLLAND, Rosa.—Marcella Grace. An Irish Novel. Crown 8vo, 6*s.*

A Fair Emigrant. With Frontispiece. Crown 8vo, 6*s.*

OGLE, Anna C.—A Lost Love. Small crown 8vo, 2*s.* 6*d.*

PALGRAVE, W. Gifford.—Hermann Agha : an Eastern Narrative. Crown 8vo, 6*s.*

Romance of the Recusants. By the Author of "Life of a Prig." Crown 8vo, 5*s.*

SEVERNE, Florence.—The Pillar House. With Frontispiece. Crown 8vo, 6*s.*

SHAW, Flora L.—Castle Blair : a Story of Youthful Days. Crown 8vo, 3*s.* 6*d.*

STRETTON, Hesba.—Through a Needle's Eye. A Story. With Frontispiece. Crown 8vo, 6*s.*

TAYLOR, Col. Meadows, C.S.I., M.R.I.A.—Seeta. A Novel. With Frontispiece. Crown 8vo, 6*s.*

Tippoo Sultaun : a Tale of the Mysore War. With Frontispiece. Crown 8vo, 6*s.*

Ralph Darnell. With Frontispiece. Crown 8vo, 6*s.*

A Noble Queen. With Frontispiece. Crown 8vo, 6*s.*

The Confessions of a Thug. With Frontispiece. Crown 8vo, 6*s.*

Tara : a Mahratta Tale. With Frontispiece. Crown 8vo, 6*s.*

Within Sound of the Sea. With Frontispiece. Crown 8vo, 6*s.*

BOOKS FOR THE YOUNG.

Brave Men's Footsteps. A Book of Example and Anecdote for Young People. By the Editor of "Men who have Risen." With 4 Illustrations by C. Doyle. Ninth Edition. Crown 8vo, 2*s*. 6*d*.

COXHEAD, Ethel.—**Birds and Babies.** With 33 Illustrations. Second Edition. Imp. 16mo, cloth, 1*s*.

DAVIES, G. Christopher.—**Rambles and Adventures of our School Field Club.** With 4 Illustrations. New and Cheaper Edition. Crown 8vo, 3*s*. 6*d*.

EDMONDS, Herbert.—**Well Spent Lives:** a Series of Modern Biographies. New and Cheaper Edition. Crown 8vo, 3*s*. 6*d*.

EVANS, Mark.—**The Story of our Father's Love,** told to Children. Sixth and Cheaper Edition of Theology for Children. With 4 Illustrations. Fcap. 8vo, 1*s*. 6*d*.

MAC KENNA, S. J.—**Plucky Fellows.** A Book for Boys. With 6 Illustrations. Fifth Edition. Crown 8vo, 3*s*. 6*d*.

MALET, Lucas.—**Little Peter.** A Christmas Morality for Children of any Age. With numerous Illustrations. Fourth Thousand. 5*s*.

REANEY, Mrs. G. S.—**Waking and Working;** or, From Girlhood to Womanhood. New and Cheaper Edition. With a Frontispiece. Crown 8vo, 3*s*. 6*d*.

> **Blessing and Blessed:** a Sketch of Girl Life. New and Cheaper Edition. Crown 8vo, 3*s*. 6*d*.

> **Rose Gurney's Discovery.** A Story for Girls. Dedicated to their Mothers. Crown 8vo, 3*s*. 6*d*.

> **English Girls:** their Place and Power. With Preface by the Rev. R. W. Dale. Fifth Edition. Fcap. 8vo, 2*s*. 6*d*.

> **Just Anyone,** and other Stories. Three Illustrations. Royal 16mo, 1*s*. 6*d*.

> **Sunbeam Willie,** and other Stories. Three Illustrations. Royal 16mo, 1*s*. 6*d*.

> **Sunshine Jenny,** and other Stories. Three Illustrations. Royal 16mo, 1*s*. 6*d*.

STORR, Francis, and TURNER, Hawes.—**Canterbury Chimes;** or, Chaucer Tales re-told to Children. With 6 Illustrations from the Ellesmere Manuscript. Third Edition. Fcap. 8vo, 3*s*. 6*d*.

STRETTON, Hesba.—**David Lloyd's Last Will.** With 4 Illustrations. New Edition. Royal 16mo, 2*s*. 6*d*.

WHITAKER, Florence.—**Christy's Inheritance.** A London Story. Illustrated. Royal 16mo, 1*s*. 6*d*.

PRINTED BY WILLIAM CLOWES AND SONS, LIMITED,
LONDON AND BECCLES.

SHAKSPERE'S WORKS.

THE AVON EDITION.

Printed on thin opaque paper, and forming 12 handy volumes, cloth, 18*s*., or bound in 6 volumes, 15*s*.

The set of 12 volumes may also be had in a cloth box, price 21*s*., or bound in Roan, Persian, Crushed Persian Levant, Calf, or Morocco, and enclosed in an attractive leather box at prices from 31*s*. 6*d*. upwards.

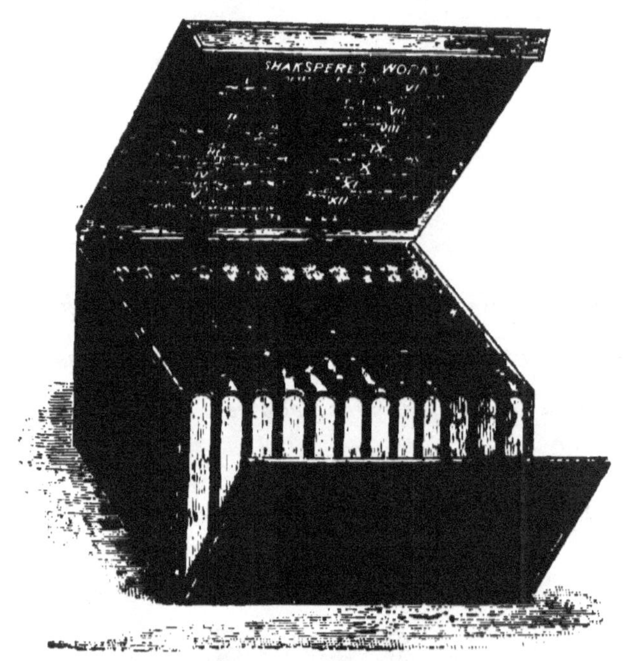

SOME PRESS NOTICES.

"This edition will be useful to those who want a good text, well and clearly printed, in convenient little volumes that will slip easily into an overcoat pocket or a travelling-bag."—*St. James's Gazette.*

"We know no prettier edition of Shakspere for the price."—*Academy.*

"It is refreshing to meet with an edition of Shakspere of convenient size and low price, without either notes or introductions of any sort to distract the attention of the reader."—*Saturday Review.*

"It is exquisite. Each volume is handy, is beautifully printed, and in every way lends itself to the taste of the cultivated student of Shak-spere."—*Scotsman.*

LONDON: KEGAN PAUL, TRENCH & CO., 1, PATERNOSTER SQUARE.

SHAKSPERE'S WORKS.

THE PARCHMENT LIBRARY EDITION.

In 12 volumes Elzevir 8vo., choicely printed on hand-made paper, and bound in parchment or cloth, price £3 12s., or in vellum, price £4 10s.

The set of 12 volumes may also be had in a strong cloth box, price £3 17s., or with an oak hanging shelf, £3 18s.

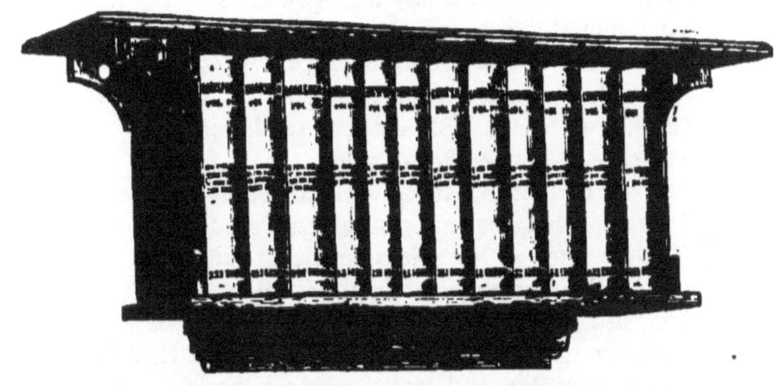

SOME PRESS NOTICES.

". . . There is, perhaps, no edition in which the works of Shakspere can be read in such luxury of type and quiet distinction of form as this, and we warmly recommend it."—*Pall Mall Gazette.*

"For elegance of form and beauty of typography, no edition of Shakspere hitherto published has excelled the 'Parchment Library Edition.' . . . They are in the strictest sense pocket volumes, yet the type is bold, and, being on fine white hand-made paper, can hardly tax the weakest of sight. The print is judiciously confined to the text, notes being more appropriate to library editions. The whole will be comprised in the cream-coloured parchment which gives the name to the series."—*Daily News.*

"The Parchment Library Edition of Shakspere needs no further praise."—*Saturday Review.*

Just published.   Price 5s.

AN INDEX TO THE WORKS OF SHAKSPERE.

Applicable to all editions of Shakspere, and giving reference, by topics, to notable passages and significant expressions; brief histories of the plays; geographical names and historic incidents; mention of all characters and sketches of important ones; together with explanations of allusions and obscure and obsolete words and phrases.

By EVANGELINE M. O'CONNOR.

LONDON : KEGAN PAUL, TRENCH & CO., 1, PATERNOSTER SQUARE.

SHAKSPERE'S WORKS.

SPECIMEN OF TYPE.

    Salar.   My wind, cooling my broth,
Would blow me to an ague, when I thought
What harm a wind too great might do at sea.
I should not see the sandy hour-glass run
But I should think of shallows and of flats,
And see my wealthy Andrew, dock'd in sand,
Vailing her high-top lower than her ribs
To kiss her burial.   Should I go to church
And see the holy edifice of stone,
And not bethink me straight of dangerous rocks,
Which touching but my gentle vessel's side,
Would scatter all her spices on the stream,
Enrobe the roaring waters with my silks,
And, in a word, but even now worth this,
And now worth nothing?   Shall I have the thought
To think on this, and shall I lack the thought
That such a thing bechanc'd would make me sad?
But tell not me : I know Antonio
Is sad to think upon his merchandise.

    Ant. Believe me, no : I thank my fortune for it,
My ventures are not in one bottom trusted,
Nor to one place ; nor is my whole estate
Upon the fortune of this present year :
Therefore my merchandise makes me not sad.

    Salar. Why, then you are in love.

    Ant.   Fie, fie!

    Salar. Not in love neither?   Then let us say you
    . are sad,
Because you are not merry ; and 'twere as easy
For you to laugh, and leap, and say you are merry,
Because you are not sad. Now, by two-headed
    Janus,
Nature hath fram'd strange fellows in her time :
Some that will evermore peep through their eyes
And laugh like parrots at a bag-piper ;
And other of such vinegar aspect

LONDON : KEGAN PAUL, TRENCH & CO., 1, PATERNOSTER SQUARE.